CODE OF THE HEART

Joel Badger

CONTENTS

1

CHAPTER 1

Raghav's POV

"Clink, Clink", the card reader's swipe machine beeped and so did the access detector light turn green but the glass door didn't open to Raghav's dismay. There I, Raghav Srivastav, was standing and looking through the stripped see-through door to check if anyone was there in the floor to help me with the access. I had just been shifted to Block 10B at the office campus. The cubicles were a few meters away from the door and the lights on the passage connecting it to the door had not been lit up except for the two closer to the door. The needle had just struck 8:20 in the morning and I knew I would have to wait for a very long time for even a fly to arrive here.

"Great! Raghav! Now enjoy standing like a watchman at the door. Why did you even think of coming early on the day of shifting", Raghav was talking to himself, like enacting a monologue. "It's b ecause... Raghav, you fool, had come into the Lady HR's words of maintaining the great 'Work-Life Balance' and enrolled for the evening GYM sessions sharp at 5:30 pm. Now how on earth are you going to finish your work before the session?"

I started banging my head with my closed fist when I remembered that my own manager, Mr. Selva Ganesan, was the gym instructor too. Both ways I was doomed. If I didn't finish my EOD (End-Of-The-Day) task, my clients would escalate it to my manager and if I stayed back to finish it and bunked the Gym session, all the vicious tentacles would come out of my man-eater-manager. I was trying to figure out how I had dug my own grave? Like they say, when a Girl says something with her fluttering eyes and mesmerizing voice; we dumb guys always nod our heads, that's the beginning of the end of something.

I was looking down at the floor, busy cursing myself, just then a pair of blue and white sneakers with untidily knotted laces came into the scope of my vision. The sneakers were moving towards me with a scuffed jogging speed. A thin tall person in blue jeans with maroon and white checked shirt dashed into my right arm to swipe the card. My pupils dilated with joy and my face beamed with glee, as the door to the ODC (Offshore Development Centre) opened. Without any haste, I sneaked through the open door and now I could see myself getting the golden brownie points from my man-eater manager cum gym instructor. Tailgating was not allowed at office but desperate times require desperate measures. I let out a relieved sigh as I made my way in. I had to thank my savior for the day, so I hurried to catch up with Mr. Sneakers.

Once our footsteps were in line, I put my hand over my savior's shoulder and continued our forward stride. With each step we took, the lights above us were automatically switching on, as if it had a motion detection sensor. "You don't know what you have just done for me. Thanks a ton, Bro! Your deed will not go unpaid. Call me anytime, in need, ok Bro?" I exclaimed in a happy tone and about to turn to give a bro-hug.

"BRO???... Excuse-me!", as I heard this authoritative voice, I turned to come face-to-face with my savior. I saw two jet black eyes hidden behind a geeky, the-jetson's-cartoon-inspired, black spectacles.

"Excuse-me!", again the words came out and the head titled towards my arm over the shoulder. Only when the shoulders shrugged, the jolt woke me up. I noticed the black line on the upper eyelid extending in a pointed upward curve along with the deep red painted long nails on the hand which pushed me, to take a step back. "What the hell, you think you are doing?", as the words came out from her mouth, she tripped over her long untied laces.

She bent down to tie her laces and tucked her fluffy one-sided fringe behind her ear, I continued to look at her, only then I realized my savior was not "Mr. Sneakers" but "Ms. Sneakers". How could I have been such a blind idiot to mistake a girl for a boy? The answer to it was, her dressing sense; it was so tom-boyish along with her short haircut, it made up for a perfect camouflage. On Google-ing it later, I found out that it's called a pixie hair style with bangs, which is quite a craze among a few girls. I was so embarrassed with my act and I had to apologize to her for it but she was gone, disappeared into the thin air and lost among the bustling people entering into the floor.

I walked up to my desk and logged on to my workstation with her visuals, of tucking her maroon streaked bangs behind her ear whilst tying her laces, flashing in front of me. Now the only thing in my mind was to find her and convey my apologies.

I narrated my magical morning encounter to my friend, Vikram, over the phone, after our discussion about the coding defect raised against our names by the client. He laughed out a loud, and didn't leave any stone behind to ridicule me for my fairy tale myth. He said, "Idiot! those lights are scheduled to switch on by itself at 8:30 am. Looks like soul swapping happened in the morning, you turned into a girl with your fairy tale imagination." Vikram continued to snort out loudly.

"Hmph! You are just being jealous Vicky. Whatever it was, but one thing is for sure, I have to find her and apologize. I already have a starting point. She's got to be somewhere in this floor only, I can find her easily"

song:Oh, baby, when you talk like thatYou make a woman go madSo be wise (sí) and keep on (sí)Reading the signs of my body (uno, dos, tres, cuatro) I'm on tonightYou know my hips don't lie (no fighting)And I'm starting to feel it's rightAll the attraction, the tensionDon't you see, baby, this is perfection?

All of a sudden Shakira's Hips don't Lie song was booming on the phone and I know Vicky was upto his antics. God! that boy doesn't wait a second to poke fun of me. Can't expect anything less from a man who was not only my best friend for the past four and a half years but also my mentor and confidant. If I would take away, anything from this office, it would be our friendship. Friends till we die! Though he means a lot, he is annoying to the core. Just like now.

"Vicky! Vicky!...... VICKY!" I had to call out his name repeatedly, raising my voice up an octane, each time, so he could hear me. I have known him enough to be sure that he was just pretending not to hear me.

" VIKRAMENDRA YARLAGADDA, I say shut it!", I screamed, knowing that ought to stop him. There, the music died out. If you need to get his attention, all you have to do is call out his full name, and you will be awarded with his dull voice. He disliked his name, stating it didn't sound cool. Can't blame him, it took me two weeks to learn how to pronounce it properly.

"Ok, ok! All the best Bro! But one last thing, before you say sorry to her, go wash your eyes and see first if there is a moustache on the face. Who knows who you'll go and apologize to...hehehe."

"Enough! Bye!" and I cut the call.

2

—— ◆ ——

CHAPTER 2

Raghav's POV

song:Birds don't just flyThey fall down and get upNobody learns without getting it wrong.

Totally immersed in my coding task, I kept checking the clock, every now and then. I felt it was ticking on a faster rate, than usual. I had only two more hours for my deadline - 5:30 pm to arrive and I was so tensed whether or not I'll be able to finish it on time. I remembered "Ms. Sneakers" and said to myself, "No man! I can't ! I just cannot lose like this, after the morning miracle followed up by my embarrassing goof-up!" I gave myself a self- boost and nodded to reassure myself, "I can do it! If I can't, who can! I have two tasks for today not only this stupid coding one but also 'Finding Ms.Sneakers '." I smiled to myself how my self-imposed task coincided with the Finding Nemo movie. "Get back on Track Raghav ! 2 hours to go and 2 tasks to finish! buck-up man, Buck-up!"

song:I won't give up, no I won't give inTill I reach the endAnd then I'll start again.

The second task had infused extra energy into me. My technical and reasoning sections of my brain looked like they had suddenly woke up after being dormant for the whole day. I knew I was just beating around the bush instead of trying to approach the issue with a different outlook. I leaned back on my chair, to make a full 120 degree angle with the ground and closed my eyes for few minutes, with my fingers interlocked and pressed against the top of my head; to re-collect the defect scenario. At last I had found the bug in my code and Voila! I fixed it and now the code was working as expected.

Uff! Thank God I have one and a half hours, which I thought was ample enough to find a girl, no a Tom-Boy. That too I just had to search in my wing, how difficult was it going to be! All I had to do is walk past a couple of bays and spotting Ms. Sneakers among a couple of people, was going to be like picking out a colored stone from a pot full of black stones. So I got ready to start working on my second task. Just when I was about to step out of my cubicle, I thought lets not just jump into it like a direction-less-donkey. My algorithmic brain started churning out the fastest approach of finding her. Should I go with Linear Search or Binary Search? I took the Linear search approach, just to make it simple and considering that the wing would not be too big, I would complete my search soon.

song:No, I won't leaveI wanna try everythingI wanna try even though I could failOh, oh, oh, oh, oh! Try everything.

As I walked past bay-after-bay, scanning the left side and then the right side, to find my savior-of-the-day; I hadn't realized that I had just tail-gated myself from Wing- C into Wing-B. "Oh! It's ok, sometimes it happens", I comforted myself and carried on. I was scanning each square of the floor, if anyone had noticed me, they would have thought I was a human-look-alike search robot, with head turning from side to side. It was just a matter of forty minutes, and I was back to square one- My cubicle's bay. It was confusing like

I had lost my path and suddenly back to the place where I belong; I turned fully two to three times just to figure out how I landed here. Only then I found out that this building had all it's four wings along its circumference and they were inter-connected. I was astonished that I couldn't find her in my Wing, neither in the three other big wings, "Then where the hell, she disappeared?".

song:Baby you've done enough, take a deep breath. Don't beat yourself upDon't need to run so fastSometimes we come last, but we did our best.

The vibrator in my mobile started buzzing and I saw my GYM reminder I had scheduled, "Oookkk! It's evening coffee break time that's the reason. Hmm now I have to continue, tomorrow only", with a dejected look I made my way to the changing room and then to the Gym. There my Boss was standing in front of the mirror and warming-up. He saw me entering the room and smirked, I understood his strategy. He had chosen that spot so that he could see the attendees for his session without making direct eye-contact, "What a loser!", I thought to myself. I turned to see where I could take my position. Around 10-15 people had already come and seeing people still flowing through the door. I had to agree with my Boss's intelligent idea of how to cut the nervousness, he was going through, seeing so many attendees in his first session. The session was awkward for me in the beginning then I loosened up and forgot that he was my reporting manager and was just a trainer.

It was a hectic first session, I guess it was because all of a sudden my dormant muscles were made active today. My full body was already rattling by the end of the session and I literally thanked God for bringing the closure of the session. I knew there was going to be full crowd in front of the shower-cum-changing room; and I needed a nice long hot relaxing bath, without people banging on the doors to speed up. I just grabbed my towel and dabbed myself and headed towards the cafeteria to get myself a nice hot cup of coffee and more importantly to get a place to sit.

I collected my coffee token and was looking into my smartphone to check my mails and messages. On reaching the counter, as I was putting it back into my track pant's pocket, my elbow nudged another elbow. "Ooops! Sorry.... are you ok? Did your coffee drop? Shall I get you another one?", I asked. My pupils enlarged and gleamed in sheer happiness on seeing the pixie-haired-girl. She was busy brushing out the coffee droplets that had sprinkled on her shirt. "It's ok, no problem", she swiftly turned her head to me and walked away. My eyes were following her as she walked away and did a happy dance in my mind, "You did! You found her! Second task completed."

"Hello Sir!...Sir? Sir??", the voice came from the guy behind the counter. I cleared my throat and said, "Uh! Yes .... Ssorry. One large cappuccino please!

3

CHAPTER 3

R aghav's POV

song: You're turning heads when you walk through the door Don't need make-up to cover up Being the way that you are is enough. Everyone else in the room can see it Everyone else but you. Baby, you light up my world like nobody else The way that you flip your hair gets me overwhelmed.

For the on-lookers, I must have looked like a joker with a wide smile on my face for no reason at all; but they didn't know that I was beaming in my glory. With my cappuccino in my hand, I went ahead looking for a suitable place to sit. Just then my eyes fell on the pixie-haired person and the empty chair in front of her. My legs automatically took me to that place but I was standing in between two rows and hesitant on whether to sit with her or not. I saw someone walk past me, I literally pounced to reach "the" chair, thinking my chair would be taken. A sudden rush of blood was within me and I felt if my performance was being rated, I was not just "meeting the expectations" but I was "exceeding the expectations".

"Oh man! I'm again making the same blunder as in the morning". I had already sat in the chair in front of Ms. Sneakers but forgot my courtesy. She was looking into her purse below the table so she mustn't have noticed anything, so it was OK, I reassured myself.

"Hi! Sorry I forgot to ask if you are expecting someone to join you here."

She looked up and adjusted her spectacles, "Uh?... No, you may take it."

Thank God, I heaved a sigh of relief. Now I had to make the next move nice-n- smooth, before it becomes too late and looks like the "forced conversations" people have with the elders.

"Oh ! Hey ! I'm Raghav, I think we met each other today morning?", trying to be as casual as I could and hoping I had delivered my dialogue of a sudden realization with conviction.

"Uh?" she said with a what-the-hell kind of a look and turned towards the Television on her left, trying to ignore me.

I realized if I try to be uber cool and try all kinds of stuffs, nothing is gonna happen. So I decided the best way is to be honest and pour my heart out, but obviously in a decent way.

"Yes, seriously !", swaying my body slightly to be face-to-face with her.

"Don't you remember the morning dash while swiping the card at the floor? ...You may not remember me, but how can I forget my savior of the day"

That caught her attention and she turned toward me. It was like those 5 penalty shootouts the team gets in a FIFA match to decide the winner and each time she gave a positive response, it was like a score for me.

I went on ,"Sorry and THANK YOU!"

Her first reply, "Both? Sorry and Thanks?"

"Thank you was for being my savior for opening the door and saving me from my man-eater manager." She giggled and I was like, I'm on the right track, just keep going.

"If it wasn't for you, it would be Hell for me, today and for the next few days ; not only from my manager but from my clients too. Escalations after escalations, meetings after meetings and still the pending work lying right just there, in front of my eyes", I smirked. I didn't know while talking about my day's tension, I would be so involved and animated with so much hand gestures.

She gave a reassuring smile that said I-have-been-there and I-can-understand. I guess everyone can relate to the escalation and meeting round-the-clock in the IT world.

"And sorry was for...?", she asked with a puzzled look and took a sip of her coffee.

"That's for two things", I smiled, "One for not able to thank you at that time and..."

I didn't know how to articulate it in an unoffensive way about thinking she was a Guy. I needed some time for my brains to churn out something good, so hurriedly I sipped my coffee.

"And the other one was for misbehaving with you", I said in my soft, innocent voice with my I-didn't-do-it-wantedly charm; which always works with my mom, when I own up to my mistakes and helps me escape from the punishment. I was hoping It would work with her too.

She must have had a very long day because she was trying to recollect what had happened exactly in the wee hours of the day.

I continued, "and for calling you a 'bro'", and was so embarrassed with my guilt that I didn't realize that I was fidgeting with my hair at the back of my head. "I didn't do it purposely, I'm such a fool, how could I have mistaken such a beautiful girl for a Bro, it must have been the dim lights".

She burst out laughing for a good whole minute, "Now, now, now... you don't have to put so much flattery into it," her words were hardly audible with her giggling speed-breakers. "Obviously, everyone knows, "How", the mistake happened", she said with both her hands pointing to herself and moving her hands up and down, gesturing her get-up.

song:But when you smile at the ground it ain't hard to tell. You don't know, oh ohYou don't know you're beautiful.

"So ... then.. All's OK between us?"

She nodded and said with a raised left eyebrow, "But, that doesn't mean you can get away with it."

I was dreading this.

"Might be you should go in for an eye check-up and get it tested for night blindness", she said with a naughty laugh.

Now it was my turn to let out a laugh and I was happy it ended on a such a good note.

"Thanks once again and Sorry, it won't happen again... Friends?"

"Ok! :) Raghav is it?"

"Yes", my smile was touching ear-to-ear and I could feel it.

"Sasha", and we shook hands. What a beautiful and unusual name it was, I didn't want to say it aloud and make her feel I was trying too hard.

song:Right now I'm looking at you and I can't believeYou don't know, oh ohYou don't know you're beautiful, oh ohThat's what makes you beautiful.

"To US!" I raised my cup and we clinked our coffee cups together to mark the beginning of our friendship.

Afterwards we exchanged pleasantries and went our ways.

While I was driving back home and replaying the chat over our coffee, I realized that girls do like honest men with a dash of humor.

And that's how we got to know each other's name over our first coffee date. Yes, a "Date", a smooth conversation between a guy and a girl getting to know each other's names, over a cup of coffee and throw some giggles here and there; doesn't that count as date. So yes it was our cute little Coffee Date, I reassured myself while rolling over my bed and went to sleep.

4

— ◦ —

CHAPTER 4

Raghav's POV

song:Hey, go, uh Bring me down, can't nothin'Bring me downMy level's too high to bring me downCan't nothin' bring me downI said. Because I'm happyClap along if you feel like a room without a roofBecause I'm happyClap along if you feel like happiness is the truthBecause I'm happyClap along if you know what happiness is to you, eh eh ehBecause I'm happyClap along if you feel like that's what you wanna do.

The next day, for the first time in forever, I had gone to office with a smile on my face and no morning blues. I didn't know what was the reason neither did my mind or heart try to find it out. In fact, I myself was unaware of the constant smile stuck on my face; only when my colleagues started pulling my leg to spill out the beans, I realized that I had suddenly turned into a happy-go-lucky guy. No, No, no! Don't you guys get the wrong idea, it was just the effect of a good night's sleep.

It was a rather busy day, with meetings after meetings; somehow we had managed to squeeze time for a bite around lunch time. That's the reason my mind hadn't gone wandering around to Sasha and our little date. We, a group of four, who had just met and interacted in the roller coaster meetings from the morning; slumped down with our coffee mugs at the coffee zone.

The sip of coffee and its strong aroma triggered back yesterday's visuals into my mind. I was re-living those memories with each sip. Mid-way, I tried to pull myself together from my day dreams, "Raghav, my boy, nothing's gonna happen. It was just a one-time lucky stroke, who knows whether you will meet her again here in this office with 5,000+ employees. So boss, Come down to the earth and don't fly around."

Exactly when I reached to the point when she had giggled for the first time; the same spunky giggle came from across the room. My eyes shifted focus towards the giggle and saw the familiar pixie hair, glowing with the sunset beams passing through it from the translucent window. It made up for a perfect sunkissed Instagram photo. The vibrancy of her smile and her positive aura was spreading across the whole room. It felt like a cool refreshing wave lapping towards me and just hit my face instead of my feet. There was our #First Glance.

I had raised my mug for another sip, and looked at her through the circular rim of the coffee mug. I was mesmerized by the twinkle in her eye and how her big round eyes had shrunk into cute little half closed eyes, while she laughed her heart out. My constant glare towards her must have made her conscious as she looked towards me. Our eyes met for a fraction of a second and I knew she had seen me.

Like a guilty ridden person caught red handed, I instantly moved my head away from her gaze. I was so fidgety that I was looking at the ceiling as if it was some kind of masterpiece. Now I couldn't resist and was curious to know if she had spotted me and was still looking at me. So, I turned towards her, only to meet her big black eyes again. My cheeks were flushed with embarrassment, I had to dip my head down to hide it. I had to act quickly and quit being such a sissy. Instantly I looked up to see her giggle at me, with her hand covering her mouth. It would have been game over for me, if I hadn't raised my coffee mug to her with a slight nod and a decent smile. She saw my gesture and immediately acknowledged it by lifting her and did air-cheers-up with a laugh.

The next morning, I reached office to greet my colleagues "Good Noon". As I was late; I was taking long brisk strides, holding on to my college sling bag worn across my chest, to reach my desk. Slightly ashamed of coming to office at this odd time, I was looking down at the floor and walking. My phone started vibrating in my pant pocket and saw Vikcy's name flashing on the screen.

If it had been some other teammate, I would have left the call unanswered. As it was Vicky and I wanted to know what was the team's mood today - normal tide or full moon's high tide; I attended it. I brought the phone to my left ear and half-minded turned my face to the right. My eyes; like a magnet drawn towards any iron material due to its attractive force, got stuck to the girl seated on top of the desk adjoining to two computers. "It's Sasha!! Wow! Way to go lucky boy, second glance was not too far. Two in row", squealed my inner voice. Her presence in the same room as me, was enough to make my heart skip a beat. She looked like she was having a fun time and was a carefree college girl sitting on the desk, giggling and kicking her legs in the air.

"DO YOU GET IT RAGHAV !!", someone yelled into my ear from the other side of phone.

"eh! WHAT?", I also replied in the same tone unknowingly, that got Sasha's attention towards me.

For a second our pair of eyes met in a perfect line-of-sight, though not long enough that's required for any satellite to make a connection with it's receiver. But, it was more than enough to make "our " connection. I somehow managed to give her a small weird smile after my sudden outburst. I didn't want to give her a wrong impression of me being arrogant. She, on the other hand, gave me a clueless look, with the sudden break on her giggles.

I just prayed to God internally that, what just happened few minutes back wouldn't ruin anything for 'us'. Not that there was anything between her and me, for there to be an 'us'. Not that I was in love with her. Not that I wanted something to happen between us but I just didn't want her to see me in any kind of bad light. Damn It! I yelled only a single word and not a swear or anything, and it didn't last for even 5 seconds. Why was I over-thinking, over-analyzing over such a petty thing, was beyond my mind. What is this girl and her gaze and giggles doing to me!, I questioned myself.

"RRRRAAAAAGGGGHHHAAV!!!", again the person on the other side of the phone was yelling only with double intensity.

I took a deep breathe and trying to be calm. "Ya Vicky, tell me", I replied back and moved my attention back to the call and continued striding to my desk.

"What the hell TELL ME means ! Am I talking to the walls. GET LOST!", Vicky burst out and cut the call.

"There goes my last saving straw to the drain", I mumbled and grumbled to myself as I slouched into my office chair. I ended up doing most of the work, as it was pushed into my kitty; thanks to Vicky's grumpy attitude towards me. It felt like it was one of those days, where it was the team vs me. So much for being a "team"! Everyone thought I was taking work liberty by coming to office late. They were taking a united front against me by avenging my work etiquettes, and they won it hands down as my only friend had joined as their ally. I prayed to God hopefully the betrayal from Vicky would only last for a day.

By the time I was able wrap my work, the needle in my wristwatch had ticked to 9:30pm. I lent out a loud yawn and stretched out my hands and legs into the air to ease out my muscles crumpled posture. I continued doing some in-the-chair-stretches and rotating my neck, I could hear crackling sounds of the bones. I didn't mind it, as the bay, correction, the entire wing was empty. I could have even jogged around the wing or danced to loud music emanating from my phone speakers and no one would have objected; except if the security guards were looking into the cctv camera footages covering my bay. I let out a low chuckle thinking even those guards would be snoring in their chairs. Crackling my knuckles and waiting for my deskstop screen to die down to a black dead screen, I picked up my bag and left.

The parking lot at the second floor was eerie and cold. It was a closed parking lot, but the four sides of the building had huge open windowless slots to let the cool breeze to fill in the space. Whoosh! Whoosh! Sounds of the cool breeze were sending chills to my spine. I usually don't end up so late at office and I'm not afraid of the dark or anything but it just felt chilly. Before it could get to creep me out, I walked towards my car and pressed the automatic key to open it. Just wanting something to distract me from my thoughts.

The blinking yellow headlights, disguised as spotlights in a party seemed to usher the entry of a slim figure into my vision. My eyes roamed up the figure till it met my other companion's eyes in this eerie parking lot. And there it was..... STRIKE THREE!

5

CHAPTER 5

Raghav's POV

song:You held me up, held me downMade me crazy, then you brought me aroundWere my darkness and my lightYou were my blindness and my sight.

I just froze in my place, I was surprised to see her at this time, over here, in this lonely parking lot. I gave a quick glance to my watch and looked around to see if she had company, a sudden concern for her well-being had taken over me. Her car was parked a few slots away from mine. I was as still as a board, pinned down to its place, not able to move my damn feet towards her.

On the other hand, she was oblivious to her surroundings, and like it was just any another day for her, she went towards her car. Her face was leaning to her right side clutching her phone between it and her shoulder, as she was rummaging her backpack for her car keys. Don't know what took over me, and I kept on pressing the automatic lock on my key, repeatedly locking and unlocking my car. I guess, even though my feet were not moving, atleast my hands were doing something useful and trying to give her whatever little light that could be provided, in this pitch black ambience. The parking lot was poorly lit, but the place we were at was not ideal. When she found her keys, a warm smile spread across her face and she locked eyes with me and blinked, as a token of thanks.

song:Were my shelter and my stormMade me cold then you made me warmYou were my fever and my cure.

The imaginatory frozen ice surrounding me, making me immobile, had melted with her gaze. It felt like the unintentional, freeze game, I was playing with myself was over and I returned her smile. I took a step forward, while watching her switch from phone to her Bluetooth device on her ear. I stopped when I heard her laugh, with her head bouncing backwards. I was able to hear her side of the conversation and watching her at ease, I realized I was not needed there.... atleast not for her and not now! Bummed and sad, my heart sank. I turned abruptly towards my car and watched her speed off.

song:Made me doubt then you made me sureOne step forward and two steps backNobody gets too far like thatOne step forward and two steps backThis kind of dance can never last.

While manoeuvring my car to get out off the multi-storied parking lot, her words and reactions were replaying in my mind.

"Dude, ... you... are... on fire", her words were bearly heard, amidst her rolling laughter.

She shrugged innocently and said, "I'm fine, just the usual, no problem."

Her eyebrows forrowed together to and questioned, "Anyways, you are gonna be on the line with me the whole time, right?"

" Ya ya ya, I know we shouldn't use the phone while driving", she rolled her eyes and stated like it was an oath.

"I won't talk, just be my background music, alright! Guess what, this is your lucky day?", she chirped enthusiastically.

"I will give you liberty to talk all the nonsense you want, and the cherry on the top, I won't interrupt you.", she proudly declared, wiggling her eyebrows mischievously.

Tap! Tap!

The sound against my glass window, made me turn to the security guard standing next to me. I looked at the car in front of me, making its way out of the gate. I was wondering what kind of security check they are doing at this hour of the day. Might be checking for drunken driving,..... but at office?, my mind questioned. Nevertheless, I rolled down my window.

"Sir, company sticker... Where?", came out the broken english words of the security guard.

I pointed to the worn out sticker on my car and he gave a dis-approving nod. They made me park the car at the side and guided me to speak with the person in-charge. After a few back and forth exchanges, they came to a conclusion that they won't fine me. My company name, employee ID and parking slot details were noted down and at last, they stuck the brand new sticker on my car.

The security guard, who had stopped me, was smiling happily like he had just achieved his mission for the day. I was buckling up and waved to him with a warm smile and drove off.

Atleast, it was someone's lucky day.

Once again, even after the slight distraction, Sasha's words, "Guess what, this is your lucky day?", crept back into in my mind. I sighed, "Not mine, even after three strokes... But some other dude's, for sure..... May be.. May be... Her boy... friend". The word 'her boyfriend' hesitantly rolled out of my tongue leaving behind bitter taste. Like it was a punishable sin, just to say it.

song:And we were never really meant for each otherWe were never really meant to lastIn the years that we danced togetherEach step forward we took two steps backEach step forward we took two steps back.

My stomach grumbled and I let out a laugh, "don't worry buddy, I didn't forget you, lets go home and order some yummy food". That's what happens when you are exhausted after work, you start doing weird stuff like talking to your own tummy.

The next day, I stood in front of the mirror, while styling my hair, I gave myself a self-boost. "Raghav, come on man! Let's make things right today! Let's do it man!". I took a last glance of my office attire and left my home.

I clasped my hands together and said," first things first". I logged into my computer and swiftly scanned through all the mails. Replied back to the ones that needed my action. Slowly as I marked all the 25 mails recieved as read, I saw an appreciation mail for me, for my yesterday's work. A thats-how-do-it confident smirk turned to smile, crept across my face. I leaned back on my chair and reclined it till the squeaky noise came and clasped my hands, at the back, to rest my head on it.

"Great! After yesterday's work marathon, today I'm free, just one small task that hardly takes a hour or two for me", I told myself. I was contend, that I had enough time to execute my plan.

Quickly I completed my task, and checked the time. The clock had struck twelve in the afternoon, the perfect time for lunch. Surfing through internet on my phone, I searched for home delivery from a famous restaurant.

"Hmmmm, will one full plate of chicken biryani be enough?.... Nah! Let's top it up with dessert and a bottle of coke."

Scrolling through the dessert menu, trying to search the perfect fit for the meal, "What should I get, what should I get...... Bingo! Carrot Halwa it is!". I quickly added them to the cart, entered the office address and paid it. It was scheduled to be delivered by 1pm the latest. " No prob. As long as the food is delicious and reaches before 1:30 pm, I have nothing to worry", I shrugged and went back to work.

I was restlessly clicking and un-clicking the head of my ballpoint pen and waiting for the call. I was sure that enough time had past. While anticipating the call, a sudden doubt crossed my mind, What if, I mentioned the wrong address? I re-checked the order, everything looked fine, name, address, phone number... Everything! I was loosing my patience, I got up and went to relieve myself at the men's room. Returning back to my desk, I could hear my phone's ring-tone, "Finally!", I said out aloud and sprinted faster to anwer it.

"Awwww!..... Man!.... Thanks! And here I thought I would be receiving a bouquet of flowers and chocolates on my table", the voice came from the other end of the call, ending with a chuckle.

"Ha ha ha.... Very funny, Vicky", I replied sarcastically.

"What can I do", I knew Vicky shrugged his shoulders at that. "You have been misreading people lately. Might have mistaken me as your girlfriend", replied Vicky, purposely slurring the last word and I could imagine him winking at me.

"Thank God that idiot is in Hyderabad and not in front of me, right now", my inner voice stated. Before I could say anything, he cut me off.

"I thought your time had come, to be wooing your so called girlfriend". I knew he was hinting at Sasha, like as if something was there, I let out a frustrated sigh.

Vicky continued his teasing, "Oh Poor thing!! You are back to zeroth positon.... Ah! Are you trying to practice your wooing skills on me?!", his fake surprised voice came out. Vicky ended his wacky imagination with a whine, "Am I your trial piece? "

"Oh! Come on Vicky! you are my best bud! And you know that.....". Trying to get Vicky back on track, I asked, "Hmmm so how was it? "

Vicky left out a small laugh and responded back in his real voice, "It was yum! Just perfect and the carrot halwa was bang on! You nailed it this time!"

Now it was my turn to chuckle, "Anything for you bro!", and then with a slightly serious voice, "Next time you pull yesterday's crap on me again, you better watch out for me. Your ass will be the one paying it off", I warned him.

"Burn!.... Hey whatever happened to 'best buds', Raghav boy?"

"He and his ways of nicknaming me, Oh Lord!" , I cried to myself.

"That's a two-way ride, Sir!"

"Gottcha! Relax Raghav. You and me, know what got me pissed off."

"Hence the peace offering", I stated matter-of-factly.

"Ya, Your offering was well received, appreciated and approved!", in a commander's voice he stated.

"Good! Good!", I nodded my headand continued, "Ok, I need to go now, gotta go for lunch."

"Whoa! you waited for me to have lunch first..... Awwww.... I am so touched bro!"

I shook my head and cut the call, knowing very well that, a full fed and statied Vicky, high on his favorite biryani, wouldn't end his dramatics anytime soon.

I rushed to the cafeteria and got my food token after paying the cashier, worried that the food would have gotten over or only left overs would be there. Queuing up at the food counter, I let out a grateful sigh. I took my tray and walked back to the dinning area, looking for a empty seat.

As my eyes were busy scanning the area, they found the perfect seat. It was at a right distance and angle from the TV hung nearby, not directly under the A/C outlet, enough place between the row of tables, for people to comfortably get up and walk around without banging into each other. I took two steps forward and found a vey familiar girl with pixie hairstyle sitting in front of my perfect spot.

6

CHAPTER 6

Raghav's POV

song:Here I am this is meThere's no where else on earth I'd rather beHere I am it's just me and youTonight we make our dreams come true.

Before I could take a call on where to sit, the universe had decided for me.

"Raghav! Over here!", I heard my manager call out to me with a hand gesture.

I groaned internally and tried to keep a straight face. I felt like a gravitational pull had taken me to where he sat. "Oh God! Help me. Now I have to hear his rambling and have to attempt to make sweet talk with him. Urgh!", cursed internally for my ill fate. I looked down at my tray, "You better be good, to help me survive with him."

"You know Cathy is going to make a visit over here. Few other folks will join her, they haven't shared the confirmed list and dates", Selva, my manager, stopped while stuffing his mouth with the next morsel. Then he continued, "It's going to be busy month ahead Raghav, we need to build better client relationship and win over the new project....." Blah blah blah, he went on and on. I just nodding my head and replying 'yes' every now and then.

"Ya like the clients are so dumb, to give the new project worth of millions of dollars, just based on few days of visit. Over that, these idiots sitting in the leadership roles, instead of deciding to showcase our technical skills, wanted to put up a Bollywood inspired skit cum dance. God help us! Don't know how they got these jobs...... Can it be that after many years of working, their brains started rotting?", I was internally giving a disapproving nod but physically shaking my head yes.

In the previous client visit, I had voiced out on giving importance on our innovations and technical aspects to make an impression, but it went down the drain. The leadership team was hell bound on showing our tradition and culture, which I don't have qualms with, but just wanted to add some more meaning content for the clients. So after repeated rejections earlier, I knew they would stick to their same old and worn out trick. It felt like the world moves forward but we are stuck in a broken tape recorder, winding the same thing and reeling it out. Aren't those clients also fed up to see it too. I think that's why they send a new person every time.... Might be someone must have complained about the torture they went through time and again, I chuckled at that thought.

"You liked the idea. Are you in it?", Selva exclaimed.

"Yes, yes. It's good", I looked up to him and stated, though I didn't have a clue, but knew it was the usual Bollywood skit. Trust these people to never try anything out of the box and they expect us to think out of the box and develop some innovative tools... Double standard-ed idiots!

"Great! you took the load off my shoulder man, thanks. Will see you later", he gave a grateful pat on my shoulder and walked past me with his empty plate. I didn't give much heed to it and walked to wash area.

As I was exiting the cafeteria and making my way to the left to head towards elevator section, I could faintly hear a repeated "Excuse me!", from behind me. It was getting more louder as I could hear the sprinting of footsteps closer to me. I turned around to see and was surprised. A girl was standing in front of me with the head bent down, as she was steadying her breath. Even though the burgundy streaked fringe of her hair, was hiding half of her face, I knew who it was. Once stable, she looked up and we had identical warm smiles on our faces. "Wow! She is approaching me, for once, that's new", my mind was jumping with all kinds of thoughts.

song:It's a new world it's a new startIt's alive with the beating of young heartsIt's a new day it's a new planI've been waiting for youHere I amHere I am.

"Hey!", Sasha said.

"Hey!", I responded back.

Her smile turned to an awkward smile with thinning of her lips to a flat line, "Sorry and Thank you", she blurted out.

I cocked my right eyebrow and let out a light laugh, "Déjà vu!". She joined with a soft laugh and said, "Ya, right!"

"Sorry I forgot your name and I'm sure you forget mine too", she said and extended her hand out, " I'm Sasha and you...", she trailed off.

Accepting her handshake, "I'm Raghav and I remember your name."

"Oh!... That makes me look bad, right?", she brushed her hand over one side of her face, feeling embarrassed.

I shrugged my shoulders and said, "Nah! You were my savior, so if I didn't remember your's, then it would be bad on my part."

"Hmmmm Raghav.....but if it makes anything better, I do remember your face", Sasha stated still trying to ease out her embarrassment. "I mean, I mean you.... I remember the full you, your body not only your face....Oh My God! What am I blabbering, I didn't mean it like that....", but she was only making it worse and more visible, as she was ranting on unintentionally. She looked cute though and my smile was replaced by a wide toothy grin, "Relax Sasha, I understand."

She took a deep breath and cleared her throat, but before she could say anything people were rushing past and made her stumble. It was not their fault, we were standing, immersed in our conversation, in the middle of passage leading to the elevators at a busy hour. Everyone was hurrying up to catch one of the six elevators, split up equally at the two sides of the passage, to rush back to their desk at the end of lunchtime. I caught her left arm gently, steadying her and walked her to the side, to be out of their way. We glanced at the crowd and back to each other. She took a few steps back to put some distance between us and said,"Thanks for that!". I just gave a small smile.

"So... the earlier thanks was for yesterday.... You were the one at the parking lot, right?", she continued.

"Yeah! No problem". I was debating to whether to ask her or not but went ahead and asked, "Do you always leave office so late?... ..Sorry if I'm intruding, you needn't to answer it", I rushed the last sentence.

"No...only sometimes. What about you?"

"Mine was the outcome of ignoring my friend-cum-team lead, with a return gift of six people's work handed over to me...Doesn't happen a lot though", I laughed.

"Lol! He screwed you for screwing him", she also found amusement at my situation.

"Kind-off... But all's good now. Hmmm but try not to leave at odd hours, it's not safe", I advised genuinely concerned for her. Her right eyebrow was raised and had a don't-go-there look. I quickly added, "Hey! not because you are a girl or something. Hell! I was scared to death myself in that parking lot. Safety as in for any person - gender, doesn't matter. Mishaps don't look for gender, it just happens". With that her facial expressions calmed down, she didn't tell anything. I guess she had heard a lot of gender based advises-cum- discussions and it was asecond time from me, "Way to go! Keep digging your own grave", my mind voice stated.

Adjusting her spectacles, she ran her hand over her fringe and fluffed it , "Same here....I was also kinda scared ...but you were there and I was on the phone, so it calmed me....I owe you a coffee for it though, let me know when you are free?". Something in me was irked at the mention of her call.

"I'm free now!", I immediately answered, not wanting to lose a chance. Back in my head I was trying to convince myself it was mainly because I didn't have work for the day; don't think it was worked though.

"Now?", came out her slightly surprised voice and she looked around to the now empty passage and her watch, "We just had lunch.....Oh! It's already 4!", she exclaimed.

"You have work?"

"Hmmm, nothing major", she said absent-minded.

"I finished my team's work for the week, yesterday itself", I replied, nonchalantly putting my hands into my pant pockets and slightly leaning my back to the wall.

"Week's work?", she quipped astonished.

"Yeah! Today is Friday right", I replied with a smug smile.

She chuckled and shook her head slightly.

song:Here we are we've just begunAnd after all this time our time has comeYa here we are still going strongRight here in the place where we belong.

"Sooo?", I asked.

Her phone rang and I was left hanging for her reply while she answered her call. I felt a sudden dip in my mood like she was going to cancel it. Just as I was getting my hopes high, it had to come crashing down, so soon.

7

— ◦ —

CHAPTER 7

Raghav's POV

song:If the heart is always searching. Can you ever find a home.I've been looking for that someoneI'll never make it on my own.

Sasha hung up the call and opened her mouth, everything around me seemed to be moving in slow motion, I was eagerly waiting for her next words. She said, "Okay! Let's go!"

"Uh?!", I blurted in disbelief.

"Come on Raghav, let's have coffee. I don't have much time, I have a meeting at 5:30."

"Oh ok!"

We made our way to the snack-cum-fast food cafe, at the other end of the hallway, which was open 24x7.

"What would you like to have?", I asked while standing in front of the cashier with my open wallet.

"No, No no.... It's my treat , remember?", she effortlessly pushed down my wallet, "I'm having juice, ate too much", she said while rubbing her tummy, "You?"

"Cappuccino will be fine", I said with a smile.

After collecting her lime mint cooler and my cappuccino we settled at our table. I came to know we had few similarities. This was the first company for both of us, she joined a year and a half after me and she was also staying away from her parents but in a shared accommodation, unlike my single room flat. We shared the same hometowns too, what a coincidence.

"Which account do you belong too? I haven't seen you before...", I was cut off my her slight shriek.

"Oh Shit!", she cursed aloud and immediately ducked her head. She was hiding behind her mint cooler, like it did any good. "Stand up!", motioning me to do so with her hands, "Stand up!", the urgency evident in her voice. Sasha kept ducking. As an obedient soldier I sprung to my legs, clueless of the situation we were in. "Right! right", her black eyeballs immediately hit to the top of her eyes, to meet my confused face, "Move right one step please", she said. She looked adorable, like an innocent toddler trying to hide away from her parent's warth for something she shouldn't have done. What could that be?, my mind questioned, shrugging it off, I did as I was ordered.

"One more step.... One more step right.... Right", I complied as and when the orders were thrown at me. I gave quick glance at our surrounding ambiance and let out an inwardly sigh of relief, Thank God the Cafe is deserted. With her chin resting her right hand to avoid clashing with the tabletop, she shook her head, signaling me not to glance around.

This moment felt surreal, like I was transported to a battle ground and reprimanded from my commander-in-charge for deviating from her orders. It felt like I was the barrel gun of a tanker, and she was the commander who had its control, to maneuver it in any direction.

I was no more a human being but a piece of ammunition. Instead of using to shoot, it's purpose was to shield from the enemy. The enemy only known to her. With each step I took right, she shifted her chair left, to get maximum coverage.

After few minutes, Sasha sat up straight in her chair and let out a loud sigh. Taking a sip from her cooler, "Thanks, you may relax now. He just stepped out."

"What was that all about?", I inquired with my thumb pointing behind me and took my seat.

"Escaping from some one", she coolly replied with a slight shrug, "It's a long story, may be for another time."

She sipped through her juice, like a thirsty wanderer in the oasis who had just been handed it over to.

song:Dreams can't take the place of loving youThere's gotta be a million reasons why it's true.

Smiling at her antics and the words another time ringing in my head, I nodded my head. Anyone else in my shoes, a while ago, would been embarrassed for making a fool of himself. I, on the other hand, sat blissfully enjoying everything about this moment - the coffee, the view in-front of me and the silence between us. Truth be told, if given another chance, I would let her do the same a hundred times over. Uh hun! What did I just say?

song:Every thing's alrightWhen you're right here by my sideWhen you look me in the eyesI catch a glimpse of heavenI find my paradiseWhen you look me in the eyes.

"I'm done", broke me from my thoughts and I saw her getting up to leave.

Sasha came over to my side, "Gotta go now, meeting time. Bye Dude", she bid adieu. She double tapped my left shoulder and crossed behind me, with that she made her way towards the exit. Dumbstruck by her swift casual pat. I could still feel her fingers lingering on me as it slightly brushed my back.

"Sorry bro - Better luck next time". Coming back to my senses, I looked up to see who it was, " Uh?... What?", I said in small questioning voice, trying to regain my composure.

The passerby, who was a couple of steps ahead of my table, turned on his heels to face me and whisper yelled, "Friend zoned!". He nudged towards his shoulder, implying about Sasha's friendly pat and left the scene. Now that was weird, who was he?

song:How long will I be waitingTo be with you again.

For the next couple of weeks, Sasha's and my paths had crossed a little more than anyone could ask. Every now and then, we used to meet but it felt like we were standing at two opposite poles in a crowded crosswalk. Too close but yet too far. That sounds poetic, I'm becoming a poet now? What's happening to me?

song:I can't take a day without you hereYou're the light that makes my darkness disappear.

"Focus Raghav!", I groaned loudly and threw the pen in my hand, only for it to hit the far dead end of my desk. Here I'm supposed to be churning out ideas for the upcoming client visit, but my mind was in no mood to cooperate. Behaving like a disobedient child, it kept drifting back to my interactions with Sasha over the past weeks.

The first flashback that hit me were of the elevator meets.

Panting for air, I shouted, "Hold on!"

Skidding through the elevator passage to press the button, just in time for the closing elevator doors to open up back, I let out a relaxed breath.

Quickly I got in to the elevator and thanked the guy to my left for holding it. Before I could turn around and face the door, the door dinged, closing me in and making me immovable in my position. I awkwardly smiled at the person in whose face I was literally in. Oh Crap! How do I land up in such humiliating situations. At least it's a man not a woman.

The elevator was jam packed with all my fellow passengers facing the door and the unfortunate me had to bear with their stares. Trying not to lock eyes with anyone one, I let my eyes sweep through, from one end to the other. As it reached the far right hand side of the elevator, it rested at the pair if wide eyed black iris hidden behind spectacles, whose owner was trying hard to stifle her laugh at my predicament. I responded with a shrug of what-can-I-do innocence. We were conversing through our eyes - blinking in acceptance, widening in surprise rolling in attitude and air mouthing whenever necessary.

The door dinged at several levels, people exited, making me walk backwards, as I didn't want to break our eye contact. Before I could re-enter the elevator, new passengers boarded it, leaving no space for improvement in my elevator predicament. Now it didn't matter to me and everyone else, present in that enclosed space, were zoomed out of my vision. If anyone paid attention, they would vouch for the amazing eye chemistry Sasha and me were sharing, but our co-passengers were oblivious to it.

song:When you look me in the eyesMore and more, I start to realizeI can reach my tomorrowI can hold my head highAnd it's all because you're by my side.

The next elevator meet, the following day, thankfully turned out better. I conveniently placed myself near the elevator button board and tested my back on the elevator's lateral side. She had stationed herself at the same spot as I had left her yesterday whilst exiting at my floor. It left like our earlier day's conversation was put on pause to resume the next day.

With each subsequent elevator meets, our placements inside it improved. It felt like we were pounds on a chess board, moving one step closer, slow and steady, closing the distance between us. The next scene that rewound in my mind had to be the one that sent electrifying sparks through me, making me flush out in front of my team mates. We all had gathered at the conference room at the fourth floor, as the ones on our ninth floor were occupied. I headed the meeting to fulfill the innovation SPOC responsibilities that had been thrust upon me in the beginning of the year. We were almost winding up the meeting when we heard at the door.

Knock! Knock!

A girl's head popped in to let us know that her team had booked the room for the next hour and were waiting outside.

"Sure give us two minutes, we were just about to wrap up", I replied with a small smile and her head retreated back as quickly as it had popped in.

"Soo.... Hope everyone's in on this and understands what needs to be done..... Any questions?.... We will have a follow-up meeting two weeks from now to share our progress. Thank you all for your time."

On that note, my teammates dispersed from the room. There was slight bottleneck outside the conference room, as the other team waiting on us had gathered in the walkway between the door and the cubicles. I shook my head disapprovingly with my eyes cast down to the floor, These idiots can't they behave professionally -, my inner thought abruptly came to a stop at the sight of a particular blue and white sneakers.

My eyes traversed up the body of it's possessor, to reveal slim fitted royal blue jeans with tucked in pristine white shirt enclosed over a black open zipped hoodie. It made it's way up to Sasha's eyes and instantly wondered if, her health was not in check, for her to be wearing a hoodie. Tightly hugging her laptop to her chest, with her hands barely visible from being tucked into the hoodie's sleeves, she looked at me through the brim of her quirky spectacles. From the back of her hand she nudged it to settle in it's actual place and smiled at me.

Waiting for my turn to pass-by, I couldn't help but recollect that I have never seen her in anything else apart from jeans or formal trousers. Not even her shirts were girly. Of course you idiot! Why would she wear anything girly, she said herself, she is a Tom-Boy. Our office had shifted to business casual attire on all days, lucky for her. Our shoulders bumped lightly making us glide sideways; sending never felt before sparks all through my body. We were immersed in our little eye contact, before she hurriedly ran into the conference room.

"Raghav"

"Umm ya?"

"Come, let's go. They are holding the bay's access door for us", came Asim, my team mate's voice. I acknowledged him and stepped in line with him.

While reminiscing our memories, it struck me that whenever I meet Sasha, I'm like a lost puppy in the dreamland. Why does she have such an affect on me? I left for lunch, seeing how productive I had been for the past two hours. Lo and behold, there she was, yet again ready to invade my mind, settled at a table with a group of boys, ready to pounce on her food. Walking past their table, I was astonished to hear them singing, looks like they are having fun.

Few days later, waiting in the queue to collect my cappuccino, I heard my name being called. Fumbling with my phone to stop the music blasting in my ears, I felt a tap on my shoulder.

"Hi Raghav! ", Sasha exclaimed with a wave.

"Hi! I can hear you now."

"Oh ya after screaming your name 4-5 times", she huffed slightly and rolled her eyes. To which I sheepishly smiled and collected my cup.

We sat down together at a nearby table and chit-chatted over her plate of hot crispy samosas, which she generously shared. We were discussing IPL and placing our bets on which team would win it. She is interested in cricket!?... Obviously all girls watch it only to drool over the Dhoni's and Kholi's. However my misconception on her enthusiasm in cricket came crashing down with the knowledge she shared, as our conversation progressed.

Deeply enthralled in her fascination towards cricket, I felt something itching on my right thigh. Subconsciously I moved my hand over the area in question and placed the object near my plate. Sasha's eyes kept shooting at it, only then I apprehended that the itchiness I felt was my phone vibrating against my leg. Raghav internally face-palmed.

"Need to take that, just a minute."

Sasha gave a go ahead nod.

"Yes, tell me", Raghav spoke into his phone.

"Brooo! Where the hell have you been! We've been calling you since half an hour", Vicky roared with concern and anger evident.

"Just got stuck up with something. Why, what happened", Raghav nonchalantly replied.

"Just got stuck up", mocked Vicky, "What happened, you are asking me?" Vicky took a deep breath and continued in a calm voice, "So let me take you down memory lane, today is 9th May, Friday and the needle has struck 6:30pm IST."

Raghav rolled his eyes at the dramatic act Vicky was pulling off, instead of getting to the point.

"And that my friend marks the end of the weekly status meeting with onshore and offshore leads along with the client's management team!", with that Vicky rested his case.

"Oh my God! Oh my God! Don't tell me-"

"Yes!", Vicky cut him in the middle, "Now you panic", he said as cool as a cucumber.

"Please tell me you took over the meeting", Raghav asked with a plea.

A wicked snort was heard on the line, "Obviously you dumb ass! I wasn't going to let that dumb manager of ours to run it and take over our credit."

Raghav let out the breath he was holding in, "Thanks Vicky! Bro I seriously don't know how I missed such an important meeting. Please tell me you had the latest ppt slides right, the ones with the effort save and dollar save metrics?", questioned as another stroke of panic hit him.

"Ya, I had it.... Chill now. Everything went well and I made sure to subtly highlight to the clients that all the work was done by both of us. Didn't give a chance to Selva to hog over our hard work."

"Good good....", I ran palm over my face in relief. Sasha motioned to inquire if everything was fine and then signaled that she needs to leave. I reassured her with a smile and nod. "Sorry man to put you in the spot like that."

"OK so what was the thing that made you jeopardize our 6 months efforts?", an intrigued Vicky asked with a slight hint of annoyance.

I couldn't get myself to answer him as the consequences of my actions came down on me.

Vicky being a smart ass, interpreted the silence, "Let me guess.... what was the name.... SA-SHA!?" I'm not sure if he cut the line before or after hearing my faint yes.

I let my elbows slump on the table and raked my hands through my hair, She's going to be the death of me.

On his way back to my desk, waiting for the elevator, Raghav saw Sasha near the turnstile throwing her head backward and laughing away with someone. When her companion came into his view, he was shocked to see it was the man who had earlier branded him "Friend zoned" and wished him luck.

Who was he?

8

— • —

CHAPTER 8

Sasha's POV

song:I'm sure you got some thingsYou'd like to change about yourself. But when it comes to meI wouldn't want to be anybody else.

"Eeewwww! What is this? What the hell is hanging there?..... It's tickling me", I squirmed in annoyance.

"Wait a minute..... Just stand still for 2 minutes, will you?", Ruhi, her colleague who was helping her dress up for the Client visit in the ladies room at office, ordered in a stern voice.

Chitra, holding the safety pins in her hands burst out laughing aloud at the sight.

I whipped my head sideways to give a zip-it-up glance to Chitra. While straightening up my shoulders and back, to stand in attention, "Watch out, you might swallow the pins". Instantly the laughter booming in the room came to an abrupt end.

"That's so rude!", proclaimed Chitra.

"Oh ya right", I did my signature eye-roll minus my spectacles, "It was for your safety. We don't want to be rushing to an ambulance in the mid of Cathy's client visit, do we now?", I enunciated.

Chitra, let out a small chuckle, "Wait till you step out, Missy....we'll see who or should I say how many are going to be needing an ambulance", wiggling her eyebrows in a tease.

"Cut it, both of you", Ruhi shut the bickering pair up.

"But she -"

"I'm trying to work here. Stand straight", Ruhi me cut off and turned to Chitra, "Pass me two pins, we will pin the pallu pleats, here and here and that should do it".

After another good fifteen minutes, Ruhi got ready to showcase their creation, to the world or actually to me. She slowly turned me around, dramatically as in any movie, to catch a glimpse of my "dolled-up" version in the mirror. I came face-to-face with a blurred me, spontaneously my hand reached out for my spectacles on the slab.

SMACK!... OUCH!

"Don't you dare touch that", Chitra scorned.

Tending to my smacked hand, "Why?", I asked halfheartedly in a mellow voice, "I can't see without them."

"Use these instead", handing me over my contact lens.

"Yes", Ruhi agreed with Chitra in a tone of finality.

I huffed, "Now this is going over hand guys. You can't dictate over everything, I already abode to this outrageous saree makeover. Cut me some slack", as I put my trademark glasses on.

"Okay!", sighed Ruhi, "What do you think?", rubbing her hands excitedly eagerly waiting for my opinion.

I turned my head left and right and then my body. There I stood unable to recognize myself clad in a sky blue chiffon saree comprising of Zardosi sequence embellishmentsat the thin border along with cute tiny sequences disguised as flowers thrown in the saree's body. Accessorized with silver oxidized multi-colored enamel earnings ending in dangling multi-colored beads and a thin matching chain-set adorning my neck with similar but elongated beads. An elongated sleek moon shaped enamel pendant hung over it. A proud Titan Raga's watch was clutched to my left wrist, which I had bought from my first salary. My signature winged eyeliner and cherry red lips, kept my identity intact. The funky me added blue kajal to glamorize my lower eyelids. Like the icing on the cake, a tiny stone bindi shone between my brows.

song:I'm no beauty queenI'm just beautiful meNa na naNa na naYou've got every rightTo a beautiful life.

I must say they did a pretty impressive job and cleaned up good. I'm looking different.....decent.... Nice. But Never in my life time on this Earth will I express that aloud, or else these crazy co-workers will start including me in all ridiculous events. Urgh! I shivered inwardly at the thought of me being dragged around in such costumes. This saree is uncomfortable as hell. I need to just get through the next two torturous hours.

"Hmmm. It's ok, not bad", I gave my laid-back response.

"Not bad!", Ruhi's mouth flung open and twirled me, "It's beautiful".

"Something's missing", Chitra wandered, "Ah haa! Here you put this", with an evil smirk growing on her face.

I did a double check at what she had in hand and looked between her hand and her, with a weird expression.

I cracked up, "You gotta be kidding me right now!", to earn a dismissing nod from her.

"Where do I have hair to put it on", I slightly tugged my hair out to show, like as if they were blind bats. Wearing an exasperated expression, "That Gajra is longer than my hair for heaven's sake Chitra!"

She bit her lips to suppress the smile that wanted to concur and pulled a straight poker face to say, "Gajra is part of the Indian tradition attire, so all the ladies are wearing it to showcase uniformity and team spirit."

song:Keep you beneath the starsWon't let you touch the sky.

A muffled bull-shit! escaped from lips. She is doing this on purpose.

"Come on, be a sport and wear it. We need to go out, to receive them at the reception. Cathy and her team will be arriving soon", Ruhi stated. "Let me put it for you".

She used a sparkling silver coated hairpin to clip and the Gajra fell to my right side hanging in two uneven columns. I looked like a toddler whose mother had put the prominent flower garland to ensure no one calls her kid, a boy. I wasn't ready to go to sacrifice my dignity, just to satisfy some clients who were hardly going to glance at me for more than 10 seconds, at the expense of become the laughing stock for the rest of the year.

Pulling the flowers out of my hair to hear, "No, you need to wear them" and "It's late, wear it back soon", from my colleagues.

I rolled the garland on my right wrist and secured it as a wrist corsage. "Rule is that everyone needs to wear it but no one said where. If it was some other flowers, I would have worked with it to make a floral crown..... But I think this seals the deal and compliments okaish", I said admiring my hand, at different poses. Patting my right hand on Chitra's shoulder, to put it in her face, I announced, "I'm ready, let's get going girls". I went on to grab my belongings to stuff them in my bag and headed towards the door in my sober golden flat ballerina shoes, at least one part of my attire I was comfortable in.

We took a few quick selfies and groupies, they being girls wanted to take it before their look wears off. I silently obliged and thanked them for helping me with the saree. Now all I had to do was endure the Zardosi threads poking my body and pray that no wardrobe malfunction happens for next few hours.

Our task to receive and handover bouquets to the guest of honors at the reception, completed without any hassles. I had just started to get comfortable as we didn't have to move around. The clients were overwhelmed seeing us in traditional attire and sweet enough to walk over to us to get snapped.

Cathy said, "Wow! All you ladies are looking beautiful in these outfits. Now I feel left out!", whined slightly. On hearing, they had arranged similar outfits for the guests to slip on to after the official meetings are over, they were looking forward to it. "That will be wonderful, now that's what we call a team. We will take group snaps later then. Hopefully you guys will stick around in them till then."

Great! Another circus started, the dreaded two hours is going to be prolonged to a whole day!

With each calculated step I took to avoid toppling; I was cursing internally for whoever came up with "all traditional saree attire" and planning the culprit's execution in my head. Who knew that handling a saree was more difficult than resolving a production issue at work, my IT engineer brain marveled on it. I was so self-conscious, to avoid putting on a skin show of my hip and back, I kept pulling the flowing saree pallu to cover my body. The dangling blouse tassels tickling my back added to my discomfort. Will make that person wear this saree for a whole week. Nah! it's a flop idea, if the culprit is a lady, they will probably enjoy their punishment. Engrossed in my thoughts on how to torture that person, I bumped into a hard wall, Bang! Great! The last thing I needed is a red bump on my head.

"Sasha, is that you?", the voice made me look up to catch Raghav's surprised face. Flustered at his sudden appearance, my stomach started knotting up. Anticipating his response to my feminine ensemble, I stood before him with small smile.

"Whoa! For a minute there, I couldn't recognize you. You-"

Behind him came a authoritative voice, "Raghav, we must hurry up. Cathy and Team finished their meeting and are heading towards the ODC for the floor visiiiittt."

"Meet my best friend Vikram. Vikram-"

For the second time, Vikram cut him off to state, "You must be Ms. Sneakers..... Sasha, right?"; he extended his hand and flashed a wide grin.

"Sasha", I acknowledged him with a curt nod and handshake. "I haven't see you here before."

"He's based out from Hyderabad and flew down just for this visit. He'll be staying here for a couple of days", responded Raghav.

"You came only for the client visit?", surprise evident in my voice, "That's crazy."

"I know! Apparently if Cathy and Team doesn't get a glance of 'His Highness' ", pointing to himself, "The contract won't be signed", Vikram bragged; everyone joined in the contagious laughter. "Anyway, the joke's on them, I get sponsored flight ticket for my travel, three star hotel stay and couple of days to hang out with my friend s....Also, Raghav needed an extra hand in setting up this". He turned to Raghav and bowed, "At your service", earning him a smack on his back.

"Don't take this idiot seriously", Raghav pointed.

"I can see that", I grinned. Glancing around at the decorated floor, I asked, "So Raghav, you are in charge of all this."

"Yes, that's the site-leader-in-charge cum event orchestrator", Vikram butted in."

"YOU! you were the cause of all this?", pointing to our traditional wear attires, I accused.

He looked comfy in his Ivory Kurta-Pajama teamed with a self-designed hexagon patterned sea green Nehru Jacket; radiating a soothing view to the beholder's eyes. It's bringing out his clean shaven chiseled features, and scintillating eyes. Looking handsome. The last part of the sentence was almost going to slip out of my tongue. What am I thinking!, I ridiculed myself and brought myself back to our earlier conversation.

"Hmmm, kind-of", Raghav absentmindedly moved his hand over the back of his hair with a slight shrug, a give away of his helpless state. "I didn't know you work in this account, didn't see you around during the client visit preps?"

I let out a small laugh, "I did a good job escaping it, I guess. But couldn't escape the mandatory dress code of the day", bringing back the attention to my saree. Why I was eager to hear his comments, rattled my brain wires.

"Yeah! You look.......... different". I raised my eyebrow and titled my head for him to go on.

"Answer faster. Answer faster", Vikram's whisper chimed in the background.

"I haven't seen you dressed like this before". A frown starting creep up my face.

"Answer better. Answer better", once again Vikram's chime was heard. He moved his head upwards to the ceiling, like he was oblivious to his surroundings.

Raghav gave him a glare and turned to me, "You look like a girl now!", he stated like a conclusion to his new discovery.

"What do you mean?", I probed with a deep frown.

"I mean...You look -"

song:Who saysWho says you're not perfectWho says you're not worth itWho says you're the only one that's hurtingTrust meThat's the price of beautyWho says you're not prettyWho says you're not beautifulWho says. It's such a funny thingHow nothing's funny when it's you.

I had enough of this and cut him off, "I AM a girl, so I WILL look like a girl", I said rudely. With a marred expression, "I thought you were different, but-" and dashed out, slightly lifting my saree, towards the bay's entrance; without finishing my sentence. Tears were welling up in my eyes and I didn't want him to see it.

song:I wouldn't wanna be anybody else.You made me insecure. Told me I wasn't good enough.But who are you to judgeWhen you're a diamond in the rough.

On my way out, all I heard was my name being called out and "You screwed it, man."

9

— • —

CHAPTER 9

Raghav's POV

song:First things firstI'mma say all the words inside my head-I'm fired up and tired of the way that things have been, oh oohThe way that things have been, oh ooh.

"What just happened?", I stood with my hands stretched out, startled at her outburst.

Vicky repeatedly shook his head, "Oh Boy! Oh Boy!"

"What did I do?", I pleaded guilty.

"A two year old in your place, would have done better."

"Excuse me!", I gaped at Vicky's insult.

"I might not have enough experience in the 'girl's' department, but you could have complimented her", stating the obvious. "And what the hell was that Eureka moment - 'You look like a girl', you dumb ass'", Vicky mimicked me, displaying his displeasure.

"Hey I'm new to all this. If she had-"

Asim walked in through the door and rushed to us, "Raghav, Hurry up! You are needed at 9th floor. Change of plans, they'll be visit it first then come to 4th floor ".

Grumbling we made our way to the elevator, "Can't they stick to the plan?"

Vicky put his hand over me, "Chill Bro! Everything's set there. Asim please send a quick text in the group to inform the team that the floor visit is now". Turning back to me, he grasped my shoulders and gave it a little shake, "Snap out of it! Get yourself together, focus on the presentation and rock it! Do you hear me?"

In a lackadaisical manner, I nodded.

Whilst running through the preparations, I spotted Sasha, but she steered clear of me. I have unfinished business but now is not the time for it.

Cathy and her team of four entered the wing, guided by some senior management and of course, my manager, Selva; trying to score brownie points for our work. My blood was already boiling with all the pressure I had gone through in setting up this event, I didn't even sign up for, then Sasha's encounter, and now this. It's high time to put this man in his place. Calming my nerves down, Channelize your energy, Raghav!

song:Second things secondDon't you tell me what you think that I could bel'm the one at the sail, I'm the master of my sea, oh oohThe master of my sea, oh ooh.

Briskly walking towards the troupe, I took over the show, "Hi, Raghav Srivatsav, I'll be your host and presenter for the client engagement fun activities we have lined up at the floor."

A client named Lisa, exclaimed, "Yay! At last some fun activities, had enough of those board room meetings", she giggled.

Selva butted in, "All work and no play makes Jack a dull boy."

song:Seeing the beauty through the Pain!You made me a, you made me a believer, believerPain!You break me down, you build me up, believer, believerPain!

I resisted rolling my eyes, "The activities are wrapped around an Indian festival called Navratri, meaning Nine Nights", I stated with a smile.

"That's why the floor is beautifully decorated, oh! And I thought it's for us", came Lisa's jestful reply, lightening the mood.

"We have set up a mini carnival at the floor called - 'Navratri - an Insight'. Please come this way. "

Making our way to the said location, Vicky explained how the same festival is celebrated by different parts of India with different names and customs. The floor had total 9 bays in parallel; with each bay emphasizing on one flavour of Navratri, symbolic to the 9 step Gollu, of the South Indian custom. In short, the floor was transformed into a lateral decorative Gollu, for our carnival. This idea not only irked interest in the clients but also impressed some of my senior managers too.

"Any Indian festival is incomplete with fun, music and dance. We are at our first stop, 'Dandiya nights' ", I made way to the first bay that had colourful dupattas twirled around each other in arcs.

A team of 12, danced to the tunes of Nagadha Sang Dol, Kamariya, Chogada and Dholi Taru Dhol. The clients and few others also joined in and had few rounds of Dandiya followed by Garba. Cardboard cutouts of Dandiya, dhols and couples in Dandiya poses hung from the ceiling.

After enjoying the Dandiya Raas, we made our entry to the second bay, "Indians being big foodies, here is our food street. Feel free to visit any counter and enjoy the Navratri delicacies". We stated that people usually fast for these nine days. Counters with south Indian sundals of different kinds, chat items, sweets and bhog were scattered within the second bay; with teammates serving and explaining about them.

Vicky popped in a Gulab Jamun discreetly, but didn't escape from me, awarding him a glare. We had tried our best to safeguard them from the salivating mouth's and prying eyes of team members till the event started, as we had ordered only few. With Gulab Jamun being the hot favorite, it was declared as a high risk component.

We proceeded to the next bay, few still devouring the delicacies with the eco-friendly plates in their hands. I continued my speech, "Indian traditions have always held ladies with high regard. This festival is a living example of it as it is solely dedicated to Goddess Durga and her nine avataars. Each day associated with each reincarnation of the Goddess."

"To celebrate womanhood and re-ignite the importance of the beautiful species God has created, welcome to the 'Woman empowerment' Bay". One corner had been decorated with the Goddess, we didn't want to indulge too much into religious stuff. The other corner, elaborated the laurels of woman leaders and their achievements in our profolio and company.

The four corners, comprising other half of the bay, focused on eradication of the atrocities imposed on the female gender. 'Save the girl child' stall depicted a infant girl toy surrounded with statics of the same. 'Educate the girl child' stall had a doll of young girl standing on pedestal made of books. 'Child marriage abolishment' stall was decorated with a Mughal handfan shaped marriage invitation card, as backdrop to a Gath Bandhan hanging on top of a lotus flower candle stand, which was bought few months back for celebrating Chitra's birthday. Also touch upon Dowry. 'Violence against women' stall potraued the physical, mental, sexual abuses, their statics and how history had proved not to invoke a woman's wrath by exhibiting the killing of a lion by Goddess.

Stepping out of the bay, Cathy exclaimed, "Wow! That show had me spellbound."

"Second it! I'm speechless too. It felt like we were at a theater watching a play. You guys have done a fabulous job", Lisa added.

Ethan, their companion, said, "I have never experienced something like this. You'll highlighted the good and the bad in a way never witnessed before and through bay decoration!"

Vivek, my senior manager, one up of Selva, pat my back and wore a proud smile. I was also impressed as how my team had brought out my envision and added their own touch to it.

"Show toh abhi baakhi hai mere dost", Vicky chirped, making us laugh while the clueless clients turned to me for translation.

"The show hasn't ended yet, there's more to come", I explained and entered the next bay. "A day is also dedicated to the Goddesses of wisdom and Learning. On this day, books, musical instruments among many others are kept near the idols for worship and blessings.

Vivek added with a small chuckle,"It's also a day where we all get a holiday, since all equipment at the office is cleaned and smeared after the Puja."

Excited for my most awaited bay, I exclaimed, "To commemorate our education and skills, we present you the 'Innovation Hub' bay". Two groups gave a live demo of all the innovations developed this year. The in-house end-to-end product created on the lines of self-identification of issues, social distancing was also exhibited. Self healing was the key, where if any node or link identified a risk, it immediately disconnects from the network and the perfectly working nodes establish handshake to resume work. Meanwhile, the defective node, restores itself with smaller pieces of backup files in an iterative mode and destroys the last corrupted file. Switching of traffic among the different routes was also taken care based on capacity loading to conserve energy and effective utilization of resouces. Though some of the features are not brand new, multiple functions combined together into our product Innovation Nutshell, was cost effective compared to the number of licensed products the clients were using over the years. Cathy and Dave insisted on having a dedicated meeting the following day to discuss on it. That's how you score!, I fist pumped internally.

Already on a high, enterring into the glamorous bay, "Dressing up in our traditional attires has the youngest to the oldest person in the family excited about the festival fever". Vicky spoke with a undertone of humor, "Our protfolio is like an assorted sweets box, take a look". We had people from all corners of India, each representing their traditional attire. The most selfies were taken here. He added, "That's how we collaborate each of our unique and distinct skills to drive an efficient team". Puzzled at Vicky's first serious words during this event. He winked at me, when he caught me staring at him.

Moving on, I said, "The whole floor is a testimony of the love for decoration but this bay brings to you how we actually clean and decorate our homes during festivals."

Cathy replied,"Oh!"

"You didn't expect us to go all out like this at our homes, did you? Firstly, our mum's, 'The Home Minister', wouldn't approve of it. Secondly, it would bore a hole in our wallets considering the number of Indian Festivals", Vicky showered us with his witty insights. As the laughter died down, he lightly chuckled, "Lastly we would end up with broken backs after cleaning all the mess in the after party."

No one could be themselves other than Vicky in such situations. Many would have better comebacks, but they stood like the cat caught their tongue. All were nervous of the new invaders and well aware that one word gone wrong would be 'the story of their life' for the rest of the year. Not to mention, it being the highlighted and only point of discussion in the yearly appraisal. Vicky being Vicky, didn't give a damn about the senior management or clients, obviously because he was 'The Star Performer', nicknamed as The Untouchable Vicky.

Coming back from my thoughts, "Cleanliness is next to Godliness, stands high in our traditions, I'm sure in yours too?" I advanced further into the bay, so that they could have better view of the two beautiful vast rangoli's spread across the centre of the two cubicles. The desks had small pookolams with diyas between desktops. Fairylights twinkling in the ceiling.   Ruhi took over from here, she welcomed them to the 'Spread Happiness' Bay. She told, "As kids we look forward for festivals, to receive new gifts and toys. Similarly when ladies and girls are invited to visit a Gollu, as a return gift, they are presented with these". The team handed over bags with coconut, banana, pan leaves along with our mementos; to the clients.

Dave glanced into his bag and looked up, "Wait a minute, this Gol-lu", pronouncing it in a funny way, "is only for the lady folks?", he questioned. Amused at the latest discovery, "That means we guys crashed here uninvited?" Vicky and me were stifling a laugh. Turned to answer, Ruhi replied with a bright smile, "Yes, it's mainly for ladies. You get access to a lot of special privileged functions if you are a female, especially during Indian weddings."

"Damn it", Dave said in a humorous way.

"The team also plays an active part on their social responsibilities and here we have displayed the initiatives that we were part of. The mementos present inside the gift bag and the gift bag itself are products created by differently able people, painted by mouth and foot artists."

Lisa admiring her handicraft, "Lovely. You guys are great, as working professionals as well as humans for doing this."

"Thank you for your kind words. The company has inculcated it in us by giving us the exposure and opportunity to be part of it", Ruhi replied with pride, being one of the ESG Spoc's within our portfolio. "We try our best to participate in it as a team activity, to strengthen our team bonding."

"Let's move over to our second last bay - 'Praise to God'. The team will showcase what happens at a real Gollu visit", Ruhi told.

We had our version of a mini Gollu setup at the desk. Vivek and Lavanya, the delivery manager were grinning looking at it. It was the best we could come with. Religious items and idols, fished out from everyone's desk from both the floors, had been put on display in our three step Gollu. The items were not enough to fill the last step so any piece of decoration we found was added. Lavanya was pursing her lips not to burst out laughing, at the sight of the out of place cute baby penguin stuff toy sitting proudly on the left side.

The guests were welcomed traditionally with tikas and short Aarti, followed by lighting of the bulb based diyas. Saravana, the Pandit of our floor, came forward and chanted some religious verses while performing Aarti to our Gollu, simultaneously ringing the bell in his hand. Three girls joined him to sing some traditional songs based on praising and thanking God. Once done, they progressed to the next cubicle were few traditional games were set up.

"Let me hand over the baton to Bala, to take you through our last stop", Ruhi concluded.

Bala fumbled in the beginning, but quickly found his foot hold, "The tenth day of Navratri is called Dusshera. It marks the victory of the 'Good over Evil'."

"Is it the one told in woman empowerment bay ?", questioned Lisa.

Bala agreed with a surprised smile, "Yes! Very attentive."

Dave added, "Historic stories sparks Lisa's interests. Moreover she has an eye-for-detail, you people must be knowing better when she rejects your documents and sends them for corrections", and chuckled.

Bala was put on the spot, he didn't know how to react as he had witnessed it recently. He awkwardly nodded his head.

Dave took a glimpse at the cutouts of bats, webs, spiders hanging, "It looks spooky in here."

Going back to his presentation, Bala replied, "We know Halloween is around the corner. Honestly, this was supposed to be our bay decoration for Halloween, but it went well with the theme. We added the colorful peacock cutouts to represent the good or positive vibes ", he shrugged his shoulders.

"So Halloween is in early", with a wide grin Dave bobbed his head.

I walked forward to add, "We wanted to blend in both the festivals, a true assertion of the way we all work together."

"True that!", Dave responded, in awe at the humongous Halloween decorations done and taking pictures of it.

"That brings us to the end the carnival. Hope you liked it", I stated.

Cathy beamed, "This is the best client engagement activity I have been part of in my 20 long career and trust me I have been to a little, too many. Others did a great job too, but they focused on one aspect. You guys, here created a wholesome package from music, dance, food, games, innovation and what not. It was a like a block-buster show!"

"Thank you so much! It was our pleasure hosting it, you've been a great audience to it. Thanks to the team for all their efforts and enthusiasm", I genuinely thanked her and my team.

She turned to Lavanya and other higher-ups, "You've got a great team here. Seeing such young talent has instilled a boost in me to keep working".

Dave joining us, "Job well done! You guys should be Art directors."

Vivek shook his head in disapproval, "Now Now, we don't want to be loosing such gems? The next thing you know, we will be looking out for replacements", he chuckled. All shared their words of praise and made their way out.

Dave turned on his heels and whispered, 'Art Directors! Don't listen to him. Follow your passion!", he winked and joined his troupe.

People came, pat my back and left, all I could do was stand there in astonishment at the successful outcomes of the event. I knew the idea was unique but never expected such a response. Slowly a group gathered around me and became busy in sharing congratulatory handshakes. Vicky gave me side bump, "That's my man!", he proudly exclaimed.

"It was team work", I replied.

Asim on Vicky's left said, "Yeah! No doubt in that, but the concept was your idea, bro."

"Beautiful concept and it was that, that made us stand out", Ruhi to my right, beamed with happiness. "Kudos to you, Raghav!", she gave me a hi-five.

"Impressive!", recognizing the voice I looked up to see Sasha slightly lost in her thoughts. Ok, now she is talking to me!

song:Third things thirdSend a prayer to the ones up aboveAll the hate that you've heard has turned your spirit to a dove, oh oohYour spirit up above, oh ooh.

I smiled back at her but it didn't take long for it to start faltering, when I saw her clutching a guy's arm. Oh ho!

Wait! Where have I seen him?

Isn't he the guy who branded me as friend-zoned?

I could see the green eyed evil monster of jealousy clouding my thoughts. Gradually people started dispersing, the guy whose arm Sasha was clinging on so tightly, also left. She was also about to leave. I waved off my negative thoughts, I have things to clear, other things can take a back seat for now. Switfly, I caught her elbow, "Not again, I'm not letting you run without hearing me out", I said.

Spinning on her heels, Sasha turned to face me, with an annoyed look. Might be our faces were too close for her liking. I took a step back still holding onto her.

song:Last things lastBy the grace of the fire and the flamesYou're the face of the future, the blood in my veins, oh oohThe blood in my veins, oh ooh.

"What is it you want now?", came her impatient reply.

"I'll cut the chase", I released my grip to run my hand through my hair, heaving a long sigh. "See I don't know what upset you. But if only you had stayed for me to finish my sentence, I think it would have not ended the way it did". Pressing my temples, Why is it so hard for me to tell now?, I could feel my voice choking.

When she nodded to continue, I said, "I meant to say you look beautiful even in a saree", I blurted out sheepishly.

Instantly a smile graced her face and I let out the breath I was holding unknowingly. "Thanks!", she coyly replied and looked down at the floor.

"Sash", came a guy's voice from the door.

"Coming!", she yelled back, "Gotta go now. Bye", she gave a small smile and left me staring at guy's head slowly retreating away from the door.

What's with the name 'Sash'? For Heaven sakes, just add an 'a' to it and it'll be her full name! How hard could it be you idiot!, I spat with contempt.

10

CHAPTER 10

Raghav's POV

song:We go togetherBetter than birds of a feather, you and meWe change the weather, yeahI'm feeling heat in December when you're 'round me.

Bala walked into our cubicle where we were all chit-chatting and reminiscing the day's event. He asked, "Hey, where's Rosh?"

I pointed to far end of the floor, "Roshan's over there."

"Not him", he absent-mindlessly dismissed it.

"Oh! Roshini??", I furrowed my eyebrows and turned right to point to her, at the bay on the other side of the aisle.

"Are you doing this on purpose, Raghav?", he deadpanned, cocking his head to the left.

Ruhi giggled at Bala's slightly irritated expression and turned to me, "You recently shifted to this block, right? He's talking about Rohit and Sasha. Bala, they left sometime back."

On hearing that he walked away. Now I have a name for that stupid face... Rohit.

"Why did Bala ask for Rosh then?", I asked in confusion.

"Because that's what they call themselves", Ruhi said as matter-of-fact with a slight shrug.

"Why?", my high pitched mono syllable, sounded weird to me, but I couldn't be bothered about it right now.

"They are together -". She abruptly got from her chair, "Crap! We got an abend call on our production support mobile". She hurriedly slipped back into her heels, "Today only it had to happen. Always wrong timing! Can't let a person enjoy a fun event. Urgh!... Bye Raghav!".

She left me with so many unanswered questions in my mind.

First Sash and now Rosh?

They are together means together-together like girlfriend and boyfriend?

Nah! It can't be.

Rosh?! It's like a combo of their names

Why do they have it? Only Couples do that.

No they can't be.

Is that a love acronym like Saifeena, Virushka?

Isn't that something she should have with me not him!

Wait! What did I just say?

These were the thoughts that kept running in my mind every few minutes, till the end of the day. I couldn't figure out why I was still stuck on it like a broken record, even after two hours.

Vicky was staying with me, he plopped on the bed and dozed off within a second. I, on the other hand, was having a difficult time, tossing around restlessly.

song:I've been dancing on top of cars and stumbling out of barsI follow you through the dark, can't get enoughYou're the medicine and the pain, the tattoo inside my brain.

The next day, I went to the sports court during the evening break, sitting on the side benches, to clear my mind. Sports, my second love, could only rescue me. My traitorous eyes, fell on a quirky girl floating in an over-sized red and yellow stripped jersey teamed with baggy charcoal grey track-pants. Dipping my head lower to frantically run my hands over my hair, She doesn't leave me alone! After few minutes, I was back at watching Sasha play volley ball with a bunch of boys, my traitorous eyes!

song:And, baby, you know it's obvious. I'm a sucker for youYou say the word and I'll go anywhere blindlyI'm a sucker for you, yeahAny road you take, you know that you'll find me.

"Creep Alert! Creep Alert!", came the boisterous voice of Vicky , followed by a chuckle from Asim and they sat beside me, one on each side.

"Stop staring at her like that! She might be your girlfriend but she will run away, like Usain Bolt this time", scolded Vicky.

Titling my head towards him, "She has a boyfriend already... and that's not me", sounding like a lost puppy.

"Are you kidding me?", scoffed Vicky, "She, she has a boyfriend? I thought you might have competition with the girls... with Section 377 and all you know?"

"Hey! Don't judge", objected Asim.

Completely drained of any energy, I didn't want to fight with Vicky, "She might look like a boy but she's straight. I can see how her eyes sparkle when she talks to me", my pupils still trained on her.

song:I'm a sucker for all the subliminal thingsNo one knows about you (about you) about you (about you).

"Me too!", agreed Asim.

"Me three", Vicky said, "I have seen the look, you two shared. At the bay, it looked like only the two of you existed and the whole world had gone for a toss. I felt out-of-place like an alien just standing there.....so tell me again, why do you think she has a boyfriend?", with a hint of concern.

"Ruhi said so", my robotic voice pierced through the thin air.

"Cut it will you, look at me and tell clearly", snapped Vicky.

Heaving a long sigh, I narrated the 'Rosh' incident. It felt like someone had jabbed thorns into my heart, in the process.

"Hmmm, before you could get a clear picture of what she said, she was gone", Vicky repeated the last part of my narration, going into deep thought.

"Umm", I said dejectfully, as there was nothing we could do.

Clasping his hands loudly to garner our attention, Vicky said, "I came here looking forward to party and I am getting one tonight. Here's the thing.... Let's clear the doubt that's nagging you by hearing it directly from the horse's mouth."

"Sasha?", Asim asked.

"No, let me rephrase, clearing it from cause of this disturbance - Ruhi."

"I have her number, we can call and clarify", Asim offered.

These two were discussing like I wasn't there in between them,"Wait. How's that going to end in a party?", raising my right brow, I questioned.

"If the answer is in your favour, party on the rocks, for sure and if it goes the other way....", giving an understanding clap on my back, "hard drinks are the best to go with. So party is on, either way."

"Hey! I'll just help to connect with Ruhi, after that I'm out", Asim washed his hands away from the hardcore party Vicky was planning.

Switching the phone in speaker mode, Asim spoke, "Hello Ruhi, are you free? We wanted to clarify something with you. "

"Yes tell me", Ruhi replied, probably thinking it was work related. Already dreading this confrontation, I face-palmed. Asim nudged Vicky to ask.

"You said Rohit and Sasha are together, since when?", Vicky inquired, "Like a couple, I mean." Thud!, there goes my second face-palm, at this rate I'm going to have migrane and a bruise on my forehead. Way to go smooth, Vicky. Why don't you just push me under a running truck. The silence on the line, proved, she was taken aback.

Ruhi snickered,"Couple my foot!", she burst into a fit of laughter, "Which idiot told you that?". I signaled Vicky not to let a word out, "I meant they are always spotted together, like friends or siblings". Opening and closing my mouth to find my voice, I finally settled with my mouth shaped as an 'O'.

"Thanks Ruhi! Meet you tomorrow. Bye", said Vicky. With the line going dead, I was awarded a smack at the back of my head from him.

"You and your stupid assumptions ", he scoffed, "You were just trying to escape from the party.... The party is on you, you owe it to me!", he ended with a smug face, folding his arms to lean back in satisfaction.

Just then a ball came rolling to us, "Hey Guys", Sasha greeted, while grabbing the ball and bouncing it between her hands, "Didn't know you all were here, wanna join us?"

Vicky and his smart tongue, beat me to it, "Sorry, he's booked for today, maybe tomorrow."

"Okay!", she shrugged and turned to walk away, to reveal 'Rohit' proudly written in yellow on her back. If we were part of a cartoon program, my character's eyes would have popped out and falled to the ground.

song:Don't complicate it (yeah)'Cause I know you and you know everything about me.

Smacking my forehead as it downed on me, this is not going to end anytime soon.

Looking at her play and match up with all the hulks there, a proud smile grew on me.

"Whipped", I heard Vicky shout, which fell flat to my ears and I couldn't be bothered, due to my fixation on Sasha's game.

"I see, it was love at first sight", Asim casually mumbled close to my ear.

Giving a disapproving nod, I responded, "It wasBlunder at First sight, Curiosity at Second sight, Apology at Third sight, And.... Love at whatever sight later", waving my hand in the air aimlessly.

"Yay! Double treat today, my boy's in love". Seeing Vicky's ecstatic behavior made me wonder, Is it for the treat or my love life?

"I didn't say I'm in love", glaring at him.

"Yes you did", Asim too nodded in agreement.

Rubbing my hands over my face, "I wasn't paying attention to what I was saying, so it doesn't count."

Vicky tried not to let his grin take over, "You are in denial, my friend", he put his arm over me, "Let's go now."

We left the scene, only to make a re-entry the next day. It was tiresome, convincing Vicky and Asim for a game of volleyball, but they gave in. Luckily we came early, to find the court empty. Booking of the court was based on 'First come, First serve' rule, tracking it via a register and was time bound. This was done, due to the limited space constraints, preventing one group from annexing the place.

Spinning the ball over my index finger, while the others took their positions, I anxiously searched for any sight of Sasha.

"We are Ready", clapped Asim loudly, bringing me back to my friends.

The voice, "Oh, you guys came in early today", broke my serve.

Helpless to the smile conquering over my face, I said, "Hi, yes. Wanna join?", ignoring Vicky's faint grunt, from across the net.

"Umm, actually we have a tournament today and I kinda forgot to book the court", Sasha said hesitantly, fidgeting from one foot to the other.

Without any second thoughts, "No worries, it's all yours", I said throwing the ball over to her. Her strained posture relaxed and air-mouthed a Thanks.

"Great!", shoving his heads in the air, Vicky yelled and stormed out. She turned to me with creased lines over her forehead. I murmured into her ears, "I'll handle it", as I passed her to join Asim.

"Dude, that's going to take you - a BBQ party, pizza treat, might be throw in some t-shirts and some really good shades.... That should do it", Asim listed them all, poking fun at the catastrophe I had created.

"Do you think he'll be mad for breaking the Mates before Dates bro-code?", worry and disappointment evident in my tone.

Asim turned to give me a weird look, "Don't worry, he won't disown you from his brotherhood". I resisted the urge to ask if he was serious or making fun.

He let out a long sigh, "Off all the people, Vicky's is the last guy to judge anyone for choosing love". When I opened my mouth to object, he raised his hands in surrender, nodding his head, "ok ok, girls... Happy?", he retorted. "Especially not you. You don't know his past. Before you joined this team, we all saw him go through a bad phase in his life. The light within him was burning out, we all were on the verge of losing hope. Then, you came and literally brought him back to life. He saw you as his younger brother. What I'm trying to say is, Vicky can't stay mad at you for long and surely not due to what just happened". He placed his hand on my back to ease my tension.

Shock over took me, never in my weirdest dreams would I have thought about Vicky's lifeless past. Asim knew Vicky before me, as they were batchmates and I had joined a year or so later. I blinked my eyes to let it sink in, "What happened?", I asked in a small voice.

Vigorously shaking his head, "That's not mine to tell. Let it go, it's all in the past."

I made a mental note to check on it later. Not trying to be nosy, but if he had gone through a dark phase, I needed to make sure it doesn't re-surface and he is not just putting the happy-go-lucky disguise to cover his true feelings.

Asim's word turned out to be true, it didn't take me long to cool down the fuming Vicky, I last saw. Just needed to sit through with him for his favorite Mahesh Babu's telugu movie, which I couldn't understand head or tail. No subtitles also! I couldn't complain though, this was the pocket friendly way out.

For next few days, we went religiously to the court, at the strike of 5 o'clock in the evening. The inter-business unit volley ball tournament was running through the week. In between the matches or time-outs, Sasha would come over to our side benches for small talk. I was rooting for her from the sidelines, wondering how they had agreed in allowing a girl play a all-men tournament.

I would stay back sometimes for their practice sessions to play with her, majority of the time loosing to her. No, I didn't do the cliché - 'let her win' thing, she really was a pro and strong. Thank Godness, the other two, especially Vicky, didn't see me failing miserably to return her serves or hold a good rally. I was marked as the unwanted soul in my team and the opponent team marking me as the weak link, kept targeting me. In my defense, I hadn't warmed up, I needed practice for the practice session. I couldn't care less to the disgusted glances thrown at my way, from my team mates. I was getting to spend some extra hours with Sasha and that's all that mattered to me.

song: And you're making the typical me break my typical rulesIt's true, I'm a sucker for youI'm a sucker for you.

11

CHAPTER 11

Raghav's POV

song:Living in my own worldDidn't understandThat anything can happenWhen you take a chanceI never believed in What I couldn't seeI never opened my heart (Oh)To all the possibilities.

With the tournament's facilitation, wrapping up; I walked over to Sasha and her band of boys, to congratulate her for securing the third place. Pretty impressive.

"Hey", I called from behind her.

"Hey, Hi!", Sasha turned, beaming in her victory.

"Congratulations, Sasha!", I wished stretching my hand out. Expecting her slender fingers to glide into mine, but met with a moist palm slamming into mine with force. I flinched slightly at the impact. Closing in the handshake, it felt fleshy, round and big... Bigger than mine. Wait!

"Thanks Man", the grumpy voice made me snap towards my hand. Running up the extended hand, I met Rohit's blazing glare.

Yikes! I yanked my hand away, muttering non-cohorent words under my breath while he was sizing me up.

"I haven't introduced you guys?", asked Sasha and waved to the others standing few meters away, "Guys, over here", she shouted.

Three more brooding men came over and stood in line, with her at the centre. It felt like a conglomarate's heiress, with her four bodyguards, were standing in front of me. Like I said Sasha and her band of boys.

"Everyone, this is Raghav", she announced.

"Raghav, meet my gang. Rohit, from our portfolio. Daniel, AJ aka Arjun Jaitley and Simbu; you might not have met them before as they are from other portfolio's. We've known each other since induction and were training mates. We stuck on to each other, even after the training period got over and have each other's back since then", Sasha introduced them with a proud smile.

I gave a short nod and shook hands with everyone, exchanged a few words on the games and indulged in small talk. Everyone's expressions had mellowed down by now, except for Rohit, What was his problem? He looked even more devilish with the streetlights bouncing off his sneered face.

"Join us, Raghav, we are going over to Domino's for our victory treat. Call Vicky and Asim too", she insisted, while Rohit bore a pissed off look.

"You guys go ahead and enjoy your day. Maybe some other day", I smiled. Before parting, "Don't forget, this treat is pending", widening my smile to a grin and signed off with a wink.

"Your's too!", she chirped, stopping me mid way, "for the successful client visit."

"Sure, sure. Whenever you are free."

song:It feels so right to be here with you (oh)And now looking in your eyesI feel in my heart (feel in my heart)The start of something new.

We barely said our goodbye's, when Rohit slightly pulled her to him to walk away; tearing us apart. Clearly irritated by our endless departing chatter, as neither Sasha nor I, wanted to bid adieu anytime soon. She stole a glance at me and I was left watching her fading silhouette disappear into the dark.

I didn't want to be a part of her 'band of boys', I wanted to be apart from them and nor did I want to share her attention with four other guys.

song:Now who'd have ever thought thatWe'd both be here tonightAnd the world looks so much brighterWith you by my sideI know that something has changedNever felt this wayI know it for real.

Vicky's temporary workstation being setup diagonally across mine, I had to walk over to his bay as a glass barricade separated our desks. It was like old times - knocking on the glass to catch the other's attention, chatting through it and playing hide and seek, as we hide in between the transculent design stuck over it. Childish, but it was a stressbuster and our ways of cooling our eyes off the screen light.

Boredom taking over me, I went to his desk to see a chat window open. Seeing the name, I flicked his forehead as a reflex.

"Hey, what was that for?", complained Vicky rubbing his forehead.

Leaning back on his desk for support, I nudged towards his screen, my eyes shooting at the chat window.

"Ooohh! Don't worry I'm not flirting with your girl", Vicky passively dismissed my glare.

I hardened my stare at him and folded my arms to emanate an intimidating stance.

He snorted, "Look, I am running a defect triage chat for the E2E (End-to-End) testing and I was given her name as point of contact for her application. How would I know that your Sasha is Sasha Hedge?", feigning innocence.

Hedge, that was news to me but I wasn't going to give it off and kept a cool facade.

"You didn't know her surname?", he whelped with an accusing undertone.

Relaxing my tensed shoulders and back, Who am I kidding, this guy sees through me like laser. I leant over the barrier to reach for my coffee mug at my desk, while he praised Sasha.

"For what it's worth, she's a badass not only in the field of volleyball but in the field of of IT too. I gave her a heads up about the issue and when she joined the triage chat, she started shooting questions one after the other. The way she dug out from the Middleware team that their logs didn't prove anything, instead only contradicted, that the message had not routed out from their end, showed she's a force to reckon with. She easily put all the two weeks back and forth speculation on the issue to rest in a matter of ten minutes".

Vicky spoke in awe of her work and let me tell you to get that from Vicky, is not an easy task. He eased back on his chair and sighed, "Now the Middleware Team is working on the fix. Pity them, if only they had seen it earlier, there wouldn't have been such a large audience to witness their mess up", letting out a chuckle.

That's my gir--, I couldn't bring myself to complete it.

I nodded mutely, and left to get some of the caffeinated drink from the coffee machine. On my return, I found Sasha sitting on Rohit's desk, so he's the reason she comes to this floor often.

Engrossed in my work, I felt someone tap my shoulder, "Hey, What's up?", Sasha said. Waving to Vicky, "All good, defect tension's over?"

"Yes, all thanks to you", Vicky smiled back, "they were driving me crazy for past few days."

"I know, it always happens with them. Been there! That's why I get straight to the point with them", as she was talking she climbed onto my desk next to my workstation facing me, clutching her palms on the desk.

This desk is way better than the previous one!

A weird sense of warmth filled my heart observing her get comfy so close to me.

song:I never knew that it could happen till it happened to meI didn't know it beforeBut now it's easy to seeIt's the start of something new.

"Poor things got hit blue and black, with all the statistics she was asking them", letting out a evil grin, Vicky said.

"Hey!", she turned right to face him and plucked the pen out of my hand to throw it at him, "Don't make me sound like a strict professor".

He let out a chuckle and taunted playfully, "I meant - boring!". She took a quick scan of my desk and threw the smiley ball at him.

How the situation had escalated from praise to tease in a fraction of a minute, marveled me. I was content being their silent spectator.

Their back and forth halted at the sound of the 'Year End annual celebrations' hailing from the speakers across the floor. They listed out the events that were going to span out the week before the D-day.

As the announcement died down, the back of Sasha's hand, in an impulse slapped on my chest, "Be my Cat walk patner, Raghav".

My eyes doubled in size taking her words in, after watching her hand leave my territory. Stealing a quick sideway glance to Vicky, showed his surprised expression too.

What! I tried to voice it out but only air was blowing out.

"What happened?", she jerked her head back.

"Shouldn't I be asking that?", I asked in disbelief.

"Are you slow Raghav?", she asked being preoccupied with rummaging through the stuff on my desk.

When she was back to my questioning black orbs, "Lets participate in the Fashion show together."

"Uh? U and me??..... NO", I said sternly, going back to my work.

A few heartbeats passed, when Vicky decided to butt in, "Why, Raghav boy? Do you want to go with someone else?". The innocent question had an underlying mockery, which only both of us knew due to my stage fright. Giving a presentation in a closed room is fine, but standing on a stage with hundreds of eyes on me, Nah, that's not happening.

"Ooh!", she hummed.

Asim walked back in to our cubicle, after helping a colleague, seated in the adjacent cubicle with a query, headed towards his seat behind me. Each bay had two cubicles, with workstations embracing the four corners. Whenever we wanted to have a quick discussion, all we had to do is turn around our chairs along with others from adjacent ones rolling in theirs, for our impromptu round table meeting.

"Take Asim instead", I suggested in an elated tone, while he cocked his brow in annoyance throwing me a digusted glare and his eyes were flaring up in anger.

I have never seen him fire up so easily, he was the calm and composed one among us. Such an explosive reaction for a mere proposition of participating in a Fashion show?

Vicky threw me a deadly warning and said, "I'll partner with Asim on it", it felt like huge bucket of cold water was splashed over; easing out the burning tension in the air.

For the bystanders like Sasha it would have sounded hilarious but I couldn't be fooled. What the hell is happening? Are these two hiding something?

"If you wanted to participate with someone else", huffed Sasha in agonizing ache while climbing down the desk, "..... Like with Ruhi, you could have just said it up right."

"Where did Ruhi come into the picture now? ", clearly clueless of the ridiculous idea.

Her shrug seemed to be her only answer but it didn't convey anything to me, with that she walked away.

Just when I thought we were getting closer, I had to ruin it all.

After bringing my work to a logical end, I went in search of her at her floor. Unsuccessful in my quest, I charged into the floor's breakout area to grab some water from the cooler. Turning towards the news telecasted in mute on the TV, my eyes fell on Sasha seated at the corner sipping through her drink, deep in her thoughts.

"Fine! I agree", sighing as I flopped into the chair opposite her.

Her stance broke and her eyebrows shot up, almost hitting her hairline.

"See, I denied at first only due to my stage fright, nothing else trust me", I leant forward to push the object wrapped in a small brown bag towards her.

The reveal of the object brighten her mood, as she excitedly started ripping off the cover from her mango duet ice-cream.

"How did you know?", she quipped while licking her favorite ice-cream in joy.

Smiling generously at her, "Remember our first da-", mentally face-palmed myself and immediately corrected, "coffee meet at the cafeteria, you were grumpy that the mango ice cream had exhausted at the counter".

"Oh!"

The way she was relishing the ice-cream, providing her undue concentration to it, so as to not let it drip down and even let a drop of the melting ice-cream go to waste, pulled me in. Her tongue was doing an amazing job at it.

My breath hitched at that thought, ringing all warning bells.

Clearing my throat and thoughts, "But why me?", I asked the question lingering me my mind since her invitation.

Uh, uh! No way was she going to leave devouring her ice-cream mid-way to answer me.

Leaning comfortably on the back rest of my chair, gauging her expressions, I gave her all the time she required. I wanted to capture this moment forever in a snap, preferably a video would do more justice. My fingers were twitching to grab my phone but I restrained from any more embarrassing actions. To keep them occupied, I kept rubbing my fingers against my thumb rapidly, with my hand resting on the table.

She's something alright!

"Hmmm, so where were we at?", she asked when she secured the barren stick into the cover, "Thank you for this", lifting it.

She stood up and as she crossed me, lightly ruffling my hair at the crown of my head, "I'll help you with your buck fever, Raghav Boy". She playfully stressed on the newly discovered nick name of mine.

Chuckling at her use of it, I highlighted in my mental notepad, to keep Vicky at an arms distance from Sasha. Not due to any jealous but of pure fear of letting out, all my well guarded secrets, in the open. Trust him to be the annoying parent who would recite all embarrassing incidents of their child's life to anyone thinking it's funny and it required an audience to it. They had just met a couple of times and gelled along so well leading to the disclosure of my moniker. The dam needs to be closed before anything else spills out.

"By the way, I'm shifting to your floor", her words fell into my ears from behind me. Like a deer picking up a sound, my ears perked up in attention.

Turning around in my chair, the twinkle in her optical spheres couldn't be masked even by her spectacles.

"This was a good farewell to this floor. We will meet you more often, from now on", with that she waved and took her leave.

song:It feels so right to be here with youAnd now looking in your eyes I feel in my heartThe start of something new (The start of something new)The start of something new.

12

— ◆ —

CHAPTER 12

Raghav's POV

song:Every night in my dreamsI see you, I feel youThat is how I know you go on.

With Sasha moving into the same floor and wing as mine, my desk became her favorite spot to hangout, after Rohit's of course. She had called dibs on my desk.

Her desk was at the other side of the aisle towards the farther end. Though there was a good amount of distance between our desks, luckily if I stood up at mine, I could see her face crowning from her workstation. Yes, our starry glances were not going to end anytime soon, to my benefit.

song:Far across the distanceAnd spaces between usYou have come to show you go on.

Vicky had come over to my cubicle, to while away sometime with Asim and me. Casually he sat on the desk which was her spot.

"Uh-huh! No! That's not happening", Sasha hot on her heels strode towards us, half-mindedly shaking her head as her gaze was on the floor with her index finger wriggling in the air. All of us turned to look at her with puzzled looks.

"Get down this minute, Vicky", she said looking straight at him. He cocked his eyebrow in question.

"Oh! Look who's here, the great spy with her sniffing nose as a radar", he let out a sarcastic chuckle, teasing her. "Are you sure you are employed at the right place, this is an IT Company, not a secret agency, where your snooping skills can be used?"

Seeing that he didn't budge, she took it in her hands to literally push him down, "Trespassers are not allowed here". Making us all laugh at Vicky's pretentious annoyed look and her triumphant smile as she took her rightful place, as she claimed.

"Give me your phone", Sasha said, more like commanded with her hand extended towards me, impatience ticking off her fingers.

"Why? What happened?", I inquired while fishing it out from my trouser's pocket.

"If you are looking for any games to play, lover boy here doesn't have any", Vicky enlightened us with his superfluous information, as always.

I have him a pointed look, which made him bite back his words, "Oops! I meant Raghav boy".

Can he be more discreet?, I rolled my eyes in frustration. Thankfully, Sasha was busy with my phone, immune to Vicky's words. I should give it to her, for mastering the skill of muting Vicky's voice when not needed.

"Here you go", she said and shoved it back into my hands. Her smile widen, when her ringtone was heard. Like a blinking tubelight, it took me sometime to grasp, that we had just exchanged our phone numbers. Studying my stunned look, Asim dragged Vicky out, before he could come up with another smart retort.

"Hmmm, I'm taking a week's vacation to attend a cousin's wedding..... So if u need to reach me....", she trailed off and slightly shrugged.

song:Near, far, wherever you areI believe that the heart does go onOnce more you open the doorAnd you're here in my heartAnd my heart will go on and on.

"Your going home then? Or some other place?", I eased myself and asked.

"Yeah! Home sweet home. Wedding's in Bangalore".

"Nice! Enjoy yourself", I smiled at her, "When are you leaving?"

She cringed and scrunched her tiny nose, "Tomorrow evening, after office. I'm going home after 3-4 months, I guess. Trust me there's nothing to enjoy, weddings are gruesome..... I'm happy for the couple but if the wedding was minus all the nagging aunt's and grilling, I would enjoy it.... I'm walking straight into hell I feel. Wish me luck that I'll be able to survive the week. Or else I'll need another week's leave to recover from it".

I let out a hearty laugh, "I sympathize with your situation, it happens to all, even me..... No worries, I'm there. Anytime you need me to cheer you up", I waved the phone in the air.

"Thanks Raghav! Will be needing that a lot. Okies, my daily scrum meeting is calling me now. Bye", she huffed and got down to leave.

"How are you going home? Do you need any help with luggage or transport?"

"Nah! I'm good. I'm tagging along with Rohit and AJ, the boys are going on a road trip so they will drop me at my door step, on their way", she waved and scurried away to her desk.

The next day, on our way home from work, sitting in the passenger seat of my car, I was in dilemma whether to ping Sasha or not and enquire about her travel. Though she went with her trusted friends, you can't be sure of anything. To stop my brain from thinking all kinds of trouble they could have gotten into, I hit the send button of my message.

Hi! Raghav here. ~R

Within few seconds, her swift reply came

Hi! What's up?! ~S

Leaving office..... How was your journey? Reached home safely?

Oh! Not yet, another 30 minutes to reach my home. These guys are a nuisance!!

Ok. Why? What happened? Any problem ?

Yes!! They are the problem. I shouldn't have agreed to this, I knew this would happen..... Just imagine 5 freaking hours of listening to metallic music blasting in a closed car.

Lol!

You are not helping, Raghav! These guys ganged up on me,I thought atleast AJ will take my side... But Rohit swayed himto his side with a promise of few drinks.

Relax!Only 28 more minutesof suffering Had dinner?

Ya right! We stopped for snacks, & I ate a little too much. Now I'm dreading it. Ma would have made a lavish meal for my welcome& I bearly have space to drink a glass of water.She will throw a fit, if I don't eat her cooked meal

Rofl! Looks like your vacation is turning out great from the word go!

Ya poke more fun, Raghav.

Chill!It's just one meal. Walk for something beforeeating you'll feel better.

Hmmmm....

Take care. Let me know whenyou reach home safely.

Sure. TC!

While we were eating our hearts out with the Paneer butter masala and Naan ordered from a hotel, my phone lit up with a notification from Sasha.

Reached home. Tired out!

Good. Take restSleep well. Good night!

Good night!

Hardly, forty-five minutes would have passed away, since I arrived at office and I was already missing Sasha and our morning coffee-breaks. I decided to check up on her.

Rise & Shine. Good morning!

Good Morning!!! You didn't leave for office yet??

I'm at office. Having coffee without you.

Lol!Sure Vicky's entertainingyou enough.

Does he evenknow to do anything else!?!

So what's the plan for today?

Busy day ahead. Going shopping with my cousins

Cool! Enjoy!

8hrs of running in-and-out of shops to skim through numerous outfits, cosmetics & accessories, to return home with 15+ bags, is not my kind of "fun"

I can only imagine.Don't tire yourself. Have a nice day.

You too! Have a great day!

Our casual chatting went on for the next few days, discussing her day with the wedding preparations and my day at office. The horizon of our conversations used to expand to our childhood days, college memories and general likes and dislikes. How our round-the-clock chats used to flow from one topic to the other so naturally, stunned me. It's been three days since I've heard her voice and I don't know what took over me, instead of sending her a text, I called her, in the evening.

"Hi Sasha! Hope I'm not interrupting anything", my voice had a little extra dose of happiness, if I had to say so.

"Hi Raghav!", she replied with equal fervor, "oh! Not at all Raghav!"

I love the way my name rolls out from her mouth.

"Wedding preps keeping you busy? When are the functions starting?"

"Don't remind me!", I heard her huff and flop down onto her bed, I guess. "To think, coming only three days prior to the wedding functions would help me escape from doing all the work, but it back fired on me. These people are so cunning and outsmarted me, they piled up everything I hate, for when I come home." I heard her hit the pillow in exhaustion.

I let out a good laugh,"You can't always escape from preparations. Same trick won't work all the time", I jested.

"I know what you mean, the client visit and wedding preps are not my cup of tea. Can't help it, if they repel me..... Ok enough of me though, how's everything at your end?"

I smiled at her concern, "All's good here. Our lives are not has happening as your's right now", I teased her. It was fun getting her all riled up for the upcoming festive events.

"I can see Vicky's rubbing off on you, but it doesn't feel nice to be on the receiving end", she replied jovially.

"It's not my fault", I shrugged, "you left me all alone here with the devil. Like they say - 'One rotten mango, can spoil the others'", in my all-so-innocent voice.

She burst out into her peculiar laughter with speedbreaks in between and I could solemnly confirm that it's echo would reverberate in my ears for a long time.

It came to a halt, when I heard a third person's voice in the background, "Sasha beta, is that you?", I figured out it was Mrs. Hedge, her mother.

"Ya! Ma", Sasha yelled back.

"What's so funny?", the door creaked open, "Care to share?"

"Nothing Ma, just on the phone".

I could hear footsteps nearing, "I can see you are spending a lot of your time with your phone over there. No time for us, parents?", Mrs. Hedge's voice sounded hurt and I felt bad for monopolizing Sasha's time during her vacation. I didn't know whether to stay on the line or cut it.

"Sasha, I'm sorry. I'll call you later", I said rushing to wind up the call, in case I'm putting her in a difficult situation.

"Hmmmm. No problem, Raghav -", she said softly but was cut-off.

"Raghav?", Mrs. Hedge quipped, "Boyfriend?"

"MA! Please!"

Gosh! What did I do?

"Boyfriend!", Mrs. Hedge repeated, I was having a bad feeling about all of this. "Ō dēvarē! Ō dēvarē!!! Thank you, thank you!", she exclaimed loudly in a bout of happiness; I was shell shocked hearing her response.

"Carry on Magu, you made me so happy. I need to go to the pooja room and thank God and offer prasadham. Tomorrow will go to the temple and donate. Atlast God showed mercy and blessings on us", Sasha's mom waas rambling away in jet speed, unable to contain her happiness. I could hear her clasp her hands together and was imagining her, looking heavenwards with her clasped hands moving swiftly between her mouth and above her head.

"MA!", Sasha shouted in a warning tone.

"Ok ok, sorry. I won't disturb you. Thank you Raghav Beta!", I could visualize Mrs. Hedge stepping closer to yell the last sentence into Sasha's mobile. I stifled my evolving laugh.

Just when we were about to resume our call, I heard the door creak open again, "He is a good guy, right?", her mother's voice was heard faintly. The silence only justified that Sasha wore an annoyed expression.

The door closed and opened again within a fraction of a second, "He treats you right, Magu?", questioned her daughter with worry.

"MA! You are embarrassing me! Please stop this."

"OK! As long as he is good guy belonging to a good family and treats you right with love and care, you two have my blessings", announced Mrs Hedge merrily.

With that Mrs. Hedge's cameo appearance attended and we returned to our call, "I'm so so sorry for this", Sasha apologized with a heavy sigh.

"No problem. I didn't hear much", I lied because I didn't want to make the atmosphere awkward and uncomfortable, "Relax, Don't think too much into it. Have dinner and sleep well. We'll talk tomorrow, I know you are exhausted."

"Thanks Raghav! Oh God that was so embarrassing. Take care. Eat well and sleep well. Good night!"

As I pressed the end icon on my smartphone, I needed to remind myself-Don't think too much into it.

The following day, the three of us had assembled in the conference room for an early morning meeting. Vicky and Asim we figuring out how to set up the projector, while I was busy exchanging good morning pleasantries with Sasha over text messages. With their efforts turning futile, Vicky was getting restless with every passing minute, he kicked me under the table, "Oh come on, give it a break and help us here."

"No can do! Just call the admin team, they'll set it up", I replied nonchalantly without taking my eyes off my chat screen.

"Oh! Why didn't we think about that?", Vicky snorted, "You think, you only have brains. We tried their extensions and mobile numbers, no one is picking it up."

"Hmmm", I hummed without paying attention and that clearly ticked him off.

Asim came to my rescue, "Leave the poor thing alone, we will arrange it."

"This is is how u repay me? Remember the fashion show fiasco?", Vicky raised his brow at Asim, who sat beside me; across Vicky.

Asim abruptly stood up, sending his chair rolling off to hit the glass wall, "I'm not getting in between the two of you", he stomped away to read the set-up instructions for projector at the other end of the room.

"Remind me again, why are you still here? Client visit got over two weeks back", I questioned.

Vicky grinned evilly, "Boy, sorry to burst your bubble, I'm going stick around for a longer time, probably till your ship sails. By the looks of it, it's still anchored at the docks", he ridiculed me

"Tell me, Why again?", I asked in disbelief.

Asim came back to his seat, when a notification in his smartphone caught his attention. He gave a disspproving nod, "For the same reason he asked for transfer to Hyderabad, few years ago", he spat out in disgust.

Vicky sent him a murderous glare and gritted his teeth while crumpling the paper in his notepad, whereas Asim matched up his stare with a piercing look. I, on the other hand looked like an umpire for an eye stare off match. I need to get to the bottom of it, what are they talking about? Our teammates bustled inside the room, putting the tension, between my two friends, to the back seat.

The same evening, the wedding functions were kicking off. Some pre-wedding celebrations - Sangeet, Mehendi, What name did Sasha tell?, I tried re-collecting, but was of no use. I didn't care, I was only curious to know what she would be wearing. The last time I remembered, she accused me of putting her through hell for the traditional attire. She cannot wear jeans and oversized t-shirts to a wedding, so what would she wear?

Hey!! All set to rock the party

I knew I was inviting trouble with my message but couldn't help it.

Oh ya! The party of the century

Lol! What are you wearing? Any photos for us peasants, who were not invited

You want I can ask my grandma to send you an invitation, then they'll get busy with their new Bakra & leave me off the hook, what say?

No thanks! So what you're wearing for the function?

Why? Are you worried, I'll go in jeans?

RAAAGHAAV!

Ok Truce! I just want to know who's getting murdered in your head for your evening outfit?

No one. I picked it to my comfort! Unlike some ruthless people who imposed their deisre on others

Great! So I'm not sharing the punishment with anyone?

You wish!

Why do I get not-so-good vibes from you now?

As you sow, so shall you reap, Raghav boy! Your punishment awaits you, when I'm back.

Oh! Great! I'm so *not* excited for your return right now.

Ok, it's getting late for me.

So no photos?

Uff! Here you go & BYE!

song:You're here, there's nothing I fearAnd I know that my heart will go onWe'll stay forever this wayYou are safe in my heart andMy heart will go on and on.

She posed with her tongue out at the edge of her mouth, in a white based pastel colored floral printed peplum top with elbow length sleeves teamed with mehendi green heavly pleated dhoti pants. She wrote the outfit's description in the photo. One ear was adorned with thin mutli string pearl drops cuff earrings, while the other earring was pinned as brooch on her top, to add a little bling to it. Give it to Sasha to do things differently and stand out of the crowd. Her prestigious watch clamped in one hand and a thin golden charm bracelet with tiny butterfly crinklets, rested on the other. She looked gorgeous even in her minimal look.

For the remaining functions, she shared her look before heading off to the venue. The cousins had decided, for the Sangeet Cere-mony, to wear same dress in different styles. It was a deep red satin cloth with heavy embroidered motifs on the body. Sasha made hers into a long knee length cape, with hand cutouts and matched it with black churidhar. She poked fun at her self, saying she looked like ghost, more like Casper, in a red bedsheet with her head popping out. Her jab took sometime for me to restore myself to normalcy, after my laughing riots died down. She never seizes to amaze me. She even recorded herself doing a March past in it, to show how happy she was with the unrestricted access to hand movements, the dress was providing her.

Her look for the wedding was a waist length cape in rust, golden sequences running along the border with a raw silk creme semi dhothi pants. Accessorized with Kundan stone loop earrings, in the size of a ten rupee coin and double ring -- consisting of a tear drop Kundan ring and simple emerald ring - with adjustable pearl chain; proudly circling her index finger and ring finger respectively.

Lime yellow waist length crop top with straight pants and gold foiled geometric patterned floor length jacket was her outfit for the wedding reception. She wore triangular red studs and tiny red roses arranged beautifully as a wrist corsage, just like during the client visit.

Sasha went in black pencil pants and t-shirt under a open-front grey-blue-and-black checked asymmetrical shrug, for the after party cum disco party. She so needed the cooling off period from all the heavy apparels she wore over the past few days. Grey button studs with silver border were her only accessory with her trademark white sneakers.

Looking like the Sasha I knew, all comfy and natural, so serene; I kept starring at her last photo she shared. The night ended with my last message to her.

kiss.~R

13

—◦—

CHAPTER 13

Raghav's POV

song:Baby, lay on back and relax, kick your pretty feet up on my dashNo need to go nowhere fast, let's enjoy right here where we at.

Sitting up on my bed, after a good night's sleep, I stretched my arms and cracked my neck to release the stiffness. Stifling an emerging yawn with my hand, I let my free hand take possession of my phone. It had become a routine — to send Sasha a Good morning message, even before I left my bed. The best way to start my day and the recent photos she had shared were a bonus; a grateful blessing that was showered on me by an angel.

"Oh No.... Ooohh Nooo!", my voice scaled from a whisper to an ear-splitting howl, followed by a string of curses.

Vicky rushed in with a toothbrush in his mouth and toothpaste mixed with saliva was dripping off his half-open mouth. "What happened?", his wobbly voice muffled by the toothpaste, was heard as he dislodged his brush from his mouth.

"Yuck!! Get out of here before you turn my roon into a mess.....
What the hell are you doing here, like that–", circling his mouth area, "Go to the washroom you dumb creature."

"Hey! I thought you were in some sort of danger, heard your shrills.....like someone was kidnapping you or something worse..... So much for the concern", Vicky huffed.

"DON'T. START. IT ", I warned him, not wanting my emerging headache to worsen with his snappy rebuts. Thank God he got the message loud and clear and left quietly.

While happily chomping away his food loudly, "Stop digging holes in the floor and your bank account — your landlord will not let you escape without fixing the damages", Vicky commented on my vigorous pacing in the living room.

"Won't you ask, why I'm like this?", I turned my head sideways to face him.

"Nope!", came his instant reply, "Let me refresh your brain, you asked me to stay out of it and I'm doing just that", he gave a wide smile which had hidden intentions.

I know he was dying to hear it, but wanted me to divulge the details without him asking directly. Trying to be subtle, Vicky.... But I know you inside and out. No wonder he was eating loudly to make his presence known.

Not able to determine how to resolve the issue in hand and desperately in need of a third person's point of view, I showed him the message. I had checked it numerous times to see if Sasha had replied. What was worse, she had seen it fourty-two minutes earlier but still nothing from her side. Was she giving me the silent treatment? I'm in trrr-ooouubbbllle!!

"So?", Vicky's nonchalant reply dragged me out of my thoughts.

"That's it? That is your response to it?"

"Yeah!", he went back to his food and fisted a thumbs up with a fork in his hand, "Good, I see you have at last, got your balls together and made a move."

"It wasn't my move", I yelled exasperatedly.

"Then make it one." I cocked my brows in annoyance to his one-liner.

This is the time he chooses to be reserved, a 360 degree turn to his chatty nature.

Heaving a small sigh, he continued, "See Raghav, there's only two ways to go about it. Either own up your mistake or like they say — When life gives you lemons, make lemonade", he ended with a shrug.

I thought about his suggestion, my mind kept playing games, switching between the two options. I felt like an indecisive toddler dilly-dallying on which ice-cream flavor he wanted. Even after I got to my desk, there was no concrete decision. Moreover; today, Sasha was to report back to office, I was dreading to face her.

Thud!

The loud sound on my desk disturbed the parallel space I was driven into due to my concentration on my work. I traced the object in question and saw the slender figure in greyish-blue limestoned button-down, short sleeves shirt neatly tucked into white skinny jeans, tightly secured with a slim brown weaved belt. I couldn't help myself from staring at her and let my eyes roam over her face, memorizing her features. It felt it had been ages since I saw her in flesh and blood. Photographs didn't do justice to the living and breathing original piece standing in front of me.

song:Who knows where this road is supposed to leadWe got nothing but timeAs long as you're right here next to me, everything's gonna be alright.

"These are homemade sweets and savories, Ma sent them specially for you. Some are from the wedding celebrations", Sasha broke the calm lull enveloping us.

Her voice brought back the tension of my message, which had temporarily taken a back seat on her arrival. Trying to analyze her, to weigh our current situation and check if she wore a cloak to mask her real emotions; due to the awkwardness I had suspected, but it was of no vail. Just like she had appeared from nowhere, she vanished from my sight.

"Oh-ho! Damaad ki khateerdhari abhi se, Wah-ji wah!", Vicky teased with his chin resting on the glass barrier separating our desks. His eyes were zooming onto the three circular shaped medium sized steel containers.

"It's off limits for you, Mister", for a moment there I was under the impression that Asim was on my side, until he continued. "That's specially cooked and packed for Hedge family's soon-to-be Damaad. Stay away from it, if you don't want to be in the bad books of Mrs. Hedge..... Heard she has some special connection with the Almighty."

"True! I also heard that it took only a minute for their would-be-Damaad to secure his place in Mrs. Hedge's heart. Look she has personally sent her acceptance whole heartedly, for their alliance."

"Ya!", Asim's voice filled with enthusiasm came from my left side, "Not one but three-three boxes.... Way to go Raghav", he gave me an appreciating part on my back.

My eyes did a somersault on my friend's ridiculous exaggeration. It felt like being caught in the crossfire of neighboring aunties's and I was their hot piece of gossip.

"The aroma is so inviting, my mouth has started to water", Vicky honestly confessed and none of us could deny it. "I'll just ask Sasha's permission if we could share it— I'll be back".

I sprung to my feet and leaped over to grab his arm, "No! you are not— you are not going anywhere. "

"I knew it! You grumpy, ungrateful, selfish man", Vicky said with accussing eyes, "That's why I was going to ask Sasha, if she would mind. She gave it to you, so technically if she's ok with it... you don't have a say in it".

"I don't care about the food..... I mean I care.... I don't mind sharing it...But I need to talk to Sasha first, about the little situation I created", I said hesitantly.

Vicky gave me a knowing nod, "Walk your way then lad".

Approaching her desk, I tapped her shoulder and asked, "Can we talk?".

"Yeah sure", she rolled back her swivel chair and leaned back on it, so that the whole of me, was within her vision.

I gave a quick glance around and shook my head, "Not here, somewhere less crowded", and jerked to the hallway connecting the wings.

Once we were at the said location, I tried formulating what to say. Running my hand through my hair, "H-How was your journey back?", I stammered.

"Good."

Letting out a deep breath, "Did you see the last message, I mean the emoji that I sent.... It was an accident... I must have falled asleep with the chat window open and by – mistake – it – got – sent", I enunciated the last few words carefully.

Sasha took everything in quietly with a stoic face. The sag in her shoulders for a fraction of a second was her only visible reaction, if my eyes weren't searching her intently for any signs, I would have missed it too. She gave me a small knowing smile, "I understand. Accidents happen..... After all it's just an emoji... Nothing to worry."

A wave of relief lapped onto my tensed body, She is so calm about this.

"If that's all, shall we?", she suggested to return back to our cubicles; to which I nodded.

On reeling our interaction to my friends, Vicky had a stunned expression, "That's all?.... No drama... No howling....No exchange of accusations or threats??". Even Asim couldn't believe her easy-going response and stifled a laugh, "Looks like Vicky was ready with popcorn for some drama to unfold."

"You bet!", Vicky damned.

I let out a chuckle, "She's not a drama queen, you guys should have known that by now", I said while sitting down and grabbing one of the boxes. "Yummmm", I slightly moaned unhindered with the fact that I was in office. "These are great.... You know, you guys, if only you stop dipping your nose in my business and look out for your better-halves, you would also be awarded with such tasty moothichur laddoos". Shrugging, I lifted the laddoo like a prized possession and rotated it with a playful look, "Want some, guys?"

On meeting Asim's face, sadness overtook his eyes and without a word, he spun his chair to go back to his work. Turning to Vicky's side, his eyes were blazing with anger and he tightly clutched his armrest. To soothe his heavy breathing, he gulped down water from his flask. Bull's eye! Gotcha guys. My plan worked, revealing that all the mysterious talks that was resurfacing for the past few days, were to do with a girl......both have some lingering feelings.... And they succeeded in hiding it from me, for four freaking years!!! I gasped internally, not sure when I was going to take them down for it.

As the day progressed, the air between us had thicked, gloom had clouded over the usual frolic atmosphere. Everyone kept mum and did their own work and spoke only when they had to. I felt bad for ruining it, but things just had to be done, I was trying to open the doors to their mysterious side, which they'd managed to turn into a no-man's-land for so many years.

At sunset, came in my Sasha as usual to knock out the gloom with her charisma. She swiftly shooed away my hand over the mouse and shifted the control back to my local system, from my remote client machine. Clicked on the top most mail in my inbox and the link in it, took her to another page, where she checked nearly all of the checkboxes, as she scrolled down the page. She freed herself from my workstation and mouse, "Your employee ID and email address", she said while crossing her hands. The sudden feeling of being held at gunpoint crept in me. The layers to her personality were peeling off one by one slowly. Who would have thought she could be this intimidating.

"Uh?", after reading through the open page, it looked like a sign-up form, rolling back closer to my system and entering the required details, I questioned, "What's this?"

"Your punishment", she said with a wicked smile playing on her lips and her charcoal eyes glittered like diamonds; as if crystallization of carbon atoms occurred within a fraction of a second.

"Oooohhh! I thought you would forget", I returned a sheepish smile.

"Never!... Roles swapping happened last week and I'm one of the new ESG (Environmental, social and governance) spoc for this portfolio..... You'll be attending all the events scheduled for this month", she announced happily, while fluffy her bangs.

I hid my smile, even if she hadn't forced me, I would have provided my full support by self-nominating; after all it's her new role and I wanted her to excel in it. Punishment??... Doesn't sound like one... Only if she knew!

song:So, won't you ride with me, ride with me?See where this thing goes.

"Sure-sure. It will be a child's play". Skimming through the ten events, my eyes popped up, "50 kilometers Marathon and beach cleanup", and came face-to-face with her, "No way! I can't run for heaven sakes, that too for 50 kilometers?"

"It's called Marathon, Raghav, you don't need to run. I'm not asking you to win the trophy for me, just make it to the finish line... It's for cancer awareness, all for a good cause", she pat my shoulder comforting me.

"And the Beach cleanup", I scrunched my nose in slight disgust, like I had got a sniff of all the weird smells and things that were at the beach.

"Ya, What about it?... Don't you remember - 'Cleanliness is next to Godliness'?", she smirked in my way. It felt like the fitting revenge, throwing back words from the client visit to me.

"Okayyyy", I slumped in my chair accepting defeat.

Obviously all of this didn't go without two pairs of eyes and ears trained to it, I could also hear faint snickers. After emerging a winner from the brawl and all the ruckus we created while trying to sign-up my two buddies from their respective systems, "If I'm going, you guys are coming in tow, too". They thought, they could escape from having fun at my expense.

The day had come for the first activity — 50km Marathon. The three of us practiced daily, we used to go for an early morning jog. Slowly increasing our race distance and building stamina for the day, including late night walks too. Whatever preps we did, we were aware that, there still was a huge shortfall, due to the short preparation time.

"Urgh! It's 4:00 am Raghav, that too on a weekend", Vicky groaned while resting his head downwards on my shoulder, "I can't even see anything."

"Me too", I exhaled, looking around the assembling point of the marathon for Sasha, she said she would be participating in all the activities too. "I just hope I don't step on a pit-hole and fall down."

"Don't worry, I'll make sure you do fall", Vicky scoffed, lifting his heavy head from shoulder. Was he tryimg to tire me even before the Marathon starts?

"What I don't understand is, why do we have to be dragged into this —punishment or winning her over thing — whatever you are trying to do", Vicky whined in his half sleep.

"Because you wanted to", Asim's curt reply came, "Now stop being a whiny child."

I left them alone, if they wanted to pull each one's hair, they were welcome to do it, without me being their referee. I walked over to Sasha who was wearing a military cap teamed with similar tracks and maroon t-shirt, comprising our company name and her new role - SPOC printed on her back.

"All ready, Raghav? Nice look", she complimented me for my knee-length khakhi shorts with identical maroon t-shirt, representating our organization. Before I could return her compliment, she made her way for checking the attendees list.

The race had started, as predicted we were struggling. Snatching every water bottle, glucose drink and whatever item that was kept at stalls to energize ourselves. Mid-way we halted and just walked, it felt like we were at a never ending road. If not for the crowd encompassing us, we would have thought we had lost our way, as the red finish line was nowhere to be seen.

Huffing and panting, I stopped to bow down and held my knees.

"You alright, Raghav?", Sasha's voice filled with concern was heard behind me while she rubbed my back gently.

Oh-My-God!!

The tingles her fingers were leaving behind made me shiver and squirm under her touch. She didn't know what her innocent act of caring was doing to me. I stepped aside and stood straight to stop it.

"Yes I'm fine, just exhausted", I said between breaths.

"Here have some water. Calm. Down. Breathe with me..... Breathe in... Breathe out... Breathe in... Breath out."

We continued her breathing exercise till I felt better. "Come let's continue", she turned to jog.

"Wait! I can't jog yet".

"Oh! Come on, you'll be fine", she linked our arms and started her brisk stride, dragging me along with her.

As the time passed, when our interlinked arms settled into holding hands, neither of us realized, nor objected. Only when I heard snaps being clicked —like sounds emerging from a surround theater system — from behind us, from our sides and when Vicky and Asim's pair came into my view, it dawned on me, how the public demonstration of the support we were providing to each other would be perceived by others. Vicky's wicked grin while snapping us from front was enough to prove it. I felt like Sasha and me were subjected to the scrutiny of the paparazzi. Before any awkwardness could creep in, I suggested to take some groupies.

The enjoyable time had to be halted by none other than Rohit. He casually put his arm over her shoulder, "Sash, what are you doing here? Don't you want to make it to top twenty list like always? Especially now that you are one of the spocs."

"Ya, go ahead. I'm feeling better, Vicky and Asim are there any-ways", I told her when she glanced over me with sad expression. I didn't want to hold her back, I was here to encourage her to push forward not pull her down.

To gain possession of the Marathon snaps, I had to bribe, run errands and do what not, for the avenging duo. At last, after three long days the snaps found their place in my phone's gallery and I had to applaud their photography skills for the picture perfect snaps taken. I couldn't stop myself from going through them time and again, after all it was our first snaps together.

Our next weekend was occupied in the beach cleanup event at the Snehatheeram Beach located 138 kilometers away from our city, Coimbatore. Just like the Marathon, we had to wake up early this time too but Thank God for the two and a half hour bus journey arranged by the company, I escaped Vicky's scuffle. As spoiling two of his weekends in a row, had a guaranteed stamp for a squabble.

We reached our destination, with most of us using our travel time to gain our lost hours of sleep and everyone disembarked the bus, stretching themselves up. Sasha was busy with her band of boys, they had tagged along, no wonder — being her besties it was called for. Today she was dressed in an over-sized white t-shirt with sleeves, rolled up a in a notch at the edges, tucked into her black ripped bootcut jeans. A red and black checked flannel shirt tied around her waist, perfecting her low-key casual look to the tee. Just looking at her, feels so refreshing and comfy, an instant mood booster.

Sasha and me hadn't interacted yet, she was assigned a different section of the beach along with her boys and the three of us along with few others were assigned a section that was at opposite poles to hers. The scorching sun and wind blowing the dust wasn't being helpful at all.

Roughly, on top of an hour, Sasha came to our side and plumped down on a stone seat few steps away from me. "Tired?", I quipped, glancing over at her while picking up the debris with my glove covered hand into the huge black disposable garbage bag.

"Hmmmm... Yeah! The guys volunteered to do the remaining so I came over to check upon on you guys", she said after splashing the non-drinking clean water on her face to beat the heat.

"We are fine. Look at Asim and Vicky, they are having fun over there; they made a bet on who ever fills the most bags with thrash will earn a treat from the other", I let out a genuine laugh looking at them. Turning back to Sasha's attention, "I half expected them to sit by at the sidelines or jump in to the water for a swim."

Sasha joined me in my laugh, "It's all about food with them", shaking her head she said with amusement.

"And competition", I added.

Taking a break, I sat down next to her. With our gaze focused on the turquoise water turning to pristine white, as it picked up velocity and witnessing it mellow down, on it's collision with the golden sand at the seashore, we let the prevailing tranquil atmosphere prolong. If I could vanish everyone at the beach with a snap of my fingers, the picturesque location basking in the glory of the scenic beauty along with the one sitting beside me, would be a memory engraved in my mind forever.

My gaze caught the blooming of Pentas flowers in an out-of-place shrub adjacent to our seat. The bunch of tiny star shaped red flowers tightly bundled together, in the shape of a dome mounted on a single dangling stalk — on the verge of being blown away with another puff of wind, was plucked by me. Handing it over to Sasha casually, she wore a stunned look with her brows knitted together in contrast to the sweet smile over her lips.

"Thank you!.. Oh look it's matching my shirt", she exclaimed in joy.

"The pleasure is all mine".

Delighted that my spur of the moment idea had been well received, my heartstrings tugged when she lovingly examined the flowers and her previous tired look was fading away.

song:If it's meant to be, it'll be, it'll beBaby, just let it belf it's meant to be, it'll be, it'll beBaby, just let it be.

The volunteers wrapped up the event and went back to the bus for the return journey. Sasha was seated in the second last row at the aisle while we were seated in middle of the bus. I stole some backward glances at Sasha and saw her cradling the flowers with care. I never expected that under the rough and tough Tom-Boy, there existed a soft side of her too. The Snehatheeram beach did uphold the dignity of it's name - The love shore. This felt more like a team outing than a social service activity, even though it did take the whole day, it was all worth it at the end.

The next few activities were uneventful, it was a downer but the feeling of helping the needy even in the smallest way as possible, puffed up my chest with warmth and gratitude. Teaching at a government school was the last activity listed for the month. This one had two session during work hours, so Asim gladly came to get a break from the hectic work, or to say break from the incessant trivial queries put forward by the juniors. They had somehow managed to break his rock solid patience; surprising all of us. Vicky and me wouldn't have lasted so long if we were in his place and surely with the anger unleashed by us, we knew we would have a round of sessions in the discussion rooms from Selva and the Human resources team.

The interaction with the school kids went smooth. Some of us took English classes, some Mathematics, storytelling sessions on — importance of education, career fair, health and hygiene awareness and some fun activities.

One kid made fun of Sasha and her boyish attire, so I took it upon myself to make things better.

Addressing the whole class, "Kids, if you are given two dishes to eat, one that's looking really good but doesn't taste good and the other which is not that decorated and plain but tastes delicious, which one would you choose?"

"Plain one", "Second one", "Tastier one" — came the unanimous replies from the children.

"Same way, what matters the most is a person's character inside and not the outer looks. The girl standing there, who some of you laughed at, is a gem of a person, if not for her we all wouldn't have come here to spend time with you. In fact, she is the leader of the group standing in front of you. An all-rounder topper I must say - workwise, sportwise, social servicewise. We boys didn't stand a chance to her when she secured the 22nd rank in a Marathon race..... There is very good poverb in English — Never judge a book by its cover."

"Sooorrryyy ma'am", chimed the students in chorus, without any-one urging them to do so.

My speech ended our storytelling session and moved on to laying out the snacks we had arranged for them. Rohit came over to me and awarded me with a clap on my shoulders. Though we didn't exchange any words, it was undeniable that we were entering into each other's good books. While Sasha threw me a grateful look when the kids crowded at her legs shooting questions one after the other.

Later, a second standard kid walked up to me and tugged my trousers to ask, "Is she your girlfriend?"

Taking a brief glimpse of Sasha— pre-occupied in her chat with a school teacher, I knew that I had danced around the topic for way too long. However, I didn't want to compartmentalize the relation we shared and label it; I was content with going with the flow for now. Going back to the curious kid, I flashed a smile at him, neither denying the fact nor accepting it out in the open, though my heart was clear about what it wants.

song:So, c'mon ride with me, ride with meSee where this thing goesSo, c'mon ride with me,ride with meBaby, if it's meant to be. Maybe we doMaybe we don'tMaybe we willMaybe we won't.

14

CHAPTER 14

Raghav's POV

song:I know how it goes.I know how it goes from wrong and right.

"What's your weekend plans?", Sasha asked whilst getting all comfy at her station in my cubicle.

It took me sometime to drag my vision off the monitor and focus it on her, "Nothing much. I guess it's going to be a boring weekend.... I think we should sign up for some activities like last time.... It was fun". I smirked and she snorted while recollecting how her so called 'punishment' didn't go down as she planned.

Letting out a chuckle, I went back to reply on the official communicator; where a serious issue was being discussed and needed my attention. Sasha didn't mind my slight inattentiveness, as she was busy solving the Rubik's cube at my desk, picking up from where I had left it. From the corner of my eyes I briefly checked on her, "What about you?"

"You remember Simbu and Daniel?"

"Hmmm".

"They have some crazy plans for the weekend. If I may quote them — 'Life's boring machcha, let's rock this weekend when we are still alive'".

Nodding my head as her words seep into my preoccupied brain, she continued to babble, "Movies, Go-Karting, might be bowling too at the arena, Heck! They'll surely want to hit up all the games at the arena..... Oh! And the clubbing tonight....so all-in-all, it's going to be one hectic but fun-filled weekend".

"What did you say last?", my thick eyebrows shot up, which had nothing to do with my office work.

"It's going to be one hectic but fun-filled weekend", Sasha repeated while rigorously shifting the cubes on the three dimensional puzzle game. It's evident both of us where giving each other, half of our attention but none of us had any qualms to it, until now.

I pried my eyes away from my workstation and looked straight at her, "No, before that?"

She started, "Movies, Go-Kart —", she stopped midway becoming aware of my gaze narrowing on her. Sasha glanced at me through the rim of her spectacles, that had slid down her nose slightly, to get a view of my deadpanned look.

My eyes seemed to have communicated, what my words earlier didn't, she furrowed her brows, "Clubbing?".

There — she got it.

"You are not going", I announced curtly and returned to my work. There were a few pings on the communicator asking if I was still there and if I could complete a minor task, in the next hour before the project goes live at the scheduled time — two hours from now.

"Who said so?", she quipped with her shoulders rising and falling.

"I'm saying", I replied with an emotionless finality in my voice. If I thought, it was the end of the discussion, I was wrong.

"I don't think I'm following correctly. You, don't want to me to go clubbing", she affirmed. "You don't have any rights to order me around, last time I checked, you are not my Dad", she taunted hotly, "Raghav, look at me, will you!"

song:Silence and soundDid they ever hold each other tightLike us? Did they ever fightLike us?

The way my name rolled out from her tongue now, made me shudder involuntarily. I don't think I was liking the way this was going. She grabbed my armrest and rotated my chair — our faces made the perfect line of sight now.

"I'm in the middle of my work, woman!", my frustration got the better of me.

"Then clear what you have to say as fast as you can", her voice turned cold. Both of us took deep breaths to calm our sudden escalated nerves. "May I ask why you don't — scratch that — you forbade me from going to the club?", she jerked her head.

Didn't she get it. What was so hard to understand in this.

song:You and IWe don't wanna be like themWe can make it 'til the end.

I starred at her in disbelief, "It's not safe."

"I'm going with my close friends, who by the way are four over-grown athletic men. Try again", she challenged me while cross-ing her arms.

"Okkkay... You guys will be under the influence of alcohol and any sturdy man or mind can stumble with it, so — it's not safe!"

"We are not drunkards or addicts, we are just going to unwind ourselves together after a very long time. Most probably we will take a sip or two and end up dancing whole night.... Next", her right eyebrow made a perfect high arch.

Sasha and dancing, that would be a sight to enjoy.... Not now Raghav, get back on the track.

"You are the only girl in your gang that's going there, won't it be awkward for you?"

"I'm not going there to meet people and make new friends.... Atleast not with girly-girls out there", her fingers were tapping her arm, a signal for me to move on to my next counterattack.

"I didn't mean that", my brain was running out of ideas in this stressful environment."

Nor did I want her to meet any guys at the club, that too. Her four hulks were more than enough.

song:Nothing can come betweenYou and INot even the Gods aboveCan separate the two of usNo, nothing can come betweenYou and I.

Why couldn't she just have friends who were girls like any other normal girl.

"Having some known girl's company would have been better", I tried reasoning out.

Sasha huffed, I'm sure I heard here mutter something under her breath.

"Huh?!? We are not going to an 'all-boys' club that I'll be the only female in the club...Try better Raghav".

I felt we were airlifted and dunked onto a wrestling ring where I was the attacker, hurling punches morphed as words whilst she held her defence stance, blocking them with ease. After each battle round, she was provoking me to come on harder and give her some real valid reason.

"Right! There's still chances that there might be less ladies around and you'll attract more unwanted and uncalled attention from drunk people."

She let out a humorless laugh and made eye contact, "I garner attention everywhere I go Raghav, not only in clubs from drunkards, and you very well know why", she pointed to her attire.

She raised her finger to stop me from interrupting her. "Not that I need any protection as I can take care of myself very well.... My friends won't let any harm come upon me....".

"I acknowledge that", I said in a calm and composed tone, "It's not safe means it's not safe", I shrugged.

Trying to coax Sasha from not going for clubbing, felt like we were on a merry-go-round, going round and round on the same topic. I needed strong reasoning to create a trajectorial path to remove us from this whirling situation before it brings doom to us.

"Do you have a problem with me — drinking or drinking in general? Didn't Vicky and you have a party recently? You have got some double standards there, I must say, Raghav."

"That was at our home, safely secured within our own four walls. You are going to a club, so it's not safe", exasperation evident in my voice. I felt that the phrase — 'It's not safe', had become the period marking each of my sentences.

"If you are hinting about safely returning home, we will assign a designated driver, we are responsible citizens", she lifted her chin to state it.

"The 'club' is the risk factor here", I replied with my voice notching up an octave, now getting tired of this back and forth.

"For your kind information, we are going to a reputed club — The Re-charge, hope you've heard of them?", she titled her head to the right.

It did have a good reputation, the security does a thorough check at the reception, before entry is granted. Till date there were no cases of any kind of hanky-panky occurring there, the owner was a no-non sense person and had zero tolerance for any wayward behavior or illegal activities. Sure it was a happening place amongst youngsters and draws crowds of all kinds. It boasts of their delicacies, the relaxing book club slash football club vibes it offers in the afternoon while transforming into the upbeat nightlife club, as the sun sets.

"Yes, Still.... It doesn't hurt to be cautious, Sasha", mellowing down and feeling slightly better for their choice of the club.

"There's something called cautious and something called 'over -cautious'....."

"But—", I was at a loss of words, "You can't be sure of anything, the crowd I mean. We don't know what kind of people will be there. "

She rolled her eyes, "Hence the Boys.... Can you please stop over-analyzing it, it's not some piece of code that you can't under stand....."

"Oh God! How do I make you understand?", rubbing my tensed temples I exclaimed in angst.

"If it's bothering you so much, you can tag along with your friends", Sasha suggested. Now making some sense and offering a standoff to put an end to this unintended combat session of ours.

song:I figured it outSaw the mistakes of up and downMeet in the middleThere's always room for common ground.

"Okay, when are you guys going?", slightly relieved that we were finally making some progress.

"Tonight, at six".

I nearly jumped in my seat, "And you are telling me that now? Only an hour before...... I can't...... I have to support production release — deployment and post-production activities, as the project is going live tonight. It won't be until midnight, that we'll be able to wrap up", ending in a dejected tone.

"Oh!", Sasha pursed her lips in a tight line.

"Can you'll please re-scedule the clubbing?", I pleaded.

She shook her head, "Sorry I can't. This is the only night everyone's free. Moreover past few weeks were hectic for Daniel and Simbu at work and they, very badly need to blow off their steam to maintain their sanity."

"Great", I said with lack of enthusiasm, nothing was on my side today.

song:I see what it's likeI see what it's likefor day and nightNever together'Cause they see things in a different lightLike us, but they never triedLike us.

"Better luck next time, Raghav. I'll take my leave now so you can finish up the task and hope you have a smooth release."

"Thanks", I mumbled.

"Don't stress yourself out. We will be fine, trust me...... Take care and have dinner on time. Bye."

"You too. Take care, be alert. Don't roam around alone. Go early and come back home early. Keep me posted if anything happens and when you reach home, ok. Can you do that for me, Sasha?".

She gave a small smile and went back to her desk. I prayed, Please God, let tonight be uneventful for her and me.

The project that was getting implemented today was huge and required three resources to be on call. Asim extended support from home on the office laptop, in case the deployment drags into the wee hours of the next day and Vicky and me can no longer support from office.

Apart from the initial hiccup of missing few components from moving to the pre-production environment, identified by Asim in his checklist; the remainder of the release was smooth sailing. Though we didn't have any issues, we needed to be online for co-ordination. Updating the status of the release tasks in the portal, as the deployment progressed to next stages; sending out email confirmations and screenshots for evidence.

The clock has struck nine in the evening, my mind drifted off to Sasha and her whereabouts. Thinking of it, she hasn't sent a single text message till now, that irked me. Asim's name blinked on my phone, jolting me from my slight diversion. Thinking something had gone wrong in the release, I picked up the call.

"Ya Bhai, everything good?", I questioned.

"Hmmm, you might want to sit down for this Raghav", Asim said over the phone.

Sensing trouble, I stood up and put the phone on speaker for Vicky to hear too, "Ya go ahead, Vicky's here too."

I heard him sigh, "I got a forward in one of my chat groups from college..... It was a video from the Re-charge club dated tonight.... Showing that some drug raid happened over there", he said slowly in a calm tone to mitigate sudden tense emotions from building up upon disclosure of the new found information. "Sasha's in the same club, right?"

It didn't work though, my heart started racing with his words. Frantically pulling up Sasha's chat on my phone, I flooded it with texts to know how she was and to call me immediately. "Yes!", I finally answered Asim.

"It could be an hoax, Raghav", Asim tried explaining.

Looking at my state, the level-headed Vicky took over the phone and said, "Asim, do one thing, ping the on-site counterparts — Andrew and Ashish, to take over the release activities, anyway most of it is already done. We will come pick you up on the way to the club. You pack up your laptop and wifi dongle and be ready, just in case of any release related emergencies. We'll be there in ten minutes."

I didn't hear Asim's reply as I took my office extension and started punching away Sasha's number only to hear that it was out of coverage area."Damn it!", I yelled while slamming back the phone's reciever.

After picking up Asim, Vicky behind the wheels, drove us to the club safely in record time. Meanwhile, Asim and me were trying to get updates from Sasha and his friend who had shared the video. It looks like the video was a genuine one.

On reaching the location, I wasted no time and strode towards the entrance. There were police vehicles parked haphazardly with their red and blue lights blinking away. Oh God! What's happening here!? The porch area of the club was barricaded and no passersbys were allowed. Sasha's phone was also still unreachable. The ambience was straight out of a crime scene from a movie. We caught hold of a police inspector, who initially didn't divulge any information stating it was confidential.

However, looking at my panic striven face and Asim's persuasion, he said, "The police were alerted by the club officials two hours back that a pair of drug dealers had hit their club. Our specialized team and the club authorities were in contact till we reached the place. Thanks to the swift and tactful actions of the club authorities, we caught them and confiscated the drugs."

"What happened to the people inside the club? Where are they? Are they safe? Is everyone safe?", I bombarded the inspector, with question after question.

He gave me a small smile, "Relax son. This club seems to be well trained and equipped for such situations. As soon as they got a hint of suspicion, they sealed the entry and exit points of the actual club area, making sure that the people inside were unharmed. The reception area being a little far away, gave them the advantage..... Right now the club attendees are being checked and let out from the rear entrance.... We need to make sure that no drugs were slipped inside unnoticed, so it's taking time."

"Thank you so much Sir, Thank you!"

Patiently waiting behind the barricades at the rear entrance, as soon as a slightly staggering form of Sasha came into my scope of vision, I let out a relieved sigh. With the help of Rohit, she was able to move forward. I quickly stepped in front of the free passage between the barricade and her eyes widened when she saw my angry face.

"Rrrrraaaagghav!", she slurred. Her hand flew to her mouth, astonishment written all over her face.

"Sasha!", I minced her name harshly. "Are you hurt? Is everything okay?"

She looked down and nodded, while folding her arms, to cover herself up from the cold sting of the blowing wind.

Daniel broke the silence, "Everything's fine. We are all safe and sound, Sasha too", he emphasized. "Thanks bro, for checking on us."

Among all of them, Daniel looked like the one who had consumed the least alcohol. He went on to say, "We were going to call for a cab home.... But since you guys are here, can you please help me drive them home?"

"Sure", I replied in a harsh tone as my eyes were still on Sasha and her stumbling form.

"Thanks a ton, man! We have two cars here... I can drive one, just need someone else to drive the other.... I don't think anyone else is fit to drive now!", Daniel glancing over at his friends, he stated.

Gritting my teeth, I said, "I can see that!" and felt my blood boil.

Vicky joined in, "Hey, Asim and me can drive you guys. Let me know the addresses then tomorrow or whenever you are free you can pick the car up from us..... Is that fine?"

"Ya, That will do.... anyways I doubt anyone will be up tomorrow to go out", Daniel sighed, "Will let you know bro.... Here", he gave the spare car keys to Vicky.

"I will drop Sasha, just text me her address", I volunteered leaving no room for any negotiation. I made sure to get all of her four hulk's numbers too, as a precautionary step, in case her number is unreachable next time.

"Get in the car, Sasha!", I grumbled lowly, while holding the passenger door open.

"Uh-huh", she shook her head and caught the car to steady herself, "Not when you are snarling at me, Raghav", slurring a bit.

"I'm not! Get in the damn car now!", I yelled at her, making her literally jump. I could see goosebumps forming on her but I didn't sober my annoyed expression. She winced but did not protest further. The moment she got inside, I slammed the door shut and walked over to the driver's seat.

"Seat-belt!", I barked.

"Seat-Belt", she mimicked me while making a face.

Her current inebriated state and her attitude, was of no help in subsidizing my boiling resentment towards her decision to go to the club, despite my displeasure. "Here", I handed her a bottle of water to dilute the dizziness she might have, due to dehydration.

"Grumpy grandpa", she leaned forward to shout into my ears.

The car was already on the move, I briefly glanced at her, gulping down the water and back to the road, "Did you just call me grandpa?", I gagged.

"Uh-huh!! Watcha going to do grumpy grandpa!", punctuating each word with a jab on my chest.

"Stop that!", I slapped her hand away, "I'm driving her woman! Do you want us to have an accident? Didn't the mishap at the club fulfill yourdrama for the day?" When we had halted for the red light at the traffic juncture, I turned in my seat to face her and threw a pointed look.

She stuck her tongue out, "Quit being so up-tight, Raghav bo oooyyy.... Look at those jet black pupils... the overgrown eyebrow bushes above them", she giggled. "The smooth tanned skin and the trimmed French beard.... The cute medium sized ears.... Sparkling white bunny rabbit teeth.... The small button nose—". Wearing a dreamy look, she started blabbering stuff and trailed off. Starring at her extended right hand, making its way to me, a frown grew on my puzzled face.

Honk! Honk! Honk!

The car behind us started honking rapidly, it woke her up from whatever trance she was in and her hand sped back to it's place on her lap. I resummed driving, on and off sneaking a peep at her. She was now hugging the water bottle with her head rested against the window, eyes closed and a smile affixed on her lips.

The car jumped at a speed breaker I had missed to guage. Within few seconds I regained the car's control and checked on her. The jerk seemed to have woken her up and water from the open bottle splashed on her face and the dashboard. "Careful there!", I said in caution, the water dripping down her face and bangs along with the cute stunned look that took over her face, made me want to laugh but I controlled myself.

"Jerk!", she murmured and seemed to have read through my masked expression. "You want to laugh at me now, go ahead Raghav!", her voice had an edge to it.

"Take this", I handed her the bottle cap, "If only you had closed it, it wouldn't have happened", I said calmly while looking at the road ahead. Another five minutes and we would reach her paying guest accommodation.

She snorted and said with a nasal voice, "If only — If only — If only.... Sasha this..... Sasha that.... Ufff! Raghav. You are giving me an headache!"

Was she trying to imitate my voice? I don't have a nasal voice... No way!

Bringing my car to a halt at her gate, I turned to her.

"For the whole ride here, no scratch that, for the whole time since you learnt about the clubbing, you've just been picking on me."

Opening my mouth to give my reply, she cut me off, sensing that I would disagree.

"No, let me finish!.... I know now that going to the club was a big mistake. But, Raghav, that doesn't mean you have throw it at my face every freaking second!", Sasha spat out the last words.

She continued like any enraged woman would have on being irked beyond their level of tolerance.   "Mistakes happen, we can't control everything in the universe", she spoke animatedly in anger.

Heaving a deep breath, she added, "You made mistakes too, Raghav. I didn't make a mountain of a molehill." She opened her door, while she slid out, her back towards me, "Quit being a prick.... Hmmmm thank you and no thank you for the ride!", disgust evident in her tone. Slamming the door shut, she walked away leaving no room for me to justify her allegations.

song:I figured it outI figured it outfrom black and whiteSeconds and hoursMaybe they had to take some time.

15

CHAPTER 15

Raghav's POV

song:I don't wanna know, know, know, knowWho's taking you home, home, home, homeAnd loving you so, so, so, soThe way I used to love you, noI don't wanna know,know, know, know.

While placing my bag on my desk, the infamous giggles of Sasha found their way into my ears. My instant response of glancing at her desk, proved to be a mistake. God knows what, her new team-mate - Madhav, had uttered to her, to send her rolling in laughter for past 20 seconds. I refrained from letting my loathe for Madhav, who was sitting way too close to her and having the time of his life with her, to emerge out.

It should have been me making her laugh and it should have been her, right by my side, on her designated spot on my desk.

Here, I was sulking for the setback in our camaraderie, while she's enjoying another man's company.

It's been two weeks since our dispute, on that dreadful night. Sasha and me, have not been on talking terms, following that. She stopped her daily visits to my cubicle, leaving my desk, barren of any warmth. We were at loggerheads, with no one backing down or owning up. With our ego's as huge as the entire galaxy, expecting the other to make the first move to apologize; days ticked into weeks with not even an iota of improvement. The famous proverb - Time heals all wounds, didn't hold good in our situation.

"It could have been you", Vicky's words brought me to face him.

I shook my head, "Excuse me".

"Not excused. Don't take me for a fool, Raghav. Both of us know what I'm talking about and what you are thinking about."

I groaned and let out a frustrated sigh, "I have work piled up, I don't have time to chat". Let's start another long day. Wearing a grim face, I buried myself with work.

Vicky raised his eyebrow and shot me a what-the-hell-you-are-doing look through the glass barrier. I had just committed, over a conference call, to do a week's long work within 3 days. After all, now, I had all the time in the world! To escape from Vicky's wrath, as soon as the call ended, I snatched my coffee mug and made my way to the breakout area to fetch some bitter coffee. Yes, bitter, just like how my prevailing feelings were, for the past few weeks.

Sasha and me crossed paths at the coffee machine, with me - walking towards it and her - walking away. Without as much as a second glance, we continued our paths, like two trains crossing each other in a jiff. While the machine was brewing the coffee, my mind drifted to the day that built the invisible wall between us.

song:Wasted (wasted)And the more I drink the more I think about youOh no, no, I can't take itBaby, every place I go reminds me of you.

Why can't she just accept her mistake of going to the club and apologize.

I pressed the expresso button forcefully, jolting the machine slightly.

She even called me a prick! What was that for?

Stabbing the botton, for another shot, whilst my mind was figuring out, the puzzle to our quarrel and its aftermath.

Was caring for her and her well-being, wrong??

Click! The button squeaked, when it jumped back to it's state of inertia, after my third stab.

She had the nerve to shift the blame game on me, acting like she was the victim. When everyone knows who it was. She even -

I went on to press the button for the fourth time around. My thoughts halted mid-way, when the machine started grumbling to brew the next batch. I took it as my cue, to make a move. Absent-mindedly, grabbing the cup, the steaming hot deep-brownish liquid splashed on my hand and shoes. Jumping a step back, to move my body away from the cup, I was able to save my office attire from ruining. The burning sensation lingered, for quite some time, even after shaking off the injured hand and running it through the nearby tap water. I couldn't help but think, Is this what they call Karma?

Sasha' POV

"Hmph", I snorted while returning back to my work-station.

Such a thick skinned -.... What should I say, what should I say..... ?

Tapping my index finger on my right check, to find the right word to fit in.

Buffalo.... Yeah! That's what Raghav is.... A thick skinned buffalo!!

I exclaimed internally, happy to have finished my quest and went back to my work. My mind had churned out so many colorful descriptions for Raghav in the past two weeks, that words and fallen short. It was active 24/7, running around the incident.

Couldn't he just say sorry for being so rude to me? I questioned myself while hitting the enter key of my computer's keyboard.

"Hey..... time for lunch, let's go", Madhav tapped my chair, bursting the bubble I was wrapped in, with my thoughts clouding with Raghav's indifference.

While riding the elevator and getting our lunch at the cafeteria, looking at my friends jabbering away. Thank God for Madhav and the gang, or else I would have surely lost it. They are so caring and friendly unlike someone I know.... What does he think of h imself.....The King of mankind.... I grunted out loudly, setting my meal before me. More like King Kong, beating his chest and yelling around unnecessarily..... Playing innocent all these days, only to turn out to be a devil in disguise. I shook my head and dug into my food, as my stomach had started making grumbling sounds.

Only Madhav and me had settled down at a table and reserved four seats beside us for the boys, they were waiting at their respective stalls to collect their chosen meal. I looked up from my plate to smile at Madhav, when he complimented the food he had purchased. Glancing at the aisle to check if our friends were finally joining us at the table with their food, but instead spotted - Raghav! He averted his eyes from me, within seconds. Who knew that this unintentional cooling period we had offered each other, would turn out to be so long. By the looks of it, it'll last forever.

Look at him! So indifferent! So egoistic! So...... How dare he just look away like that..... If he can act so superior and highly of himself, let him!..... Two can play the game..... I'm not dying to spend time with him, anyways....

Does he not miss me??

song:Do you think of me?Of what we used to be?Is it better now that I'm not around?

"You know -", Daniel nudged me with his elbow. Only then I realized that they had all arrived and were half way through their meal. "You know, you could just go and talk to him", Daniel continued.

"Who?", I asked, unaware of their prior conversation.

"Raghav, who else!"

"And, why should I do that?", going back to the food, as I didn't like the sudden turn in the topic of discussion. They hadn't picked it out, until now. Why now, then?

Heaving a long sigh, he slowly dropped his spoon and turned his body sideways to face me, with one arm resting on the chair, while the other on the table. "Believe it or not, Raghav was worried about you that day. I was sober enough to see his state and -"

I was about to contradict but he stopped me. "Hear me out, Sasha. He did what he knew was the best". He briefly glanced over behind our row. "From a boy's point of view, I can relate with his reactions.... I get it, it wasn't the ideal one", slightly raising his hands gesturing me to calm down. "But what can you say, we, Boys are dumb sometimes", he ended with a casual shrug.

AJ, sitting diagonally opposite to Daniel, objected, "Hey, don't call me dumb. Call yourself dumb". That got him a zip-it and I'm-trying-to-make-a-point-here look from Daniel, while others snickered. Atleast it eased out the tension a little.

"Boy, got a point there", pitched in Rohit pointed his spoon towards Daniel, seated right across him. Mixing the dal with rice, Rohit added nonchalantly,"Raghav was concerned for you, that day, even I agree."

That caught me off guard, Rohit talking about Raghav without a hard expression on his face.

"Whoa! So now you like, Raghav?", perplexed by Rohit's support for him. "When did this happen?", crossing my arms, I leaned back at the chair.

That sly fox.... Now he is turning my friends against me. I narrowed my eyes at that thought. Ready to shoot out daggers from them, if I had to, like the automatic tennis-ball launching machine at sophisticated, indoor closed courts.

"I'm just stating the fact, Sash. Don't look at me, like I'm a traitor. ..... By the way, he seems to be a good guy, for what he did for you at the school and we do need to be thankful for his help that day. He did come over to check on you, even though he had an important project release. Though nothing bad happened to us, he was there for support, and we can't deny that......That says a lot", stuffing his mouth with a spoonful of food, he concluded.

Scoffing at his impromptu lecture, "Guys will support guys, should have seen that coming... So much for our years of friend-ship."

"It's not like that Sasha, we are your friends first", Daniel tried to comfort me.

"He just got over-worked in that tensed situation..... We were safe inside but he didn't know that. Put yourself in his shoes. He was out there, amidst the police, the sirens, the drug raid and the rumors floating around him". AJ also contributed his insights, feeling left out, might be.

I nodded and leant over the table to peep at Simbu, seated beside Daniel, on the other side. "Do you also have something to say? Might as well spill it, just like how the other's over here, who are imparting their gyaan on it". Simbu shook his head. Throwing an annoyed to all of them, when I went back to rest comfortably on my chair.

AJ seemed to have not understood my underlying warning, he revealed, "The look he had, said it all, Sasha. Just the way, he has one, now. So cut him some slack."

"I didn't get you", confusion written on my face.

"You will, when the time is right", he said cheerfully and flashed a naughty smile to me.

Letting it go, I said, "I'm suffocating here, so much bromance is in the air". Waving my hand in front, like there was some smoldering smoke looming around. Rohit and AJ, chuckled, while Daniel was waiting for it to die down.

He nudged me again, "Now you are behaving unrealistically. You are doing the same, to him now."

"How's that? ", I cocked my right eyebrow, to which he responded "Really -"?

"Ok - ok, don't start your lecture again. I get it, he did it out of concern", I emphasized, "but you guys didn't see everything. You'll witnessed the aftermath not the start of it, at the office..... If he thinks he can just order me around or walk all-over me, then he is in for a surprise". Blinking my eyes innocently with a devil's smile. Slamming my palms on the table, I stood up slowly.

Daniel massaged his templates, clearly frustrated that all his work for the past twenty minutes went down the drain. He hunched a little and looked up at me, wearing a pleading look. It felt like he was hell-bound in patching us up. If I didn't know better, I would judge that he thought it was all his fault, for ruining things between that idiot and me.

Raghav's POV

Wherever I went, the images of Sasha sitting with Madhav were sprouting in front of me. Their recent luncheon together, added to it. Where were her bulky bodyguards now? And Rohit?.... He seems to have a problem only with me?! Speak of the devils and they arrived at the table that caused me discomfort.

Vicky today suggested to have our evening break at the sports court for some fresh air. So here we were, seated at the sideline benches, Vicky on the topmost, Asim in the middle and me at the one closet to the ground. Vicky sat in the centre of us, we would have looked like a pyramid from afar.

song:My friends are actin' strangeThey don't bring up your nameAre you happy now?Are you happy now?

"Enough is enough!", Vicky groaned. Turning behind to glance at him, he asked, "How long are you going to be like this?"

Clueless, I replied back with a question, "Like what?"

"Like a walking-talking disaster. You are reminding me of -", he trailed off. Asim patted right above his knee, reassuringly; making him blink away the sadness that was creeping into his eyes. He turned his focus back to me, "You are taking up work like there is no tomorrow, at this rate, you will finish all the work required for next three months", he stated.

"Stop exaggerating, Vicky... And for your kind information, I'm f-i-n-e", I grimaced when I heard it myself. When I didn't convince myself, how would it do for those two. Vicky sent me a told-so look.

"Yes, it's about time, the hatchet is burried", Asim teamed up with Vicky. "What was it about anyway? They were unharmed at the club and you dropped her home safely... So what happened?", enquired Asim.

I couldn't agree more with them, even I wanted the thick air between us to clear out. Only if I knew, what I did wrong? Vicky laughed his ass off. Great did I just it out loud?

"Raghav Boooyyyy", yodeling out his favorite nick name for me, "What would have happened to you, if I wasn't there?"

"Make your point, Vicky", I said through gritted teeth.

"Raghav, Woman are never 'wrong' and it's taken, that men have to say sorry first, always... Always", he stressed.

"What? Why? ", I asked.

"That's the thumb rule, dude. A veerrryyy important one too", Vicky said with a knowing smile.

"So even if they are at fault, we need to be the one to apologize? ", not understanding the rationale of this new found rule.

"Oh no!", Asim shook his head repeatedly, "Women are never at fault. Didn't you hear the the first part of the rule?", he retorted. "The faster you adopt to the rule, things will be better between you and Sasha."

"I still don't understand."

"Uh-huh! Just blindly follow it, because women see things, we can't", Asim's eyes gleamed with a small secretive smile cropping up.

I was skeptical at first, whether or not to follow their suggestion, later I threw all the inhibitions out of my mind. Watching the two of them impart their so-called knowledge, gave the impression that they had been first hand witnesses to this solution. They were giving out 'been-there, done-that' vibes. It looked like a tried and tested formula, no harm in giving it a shot.

"So, you guys are telling me to apologize to Sasha?"

"Yes, dumbo!", Vicky exclaimed.

"But how do I say sorry, if I don't know, for what I'm apologizing for?". I brought out the same question that was doing it's round from the time I dropped her at her place. I would have already asked for forgiveness way ahead in time, and not waited, for two dreadful weeks to pass by.

"The magic word is sorry, that should do it", Vicky proudly stated.

Asim begged to differ, "Start with sorry, it's the entry ticket. Once the closed doors open, you guys will start talking and she'll send you subtle hints on all the reasons you should repent for. Be sharp and alert to pick it up and accept it or talk it over."

OK, This rule had two sides of it.

"Trust me, it'll be the extinguisher to the fire keeping the two of you apart", Asim gloated like a pro.

And, trust me, I will dig out how you guys came to know about this rule.

I smiled wickedly to myself. They were reliving their sweet memories and the happy aura emerging out from them, I had never witnessed it before. The sudden happiness soaring in me, fell flat as soon as I remembered something.

"B-but there's nothing to rejoice about. Things might clear up but not my path", I said sadly.

"Why?", Asim was the first to come out of his daze.

"Something happened in the car."

"I knew it! Everything seemed normal when we were around. What did you do to jeopardize it?", Asim sternly asked.

"I didn't do anything", I pleaded not guilty to the two pair of eyes watching me like a hawk.

"Hmmm, ok. Tell us what happened in the car, but please keep it PG -13", Vicky kept his hands over his not-so-innocent-ears. I threw him a deadly glare. Here I'm talking about something that was life and death for me and he just had to butt in with his witty remarks.

Ya, like as if something of that sort happened in the car. Nothing rated G (general audience) also happened.

"Nothing happened", I said.

"Ya ya ya, just like that the disagreement wouldn't have sky-rocketed. Try to recollect, might be something you guys spoke sparked it", Asim suggested.

"Right! Your Ms. Sneakers was under the influence of alcohol, she would have blabbered something", Vicky tried to push my buttons.

"Alright! Alright!.... She was drooling over another man....in my presence", I disclosed.

"Rrraaagghaavv! If you once again say Rohit's name, I'll not stop from bashing you up blue and black". Vicky warned, showing his balled up fist, ready for some action.

"Calm down you maniac, I didn't say it was him. Initially I thought she was talking about me, but -"

"You better finish that sentence and cut the drama. We are not sitting here to watch an Indian television show", Vicky's tone from earlier continued.

"Until she fancied a guy having a button-nose", I pinched my nose, "I have a normal, mediocre sized nose." Heaving a deep breathe, turning to face Vicky, "That proves it's not me... "

His eyes had a mischievous shine to it and lips were tightly pursed. Asim seemed to be stifling a laugh. They wanted to poke fun at my sticky situation, how supportive! Shrugging it off, I'm going to soon join their club of Doomed love, I guess.

Just Perfect! Three guys, three friends, having three love stories that didn't see it's fruitful end.

Vicky on a serious note said, "She's clearly wearing the pants in the relationship - ". Glaring at him, made him bite his words, Did he suffer from short term memory loss? Just three minutes ago, I opened up on my one sided feelings. " - or, whatever you guys are calling it. She takes the first step, all the time. She gave the first treat, invited you to be partners for the fashion show. Heck! She even made the first move to exchange phone numbers.... To name a few", Vicky pondered.

I argued, "Hel-lo! You are forgetting the most important thing, I searched for her after our chance meet. Secondly, it was me, who texted her first, okay!"

Vicky jerked his head, "Really, that's all you got?", he deadpanned.

Wearing a meek smile, I knew that I put up a weak case, it's always been Sasha's step forward. What good would it do, if after months of our association, we break our bond on a single silly issue. Everything could be resolved by talking, being mum didn't show any results. Then there was thier infamous 'result guaranteed' formula.

Swallowing my pride, I approached her but she overlooked, giving me the cold shoulder. This one, pierced my heart deeply, as I was standing toe-to-toe with her and she straight up neglected me, like I was Mr. India.

Her fading strides, increased the thumping of my heart, "SOR-RY!", blurted loud and clear. She froze and spun on her heels with a Did-I-hear-it right expression. Catching on her look, I nodded vigorously, half-bothered about how shabbly my hair would turn out to be. She broke into a smile that could melt a glacier with it's warmth. Oh God! How much I missed this! This felt like the awakening from months of hibernation. Can't believe that I was sent into a deep slumber that had dampened my body and soul. Internally kicking myself up for not doing this earlier.

Closing the distance between us physically and emotionally, I repeated, "I'm sorry Sasha. You were right, I was a jerk.... But please not a prick". I pleaded and frowned, showing my dislike for that word.

She let out a loud laugh, "Oh! Raghav, you've been called, far more creatively in my head in the span of two weeks".

I grimaced, "Anything is ok... Stupid, idiot, fool... I would rather be your idiot, than a prick", I shrugged.

"Ah! there it is, within seconds, the smooth talker is back", Sasha rebuked.

"Hey!", acting offended on the recent accuse.

"Objection overruled!", she giggled while mimicking a judge and slamming an invisible hammer against an equally invisible table.

"My Lord, if I was what I'm accused of being, would it have taken so long, for me to seize fire?", stepping closer to her. I played along with her courtroom skit and seeing her resolve fall, my playful smirk turned into a wide grin.

"Your plea is accepted! The Court is adjourned!", she beamed energetically.

"Phew! Thank God", wiping off the imaginary sweat off my forehead. "So-"

"My work is calling me", she signaled, pointing her thumbs towards the door.

"Is it urgent? Can it wait for half an hour to an hour, max?", I asked hopefully. When she shook her head no, I said, "How about going for my long pending client visit treat and also celebrating our getting back on good terms?"

"What makes you think, we are back to where we left?", Sasha confronted me with her hands on her hips. Her wrestling stance was on.

"I-I,.. Uuh...", I stammered. The real sweats were beginning to form on my tensed temples.

"Chill Raghav! I was just pulling your leg. Wanted to see you squirm a little", wriggling her brows, she smirked wickedly.

"I should say phew! now then", trying to regain my composure. "Domino's at 7, is that ok?" Accepting my invitation with a nod. "Okay, I'll pick up at 7."

"What? Are we going to fly over there, in your helicopter?", she chided.

Chuckling, "Nope! I'm an eco-friendly person. I wouldn't waste fuel on a short ride. We'll go on my most trusted vehicle.....legs."

With that our paths forked, only to rejoin at seven, in the evening. Strolling down the lane connecting our block with the central food court of the IT campus, hands down this was the best walk I had in a loooong time. Wishing the five minute walk, wasn't so short lived. The bright moonlight and the light streaming from the halogen street lamps, illuminated the expressive Sasha, when she animatedly spoke. She's like the Tesseract from the Marvel's movies, so still as ice some times, and suddenly bubbling with unlimited enegry unable to contain in her body. She was my bundle of energy.

After placing our order, we took the tiny cozy table for two at the floor-to-ceiling window. She had been talking non-stop, catching me up with all that, I wasn't part of, of her life.

"I missed you", I blurted with a sad smile. Sasha, reflected back my smile, just then our order number was called out. Returning to our table with the pizzas and tacos, we immediately dug in.

Surprised that she had ordered pizzas loaded with all kinds of veggies, I looked up to meet her gaze.

"I'm on a healthy diet", she exclaimed after taking a bite of her pizza. The stubborn cheesy strings kept on reeling out. She took her fingers to cut it. Letting out a chuckle, I handed her a tissue. Always a delight to watch her devour her food.

"Ya right, pizzas and cheese are the way to go for it", biting into my triangular piece.

"Hmmm??", she raised her eyebrow in slight annoyance.

"Hey, that's just a harmless retort. Truce! Truce!.... Happy Pongal!", I whisper yelled to avoid any kind of escalation. A stitch in time, saves nine, right!

She chuckled at my plight, "Scared to pick up another fight?" Turning her raised eyebrow to a frown "Happy Pongal? There's 3-4 months for it".

"Yes, no more quarrels please.... I intend to kept it that way.....let's use 'Happy Pongal' as our truce code word.... What say?"

"Oh! Like a resolution not fight till Pongal?! Sounds good", giving me a thumbs up.

Or like forever.

Everything, back to normal, the urge to wear my heart on my sleeve and come out clean, built up momentum inside me. "Actually, Sorry for not being truthful... I don't know for what you were angry on me, but I know I was an idiot so I had apologized". Praying internally to the Almighty that speaking the truth didn't backfire on me.

"I know", Sasha replied casually.

"U know?", surprised at her words.

"Yeah! The boys sat me down and explained it to me that sometimes 'Men' are dumb", the words rolled out like she was stating a theorem.

"Men are dumb?!?", not sure if it was a question or just an echo of her words.

"Uh-huh! Can you believe even Rohit took your side?", she said with amusement.

"Rohit, took my side?", that was a real shock for me.

She deadpanned, "Are you just going to sit there and repeat everything I'm saying?"

The hulks weren't that bad after all.... Calls for a treat to them.

Coming out of my daze, with the reason for the apology, out in the open, it set a clean slate for what I was going to tell her. I wanted to start afresh. She might not reciprocate my feelings, but I wanted to give it a shot and let it out of my system. Fidgeting in my chair and with nervousness crawling it's way in my blood stream, I took a couple of deep breathes.

I looked straight into her eyes, "Sasha, I like you", I confessed. It surprised me that it came out so confidently, when the feeling within, was a total opposite.

Obviously, it stunned her too. Placing my hand gently over hers's, resting on the table, I repeated again. "I like you as a man would like a woman".

16

CHAPTER 16

Raghav's POV

song:It's been said and doneEvery beautiful thought's been already sungAnd I guess right now here's another oneSo your melody will play on and on, with the best of 'em.

Sasha froze, with her mouth ready to clamp onto the pizza half inside her mouth, when my declaration found it's way to her ears. Seconds turned into minutes, I was hoping it didn't turn into hours, before she woke up from her shock. I didn't take my eyes off her, who knew the second I blink, she would run for the door and disappear without a word.

Patiently waiting for her response, after all, I had gotten a PhD in it. This moment in the restaurant, hands down, topped the list of the most grueling scenes in my entire twenty five years of my life. My future depended on it, I never felt this anxious, even while facing my job interviewer. God Bless that man who selected me to be part of this organization. Indirectly leading me, five years later, to meet the girl who had made her way into my heart. More like swiped her entry into my life, I smiled internally while recollecting our first meet at my floor's entrance.

The wait was killing me. I gave a light shake to her hand held below mine. Like how I do with my mouse; to check if my computer is hanged, when it's not responding as expected. That seemed do it and she removed her hand trapped under mine in an instant. She slowly placed the pizza back on her plate and gulped down a glass of water. Scanning the table for more water, I offered her the iced lemon tea near me with a smile. Sipping through it, her eyes didn't leave mine. Clearly buying her more time. She slurped through the straw till only the air getting sucked through her empty container could be heard.

Slurp! Slurp! Slurp!

I had enough of hearing the noises, I gently took the container from her hand, making her frown at me.

Wrong move, Raghav!.....

I don't care, her rejection would be better than this slow death I'm going through now.

My thoughts were internally battling. "Eh.... Sasha do you have anything to say?..... You don't have to worry about spoiling our -"

"Me too", were the first words from her mouth.

I nodded my head, just as I had predicted, giving her a sad smile, "I get it. You don't need to worry, we can still stay friends...if it's ok with you?"

Narrowing her eyes slightly, "I said... I like you too."

song: You are beautiful, like a dream come alive, incredibleA centerfold, a miracle, lyricalYou've saved my life againAnd I want you to know babyI, I love you like a love song, baby.

A wide grin overtook my face, showcasing my sparkling white teeth. I immediately closed it when the logical side of my brain voiced out - You are eating, Raghav! What if something is stuck between your teeth??

After the initial silence was interrupted by the couple at our neighboring table, who wanted the ketchup bottle to be passed over; our conversation flowed freely, refraining from touching upon 'our confession'. Both of us, equally shy but contend with it. It wasn't the usual four letter L-word that anyone would have expected but it was enough for us. We were embarking on our journey with small baby steps.

The next day, I planned to treat Sasha's hulks, as a token of appreciation for their timely intervention. Vicky overhead me while placing the order for the pizzas.

"I think that's too much for the three of us, Raghav. Reduce the quantity by one", turning to Asim to check if he is fine with it, "Right, Asim?"

The call was put on-hold by the pizza outlet, I replied casually, "It's for Sasha's friends for helping me, not us".

"What about us?! Didn't we also put some sense into your head yesterday, Mister?", Vicky arrogantly asked while crossing his arms.

"Leave it Vicky", Asim walked over to him and clapped his shoulder, "Ghar ki murghi, dal barabar", and shook his head disapprovingly.

Sighing, "Please add two more to it..... Yes to the sides too..." After they repeated the order for confirmation, "Six pizzas.... That'll be all.... Thanks!"

On ending the call, Vicky had a satisfied look, "Drinks tonight or over the weekend?", he questioned.

"Oh no! No drinks. I had enough drama with it. Don't want to go down that lane again. If I drink, it might be used against me later.

Better to stop and stay away from drinking. There's no place in my life for things that are going to cause any rifts between Sasha and me. So no more drinks, no more fights". I concluded with a wide beam.

song:Constantly, boy you played through my mind like a symphonyThere's no way to describe what you do to meYou just do to me, what you do.

"You got it real bad for her", wearing an amused smile, Asim commented.

Responding him with a smile, "It's either food or no treat at all." Vicky had no choice but to nod in agreement.

Making a move to head out of our ODC (Offshore Development Center), Vicky's outstretched hand hindered my path. "Wait a minute!", after calculating something on his fingers, he looked back at me, "Aren't you forgetting someone? The person on whose honor you are bestowing a treat, upon all of us.... Sasha?"

"No worries, I got it covered", I reassured, dismissing his query and continued our way out.

After collecting the delivered food at the reception, I sent them to block a table for everyone in the breakout area, while I excused myself to return in a few minutes. On my return, I was able to easily spot our table among the crowded tables, spaced out in a checkered board fashion. Our's was the only table for four, overloaded with occupants. I took the chair next to Sasha. To her left was Rohit, AJ, Vicky, Asim, Simbu, Daniel and then me, all seated in clockwise direction. Sasha, being the only girl at the table, looked like she's stuck in between two MC (Motorbike Club) gangs, considering all of us were well-built, especially her hulks.

Everyone was busy opening their delivery boxes, just than Madhav squeezed himself in between AJ and Vicky. Squinting my eyes at him for his unwanted presence here, he said, "Looks like a treat... Don't bother, I have my food from home with me", tapping his box.

Ignoring him, I handed over Sasha, two tiffin boxes. "For you", pointing my gaze to the boxes, I said, "It's homemade food prepared by me. Hope you like it". Sasha's eyes lit up and I could see she was cutely surprised-cum-impressed by my gesture.

Song:And it feels like I've been rescuedI've been set free, I am hypnotized by your destinyYou are magical, lyrical, beautifulYou are, and I want you to know babyI, I love you like a love song, baby.

Before she could catch a hold of it, Rohit grabbed it, "I wonder what's in it?", rotating it to examine the bigger tiffin box.

"Give it to me", AJ snatched it, "Let me check", he shook the box slightly near his ears.

"Careful!", I reprimanded him. I didn't want all my efforts in making the food, specially for her, to go down the hill. What's he trying to hear, stones inside it huh??

Sasha was already leaping over the table trying to get it back, "Give it here, you moron. It's not for you!...... Give it, I say", she yelled. Though her efforts were unsuccessful, her vigour to snatch it back, didn't die soon. I tried to calm her down, "Relax Sasha, it'll come back... Guys just ensure nothing spills out of the box,... Or else-", I trailed off with a warning.

"Or else, what?", Vicky challenged me jerking his head, when the box landed in his possession.

Just like that, it did a full round around the table, as if it was the object we used for the 'passing the parcel' game. None of them spared us, pulling our legs to the core. Finally it found its place, back in Sasha's hand and she huffed while opening it. "Will get you all back, for this, just wait and watch". On seeing the veg biryani tightly packed inside, she turned to smile in my direction, "Thank you."

Sasha happily scooped her spoon into the biryani, when it was mid air, Rohit spoke again. "Sash, aren't you on a healthy diet these days? Biryani's have a lot of oil in, it's not good for you.... Here let me have it". He slowly, very carefully took the spoon from her hand. The horror on my face was prominent, What! I was ready to pounce on Rohit anytime.

AJ burst out laughing, clamping his mouth with one hand while the other was thumping on the table lightly. "Look...look.... Look at the poor guy's face", he said in between his laugh. "Raghav you have such a comical expression. Did you by any chance mix a love potion in it and scared about the consequences if Rohit has it?", he jested.

"I think I just found my long-lost twin", Vicky chirped and gave a wassup nod to AJ. "No wonder he didn't want us to eat it. From the day I'm crashing at his place, I'm the one doing all the cooking". Facing me, "And now you miraculously turn up with Veg biryani, huh?!"

"That's your payment for letting you stay with me. I think I should increase your payment fees. How does shoveling washing the dishes chore to you, sound?", I retorted with a scowl.

Daniel glared at Rohit and sternly said, "Return the spoon."

Elated by his suppport, I flung my arm around his shoulder. "He is the only friend I have, over here. My friends became enemies and my 'enemies' who recently became friends, where only hiding behind a mask."

Getting back the spoon filled with rice, Sasha scoffed. "Oh pluh-ease!", taking her first morsel of my prepared food. "He is feeling guilty for coming up with the clubbing idea and landing us in trouble......Causing all the differences between us, so he is taking your side". She became busy digging into her food and scooping spoon, one after the other wholeheartedly.

Letting out a longing sigh, "It's ok Daniel. Sometimes accidents happen and it's not in our hands". Tapping his shoulder, I ended out brotherly side hug.

"Really?!?", Sasha shot a glare at me, cocking her right brow. "I don't think it was your words, you chameleon!"

"I learnt it from someone and realized my mistake", I replied apologetically.

"From what I remember, you said you didn't know the reason for your apology", she replied back sharply with a pointed look.

Softly cooing to her, "I already told I'm sorry for it. If I didn't say it, let me say it again.... I'm so sorry Sasha for everything". I said with all honesty, placing my hand over hers. The guys were enjoying a free theatrical performance on our account, with tubs of popcorn replaced with pizzas. She instantly snapped her hand out of my grip, like she had just touched a hot plate.

song:No one comparesYou stand alone, to every record I ownMusic to my heart that's what you are.

"Oh cut the lovey-dovey part. It's making me puke", the ridicule came from none other than Vicky. "Anyways, that chapter is closed Sasha, he has already given up on drinks for you", he announced with a smug face.

I awarded him with a death glare, That.was.supposed.to.be.with in.us, friends", menacing each word through my gritted teeth.

"You mean to say Sasha and me aren't friends or you and Sasha aren't friends?", Vicky pretended to ask an innocent question.

Asim tried controlling him and gave him a disappointing nod.

When I was under the impression that the discussion was coming to and end, the girl sitting next to me spoke up. "Ya Raghav, what are you implying. Say it clearly", pursed her lips with a mischievous glint in her eyee.

"Great! All of you'll are ganging up on me. I feel like I'm put on a hot seat. Let me tell you, I'm not liking this arrangement, one bit", I complained, crossing my arms and trying to put up an annoyed face.

"Get used to it Raghav boyyyy", Sasha nudged her elbow playfully on my arm few times. In a half-seated stance, she hovered over the table to give a hi-fi to Vicky, who was across her.

"Sasha!", cautioning her for her carelessness, "Food could have gotten stuck to your dress". Admonishing her, felt like a parent trying to teach table manners to their toddler.

"COULD have only right, it didn't happen", she shrugged, as if it didn't matter to her.

"Ok let's eat. No more club topic again, okay", Daniel announced. Making all of us chuckle at his guilty conscience and we went back to the food, before it becomes cold in the air conditioned room.

By mentioning, 'the club', they indirectly opened a can of worms in my mind. Button nose, Button nose, Button nose - was the only thing that was echoing in my head. Who was it? I sweept my glance through my table mates, to check everyone's nose. Nah! They are all like brothers to Sasha...... Except...except might be Madhav. As he was the only man, apart from all of us who spent time with her. He was buzzing around Sasha like a mosquito, but why did it feel like he's sucking my blood? Focusing my gaze on his nose, to get better picture of it. All I wanted to do at that instant, was to grab his face between my hands, to scrutinize and measure the size of his nose.

Vicky's voice broke the peaceful silence and dragged me out from my outrageous thoughts. "By the way, Raghav, your MIL (mother-in-law) sent 3 containers for you and you only reciprocating it with 2 for Sasha.... No boy, that's not done", he shook his head in a tease.

Simbu stunned at this revealation, "What! I didn't get any", and threw Sasha a disappointed glare.

"Yes, what can we say. With the entry of the new Mister there," pointing his pizza towards me, "all our accounts will be credited less. Accept the changes Simbu". AJ declared it matter-of-factly, earning him a kick under the table and an artificial smile from Sasha.

"Not fair Sasha. You know how much I like Aunty's savouries", Simbu sounded hurt.

"Hello, don't come into AJ's words. It's nothing to do with Raghav. You people had just returned from your road trip and were on leave. Then, Simbu, you started having indigestion problems, so I didn't give you", Sasha told him.

Turning to AJ, "Don't you dare put the blame on Raghav", she narrowed her eyes at him.

"Aww! See the love and care", AJ mocked.

Without a doubt, another kick under the table was flung but unfortunately landed on Madhav, as AJ moved away predicting it.

"Oh! I'm so sorry, Madhav!", she apologized, giving him a sweet smile.

With the establishment of peace between the two of us, it gave the feeling of two neighboring countries uniting to form an alliance. We walked around the campus like a flock of birds, traveling in weird patterns. The least we could do is, not to leave a trail of destruction behind us. From then on, we used to have all our lunch breaks, coffee breaks; altogether as one big gang.

Everyday was a chaos, especially while trying to find a table with empty seats, enough for all of us. Each of us, standing at a separate row of table, ready to pounce and claim the table along with the going-to-be vacant seats; before other waiting employees grab it. The employees eating at the table were under our death glare, mostly when our patience or hunger was put on test.

When someone suceeded gaining possession of a table, they felt like they had conquered Mt. Everest. Turning around to call the others over, only to find out someone else also had blocked a table elsewhere, was the worst part. The accomplishment which one just felt proud of, was similar to deflating a fully blown balloon.

It was a fun activity, nonetheless.

I smiled when I saw Sasha and Simbu, trying to convince each other why their blocked seats were better than the other, through sign language. Like they were in a muted debate. Obviously Simbu had to give in, to the feisty Tom-Boy.

Settling down at the table, we had converted our cafeteria into a buffet. All the dishes, spread out in front of us, for everyone to share and have variety of food. I took the aloo parathas and placed one in Sasha's plate then on mine. Serving her plate, before mine, as usual - with raita, little dal and some stir fried potatoes that were swimming in oil; for which I received a glare from her. I tried my level best to drain out the excess oil.

"It's only one day, Sasha, you can have a little bit extra oil", I tried convincing her.

"You call this, little bit?", picking the potatoes from her plate with a spoon.

I sent her a slightly embarrassed smile, "It's essential to have some fat content in our food, Sasha. See that board over there, it states the same". Pointing to the diet oriented huge banner placed near the cashier.

She huffed, only to agree, "Fine!" Back to her normal happy voice, she said, "Thank you, that's enough now, you also put something in your plate".

"Good girl!"

I started filling up my plate, with a private smile playing on my lips. Others might have failed in persuading Sasha, but I was certainly learning the art now.

Vicky had come over to Asim's desk, and both the team leads of their respective application sub-teams, were busy scanning through profiles of freshers, to select someone for our huge team. One of our teammates had put down their paper, making us begin the search for a replacement. While they were busy, my mind wandered back to the mystery man with the button nose. We were enjoying the blissful days but like a tiny ant nibbling on my skin, the unconfortable sensation of her drooling over him, didn't leave me. Like they say, people usually speak the truth when they are tipsy. It could also be a reason why she had stuck to the word 'Like' while replying to my confession.

Vicky glanced at me, while letting his erected posture casually rest on Asim's desk, "Come back to earth, Alice in Wonderland. What are you thinking about?"

"Nothing", I grunted, revealing my thoughts to him was only going make things worse.

"Come on! You've been spaced out for way too long. I bet it has something to do with S-A-S-H-A', he spelt our her name like singing a some nursery rhyme.

"Ya, she and her button nose guy", before I could stop myself, the words rolled off my tongue.

Vicky suddenly called out to Bala and prompted him to come over.

"Hey! How are you guys doing?, Why did you call me Vicky?", Bala spoke as he entered our bay.

"Hmmm", Vicky rubbed his chin, "Bala do you remember when Raghav had joined this team as a fresher, how we used to call him?"

"Yup!", Bala replied in a heartbeat. Turning to me asked, "Hey Button nose, how are you?"

Not able to register that Bala had just called me button nose, I twirled my chair in the direction of Asim and Vicky. They were busy stifling their laugh, as if they were enjoying an inside joke. I couldn't believe it.

"Why didn't you guys tell me this that day?", I literally yelled at them but it was of no use.

"Raghav, if all the drama wraps up on a single day, how are we going to be entertained for the remaining 364 days?", Vicky said, laughing away.

That was acceptable from Vicky, but Asim, why did he hide it, I turned to him with questioning eyes.

He raised his hands in surrender and pointed to Vicky, "He's the culprit. Anyway, with everything settled between the two of you, we thought it was enough of our meddling. Somethings you should discover by yourself, Raghav", he said with a smirk growing on his face.

I grunted, while Bala standing next to us was clueless. "I can't understand head or tail of what you guys are speaking. It's like astrophysics, it's going way above my head.... If my work is done here, I'm leaving, bye."

The next day, Sasha came with two microwave friendly containers in hand, to my desk. She placed one in front of me, "I also made something for you", she said demurely while shifting between her legs. "It's nothing special, just Maggi."

Sasha and feeling shy, what a surprise!

Immediately I took it, to open it up, "This is just fine. Thank you".

"It's slightly burnt, sorry for that. I removed the burnt noodles... you see, it's the first time I'm cooking anything", she said while she jumping on to my desk.

Smiling at her, "The first time it's always like that. Don't worry, practice makes one perfect. No one's a born chef". Encouraging her, I patted her knee.

With the first ball of noodles entering my mouth, I understood that she needs a lot of practice. It was slightly undercooked too, I tried masking the initial cringe while swallowing the noodles with a smile. Thank God she was staying in paying guest that provides all the meals.

"How's it?", Sasha's excited voice came out. When I took time to reply due to strength I put in to chew and swallow, her excitement died down like the blowing off of a candle.

"Hey, it's not bad for the first time. Atleast you didn't burn all of it. You cooked for me, even though you haven't done it before, that's more than enough Sasha".

"Hmmmm", she hummed half-heartedly.

"Really, the gesture is sweet.... It actually makes me feel special", I announced happily.

"Special?", she asked in disbelief.

"Yes! I'm the lucky one to taste the first thing you cooked", flashing a proud smile, I winked at her.

"You - you are hopeless", she giggled

"I have heard that from my parents and from that guy sitting behind you", I joined in her laugh. "Hmmm, it's mid year appraisal time, when's your discussion scheduled?" Making small talk and trying to gobble down the noodles as fast as possible. Eyeing her other container, Eat faster Raghav, you have one more box to go. I didn't want her to eat the noodles and suffer from stomach pain. Nor did I want her to find out that it also undercooked, she would be devasted.

All you have to do is make her talk, while you eat her's too.

"Mine, is scheduled on the 15th, I think after lunch. Lets see. I don't understand why these managers keep it after lunch? How does anyone feel to talk after lunch? All are usually busy stifling a yawn... I think they are using our discussion time to avoid being caught sleeping at their desks". She chuckled and I kept nodding my head. "They aren't taking the appraisal discussions seriously then what's the use of having them in first place."

Grabbing her box, I sheepishly said, "Don't mind, I'm feeling hungry. Your lunch is on me, don't worry."

"Ya ya, go ahead, no problem."

Opening her box, continuing our conversation, I said, "Ya I agree. It's just a formality but I think the mid year discussions are a good idea, at least we know where we stand. The previous system of having only yearly once discussions, just before the appraisal usually ends up giving us surprises."

"Still, here also they are going to rant the same thing they say at the yearly ones. Moreover these mid year ones don't have any effect on our salaries too. So what's the point?"

"Ya right! In next Human Resources meeting or Employee Satisfaction Survey, we should suggest that the mid year appraisals should have salary changes."

Sasha scuffed, "Like as if they'll tale it up."

"Let's see, you never know."

"Di", someone from behind me spoke.

"Ya Madhav, tell me", she sent a small smile to him.

Di? Did Madhav call Sasha his sister? Rotating my chair to look at the new comer.

"Why are you calling her, Di?", I questioned.

"Errr-um! Sorry Sir, Sorry Ma'am", Madhav scratched his head, clearly uncomfortable.

"Sir? Ma'am?", I raised my eyebrow at him.

"Chill Raghav. He's a fresh graduate, so obviously he is stuck with Sir- Ma'am nomenclature. We have all gone through that phase while getting accustomed to the IT culture", Sasha took his side.

"Oh yes yes", coming out of my daze I said. "So you are a fresher?" Internally calculating his age and smirking within, He is no competition for me. He sees Sasha as a sister.

"Yes sir!", Madhav replied like a military speaking to his superior.

"Relax Madhav, cut the formalities, call me Raghav", I sushed him while biting into the next spoonful of noodles.

Now it doesn't taste that bad.

"I know! I told him so many times here in IT, there is no Sir's, no Ma'am's. After trying for so many days he settled with Di. I tried talking him out of it but -"

I cut her off instantly, "Leave the boy alone, Sasha. How many changes can a young boy handle. Let him be."

Sasha rolled her eyes and asked Madhav, "What did you want?"

"Are you coming for lunch?", he hesitated."If you already had it, it's ok, I'll go on my own", rushing up his words.

"Hey stop! Your Di didn't eat yet. We were just leaving, you can join us. In fact her lunch's on me, I'll treat you too. Come Madhav", standing up to leave.

"You guys head first, I'll just check my mails and join you'll at the lift", she strode away. Looking over her shoulder, she yelled, "Wait for me at the lift."

I chuckled, "Yes will wait. Come soon."

Putting my hand over the slightly stiff Madhav, "You know what, you'll enjoy working in this company. I can see your bright future ahead. Just keep learning, working and don't loose your good manners. It'll take you a long way. In this industry, interpersonal skills is very important, I like it that you replacled Ma'am with Di. I like it. The way you are rooted to your culture, keep it up. Don't let anyone sway you the other way, ok!" Giving him a pep talk, while walking towards the elevator, I felt blissful, not sure why.

At lunch, suddenly we realized that today was the fifteenth."Sh oot! Today's the 15th. Oh Gosh! Why do I loose track of the dates", Sasha exclaimed, running her hand down her face.

"Slowly, you'll choke at this rate. You still have what....a solid twenty minutes for the appraisal discussion. So calm down. It's not your first one too, so why are you getting an anxiety attack", I asked her.

"Oh! You don't know that manager of mine. If I step into the discussion room, even one minute late, he will use up the whole time, imparting a lecture on punctuality". Sasha ate her food in record time and sprinted to leave.

"Good luck, stay calm and composed. Jot down all the points you want to speak and your achievements", I reminded her before she left.

The discussion room blocked for Sasha's meeting was beside my desk. After about half an hour into the meeting, Sasha came out furiously, raging in anger. Oh God! Looks like it didn't go well. But aren't everyone's reaction the same after they come out of the appraisal discussion. Manager and employee quarrel over performance was inevitable in such discussions.

I stood up and walked towards her, she took long heavy strides and came straight to my desk. Instead of hopping onto the desk as usual, she slumped into my chair. I frowned, Something's really wrong.

"That piece of sh—", she blasted and continued firing curse words one after the other.

She's never uttered such abuses before, from the time I knew her. What the hell happened??!

17

CHAPTER 17

Sasha's POV

song:So what am I not supposed to have an opinionShould I keep quiet just because I'm a womenCall me a b***h cause I speak what's on my mindGuess it's easier for you to swallow if I sat and smiled.

I sat on Raghav's chair with a violent storm brewing inside me. My temper had reached it's limits, fuming and cursing at my Manager, after our encounter few minutes ago. Raghav handed me his flask but the cool water dashing down my oesophagus, did nothing to infuse into my boiling veins.

"Sasha, tell me what happened? You are scaring me here", Raghav's voice was heard like a faint background score.

Raghav squatted on his toes, for our eyes to be perfectly aligned. He held my hands in his and tugged them slightly. "If you don't tell me, how can I help". His voice was so soft and caring, I couldn't neglect it. If I hadn't been in such a foul mood, the twitching corners of my lips would have broken into a sweet smile, but not now. I was about to open my mouth, just then scuffling of shoes was heard and another pair of men's pointed black formal shoes came into my vision.

"What's all the commotion about? Sash, who stepped on your wrong foot?", Rohit asked authoritatively.

Without breaking our eye contact, Raghav answered, "She just came out of her mid-year appraisal discussion and walked out of it like this. She hasn't said a word yet, beside swearing".

"What the hell happened in there?", Rohit's voice mirrored his rage.

"Sasha, we are all here with you, for you. Can you please tell us why you are in this agitated state?..... Did something happen inside the discussion room? Was it related to your appraisal or performance or —", Raghav trailed off. When he saw I didn't make a move to respond back, he continued carefully, "Or.... Did he touch you or say something inappropriate?"

"That ass —!", Rohit bursted out, "Wait till I get my hands on him, he is going to be dead meat soon."

"Calm down man! You aren't helping here", Raghav cast him a warning look and nudged his head towards me. "Sasha, please open up, so that we don't jump to all kinds of conclusions..... Do you want to go somewhere else?"

Behind me I could hear Vicky's one sided conversation through the office extension, before he slammed the receiver back into it's place.

"Ruhi, are you busy? Can you and Chitra, hurry up and come to Raghav's desk.....It's an emergency....With Sasha.... Ok, good. Come soon. Thanks!"

Raghav gave a thankful nod to Vicky.

I was busy planning my next move in my mind. In jet speed, Ruhi and Chitra entered into our bay with questioning looks. Raghav was letting go my hands, to make way for them but I squeezed his, in return. Grateful for my subtle reaction, he stayed put in his place with an understanding nod.

Ruhi came to my side and scooted her chair closer to me. Placing a comforting hand on my shoulder she asked in a concerned laced toned. "Are you ok, Sasha? Do you want to talk to us girls separately?"

"For God's sake! We have been asking the same thing for past ten minutes! .... And why the hell will she go separately, to talk to you, when I'm over here", Rohit arrogantly stated while folding his hands over his chest.

Ruhi glared at him to shut up, "We know you guys are really close friends like siblings and all... but —but not everything can be shared with men, sometimes girls require a female to confide in. Will you just keep your arrogant self aside and focus on the situation."

Rohit let out a heaved sigh, "Alright!". He turned to me, "Sash, do you want us to go? You know I'm right across the hall, when you need me?"

"That's not required, Rohit. You can stay, everyone here can stay. There is nothing that is required to be hidden or kept under covers. I'm not scared and neither will I cower under fear or self-pity". Finally opening up, I looked around my friends who had formed a circle around me like a protective cocoon. "I'm fine and I will make things fine, there's nothing to worry, guys", I assured them.

"O-k! We won't force you, whenever you feel to disclose, you can tell us. We will support you in it", Raghav said.

"Hell ya!", Rohit exclaimed through gritted teeth, his anger hadn't simmered down.

"That man had the nerve to pass lewd comments to me in the middle of the appraisal discussion", I spat out in disgust. Sweeping my gaze through Ruhi, Asim, Raghav, Chitra, Rohit and Vicky, to gauge their reactions; I continued. I realized they didn't want to interrupt, when I had started to reel out what conspired within those four closed walls. "Does he not know me, after working with him for nearly three years? Did he think I'll let it pass, just like that?.... If he could do that to me, don't know, to how many other girls he would have said things that were more disgusting and demeaning."

"What did that good-for-nothing creature tell you?" Rohit asked, keeping a check in his choice of words due to Ruhi's narrowing eyes on him.

Ruhi being the mama bear, still disapproved his words with a nod. "Sasha, what kind of comment did he pass? Did he cross his lines and touch you inappropriately?"

"Wouldn't I have skinned him alive by now, if he had done that?", I retorted. "Good for him, he didn't try such cheap tricks, else there would have been a blood bath inside that room", jerking my thumb towards it.

"Let's not take violence into our hands, we can surely tackle this in better means", Asim said thoughtfully.

"What did he say to you? Did he pester you too much?", Raghav's held-in-place anger was starting to flare up.

"No, he didn't push it too much", taking a deep breathe, "He asked me how much do I want for a night". Just repeating his words made me feel dirty. I swear I'm not going to leave him without taking him down for his unprofessional ethics.

There was pin drop silence for the next few minutes. Just then my manager, Manoj, walked past by, whistling away softly, through the bay parallel to us. He was making his way to his desk, after finishing another teammates appraisal discussion. My subdued anger, shot up hearing his whistles. What the hell was his trying to project over here? I quickly caught Rohit's hand, stopping him from confronting Manoj.

song:When a female fires back suddenly big talker don't know how to actSo he does what every little boy would doMakin' up a few false rumors or twoThat for sure is not a man for me, slanderin' names for popularityIt's sad you only get your fame through controversyBut now it's time for me to come and give you more to say.

Glancing over his shoulder with an annoyed look, he snatched his hand out of my grasp. "Why the hell did you stop me? I would have punched some sense into his head and made sure he repents for his words."

Standing up, I replied, "I can do that on my own."

"You, don't need to go near him again. We four men will handle it", Raghav said pointing with his chin to the four corners, the men were at, making an imaginary square.

"Four?? Hello", Rohit waved his smartphone in the air, "I'll just call the others too. Let's see how will that creature of disgraced meat returns home in one piece. Seven versus one, he doesn't stand a chance". Rohit announced will forcefully typing the lock screen password.

"Rohit, calm down. That's not required. I can fight my own battles without you guys interfering". Raghav shook his head disapproving my idea, I went on to add. "It's a battle that needs to be fought between me and that disgusting man. It's for all the women out there. If I don't do it, then such kind of people will keep taking advantage and think that they can get away with anything because the opposite gender is too scared, too weak, to raise a voice. That, will not happen under my watch."

song:This is for my girls all around the worldWho have come across a man that don't respect your worthThinkin' all women should be seen and not heardSo what do we do girls, shout out loud.

Ruhi supported me on this,"She's right. If you guys go and confront him, he's not going to think twice about not doing it again. If Sasha stands up to him, it'll have more impact."

Chitra too added, "I'm with the girls on this. The whole point of degrading her, will be sidelined. She or some other girl will fall a victim again, when there are no trustworthy men around...... Don't worry we will go with Sasha."

"Yes Girlpower!!", Ruhi fisted Chitra's hands in agreement. "They won't back-off without being on the receiving side of a woman's wrath."

song:Lettin 'em know were gonna stand our groundSo lift your hands high and wave 'em proudTake a deep breath and say it loudNever can, never willCan't hold us down. Nobody can hold us downNever can, never will.

"You guys can come as back-up but only interfere when the situation goes out of our hands", I warned them.

Among the four men standing in front of me, everyone gave an understanding nod except Asim.

"I don't agree. I still think violence is not the best way to go with", Asim said. "There is a portal where we can report — Unfair work ethics, harassment issues and similar issues. I suggest we go through the proper channel for proper stringent actions."

"Hmmm, that does sound better. He could also be terminated for his behavior, when found guilty. That should teach him a good lesson", Vicky said thoughtfully.

"But will the justice come in time?", Ruhi questioned, "And what if he gets away, using his influence and managerial post?"

"That's a risk", Rohit pointed out, "There's no guarantee that foul play won't take place in the investigation done, after we report the issue."

Asim defended, "Have some trust in our Human Resources Team and our organization. Just because we came across one perverted manager, that doesn't mean, everyone holding authoritative posts will follow his suite."

Vicky replied, "That's the risk we will have to take. It's either reporting it officially or taking things in our hands. We also got to remember the risks of loosing our jobs, if we choose the second option". Rohit gave him a that's-what-you-are-thinking-about-now glare. "If we choose the first option now, when things go haywire, we still have the second one to utilize. But the other way round, it won't be possible. The blame will fall on us if we submit a report after taking things in hand."

"There's another risk with raising a concern in the portal", Chitra said. "All the higher management will be part of it, directly or indirectly. It'll have an impact on your appraisal, Sasha".

Everyone looked at Chitra with disappointment, she added, "Hey! Don't look down upon me. You called me to share my thoughts and support. That's what I'm doing . I'm thinking from all angles and making sure Sasha is well aware of what she's getting herself into.... Didn't I tell earlier that I am on Sasha's side!?"

"Like I care about the salary hikes or appraisal now! What's the use of having the reporting system, if the victim is also going to face the burn.... If that's so, I guess staying in this so called 'esteemed' company is not worth it, after all. I would be more than glad, to turn in my resignation but not without bringing this issue to light ", I replied hotly.

"Sasha", Raghav's palms met mine again, "I would also advice on reporting the inappropriate behavior. Think this through. If this is what you want, we are here for you. I'm here with you."

The sincerity with which Raghav said, overwhelmed my heart, body and soul. I never thought, besides my trusted four guy friends, that I would be able to trust and be close with some other male, who would eventually turn into the slightly 'more than a friend' category. Nodding my head, "Thanks Raghav. Thanks everyone. I feel better now."

"Mention not!", Raghav smiled and made me sit down, "Why don't we go ahead and file the complaint, so that action is taken without much delay."

With everyone's help, I filled in the details requested for, in the said portal. Recalling the incident, I mentioned all the details and submitted it. Letting out a sigh, I leant back on Raghav's chair. After sipping through the water, he had handed me again; I rotated my chair to face my friends, who had crowded near Raghav's workstation. "It's done! Let's see how it goes."

Ruhi, on the chair to my left, said "Don't worry. Everything will be fine". I nodded hesitantly.

"Just relax, there's no need to remember it again, atleast not for the rest of the day, Ok?", Raghav said from a chair to my right. Suddenly I felt him lean into my personal space, he brought both my hands closer to his face. I was left astonished when he gave two tender kisses, on the back of each of my palms, one after the other. Next, he settled for a tad long kiss on my forehead. The last lingering kiss, felt like Elsa's icy touch from the Frozen movie. The calmness imposed on my forehead seeped through my body, slowly from the brain till the tip of my toes.

His lips were felt surprisingly soft against my skin, apart for the slight poking of his mustache from his French beard. Till the tingles cascaded down to my toes, his lips, didn't leave my forehead. As if he could see an led bulb, flashing the green light, indicating that the goal was achieved, he put some distance between us. Rohit's faint coughs, made me aware of my surroundings.

Omg! Did we just share our first kiss in front of our friends.... So embarrassing!!... I'm really, really going to kill you Raghav!!!

"Ok! Let's disperse", Raghav said nonchalantly, like nothing happened. Rohit, Ruhi and Chitra left the place while Asim and Vicky too, went back to their respective desks. I semi-circled Raghav, from behind him. Just as I was about to move out of his cubicle, he instantly held the middle of my hand.

Turning on my heels to face him. "I'm dropping you home tonight, no if's, no but's". He completed stating his mind, before I could retaliate. "I know you came in your car today to office, so I'll pick you up tomorrow for office. Got it!?"

As if you left any room for negotiation.

I rolled my eyes, wanting to say it out loud but refrained from doing so.

The idea was not bad though, so why condemn it.

Nodding my head as an obedient child, I let him have his way this time.

At sharp, six-thirty in the evening, Raghav came up to my desk, "Time up! Time to go home".

"I usually leave at seven, because I login at ten in the morning", I reminded him.

"One day won't do any harm, anyways they take the average of a week to check the employee's clocking time. I'm sure there would have been few days, were you would had stretched and worked..... Besides! by the time we reach the reception it'll add up ten minutes. I don't think they are doing micro-management, to track even couple of unclocked minutes", he said factfully with a smug face.

"Ya, but I'm in the mid of something.... Ten minutes ok", I requested and focused on my monitor.

He peeped to see what I was doing, figuring out that I was just filing up some internal excel sheet, not client related work. He said, "Not ok! Do it tomorrow", with that he locked my system by pressing windows and the key "L" of my keyboard simultaneously.

"Rrrraghav you are just —"

"You can fill in the blanks on our way to the elevator, come now."

The ride home was quiet peaceful and light-hearted, polar opposite of the day that was on the brink of closing. Listening to my favorite songs through the CD player, we spoke about our favorite movies and songs. I could see he was trying to wade off today's events from my mind for the time being and I silently appreciated his efforts.

True to his words, Raghav came to pick me up from my accommodation, the next morning. However instead of taking my usual office route, he took a detour.

"Where are we going, Raghav?"

"To have breakfast!", the joy evident in his peppy tone.

"I already ate and came. But we could stop somewhere, if you didn't have any."

"Oh! What did the little miss eat?", he playfully asked.

Narrowing my eyes, I stated, "Cereal and coffee", lifting my chin up.

Raghav chuckled, "I knew it. That's just an appetizer". He briefly glanced at me, before returning his gaze to the road, "You need a wholesome breakfast for the busy day ahead."

Understanding his underlying meaning, it left me no choice but to agree. Today, surely would be my longest day at work. By now everyone would have been initimated that some employee from our account had raised a harassment case. The uproar caused by my complaint was waiting for me at office and I had a feeling by the end of the day, I would deprived of any energy.

We entered a famous South Indian dine-in restaurant and ordered mini tiffin. The waiter placed the plates in front of us, the aroma was tempting but how could I survive such a holistic second breakfast.

Why am I finding myself in this kind of spots often, lately? God help me, hope my stomach doesn't burst with it.

Without wasting another thought we relished the hot Pongal, Idly, vada, dosa, sambhar along with a variety of coconut, tomato and mint chutney and sweet kesari. To my surprise, I found myself hungry and a filled stomach, at the end of the meal.

Raghav placing the order for juice instead of a hot beverage, "Two pomegranate juice, without ice, one spoon sugar."

"Without ice?", I raised my brow in question.

"Yeah! With the onset of the monsoon, I don't want us to fall ill", he said with a small smile.

Did I forget to mention that we were seated beside each other. Throughout our dining in, Raghav held my hand, occasionally rubbing his thumb in comforting circular motions at the back of my hand. Thank God he refrained from pulling another act of open display of affection with his kisses, here. If he had done it, I would not wait for the ground to swallow me, I would literally dig it open, to hide in embarrassment.

The placement of the two juice containers jolted me out of my thoughts. "A pink drink for me?? Really Raghav?", I cringed and turned sideways to face him.

He casually shrugged, "Didn't you call me a blind bat when we first got acquainted with each other.....Looks like I'm colour blind too", he jested.

I shook my head in amusement, "Next time, any kind of blue crushers for me."

He chuckled, "Here they have only South Indian delicacies, you won't find your hi-fi crushers here. Moreover, pomo juice is more healthier and the colour is natural, unlike your preferred drink."

"True that!", my shoulders slumped an inch in defeat. "It's good by the way, I'm enjoying the juice", giving my honest opinion.

"Glad to hear that", he said and was smiling adoringly in my way, as I sipped through the juice slowly.

As expected, at the strike of eleven, Lavanya, the delivery manager, stopped by my desk and asked me for an impromptu meeting. We went to another discussion room, adjacent to the one, where things went down hill.

Lavanya didn't spare any minute, as soon as we sat down, "I'm sure you know the reason behind this sudden discussion..... Are you sure you want to take it up?.... The complaint?"

With full determination, I gave a curt reply, "Yes! I thought through it enough and I made the decision to log it."

"Hmmm, do you know the consequences?", she carefully asked.

"Not sure, Lavanya. But I will fight it till the end, as I need justice and want this place to be a clean and safe environment for everyone, to work in.

"I understand", she flashed a sympathy smile, "I still can't believe Manoj could do such a thing.... Whatever, if you have decided then let me go ahead and approve it right now...." I nodded in acceptance.

"As a senior manager and a lady, it's my duty to take you through the process. Not going to lie, it might have an impact on your appraisal, but I'll ensure if the complaint is taken up, no such thing happens with you. Besides that, confidentiality of the issue will be maintained within the management and Human resources, but you might get unwanted sneer looks from the ones who know about it. Be strong and don't let them dither you. If you're developing emotional stress or need assistance in this tough situation you faced, we can provide you professional counseling. That option can be availed from the complaint form. It's open to edit it, anytime, during this whole process of investigation, up to the closure of the issue. If you face additional difficulties or untoward advances from the accused or others involved in panel, you can add those details to the same complaint..... Panel discussions with you and the accused will be held separately to give the benefit of doubt, equally. Later a decision will be made after thorough investigation. It might take a week, but the organization is firm on such events and has a strict SLA (Service Level Agreement) to not drag the issue unless surprises crop up in the middle. All-in-all, it'll be a tough week ahead filled with multiple discussions.... Stay strong."

"Thanks for the detailed information and yes, I will keep in mind".

Standing up, to mark the end of the discussion, "If you need any help or to discuss anything, feel free to ping me, you can count on me".

"Sure, thanks once again for your support".

Lavanya being a pro-active managerial head, made sure the panel was set and up for discussion by the end of the day. What can you say , along with me, she wanted to clear the matter as it'll be a black mark added in her kitty as she headed the portfolio. It's not just Manoj and me, but others too would be affected.

My discussion with the investigation panel was at five in the evening. We entered a round table conference at another floor. The panel consisted of representatives from our portfolio — Lavanya and Vivek from the senior management team and our Human Resource Team lead; along with the head of the Human Resouce of the Coimbatore branch and two other cross profolio senior managers — a lady and a man. In a nutshell, they had included panelists from our portfolio for insights and unrelated outsiders to give their unbiased views.

Everyone actively participated, asking questions and jotting down things in their notepad. This discussion was recorded in the CCTV camera and extra camera and microphones, for future reference. From my point of view, it went well. They said they'll have the same discussion with Manoj the next day. Manoj was asked to work from home or from a separate floor for time being, but he had already submitted a work from home request for this week, long ago. It spared me from facing him in the floor.

They took three days to get back to me. Seems like they have come to a conclusion with their investigation. Manoj was also present this time, he looked worn out and tired. Don't feel sympathy for

him, he migh just be playing the sympathy card. I reminded myself.
Dammit! Such a good actor. If we women played that card, we would
be called out for it.

song:So-what am I not supposed to say what I'm sayingAre you
offended with the message I'm bringin'Call me whatever 'cause you
words don't mean a thingGuess you ain't even a man enough to
handle what I singIf you look back in history it's a common double
standard of society.

Lavanya adressed the gathering, "Thank you all for taking your
time out for this investigation. With everyone's smooth cooperation, we are able to close this issue within the time lines. I'll hand
it over to the head of the Human Resources Team, Tina, to convey
the outcome and related facts identified."

"I echo Lavanya's words. Thank you all and would like to re-iter-
ate that the company condemns such scenarios and provides full
support to both the parties involved, to help them cope and evolve
into better individuals — professionally and personally."

Tina glanced at the open file under her clasped hands, probably
the report and continued. "After numerous discussions with and
without the partied involved, the panel as come to a unanimous
decision that the unfortunate encounter was a misunderstanding
occurred due to the slip of the tongue from the accused in this case."

What!

She turned to me and said, "For the best interest of the parties
involved and better clarity on what led us to this inference, we would
like to replay the CCTV footage of the discussion roon during the
incident. Sasha and Manoj, based on your consent, will can go aheaf
and show it here."

Both of us nodded and the scene was projected on the screen through a laptop. The footage was captured from behind Manoj, his laptop screen was seen with me seated across him in the small circular table at the centre.

"Sasha, you are doing a good job, based on the client feedback and your superiors. Also I can see your active participation in all internal company events..... Well done, keep up your good work", Manoj praised me.

"Thank you Manoj", I smiled gratefully.

"With all that said and done, there's always room for improv ement... I can see a lot of potential in you. You should concentrate on automation and come up with ideas for innovation to get recognized from the higher management. When it drills down to our portfolio, you do stand out but to shine amongst employees from other portfolios, innovation is the key. You have surpassed the competition within our portfolio and if you need to climb up the ladders, this would be my suggestion..... Think about it... Take some steps towards it and you'll grow in no time."

Blah! Blah! Blah!, same repetitive stuff; my mind voice was stating.

Manoj side-by-side was typing in the laptop, into the various columns of the excel sheet with my name on it.

He let out a breathe and asked, half-mindedly, while typing away, "So what are your expectations this year?.....Sasha?"

"Hmmm yes?", I blankly replied as my mind had drifted away.

"How much do you want for a night?", Manoj stated

"WHAT??", I yelled in disbelief.

"Yes, how much do I want for a night?", he repeated it.

"I don't think —"

He lifted his finger, "Excuse me, I need to take this". He hardly spoke two words in the call and cut it. "If you need time to think over, you can ping it to me later. Do you have anything to discuss from your side or are we good to close the discussion?"

Hell ya! I have something to say or more, feel to slap the double faceted face of yours, I screamed those words internally.

Taking my silence as my agreement, he said," Good, that'll be all. Please send the next person after ten minutes.... You may leave now."

With that I stormed out.

Seeing the visuals, I was re-living it and could remember my internal thoughts vividly. Tina spoke again while rewinding the clip. "We have just witnessed the whole scenario, but I would like to go back to a particular scene and zoom it..... Here... Based on our keen observation, we found out that Manoj was entering the appraisal discussion details on the laptop. When he asked you the question, he was at the column filling your monetary expectations. Usually this column is filled or discussed only with the top performers, keeping in view of satisfying and retaining the best talent we have..... Request you to observe the column name, the arrow is hovering on. It's the night shift allowanceComponent", she emphasized clearly.

Oh Crap!

She continued to disclose their observations, "We are under the impression that when Manoj asked you that question, he intended to ask about your expectations for the night shift allowance... But due to some reason, he didn't phrase the question in the right manner."

Lavanya spoke, "Can also please forward the clip to after Sasha walked off?"

"Sure. As you can see Manoj, after his call, typed in the same column TBD (To be decided). Clearly stating that that is what he meant to ask from the first place..... Manoj, do you want to add anything from your side?"

"Yes. Sasha, I apologize for not articulating it professionally. Initially when I had the discussion with the panel, I was in shock and couldn't zero it out, for this misunderstanding. Now when I saw this with my own eyes, I realized how wrong it sounded and how it was misinterpreted. I apologize deeply for my behavior but assure you, that it wasn't what it sounds to be. I have always thought of you as a professional teammate and nothing else", Manoj spoke desperately.

"Hmmmm... I can understand that now. I accept your apology and thank the panel for bringing out the truth and shedding light on the facts.... Sorry for any inconvenience caused due to my assumption."

Manoj dismissed me, "You don't have to say that. It was clearly my fault. I was pre-occupied with my personal problems, entering the data, that I didn't pay heed to my choice of words. Multi-tasking is not my Forte looks like, especially when I am stressed out."

"Being compassionate to both the parties, as the management was well aware of the personal stress Manoj was going through in the past one month, we are not taking any stringent actions for the slip. However, we have identified some action items. Manoj is adviced to undergo professional etiquette, Verbal and Non-verbal etiquette, Stress Management and Multitasking trainings. He is required to complete them within a month and will be accessed with a panel on his improvement. Sasha is adviced to undergo Concentration and Listening skills training". Tina read out the conclusion from the file. After everyone signed the document, we walked out.

Manoj came up to me, "I'm so proud of you, Sasha, really. Thank Godness you didn't let the misunderstanding stay within yourself and you cleared it. I wish my six year old daughter grows up to be like you and be brave enough to voice out in case of injustice."

I smiled at him, such a good hearted person and I misread him,

"It's kind of my fault too. But glad the respect I have for you is still intact. Thank you for not being like what I thought, it was creepy", I shivered and we laughed it out.

The boys along with Ruhi and Chitra were impatiently waiting for me in the breakout area. They were eager to hear the outcome. I felt bad that I put them all through such stress for past few days, all for a mere misinterpretation.

AJ pushed the empty chair out for me with his leg, "So, all good? What was the decision?"

Sitting down next to AJ and across Raghav, taking a deep breathe, I stated, "It was a misunderstanding, just like what happened in the FRIEND's sitcom with Rachel and her blue ink."

After thorough explanation, I concluded, "and I'm awarded with some trainings to attend.... You guys better nominate yourself too.", wagging my finger around them.

"No way! I have work", Rohit whined

AJ nudged Rohit, "Uh! What happened to the 'we are in this together' ", mocking him.

"Right, Aj!", I said.

"Fi—ne!", Rohit accepted defeat, "Let me know when it is."

"I'll share the details to all, and I expect everyone to nominate", I announced brightly.

"Why me? I don't belong to your portfolio", Daniel exclaimed.

I narrowed my eyes at him, "It's not a client specific training. Moreover it'll be full day training, there will be only 10-15 seats. Just imagine, it'll be like only our gang is there in the training and they'll have some fun activities too. Plus you'll get to record your mandatory training hours."

Vicky chuckled, "She does know how to play her cards well. It does sound appealing.... Lets try to check out for similar fun training and block all the seats for us", he said with a wicked smile.

"Sure, sure.... This calls for a treat! Let's have some ice-cream, much needed stress buster after all this", Raghav announced.

We joined the tables required for all of us to fit in at the ice-cream parlor. Raghav calculatively made me sit next to him. He squeezed my hand and blinked before placing his hand back on the table. The topic doing rounds on the table was the upcoming team outing, sponsored by the company as part of our quarterly employee Motivational fund. It was one day - one night stay in a resort. Two quarters fund were accumulated for it. Families of the employees were also allowed at discounted cost, borne by the employee. Daniel and Simbu, were going to tag along with us by utilizing their funds with us instead of with their team.

This is going to be fun!

18

CHAPTER 18

Raghav's POV

song: You're the light, you're the night You're the color of my blood You're the cure, you're the pain.

The wait was over, everyone was ready with their backpacks for the overnight stay at the resort. Our combined gang had decided to ditch our personal vehicles and opt for the company transport. Entering into the 55 - seater deluxe bus, I saw Sasha waving frantically at me and patting the vacant seat next to her. A genuine smile grew on me and greeted her, while placing my backpack in the overhead.

"Hi Sasha! You seem to be jumping like an excited toddler".

She let out a shy laugh. "It's our first team outing at a resort. Everyone's here, no one backed-off..... So yeah, I'm kinda excited". You could see the excitement bouncing off her.

Nodding my head in agreement, I replied, "True! True!". While settling down in my seat, our arms brushed against each other. She took the window seat while I was at the aisle. Looking around to spot the others, only to find out, that they were all scattered throughout the length of the bus.

Good for me, those buggers won't disturb us.

It wasn't that long of a ride, hardly an hour or additional thirty minutes at the maximum. The bus grumbled to a start and kicked off the weekend gateway.

"Hey, do you want to watch a sitcom with me?". I suggested while she was mid-way in putting on her heavy-duty white-with-blazing red wireless bose headphones.

"Hmmmm, sure. Choose a good one though", Sasha replied as she placed her headphones on her lap.

I showed her the episode name in my sleek black smartphone, "How about this one?"

She leaned closer to peep into it, "Fine by me, I haven't seen it."

"Me too".

Out-stretching the right leg of my humble black wired head-phones for her, she jerked her's slightly lifting it.

"How are we going to watch it together then? Let's share the earphones. Come on it'll be fun. Here take this and I'll use the other one", I said encouragingly.

"Oh! I thought —", Sasha trailed off.

"What did you think?"

"Nothing!", she dismissed it, "Okay, you can start the video now. Just come a little bit closer".

Placing my hand on the armrest separating us, I held the smart-phone at equidistant from us. As the video played, we shared laugh-ter and constant commentary on the scenes. She tugged on my elbow and soon her arm was looped into mine. I'm sure she didn't realize her spontaneous actions.

Mission accomplished! Not a bad start right.

song: You're the only thing I wanna touchNever knew that it could meanso much, so much.

Reclining against the head rest, I let my eyes gradually roam over her face, taking in her expressions while she was engrossed in the video. I slowly opened the collapsable table that was clamped to the seat in front of me. Backtracking the phone, without deviating from Sasha's line of focus; I rested it on the tray. Sliding my hands, backwards, on the armrest till it come in contact with Sasha's palm, I squeezed it. I took the opportunity to entwine our fingers tightly. Sasha didn't seem to mind it but I caught her quick glance at me from the corner of her eyes.

The inner joy I felt was unexplainable. Last few attempts of holding hands hadn't been this successful, she had freed her hand within a matter of seconds.

How can I forget her cute alarmed look and her sharp hitch; when I kissed her in broad daylight in the office, in front of everyone. Laughing internally reliving it in my head, What were you thinking about pulling such a stunt in the cubicle.

It was a complete different situation, Sasha wasn't calming down and I just did what I thought would work at that times. It did work though! The uncontrollable itch in me to do it again hadn't fizzled out, since then. Grabbing, the seclusion the seats were offering, as an opportunity, I stole a kiss on the back of her hand.

Raising our entangled hands, I bent my head to press my lips, against her hand. Making sure the imprint of the caressing peck is felt for a longer duration. Glancing over her bent wrist, that formed the perfect optical axis, I observed her reaction. The whirlwind numerous responses Sasha displayed, all in a matter of sixty seconds, felt like she was auditioning for some play.

Her composure went from slight surprise to a shy smile, subsiding to a adorable look while meeting my eyeballs and ended with spinning her head around for onlookers.

Narrrowing my eyes with amusement in them, I let go and felt cold air hit my lips. If my lips had a say in it, they would agree, that they didn't want to depart from her hands.

Don't go too strong on her, Raghav! Hold your guns, boy. She's used to being around Guys, but not romantically. She's new to all of this ...Heck! You are also alien to all these feelings too. The angel within me, reprimanded.

I didn't need a relapse of the dejection felt after parting my lips, so I clutched onto her hands, like it had reformed itself into a lifesaving rope. A couple of minutes flew by, then Sasha trained her eyes to our hands and shook my hand.

"What?", I asked naively.

"I need to drink some water, Raghav."

"Okay", glancing at her, I replied simply and went back, unbothered, to my phone in my other hand.

"I'm feeling thirsty, Rrraaghhaav!", her tone had a hint of irritation.

"Here, take my flask", handing it to her, after grabbing it from it's holder.

"Gosh!", she let out a frustrated sigh and held both her hands in air, taking mine along with it. She turned towards me and said, "Let go of my hand, dumbo! How am I'm going to open the lid with one hand?!!"

"Oooooo!"

"Yaaa 'ooooo!'", she mimicked me.

"I see you don't possess the skills to drink from a bottle, with one hand". I jested while opening the flask's cover for her.

"Skills!!??", her piercing eyes bored holes into me, conveying the undertone of her annoyance. While gulping down the water, few droplets ran through her neck, leaving behind a thin wet trail. All I wanted to do was catch the running droplet that was teasing me, with-with—

I shut my eyes, Oh God! What is happening to me? Never felt like this before.

She thrust the flask back into my hands, dragging me out of my wayward thoughts and back to reality.

"Yes skills! You clearly are in need of learning so many new skills". Heaving a long sigh I replied, while placing the flask in it's place. I flashed her a mischievous smile, "Don't worry I'll teach you everything, in due course of time", giving an assuring pat on her shoulder.

Tightly crossing her arms, she gazed at me with suspicion, "Why do I feel like it was a pun?! ..... What's running in your head, Raghav?"

I chuckled, "Relax Sasha!", ruffling up her maroon streaked bangs, gently.

Let me atleast let of my steam like this.

"I didn't know you had such dirty thoughts playing in your mind", I devilishly smirked at her. Leaning in closer to her in one swift move, I whispered into her ears in a husky voice, "Want to share them with me?"

Her palms rested on my chest and once they found a strong holding, she pushed me away, putting some distance between the two of us. Winking at her only seemed to infuriate her more. I was thoroughly enjoying the tease and could see her put so much effort, to mask my infectious playfulness from affecting her. Anyone could tell, she was fighting herself from letting the smile spill onto her face. She was a warrior queen, wouldn't let her guard down so easily.

"Oh! You didn't just do that!", Sasha said with an underlying accusation.

"What?" Sincerely trying to recollect what just happened, then like a lightning, it hit me. "You mean this?", I asked innocently, while fondly ruffling her bangs again.

"Watch your hands, Raghav. You do not want to be doing that again?", she warned me seriously.

"Oh! But third time is a charm, I thought". I said while checking her, neating up the mess I had created.

"Uh-huh!", shaking her head, after she was satisfied that her fluffed up bangs fell in its place, properly.

It was my turn to complain, "I haven't kept count of how many times you did that to me, you know".

"So?", she asked clearly not understanding why I had raised the point.

"It means, if I can't do that to you, then you can't do it to me too", I concluded.

"Oh no, I can!", she retorted back.

"Why is that you can, but I can't?", I wasn't giving up yet.

"Be—cause", Sasha was thinking hard to come up with something. "I like doing it and I'm a girl.... Besides it doesn't hurt you, so why not!"

"It doesn't make any sense."

"Oh, it does to my ears", she said casting a wide grin.

Letting out a sigh, "Fine! You win. Girls and their weird logic." I had made a silent resolution, I wasn't going to make any more moves until she comes forward. Knowing the head-strong Sasha and the romance-deficiency she has, I could only pray.

Hope this resolution, does not bite me.

We fell back in silence, doing our own things individually. All of sudden, Sasha pulled me to her, grabbing my upper arm. She had titled to get a better view from her window.

She sounded happy, "Doesn't this view look beautiful?"

Our faces were only an inch apart diagonally, with mine slightly behind hers. My eyeballs rolled to their left and scanned Sasha's right profile.

"Yes, very beautiful!", I exclaimed.

"I wish we could seize this moment and look at it all day long."

"Me too Sasha, me too!"

I called out her name sensuously, well aware that my hot breaths were blowing on her neck. Though she was oblivious to my praise and to what my vision had been stuck on; I noticed her, involuntarily shiver, when I spoke. What is she doing to me. I cannot seem to take my eyes off her and being within her vicinity, wasn't helping at all.

From my pre-teen years till now, I had immersed myself into studies, books and making an honest career for myself. I hadn't given a thought of romance in my busy, boring geek's life. Now look how the tables had turned, I never knew I could flirt, if you go by with Sasha's accusations lately. Nor had I felt such strong attraction towards anyone before. The words rolling off my tongue and my recent actions were surprising me too.

She's bringing out all the hidden colors in me

song:You're the fear, I don't care'Cause I've never been so high-Follow me through the darkLet me take you past the satellitesYou can see the world you brought to life, to life.

Sasha turned around to face me and gasped at our closeness. The tips of our noses grazed each other, due to the lack of space. "What are you doing? People are watching us, Raghav. We are in a moving bus filled with colleagues..... Now go back to your seat and behave!"

Paying no heed to her warning, I stayed put while she retreated to rest against the window. It did not make much of a difference though. I asked her," Whose looking at us? Everyone's busy in their own world and these seats are huge. You can't practically see anything unless you stand up..... And by the way, you are the one who pulled me in."

She clearly her throat and trying to straighten herself against the window, she stated."Ok-ok! Sight-seeing is over. Now go back". Trying to shoo me away for the second time.

"Not for me", came my immediate response.

"Raghav!"

Closing the inch separating us, my lips landed on her right cheek for a quick peck. Before going back to my seat, I raised my mouth to her ears and softly whispered, "So beautiful!" Convinced that my words would reverberate through her eardrums and into her whole bloodstream, I smiled at her affectionately, like a champion.

Recovering from my impact on her, she said "That's the last time you are doing it today, Got it?

I surrendered, I agree it was going overboard and too much for both of us to handle, so soon. "Yes, got it, fair and square", I smiled happily in her direction. I didn't want her to think I was upset nor make her feel awkward. Progress is progress and this was more than I could have asked for, in our infant relationship.

song: Yeah, I'll let you set the pace 'Cause I'm not thinking straight- My head spinning around, I can't see clear no more.

The bus entered the gates of the resort and halted at the side. I took down our backpacks and let the eager crowd to disembark. As she stood up, I held her hands in mine and guided us through the aisle till we got down from the bus. Studying the bus for a minute, let's see how the day rolls out. If it was half as good as the bus journey, it would be the best day of my life.

Everyone gathered under the temporary huge pavilion set up in their vast garden. A mini stage was setup and the resort officials and staff were conveying instructions about the lodging and other important stuff. We were expected to collect keys of our shared accommodations and refresh, before the event starts. Rohit and Vicky had pulled some strings to get us all rooms on the same floor. The one's who came with their families were on separate floor, to avoid any kinds of disturbance, so Ruhi was not with us.

Ruhi, Aakash — her husband and her eight months old toddler; came over to where the gang was standing.

Vicky welcomed them in his own way, "Finally you guys made it. Looks like our bus was faster than your car."

Ruhi shrugged, "What to do, Aakash here is so scared to drive over the road limit when our kid is with us."

The guys shook hands with him and AJ, Asim and Simbu were busy fussing over the new kid.

Sasha squeaked when she turned around to see Ruhi, "You are married? I didn't know that."

"Yaaa! Got a kid too", Ruhi pointed to her toddler sitting in Asim's hand.

"How could I have been so ignorant about it? You look – look so young and fit. No way I would have missed your maternity leave absence". Sasha struggled to figure out how she missed being a part of it.

Ruhi smiled gently, "Thank you! That's because someone over here was eager to get married soon."

"Ah! I accept the blame wholeheartedly", Aakash said leaving a charming kiss on Ruhi's hands. "Who would be dumb enough to let a soul-mate spill away from their hands. I did what I had to do, it was going to happen sooner or later, so why delay". He ended stating the facts, with another kiss on his wife's hand. The love they shared was evident.

I met Sasha's eyes and we had our infamous eye-talk.

'See, damn you - people our watching', my eyes communicated to her.

Her eyes replied back, 'They are married.'

I rolled my eyes and let my eyes do the talking, 'So?'

Sasha's brows knitted together, 'What do you mean so?.... Urgh! I give up.' She ended our eye conversation, breaking it off, by looking away.

Ruhi continued talking, "And for the maternity leave, I was working from home and took it in breaks when I needed it. Thanks for the management to understand my needs and agree with it. "

Rohit clasped his hands and stated, "Let's make a move, they've given us only an hour's time to report back.... Ruhi, Aakash, sorry couldn't get you'll at our floor. If you need anything let us know, we are just one floor below yours".

Aakash nodded and smiled like a hundred watt bulb at Ruhi. Looks like they were going to have a second mini-honeymoon here, I chuckled. Good for them. If they had hinted that to Rohit, he would have ensured to get them the best isolated room in a floor where none of our colleagues were in.

Vicky, Asim and me were bunking together in one room, we just ordered an extra mattress. Rohit- Aj's room was across ours while Daniel - Simbu's was beside ours. Sasha and Chitra were sharing, but their's was on the other side of the elevator. Some dumb rule management put across to ensure no hanky-panky business happens. Geez, like the elevator separation was a real barrier stopping anyone.

The event started with South Indian traditional songs by some volunteers, followed by a live light musical show put up from the band in our portfolio. Some senior managers also participated and had genuinely good singing and piano skills. The facilitations for the long service awards, starting from 5-years up to ear-shocking 19-years, were being given away.

Who in their right mind would spend 19 long years in the same organization..... That's why they are one of the Directors now, Raghav. This kind of loyalty could be expected in people from the earlier generations.

The half day-long event was well planned and executed. They didn't make it boring with only awards. They were interrupted in the middle with dance performances, comic skits. They also lent the stage to the family members of the employees, if they wanted to showcase their talent. Some sang, did impromptu dance performances; the best was when the kids took over the stage to sing rhymes and dance their hearts out.

Ruhi and Aakash, just entered the pavilion and joined us, after an hour or so. The glow on their faces and Rohit's smirk, conveyed that the isolated room was actually handed to them. My smile stopped growing when Sasha blurted her innocent question out loud.

"What took you guys so long? You are nearly two hours late", looking up from her wristwatch she asked.

Face-palming internally, Gosh! This girl is going to embarrass herself and everyone. How can she be so naive? I swear, this is the only department she's lacking at!

Before she could make more a fool of herself, I shook my head at her. But, it I was a few seconds late.

"And to think how irresponsible you guys are, to leave a toddler amongst strangers in a unfamiliar environment", she scowled at Ruhi.

I squeezed her knee, trying to signal her to stop. I guess our communication only works when we make eye contact.

Asim spoke up, "No worries Sasha. He was with me the whole time and I had asked them to leave him to play with me.

"But still—", Sasha continued.

Asim cut her off smoothly, making the toddler stand on his lap facing him, "Keyan kutty knows me very well isn't? We have met so many times before." The toddler vigorously bobbled his head in all directions, making everyone laugh at his antics.

While Keyan had successfully caught everyone's attention with his cute actions and interrupted Sasha' questioning. Placing my fingers to her chin, I moved it sideways.

I gave her a speaking glance and dialed into our eye conversation, 'You know what they were doing?', with a mischievous glint in my eyes.

She frowned and signalled back, 'No! If I knew, why would I ask?'

I tried my best to hold in the mischievous glint and threw an equally sized smirk, for her to catch up faster. 'Really? think woman!'

'Ooo-ooo-oooh!', her pupils dilated gradually when it dawned on her. 'Oh Gosh! What did I do? This is so humiliating!'

Patting on her knee and giving it a comforting squeeze. 'Never mind, it's just us, friends'.

Then my eyes added, 'So many things to learn, I'll teach you. Don't worry.'

She snorted, 'As if!' and playfully smacked my hand off her lap.

Taking advantage of everyone's laughter, due to Keyan and his scrutiny of Asim's facial features, I let my chuckle just blend in with theirs. Though mine was due to the little baby sitting beside me.

The buffet was open to all, after the distribution of achievers of the month award, and spot awards. People had started gathering at the food stalls located at the opposite end of the stage, during the last leg of the awards. Our gang made it's way to it too. I wanted the stalls to be freed up, so me and Sashs stayed back on pretense of holding the round table for us.

I glided my hands into hers, they were so soft and smooth like silk. "I have never met anyone with such soft hands", my wondering thoughts saw the daylight.

She removed her hand from mine and folded her arms, "So how many people's hands have you held before?"

"Oh! No-No. You are getting it wrong".

"I don't think so", she shook her head.

Then a sudden thought crept into my mind. "Jealous?", I raised my brow with a happy smile plastered on me.

"Ya right! In your dreams", she lifted her chin up.

Stifling my laugh seeing her reaction, "Why do I need that, when I can see it in reality". She gave me deadpan look. "Okay, then why don't you give your hand in mine", outstretching my open palm towards her, I challenged.

"I think we need to go and get our food before it gets over". She said, bluntly ignoring my waiting palm. She stood up to leave, I hurriedly clapsed on her wrist and looked straight in her eye.

"You are the only girl I have held hands with or kissed and would like to keep it that way". I dived right to the point and spoke from my heart.

song:Only you can set my heart on fire, on fire.

She stood immobile but her eyes spoke volumes. As always, she needed a jolt to pull out from her trance and I gave what she needed. Leaving a sweet kiss on her knuckles, I looked up, "Happy Pongal!"

A faint blush crept to her cheeks and as expected she scanned for any spectators. She scurried away to meet Ruhi to apologize for earlier. From my seat afar, I could see Ruhi brushing off Sasha's sad look and cheering her up.

Making my way to them, I joined them with my plate. After serving the two ladies with me, I placed my hand on Sasha's back, guiding her to our seats. A sharp intake of breathe was heard, undoubtedly from Sasha. The placement of my hand seem to have only made her walk faster, leaving it to hang in mid-air. Quickly I pushed my hand into my pockets.

While eating, when others were busy in their own banter, she sneered, "I told you people are watching us. You promised you will not to do it again."

"You are talking about the kiss or what made you run away to reach the table faster, few minutes back?", I casually asked.

"Shush! Both!!", she said behind her spoonful of food.

"Ok! Sorry, Happy Pongal".

"You and your Happy Pongal", she rolled her eyes. "So you are just going keep infuriating me and use your code word to calm me?"

"I have many ways to calm you and it did work at the cubicle, the other day. Do you want me to replace the code word with it?", I baited her jovially.

"That's it, I'm going over to Rohit's side."

"OK - ok, Happy Pongal for the last time today, I promise. It's just so much fun to see you turn red as a tomato, when I tease you."

She let out a huff and stayed by my side, stealing sideway peeks of me.

After enjoying the plethora of dishes, we all retired at our allocated rooms. Only at late tea-time, nearly dusk did we all gather at the pavilion. The three of us slept well and watched a James Bond movie in our room. There was confusion amongst the employees, few were stating that a bonfire party had been arranged. While the remaining thought a DJ night was going to be held.

I found Sasha and we decided to stroll away from the pavilion to tour around the resort. With our coffee holders in our hands, we took in the sunset, enjoying the cool evening breeze. The atmosphere was perfect — away from beholders, dimming of the sun, casting a loving orangish- crimson red hues over the blue clouded sky, owing to the immaculate combination of Rayleigh and Mie scattering. Still something was missing, it took some time to figure it out.

"May I?". Extending my hand out to her, I asked, not wanting to waste any more time, to fix the missing element.

She smiled and nodded, sliding her tender fingers into my palm, "Yes, you may."

I bowed slightly, "Thank you for your kindness, my lady". She raised her brows in amusement.

We walked hand-in-hand and sliently sipped through our coffees from time-to-time. Encircling the resort, we joined our friends just in time for dinner. Sasha and me, decided to go light and sampled the variety of salads, soups and desserts.

A couple of bonfires were set up sporadically. Our gang claimed one and we gathered around it in a circle. I could see the flickering of the burning flames, reflecting on Sasha's signature specatacles. It looked like her eyes were on fire. The soft and shy traits of her's that I witnessed today, only proved that she was like a coconut. Hard, rough-and-tough exterior encompassing a soft, tender and unadulterated soul.

The music and laughter boomed around us. Vicky suggested we play a game of truth and dare. We were just going to go around the table, so that everyone has a chance. The person who voices out the question or dare first, gets the privilege of their idea to be executed.

My turn came soon and Vicky pounced on the opportunity. "Raghav boy, how about singing a romantic song for........ everyone to hear", he dared me.

Great! A romantic song in front of all.... This guy! Should have known he would have pulled such a thing, when he stayed clear off such stunts the whole day. It was the silence before the storm. When he drops a bomb, he always does it in a style.

AJ stopped a passing colleague with a guitar, "Hey, can we borrow that for fifteen minutes, my friend here has a dare to sing?" The passerby placed the guitar in my hands. It looked like a a trophy was handed over to me, but somehow didn't feel like that.

Sasha whispered, "Are you ok?"

Putting on a warm smile, I blinked my eyes in assurance. I starred at the task in my hands. If I was going to do this, might as well prep for it. I started tightening the strings and strummed a little to get a hang of it. Clearing my throat, I garbed everyone's attention, even the cute little fidgety Keyan Kutty. I selected 'Love me like you do' song and sang to Sasha, never leaving my gaze from her. I poured my feelings out with the lyrics.

Our group had fallen silent, except for the flickering sound and my voice along with the melody from my guitar, nothing else could be heard. As the song came to an end and the last chord had struck, our bonfire circle was engulfed with booming sounds of applause.

Sasha suddenly got up and jogged away. Not realizing what went wrong, I handed the guitar to Aj and trailed behind her. Vicky's faint complaints that he wanted a desi song and wouldn't accept that I completed my dare, fell to my deaf ears.

Panting away, I stood in-line with her. Once my breaths fell back to it's normal rhythm, I asked. "Why did you run away like that? It's not my fault, Vicky made me do it in front of everyone."

She slanted her body in my direction and said. "You—you didn't tell me about this hidden musical talent you have......You were awesome!" She exclaimed, "Now like Vicky said sing me a desi song.....your choice!"

"Oh-hello! I just dedicated that song to you, if you didn't notice!"

"Why are you getting mad, Raghav? It's not like you have a croacked voice or sang out of tune, like I feared. So why can't you sing again, for me alone?", she requested softly.

I slumped down on the lush green lawn and patted the ground beside me. She took her place. With our legs scrunched upand hands over our knees, we looked at the stars twinkling in the dark.

A yawn escaped from our mouths in synchrony, making us snap our heads at each other.

Laying my body on the ground, I saw Sasha was hesitant to follow. "Are you worried that the grass blades are going to poke you?, I questioned.

"Oh please I'm not a porcelain doll to be hurt my grass blades.. ...but", she scrunched her nose slightly. "I don't think I can rest my head down their.... Hygiene and insects and all, you know".

That instant, I stretched my arm out for her, perpendicular to my body. She got the hint and laid her head over my arm, serving as a pillow for her. We fell back to star gazing while I hummed a soft melody in the background.

Here I thought she was upset and embarrassed by the dare but it turned out for the good. She insisted that I sing specially for her alone.

Rummaging through my playlist in my mind, to select the song, I finally ended my search. I started singing Kavita Krishnamurthy and Kumar Sanu's song from the movie Khamoshi —

"Aaj Main upar Aasman niche, Aaj Main aage Jamana hai pich-heTell me O khuda abb main kya karuChalu sidhee kee Ulatee chaluAaj Main Upar Aasman niche".

She kept her eyes glued to the sky and kept playfully shifting my head back to the sky in front, whenever I tried sneaking a glance at her. Sasha, giggled away, at my song choice for our special moment.

We laid there like that for quite some time and it was getting darker and colder. It took every ounce of me to drag the next words out of my mouth "Sasha", I called out gently, once we were face-to-face, I continued. Swallowing hard, "I—I think we should call it a night and get back to our rooms."

She took her own sweet time to respond back, then she nodded and let out a meek yes.

Walking her safely upto her room, I returned to mine. Closing the door behind me, I rested against it and heaved a long deep sigh. What a close call that was! Before our logical brain could be clouded with our desire, we prevented it. Jumping onto a speed train was not advisable, especially not for the two of us.

We met again at breakfast, which flew past in a flash. The rock bottom feeling had kicked within me, as the time for us to depart from the resort had come. Taking my seat at the aisle, next to Sasha, I slouched onto it, unhappily.

Why did it have to end so soon? Why, why, why?

I felt Sasha grabbing my upper arm and looping her's around mine, as she rested her head on my shoulder. She was in half-sleep at the breakfast table and right now. Her unconscious action made me beam with glory, marking the end of the team outing with a bang!

song:What are you waiting for? Love me like you do, love me like you do (like you do)Love me like you do,love me like you do (yeah)Touch me like you do, touch me like you do.

19

CHAPTER 19

Sasha's POV

song:You and meWe used to be togetherEveryday together-AlwaysI really feelThat I'm losing my best friendI can't believeThis could be the end.

"Hey, where's Raghav?" I asked Vicky while trying to see if the person I was waiting for, was standing behind him.

Alas! No luck.

Vicky wore a grim look and pursed his lips in a tight line. "We might have to have lunch without him, Sasha. He's stuck in a conference call.... Won't be able to make it in time". He concluded with an apologetic expression, while pulling out his chair to sit down.

"Oh! Again!", my energy levels drained down in an instant. I glanced at the empty chair, beside me, that I had saved for Raghav. The missing person on it, making the chair look incomplete and lonely, mirrored my emotions. It was the third time this week, that we couldn't have lunch together. Heaving a long sigh, I went back to my food. The food, everyone was praising and enjoying, felt so tasteless and hard to swallow for me.

It's ok Sasha, cheer up!You can always visit him at his cubicle.

"Here..... For you". I announced softly when I reached Raghav's desk. I placed the food parcel, I brought for him, on his desk. He was still on the damn conference call wearing the headphones with it's microphone placed near his mouth. He looked so professional and captivating but busy too.

Good thing I brought food, at this rate, his call would never end and the cafeteria would run out of stock.

I briefly glanced at him, not wanting to interrupt his work, I exited his bay quietly. With the hope that atleast we would be able to spend sometime together in the evening coffee break, I tried concentrating on my tasks assigned for the day.

Our mis-matched routine, continued for the next few days; it had totally clocked a week. No luncheons together, no coffee break meets; sadly culminated to almost zero minutes of spending time together. Even our phone calls and chats had boiled down to the typical — "Good Morning", "Good Night, Sweet dreams", "Did you eat?" and "Take care". It felt so robotic, so wooden; devoid of any emotions, feelings and warmth.

I kept re-reading our prior chats, they were my only source of comfort at this point of time. However, as I scrolled down to our recent messages, they felt like emotionless stones reciding in our happy place. The building blocks of a wall, beginning to construct between us. The worst part was the construction felt to be on full swing, with no hindrance and no one to object. The dissented piece of construction felt like it was violating some law, atleast I had not given my permission for it.

I didn't like it,I didn't want it.I didn't ask for it,Then why the hell is this wall here? Why is there this distance between us?

The forcee of attraction had pulled Raghav and me so close but as we reached a certain point, the forces of repulsion had the upper hand. The fight between the attraction and repulsive forces, didn't let us meet; maintaining a two arm's distance of separation.

I had tried my best to build a bridge and walk over the separating distance; by giving him space, dropping of food or a warm cup of coffee. Tried to wade off the devils calling, stating —'He's taking you for granted'. Everything that I could think of, that would come out as being supportive, I did. But sometimes the bridge loses it's strength when the rough tides keep splashing hard on it. Similarly I could sense my inner resolve chipping away slowly. It takes two to build or break a relationship. With only my efforts, our ship could survive from sinking, only for a short time.

I sincerely pray that we don't have to witness our downfall and we could mend our ways before it's too late.

Looking forward to the weekend for some quality time, turned out to be unfruitful. I learnt from Asim that Raghav besides pulling all-nighters at office during the week, was working on the weekends too. Great! Just Great! Can't God have some mercy on me, it's my first relationship and such hard times at the initial stages itself.

Why God, Why? Don't you want to see me happy? Am I not carved out for being in a relationship?

I had no other option but to embrace what was being propelled at me. With a positive attitude and decluttered mind, I made my way into the office to kick start a fresh week. Our conjointed gang, met up for the morning coffee break, minus Raghav.

"So, why is it that Raghav's overloaded with work?", I questioned, glancing between Asim and Vicky. "Aren't the two of you in the same team?

Vicky replied with a small smile,"I see your concern for our boy there, but there's no reason to make us look as villains here."

Taking sip of my coffee, trying to calm my nerves. "Vicky, just reply to it directly. Sorry, I have no time or patience for your rebutes."

Asim held Vicky from replying back and said, "Vicky meant, we are in the same team, in fact Vicky and Raghav work for the same application too. But Raghav called this one upon himself and unfortunately we can't do much. We tried Sasha, trust me."

"What do you mean by, 'he called it up himself' ? Did his work result in a production issue? Even if so, others can help to fix the issue, considering it's high priority. So why can't you'll help? If you can't, I'll help out. I am good at grasping things and learning new technologies." I fired my questions in split seconds. I was, up for extending my support in solving and completing whatever work Raghav was assigned to. As it was consuming all his time and energy, I wanted to put an end to it. I can't bear if the past week's gloom proceeded for a another one.

I say, the time for the gloom is up! It needs to wrap up it's bag and get the hell out of our lives.

Asim's words dragged me back to our conversation. He said with a comforting smile, "Raghav is lucky to have you in his life. To be honest, we also have hardly spoken to him in the past week, considering we share a cubicle, it's astonishing..... To shed light on his current work, he over-committed and took up way too much. We warned him earlier pointing it out to him, that it's not as simple as the clients are portraying it to be."

"When and why did he agree to the task then?", I queried in worry.

"Remember the last time, after the clubbing incident, at that time we was taking up work like he was a machine", Vicky said. "I told him to stop, but all in vain. He under-estimated this current piece of development and informed the clients it's only one FTE's (full time employees) work."

"Even the clients were skeptical but seeing Raghav's assurance, they agreed. In fact they gave him additional two weeks of time, above his estimates to complete the new task", added Asim.

"Ok, if his calculations fell short and had over-committed, so what, that happens most of the time here in the IT field...... I still don't get it why no one else can help him and share his work, in the background?". I asked to get a better picture.

Vicky let out a deep breathe,"You think we wouldn't help him. We even shared few small tasks with him. Asim also attended some client calls with Raghav in the discussion room. But the clients are adamant. They are said we can't go back on our committed word for one resource, and ask for additional resource, in the middle of the project. They also sang their usual tune of 'short of funding and no budget' for it."

Asim too tried convincing me, "It's a new project with all new softwares and tools, none of us have it our system. We need to raise requests to get them installed in our systems, which in turn will go for their approval, which they won't approve. The client duo, part of the project are the main culprits. The lady is supportive but also nosy and plays by the rules; while the guy is just waiting like a predator, for us to do something wrong, to pounce on us and drag us down. Their eyes are trained on our full team, from the time we suggested for extra resources. Especially that guy, he had stooped down to such levels of micromanagement, that he was able to figure out, we are supporting Raghav in minor tasks."

"He started burdening us with extra tasks, stating we have capacity to do it. Little did he know, we already have automation scripts to handle those tasks. His plan backfired and we continued helping Raghav". Vicky smirked but digust evident when he spoke about that client causing trouble.

"Then he added another sly trick, keeping Raghav on conference call full time to track the work. He states it's easier to communicate in case of any queries or issues". Asim let out a frustrated sigh. "Thank God we have no video camera policy on floor, else if it was in his hands, he would have wanted video call instead of the voice call."

I patiently listened as they took turns to recite the workload story, scowl and hurl abuses at the clients. I felt bummed and blamed myself for it, as I also played a part in it indirectly. If only we hadn't taken so long to clear out the air after the clubbing fiasco, this new debacle wouldn't have come upon us. We were drifting apart due to this, God knows when it'll be back to normalcy.

Vicky seemed to have read my mind, "Relax Sasha, trust our boy, he'll finish the work by this week. Just be patient."

Asim too reassured, "Yes, I heard he is making good progress and on the verge of handing over the completed project....... All his hard work and stress is going to pay off at later point of time, for sure."

"Hmmmm. I hope so! Just seeing him so engrossed in work with no time for rest or food or break, worries me. He is spoiling his health and state of mind with so much stress", I replied.

"Don't worry, when Vicky is here", Vicky said in his playful tone, mimicking Santa Claus's voice. "You are ensuring he gets his meals and he is eating them side-by-side. And, we are ensuring he gets his breaks by forcing him to go to the dorm for a nap, while we take over the work."

"But isn't it against security policy, to use other people's system in their absence?" I immediately asked, sensing another issue could crop up.

"Oh! We have taken care of it. If the clients think they are smart, we are one step ahead of them; after all they come to us for their work". Vicky exclaimed like a proud man who knew how to play with crocked people. "They underestimated us. We know all the hooks and crooks and also the hidden gaps."

On seeing my confusion, Asim elaborated, "We make his system to go on screen share with one of us and pass control of the screen share to us", shrugging nonchalantly. "This way, his system is on, we can continue the work in his absence and it's not total violation but we can do it for our friend."

A smile slipped onto my face, for the first time since our conversation started.

"We are not sitting at his workstation so it's can't be tracked from our office and since it's on screen share, we don't think the clients will track it too. However, Raghav didn't want us to fall into trouble and risk our jobs, if this falls under the violation. So we brought it up to the higher management's notice and they agreed to do it. If complications come at a later stage, they'll take care of it, they assured. They didn't want to lose the prestigious project from the clients and also didn't want him to be pressurized. You know, with employees having heartattacks due to stress and passing away ", Vicky stated.

A loud gasp escaped from my lips on his last statement. My heart raced at the thought of Raghav's heartbeat fading.

Asim punched Vicky, "Don't scare her, you idiot". Then he turned to me, "Relax, nothing of that sort will happen. We are all here for Raghav, right. "

I nodded hesitantly, as I needed time to emerge out of the aftermath of Vicky's words.

"We have full support from our higher management, they fought for us and got extra two weeks of time, on top of the client's additional estimates. They are still having discussions on having an extra resource, if not full time, at least partially. If that happens, the work will complete faster than predicted", Asim stated with confidence.

His friends seemed to appreciate the little things I was doing for him..... But why hadn't he noticed it or thanked me? I get it, he is busy but couldn't he have sent me a thank you message, at least.

song:It looks as though you're letting goAnd if it's realWell, I don't want to know.

We left the breakout area, with mixed emotions within me. I think my inner turmoil would rest only when Raghav's project was over. Later in the day, I went to the cafe for some juice, thought to pick one for Raghav too, to refresh and rejuvenate his stressed out body. As I proceeded towards the cashier to give my order, I saw the familiar figure of Raghav, sitting with a mint-lime cooler in hand, chit-chating with a beautiful lady, across him.

It was the same drink I was going to get for him. He looked so relaxed and happy, flashing his pearly white 32 toothy grin at her. He seemed to be enjoying his lady companion.

"Hello, Miss.... Miss? Are you going to order", the cashier asked.

"Oh! Oops, Sorry", I stepped out of the line and gave way for the next customer to go ahead. The sight befolding in front of me, had taken me by surprise.

Didn't he have knee-deep of work? Even if he had taken a break, couldn't he have come to my desk? Didn't he miss me? Or...... Or, was it that he has lost interest in spending time with me..... After — after, I kept pushing him away, whenever he made advances towards me, using 'People are watching us' excuse. That, and obviously anyone would pick her as a company over me, the plain Tom-Boy..

song:As we dieBoth you and IWith my head in my handsI sit and cry.

Not able to withstand the hurt and my racing thoughts, I spun on my heels and walked away.

Raghav's POV

Sitting over here at the cafe talking to someone else, besides those clients, felt like I had just returned to Earth, from an outer space expedition after light years. It felt good to be able to speak to another human being. I had been deprived off any human interactions since the team outing.

Haaye! The team outing was just perfect.

I couldn't stop reminiscing Sasha's and our cute precious moments. While my mind drifted away to Sasha, the lady from the human resources team was talking away. She had my attention in the beginning but with Sasha entering my mind, everyone had to exit as Sasha occupied the whole space.

Thinking of all the time lost due to this stupid project, the eagerness to complete it soon and return to the blissful days with Sasha, kicked in. I excused myself and made a move, back for the elevator, with my mint lime cooler in hand. In the over-excitement, I banged into another person waiting for the samr elevator.

"Oops! Sorry... Are you okay Ma'am?", I enquired.

When she turned, I caught a glimpse of her quirky spectacles and knew it was Sasha. She was going to stumble, I readily put my arm around her waist to support her. When she met my eyes, the initial shock in her dilated pupils vanished. It was replaced by a cloak over her usual glowing orbs. Something had changed, she looked dull and distant. The ding of the elevator, made her scramble out of my grasp and she scurried away towards the turnstiles.

I let out a short laugh and sipped through my juice, as my eyes trailed behind her. Her eyes seemed to tell a different story compared to the spunky way she ran away. I had a slight indication, that it could be due to the onlookers as well as the absence of our togetherness.

Finish your damn work soon and get your act straight, Raghav. You can't keep missing out on Sasha's time.

While riding the elevator, I relived the times when she caringly dropped off food at my desk. Everytime before I could thank her, she used to leave, just like what happened few minutes ago. I was so grateful for her understanding and being supportive, when my work was so demanding. The efforts she made and for not pulling up a fight for giving her lesser priority, temporarily, were the few traits she had, among many, that I was glad she possessed. It felt like a perfect balance, when one was down, the other was there to lift up the spirits and keep the ball rolling.

I knew I missed her so much, that words couldn't express but just seeing her at office and her replies to the daily good morning and good night messages made me happy. Hearing that she had been safe and eating healthy, was sufficient for now. It was a bare minimum information but most essential to me.

When I unlocked my system, I saw two new emails from the clients stating some project specifications are changing, again. I cursed internally. These people are on a mission to suck out the blood from my body, without sparing a drop of it. I took up this project as it had some promising and challenging stuff. The tools required would be all brand new and it excited me to expand my skill set. However, they kept changing the requirements but didnt wary the deadlines accordingly.

Man! If they thought it was so easy, ask them to do it on their own.

I tugged my hair in frustration and reclined on my chair. Just then Sasha walked down the aisle, striding towards her desk. She had a tranquilizer effect on me and my nerves calmed down, the very instant. She was the only thing helping me keep my sanity intact.

She was like the shining guiding light at the end of my dark tunnel. Whenever I tried to run towards it, it felt like it was moving away from me, lately. If I'm not wrong, it was fading like the light was on the verge of diminishing.

song:It's all endingWe gotta stop pretending who we are. You and mel can see us dyingAre we?

Hope it's just an illusion.

She'll wait for me at the end of my tunnel I'm sure. I just need wrap all of this fast and catch up with her.

I assured myself that she would be waiting for me and not to worry about it. Right now my top priority had to be the project, once that's over with, everything would fall back in place. I was happy that atleast before all this project mishap, we were able to spend some good times with each other.

The clients finally gave in for having an extra resource with fifty percent capacity for this new project. The management got a new temporary workstation installed with the new softwares, stating that the system specifications of the existing ones weren't compatible or were of lower speed. Due to this extra workstation, Vicky, Asim and two freshers were working on it, time to time and extending their support, apart from the screen sharing tactics of my workstation. At any given point of time, at least two - three people were working on the project, which resulted in delivering the completed project two days before hand.

Fi-na-lly! Now I can go on a date with Sasha, I rubbed my palms together excitedly..

I went to her desk with her favorite blue crusher, to return her favors; only to find an empty chair. I found from her cubicle-mates that she had left for the day.

The next day I asked her to have lunch with me, just the two of us. She was reluctant on hearing my suggestion, then agreed to it. We picked our trays from the counter and settled down at a table for two.

"How are you, Sasha?", I broke the silence.

"I'm fine", she replied without sparing a glance at me. She was busy eating her food.

"Hmmm. I'm good too", I said, even though she hadn't asked. "Have been very busy lately, due to the pile of work thrown at me."

"I know", came her reply.

"Thank God it's over, it was hogging away all of my time and energy along with my sanity", I added.

"Hmmm, yes I know", again came her reply in a monotonous dull voice.

Her one word replies were leaving me with no room to initiate a proper conservation. They were like close-ended answers, like she didn't want to speak or continue our chat. I didn't pay much heed to it, she might be hungry that's all.

I tried changing the topic, "How's the food?"

"Good."

"I think the potatoes could have been cooked a little more, don't you think so?"

"Hmmmm."

"Is something bothering you, Sasha? You know you can tell me, right?". I spoke gently in a soothing voice, like a counselor, urging the person to disclose their troubled feelings.

She looked up for the first time and her eyes scanned my face, as if fighting an inner battle, before she spoke again. Her one word reply came out, "Nothing".

"Okay!.... You know what, I have some plan ahead..... I'm going to utilize all my compensatory-off leaves and take rest". I announced happily, "What are your plans?", I asked conservatively.

"Hmmm.. I'm planning for higher studies, abroad or in some top reputed college within India. If not, a new job, somewhere else". She replied casually, almost completing her meal.

Her reply felt like a slap to wake me up from my dream world. Here I just asked her plans for the next few days and she blurted out her future plans. By the sound of it, I wouldn't be a part of it.

Was she hinting something at me? Or just answering to my question?

"Raghav, I'm done. If you're too, shall we make a move?". She asked, like as if her revelation of her future plans, weren't supposed to send me into a shock.

I blinked my eyes a couple of times, "Ummmm... Let's go".

Might be I'm just over-thinking it and hallucinating.I am sleep deprived and haven't fully recovered from my stressed mind yet.I'll just sleep and take rest for a few days.Once I'm back to my normal self, we can continue this conversation.

song:Don't speakI know just what you're sayingSo please stop explainingDon't tell me 'cause it hurts(No, no)Don't speakI know what you're thinkingAnd I don't need your reasonsDon't tell me 'cause it hurts.

I'm just reading way too much in between the lines..... Those are her long term future plans, that doesn't mean she's going to quit her job in next two days and jump on to a flight for the overseas...

Calm down, Raghav!

20

CHAPTER 20

Vicky's POV

song:I walk in on Friday nightsSame old bar, same burned out lightsSame people and all the same facesSo why in the hell does it feel like a different place?

"When is your cat-and-mouse game going to end?" I asked Raghav, shoving my hands into my pockets.

"What game?.... I'm not playing any games", came Raghav's defensive reply.

Asim shook his head disapprovingly, "He's talking about Sasha and you. How you guys are avoiding each other".

"We are not avoiding each other. Didn't we all just have lunch together, an hour back?", Raghav answered smartly.

I let out a sarcastic laugh, "Don't try to fool us. Yes, yes, everything is normal, right? No wonder the two of you, are either sitting across each other or like the North pole and south pole of the table."

"It's too obvious, Raghav", Asim added. "So what's it, this time? Last time it was ego and pride that had put constraints in your bond..... This time around, what's the cause?"

"Hey! Just because we enjoy each other's company, it doesn't mean we need to stick to each other, all the time. Like some adhesive 'superglue' is binding us together". Raghav tried concealing the cracks that were forming in his newfound relationship, but it couldn't escape our expert eyes.

song:When they think of me, they think of youThey keep asking how I amBut they're really asking where you've beenI can read between all of the linesIt ain't just us missing all of the times.

"Seriously! .... the Ups and Downs, the two of you are creating in your budding relationship; are more than a heavily pregnant women's mood swings.... So erratic", I let out my slight frustration.

Asim chuckled, "Right! They are really perfect for each other.... 'Meant for each other' couple". Raghav's eyes narrowed on Asim and he explained. "Raghav has always been good at jumping into conclusions, like a Kang-ga-roo. By the looks of it, Sasha is not too behind in the competition."

Raghav's eyes swirled in anger, "Don't you dare say anything about Sasha!". He warned Asim sternly.

"Oh —Hello!?!", Asim waved his hands in front of Raghav's eyes. "I called you 'Kang-ga-roo' not her."

I stifled a laugh when Raghav calmed down and corrected Asim. "It's Kangaroo not Kang-ga-roo, Bhai."

Asim shrugged, "Like I care. I'm not giving TOEFL exam, here. I prefer the hindi way of pronunciating it. Seeing that it irritates you, I'll keep calling like that only......Kang-ga-roo, Kang-ga-roo, Kang-ga-roo, until you stop your jumping jack ways."

Raghav grunted, while I laughed my heart out, at their banter.

"I'm telling you, Bhai, stop spending time with Vicky. He's infec-tious". Raghav advised Asim and I couldn't be bothered about it.

"It makes me so proud that I'm having such an impact on my bro's in such a short duration". I threw my arms over their shoulders, each and shook them.

Raghav instantly removed himself from my embrace and scoffed, "Short duration, it seems. It's going to be months since you shifted over here."

"You got a problem over there, boy?", I raised my brow in question.

"No, not at all", Raghav gave a disapproving nod. "I'm out of here, before you guys start your second round of interrogation."

I quickly grabbed his arm and held him in place, "Where are you going? We are not done yet."

He wringled out, off my grasp and turned to face Asim and me. "It's not fair. You guys won't divulge anything about of your past love life to me, but you expect me to share, mine..... It's not done, yaar". He walked away after stating his mind.

I was left there standing alone, with a slightly open mouth, as Asim too stepped aside.

"He's got a point there, bro", Asim broke the silence. "You are advicing him to work on his love-life, —", his words trailed off. "Practice what you preach, is all that I can say", he spoke again, heaving a sigh.

I glanced at him, "God mirror! .... Say that to yourself, Asim Bhai". The tension between us was starting to build up, but broke with the passer-by's voice.

"God mirror?!?", Sasha laughed, "What are you guys, five?" She waved at us and continued walking towards the discussion room while hugging her laptop.

Thanks to Sasha, the tensed atmosphere broke.

Asim's melancholic voice was heard after few moments of silence. "You, still have a chance, not everyone's lucky enough like you, to have it.... make use of it."

It pained me, to hear his pensive heartbroken tone. If I could do anything for his pain to go away, I would do anything, anything.

"You too have a chance...." I swallowed hard before letting my next words spill out. "She would have wanted you to move on, Bhai."

I could see his eyes starting to water, but before it was too late, he blinked it off and cleared his throat. "Let's not dwell on our grim lives. The focus here is Raghav, let's discuss about that."

I nodded my head in agreement, just then Raghav re-entered the wing and came into my vision.

I won't let him walk the same doomed path of ours. Already two of us were down. Not one more.... No way!

song:We used to be the life of the partyWe used to be the ones that they wished they wereBut now it's like they don't know how to actMaybe they're like me and they want us back.

"I've got a plan!", I exclaimed with a evil smile gradually growing on my face.

Raghav's POV

I could sense something is going to happen, when I entered my bay. Seeing Vicky's maddening smile, was adding to my uneasiness. Vicky and Asim were standing in my cubicle. My gut instinct told me that I had walked directly into the lion's den, more like a hungry lion.

"What's with this stupid smile plastered on your face, Vicky?" I couldn't resist and asked. If something was in store for me, might as well get it out in the clear.

Asim slammed Vicky's back energetically and Vicky stumbled a step forward towards me, unanticipating it. "Vicky has some news to share", he announced happily.

What are these two upto now?

"I — I have something to say".Vicky fumbled making me knit my eyebrows together.

"I have a date! I need your help with it", Vicky continued.

"Date?", I repeated in case I heard it wrong.

"Yes, you know that thing when a girl and guy meet and get to know each other more", Vicky explained.

"I know what a date is Vicky", I sighed. "Good to hear you have a date but how can I help you with it?"

"You see, I gave a lot of thought to your advice, about moving on and to concentrate on putting my love-life back on track and all. So I decided, it was time for some action and planned out a date as my starting step", Vicky rambled on with his reasoning. "What better way to make progress, then to find a girl from our office itself, whose company I feel comfortable with."

"Okay.....Who's the girl?", I enquired.

"It's still at the nascent stage, we need to get to know each other outside this professional environment and build our companions hip....", he paused.

The feeling of slowly falling into a trap crept in me. I encouraged him to go on without opening my mouth. I need to know where this is going, before I speak out.

"Best way to go about it, is to not put ourselves in an awkward situation." Vicky let out a sarcastic laugh, "All my efforts will go down the drain, if I plan a date and we just sit there in awkward silence..... We don't want that, right!", he retorted.

"Yes.... Who's the girl and where do I fit in—in all of this?", the impatience pulsating in my nerves, made me question.

"Good, that's why I planned for a double date and I want you to come with me to it", he stated.

I jerked my head back, in surprise and looked at Asim, who had conveniently closed his eyes but nodded his head. It looked like he was listening intently with his eyes shut. If only they weren't concealed, I would be able to see if Vicky was telling the truth or buffling.

Turning back to Vicky, I said, "Why not take Asim, it would help him too."

"Might be the next date", came Vicky's instant reply. "See Raghav I have taken so much pains and pushing myself to do it. If I fail now, I won't be able to pick myself up and try again. That's why I want to do it right from the word, go...... It's ok if she and me don't click, after a couple of dates but if at the first date itself something goes wrong —". He trailed off and pursed his lips in a tight line.

"What harm is it going to do to you?", Asim turned his focus on me and asked. "He is working on your suggestion. Don't forget how much he had helped you. Can't you help him in return? If he wants you there, he must have a solid reason for it."

There it is! The emotional blackmail card, has been pulled out.

Vicky glanced at Asim and then back at me," Yes, yes. I have a strong, valid reason for choosing you instead of Asim."

"You still haven't told me, who— is— your— date?", I enunciated my question again.

"His date is....", Asim started off but didn't compete his sentence.

The suspense is killing me. Spill it out, you drama queens!

"Chitra!", revealed Vicky and a sigh of relief escaped my mouth involuntarily.

Adding to it, Vicky said, "As Chitra and me are new to this set-up, I figured out if we go on a double date with our friends, we will be at ease. Another reason why I am asking you is because you already have a date, ready to join us but in case of Asim, we need to search for one. Moreover, Sasha and Chitra are buddies too, so she will feel more relaxed. "

" You -—you mean to say..... I need to bring Sasha along with me for the double date? "

"Yup!", Asim and Vicky exclaimed in unison.

"B—but...", I stammered on trying to figure out how I landed in this situation.

"Any problem, Raghav? I thought you said all's good between you and Sasha", Asim tried digging out information from me.

How was I going to explain to them that I was the one running away from Sasha, after she disclosed her future plans. It hurts and I hadn't braved myself to continue that conversation yet. I wasn't even sure if she would agree for the date. I guess I had dodged that topic for sometime now and the time had come to face the music. Plus, I needed to do this for Vicky too. I know he wouldn't have set all this up so soon, in a matter of ten minutes, when I hsd left them alone.

Something is fishy. Though I was a novice, in front of them, in this department, my intuition never goes wrong.....Anyways, what has to be done, has to be done, Raghav.

"There's no problem. I'll check with Sasha for her availability and if she's interested in the double date", I replied.

"Great! Thanks, man!", Vicky exclaimed and clapsed my hand loudly to fistbump, before pulling me in for a bro-hug.

I waited for Sasha's meeting to get over, once everyone dispersed from the discussion room, I walked up to her. She was leaning against the glass wall of the discussion room, explaining something to her colleague. Once they were done, I stepped in, as Sasha turned to face me.

"Hey!", I greeted.

"Hey!"

"Hmmm", I rubbed my nape nervously. "Vicky has planned a double date for us, would you like to go?"

"For us?.... A double date?", Sasha waa slightly baffled.

"Yeah! You, me, Vicky and Chitra. Are you down for it?"

"Vicky and Chitra?!", she squealed loudly. When I gestured her to shush, she mellowed down and spoke. "I didn't know they were an item? Something is brewing between them and they hid it, from all of us...?"

I raised my brow in surprise. When it was about her, she was the-all-so-innocent-naive-girl and now while talking about others, she's so out-spoken.

God knows when I'll be able to crack the riddle she is and understand her.

"Not sure how much they have progressed but they want to check it out if it could become something substantial. They need our support in it. Vicky's done a lot for..... us, so I couldn't refuse..... If you feel uncomfortable, you can turn down the invitation."

"Nah! It's ok, I'm in..... For Vicky and Chitra, anytime", she happily told.

I half expected her to tell 'why would I be uncomfortable?'. But it wasn't the case....

song:It's like there's always an empty spaceThose memories that nobody can eraseOf how bright we burnedWell now it hurts, but it's true.

Can only hope we don't ruin the double date for Vicky.

"Thanks, will let him know", I nodded.

It turned out that Vicky was sparing no time, he had set the double date for the following day. It was going to be a movie date, after office hours. We planned to wrap up early and head home to dress up for the date. Sasha was going to meet us directly at the theatre. Vicky said he wanted to start off on the right foot and be a gentleman by picking up Chitra for the date. I had suggested that we could go together and pick her up in my car. He refused it outright, he said something on the lines of — his pride was intact and wouldn't go to pick his date using someone else's car. It would also give them some alone time to spend, so I didn't stress on it.

On arrival at the said theatre, I searched for the others. There was still ample amount of time before the movie starts off, I decided to wait at the waiting hall. When I made my way to the pair of beige antique Victorian armchairs placed at one corner, under the LED track lights, I spotted Sasha. A clear figure of her came closer, making me look down at my outfit and glance back at her.

She was clad in a white round neck t-shirt with faded baby blue jeggings, along with a black leather hitchhiker hip bag. The minuscule bag would have had space just adequate for her wallet, mobile and keys. Nothing extra, nothing less. Her trademark white sneakers and her hip bag where the only differences in our outfits.

We are twinning,......coincidently.I don't think so.....It has Vicky written all over this.

"Hi, Raghav", she said with a small smile as she realized our synchronized outfits for the date.

Funny, how our first official date had turned out to be a forced one.

"Hi Sasha. Just texted Vicky, he is on the way, along with Chitra", I said pushing my phone back in my jeans pocket. "Do you wanna grab some snacks for the movie till then?", gesturing at the food counters.

"Sure, let's go".

By the time we bought a mini fresh juice bottle, butter popcorn with Mexican chilli-cum-cream cheese seasoning and a tub of caramel popcorn; only five minutes were left for the movie to start. They had opened the doors of the screen for entry. We were still waiting right outside the screen door, slowly munching on the crunching popcorn.

"Let me call Vicky and check where they are. They should have been here by now", I said. Sasha just nodded her head, busy alternating between few seasoned popcorn and the caramel ones. She seemed to enjoy it, that way.

"Hey bro, where are you?", I asked over the phone, once Vicky answered it after a couple of rings.

"We got stuck in traffic....", Vicky signed. "It will take another fifteen minutes I think.... You have two tickets right, you'll go ahead and occupy them. We will join you'll at the seats directly", he suggested.

"Yes, I have Sasha's and mine. Ok we'll go ahead. Come soon... Don't miss out too much of the beginning. Let me know if you need any help, ok."

"Except for the traffic, we are good. Actually, we didn't even realize it had became late, busy chatting away", he let out a short laugh.

"Good, good. After all it's a date, at the movie or the cab, enjoy your time together". I beamed happily on hearing that they were having a good time. "Ok we are going inside now, bye."

Sasha and me checked in at the counter outside our movie's screen entrance and settled down at our seats. The titles had rolled off, even the first song of the movie had completed, still no sign of them. Fishing my phone out, I sent out a hurried text message to Vicky.

Where are you?It's going to be half an hour, since we spoke. All okay? ~R

We reached. Will be in, in another 5mins. Relax man. ~V

Ok, good. See ya soon.

Sasha was engrossed in the movie. It was a good engaging one, couldn't deny it, but where had they gone. Only when someone else took the seats beside us, we realized that they hadn't come yet. I reached out for my phone again, then it dawned on me, that we had been played by Vicky. From the beginning, his plan was to trick us into his so-called 'Double date' and ditch us at the last minute. It felt like being stood up on a date, even though Sasha was with me. I internally banged my head multiple times, to have fallen for his bait.

"They aren't coming, right?", Sasha spoke while popping the popcorns into her mouth with her eyes fixed on the large cinema screen.

I turned my head sideways and went back to face the screen to reply, "Yeah! I don't think they'll come."

"Thought as much", came her emotionless tone.

"Hmmm", was all that came out from my mouth.

We went back to watch the romantic movie in silence, felt like it was showcasing our story. All our misunderstandings, ego, love, care, the tease, everything; were playing out right in front of us. I dropped my hand to clutch the hand rest during an emotional scene, but it landed on top of hers. Our heads snapped to face each other, after starring for few thumping heartbeats, 'Sorry' spilled out from our mouths, in harmony. Our heads bobbed backwards as we laughed. We were getting coached from a movie on teenage love. I chuckled even more at that thought.

We surely were late bloomers to have caught the love-bug at our mid-twenties.

I leaned in forward, to press our foreheads against each other, while my right hand combed through her short, silky jet black hair and settled at the back of her head.

"Miss you", I murmured softly without breaking our contact.

"Miss you, more", Sasha smiled and replied back gently.

I pulled her into a bone crashing hug. I didn't want to think for what she had apologized for. Nor did I want to revoke the hanging conversation about her future plans. What I really wanted was her and her company, right now. That's what I craved for and at this moment I didn't care whatever the hell happens in the near future or 2 years fast forward from now.

Her croacked voice came out, "You are doing a good job, if you want to kill me now".

My jaws and facial muscles were paining from all the grinning, since the time we reconciled. I pulled away and rested my forehead back to its previous position.

Playfully nudging her nose, with my arms circling her slim waist. I said, "I missed you, to the moon and the back, infinite times. Can't beat that, right?". Sending her into fits of giggles as she clutched onto my shirt at the center of my chest for support. The strong hold was definitely going to leave a heavily crumpled mark.

We were so close, with only the armrest as a barrier and our lips, inches apart. I could hear Sasha's throbbing lub-dubs and vice versa too. The heart murmurs seemed to overpower the sounds from the audience as well as the boom, emerging out from the numerous dolby speakers. This seemed to have accentuated our feelings, making us part our lips slightly. I leaned in to close the distance and was about to have our first liplock, when the lights of the cinema hall flashed on.

Heavy applause was heard followed by a standing ovation. Apart from us, not a single soul was seated around us. Immediately Sasha pushed me back; shocked, embarrassed and shy were the myriad emotions her face emoted. Whereas, I had a singular emotion— disappointment.

What a timing!, I huffed.

As the cinema hall was getting empty, with the audience making their way to the exit, Sasha spoke. "You always do this, it's so embarrassing. Everyone saw us!" She folded her arms and huffed, blowing on her astray burgandy bangs, which danced gracefully in the air before falling back in place. It was like a thirty second timed dancing fountain show.

"Oh, come on! We are not celebrities, for people to stand and applaud for us. It was for the climax, Sasha", I said with amusement in my eyes.

She punched my arms with her fist, "Still—", as we got up to leave our seats.

I took her hand in mine and we climbed down the aisle. "I'm going to remember it forever. The ending of our first movie date..... So filmy." I announced happily while swinging our clasped hands in the air, enjoying the feel of the warmth transfusing into my palms. I leaned in to whisper for her ears only, "Did you notice that the climax was a replica of our scene?". Winking at her, I continued with a mischievous smirk, "But they were more successful than us, in their outcome."

Sasha laughed and rewarded me with another fist punch from her free hand. "Ya right! Our forced 'Patch-up date' become our first movie date." She titled her body to face me, covering half my body and murmured, "—and, you kinda got cock-blocked on it." After stating it she averted her eyes from me and fell back in line with the descending queue. Her unsuccessful attempts to stifle her laugh, resulted in her body vibrating with her giggles.

"Don't test the tempting waters, Sasha", I warned her with a small smile.

"Ok-ok, Relax", she dismissively patted my upper arm. We exited the building and made our way to the car parking zone. Rohit had dropped her off at the theatre, with the arrangement that I would drop her back at her place after the date. She pulled me, striding towards the car while dragging me by my upper arm, "Let's go, I'm feeling sleepy and want to hit the bed, soon"

"Can I join?", I quipped, pouncing on the golden opportunity. My eyes lit with gusto, while the corner of my lips curled in playful smirk.

Raising her brow, "Cocky much! ..... Yes, you can, Raghav. Drop me at my home while I go upto my room. Then you an take a u-turn and ride back to your home and sleep in your comfy bed, that's calling you".

"Or..... I could just come up to your's. Saves time", I shrugged, enjoying the on-going repartee. If I had my way, I wouldn't want it to end.

No harm in engaging in some playful banter.

Sasha flashed me the most fake smile I have ever seen. "Sorry, admissions are closed. Seats are full. Try again next time". Patting my shoulder, she went towards the front passenger side of my car.

"Oh!", I exclaimed. "That means, it's open for entry next time?", I asked her innocently.

"Rrraaaghhaavvvv!!", she yelled through her gritted teeth and ran behind me, with her arm ready to swat me, for pulling her leg.

After playing Catch-me-if-you-can like kids in the half-empty open parking lot, she halted near the rear end of my car to stabilize her breath. I stood few metres away from her. Walking in her direction, I brought my arm forward for me, "Here you go, go ahead swat it, as you wanted to."

She stared at my arm and back to my face, heaving a long sigh, her hands fell to her side, "It's ok, let's make a move".

Stepping closer, I took both her hands in mine and kissed them both together. Just then a security guard's voice was heard telling us to vacate the area, as the cars for the next show would start coming in.

Can't a guy have some alone time with his girl!?

As expected, she snatched her hands away from mine, puckering her brows in annoyance. Turning hot on her heels, she stomped her way to the front seat.

Shoot! All the wrong timings had to happen today only!?

"Sasha! Sasha!", jogging up to her, I called out her name. She had opened the door and I said, "I didn't know that the guard was there. He just suddenly appeared....". I ran my hands across my hair frantically knowing how annoyed she was. "See.... People will always be around and people have eyes. Do you expect me to blindfold everyone?", I tried my best, to explain.

With her palm on the opened door, she nodded her head slowly in understanding. I smiled at her and opened the door wide for her to get it. She reciprocated the smile, a sign that she was back to normal. She ducked and settled in her seat. While she was securing her seat belt, placing my palm on the car's roof, I bent down.

"I get it now. You want all your cute expressions and gestures to be for my eyes only", I sent her a tantalizing smile. She looked up at me in confusion. Lowering my head further, I pecked her cheek and placed a finger on her lips, silencing her before she starts her outburst.

"Inside these four doors, no one can see, don't worry. I would also like to be the only specatator that has the privilege to witness your cute, lovable expressions." Tapping my index finger slightly at her nose, we exchanged pleasant smiles. I closed her door and walked across to the driver's side.

CHAPTER 21

S asha's POV

song:Stranded, reaching outI call your name but you're not aroundI say your name but you're not around.

Humming along to the tunes in my favorite playlist, I started my day at work. The upbeat tunes kept me on a high, not that I was ever low, making me work at a faster pace, matching up to it. I was on a roll, completed throwing two defects that were assigned to me by my Quality Assurance (QA/ Testing) team, back to them. Scoffing at their working ways, everything needed to be spoonfed.

Who do they think they are messing with?? Defect! My foot!!That's incorrect test data setup, dear... Learn the business aspects first before throwing something at me. All they had to do is input some test data and click two buttons to verify the output.... Even that they couldn't do properly.... Ufff!

One thing I learnt in my years spent at this office, apart from mastering programming languages; you needed to learn the art of tackling and playing tennis - to smash the ball in other's court. Every task directed to you, is not meant to be worked upon by us, most of the time it's needs to parcelled back to the sender for their proper inspection.

Letting out a snort, troublemakers are there in every team. Looking over at my colleague, who had to deliver a simple piece of code last week, I rolled my eyes. If he was just warming his seat and playing games on his phone, he would take another week for fixing the pending defect. All that required was replacing the 'OR' keyword to 'AND' in one program, and Viola!, the defect would vanish. I had even hinted him the fix along with the program name, still he thought he had time, till the world comes to an end, to complete his task.

In my hyperness, I kept marking the insignificant unread mails as read, without giving it a second look. The cursor shifted slightly and clicked on a link in the mail's preview section. A page opened and some funny green colour screen appeared with a visitor's counter displayed, whose count was increasing within microseconds.

Oops! What did I do?

In an impulse, I closed the page, getting scared that it could be a malicious link. Next minute, the beep of a system sound came, along with it a pop-up from the anti-virus software installed in my computer, rose from it's icon in the taskbar.

Oh My God! Don't tell me, don't tell me it's related to some malware detection.

Crossing my fingers, I looked heavenward and chanted some slogans in bullet train speed. Opening my right eye, I moved the cursor to the pop up window.

Please be an upgrade pop-up.... Please... Pretty please!

The maximized window of it, spread across my monitor. Scanning through it for some good news to detect keywords like 'Upgrade', 'Patch required', 'scheduled' but Alas! met with the dreaded information.

"One Malware detected on your system - 22/06/2019 11:00 am IST"

My fingers were trembling on the mouse and the cursor hovered over the 'Show Details' button. An internal battle started on whether or not, to the click it. Like the decision to rip off a band-aid over a wound, I took the hard call and clicked it. Boom! There, it had the recently opened link details and time. Everything proved that the mail I had received was the root cause. Being the responsible employee, I forwarded the malicious mail to the official spam helpdesk email address, for their intimation and awareness. The anti-virus software icon was rotating in the taskbar, indicating it's busy doing some background processing.

Licking my dry lips, I reclined on my chair, before my back could hit the backrest of it, a new mail popped up in my inbox. Within a matter of ten seconds, my inbox was bombarded with five new mails. That doesn't sound good. Straightening up to have closer view of it, I could see my manager, delivery manager and delivery head of the portfolio marked in copy of the mails.

Sooooo not good!

Alarm ringing in my mind, urged me to read the mails, reluctantly. They were all auto-generated emails. I couldn't categorize their source, was it due to forwarding the spam mail to the concerned helpdesk or did it have something to do with the malware detected in my system. Never encountered a prior experience in such a scenario, panic started kicking within me. Few droplets of anxiety started forming near my temples. Wiping them off, I gulped down cool water from my flask. Grabbing my armrests, I stood up and my eyes automatically darted towards Raghav's desk. Finding his desk amd bay, spotless clean; I turned my attention to Rohit's and made my way to him.

Where is Raghav?, my hyperventilating mind voice asked on the way.

song:I need you, I need you, I need you right nowYeah, I need you right nowSo don't let me, don't let me, don't let me downI think I'm losing my mind now.

My cracked voice blurted out, from behind Rohit's chair. "Rohit, Can we talk outside? Please It's urgent."

He rotated himself on the chair and faced me with a frown. Something visible on my face, made him jump off his chair, locking his desktop and nodded. "Call AJ and the others?", he asked causiously.

Nodding my head in agreement, we walked out with his hand over my shoulder, comforting me in the process. While waiting for Daniel and Simbu, AJ grabbed some coffee from the brewing machine for us. I knew I hadn't concealed my distress properly. They were my best friends and understood my behavior. My mind flew to Raghav while fidgeting with the coffee mug's handle.

Still no clue of Raghav.Couldn't spot Asim or Vicky too. The message I had sent him, hadn't been delivered too.

"What happened Rohit? Why this urgent meet-up?" Daniel asked while pulling out his chair next to me. Simbu walked over to sit between Rohit and AJ.

Rohit nudged towards me, making them train their focus at me. I had my head lowered and mindlessly gazing at my latte, that was getting cooler as the minutes passed.

Switching to a gentler tone, Daniel asked, "What happened, Sasha? You are stressing yourself and us out?..... Did Rohit fight again?"

"Hey!", objected Rohit.

"Okay, if not Rohit.... Is it Raghav?"

I shook my head. If he was here, only then he could say something, I sighed.

AJ spoke, "Is it your manager?"

I denied it again, shaking my head, still not able to bring my eyes to look at them.

"Is it -", Simbu questioned but I cut him off.

"You can say kind of", I replied with a bitter tone.

"What do you mean by kind of, Sash?, What did that man do, now?" Rohit's typical 'ready-to-fight' mode was switched on.

Unable to get myself to reveal what I did, I swirled the latte.

"Did he do anything?", Daniel rephrased Rohit's question.

Heaving a long sigh, I sipped my perfectly temperatured latte. If I was in a better mood, would have thoroughly enjoyed it. I sent a thankful smile towards AJ for it, making a note, to get him to brew it for me, going forward.

"Yes and No", I said looking at a faraway space between Daniel and Rohit.

Rohit groaned, "Can you cut talking in riddles and spill it out in normal human language?"

Letting out a humorless laugh, oh! I'm going to miss them so much. At that note my eyes started getting blurry.

"Why aren't you looking at any of us?.... Crap! Why are you crying?" Daniel's words made the others narrow their eyes on me.

AJ gently grabbed my chin and turned my face to his concerned orbs. Dismissing his hand, I escaped his scrunity to look straight at the wall above Rohit's head.

Taking out his smartphone, admist searching for something on it, Daniel asked, "Do you want us to call Raghav?"

"His number is unreachable", I responded.

"Why Raghav, when we all are here?", Rohit's words showed off his brotherly protective side. "Sash, look at me and tell."

My focus didn't leave the plain white wall, fluffing my bangs nervously, I spoke. "Why is this happening to me?.... No! I should be asking, why is it happening only to me? My life seems to have become a roller-coaster ride with periodic rises and falls".

The last time I was unresponsive to a similar interrogation was due to the fuming anger within me. This time, it was guilt, embarrassment and fear, pure unexplainable fear. I knew my rant didn't make any sense if I didn't explain further, I was just not able to disclose it. Knowing very well it was killing them, I turned my attention to the empty space at the center of our table.

"I made a blunder..... a big one", I revealed. "I don't know how to say it. So many things and consequences churning out in my mind, it's just -". I said running my hand down my face in agony.

"Relax. Don't skip to the conclusion and don't make your own version of it. Stop over thinking. Take it one step at a time and walk us through it". Simbu spoke out for the first time.

Instantly my eyes flew to him and I took a deep breath. His calm demeanor always made me feel, he would perfectly fit in a counselor's or a therapist's shoes. He could think of it as an alternative career option. Though he didn't need one. By the looks of it, I would have to start thinking of alternatives for my drowning IT career.

All lent their ears patiently, without interrupting as I recited the events that botched up my career in a span of few minutes and in two mouse clicks.

"To err is human, Sasha.... Hell! I've made so many goof-ups in this very office, but that didn't lead me to my termination", consoled Daniel. "I'm not telling it's not a big deal. It is something to worry about, not wear yourself down."

"Yes, Sash. You did nothing wrong.... intentionally atleast", Rohit reasoned out. "You did the right thing by forwarding it to the con-cerned department. Now it's their job to look into it. Hell! If the firewall or outside office network emails were blocked, it wouldn't have reached into your inbox, in the first place." Rohit slammed his palm on the table, turning the blame to the network security team; making a small smile spread across my face.

"Rohit's right, it's their job to see that such suspicious emails are blocked at the source. So if there's been a fault, it's clearly due to their code slip - up that granted access to such emails to enter our office network." AJ too vouched for me.

These guys are - are too much I say. They are my rock solid and support system, couldn't have asked for anyone better.... But shouldn't have, a certain someone joined us at this table, too. Why aren't you here Raghav- to be with me when I need you the most, to support, to comfort, to console me?

song:It's in my head, darling I hopeThat you'll be here, when I need you the mostSo don't let me, don't let me, don't let me downDon't let me down.

"Atleast the anti-virus software is in-place and doing it's job per-fectly well. It detected the malicious link, so it's safe to assume that not much harm could have been caused by it. If it passed their fire-wall too, then the useless software needs to be uninstalled instead of sitting there taking up all the memory space and consuming CPU usage, all for nothing!" AJ continued and dammed at all the firewalls the organization had enaabled, for their pathetic performance.

Nodding my head in a happier and lighter mood, I let out few giggles. "Before you guys go out in rolling out a thesis on 'how to blame the organization's network security', let's take a breather..... Thank so much guys, I feel better now. Hope things happen just like you guys said."

After all the 'no-thank-you and no-sorry in friendship' emotional lecture I had to endure. We all hugged it out and smiles were stuck on our faces.

I said, "It's been nearly an hour it's I have kept you guys away from your desks and work.... I think we can disperse and meet up for lunch."

While getting up from my seat, I was abruptly pulled down to sit again, by AJ's tug on my wrist.

"What?", I asked.Rohit's voice made me face him.

"What's the other thing that's bothering you?" Rohit questioned nonchalantly, like it was clear as a sunny day, that two things were gnawing me.

I slumped my shoulders, "Raghav.... He is not here."

Daniel flicked my forehead.

"Ouch! What was that for?", I whined while rubbing my forehead.

"Gu-url! , put some sense in your brain", Daniel replied.

"What do you mean?", I questioned back stubbornly.

"Just because he is not here the one time, are you going to use it against him?" Daniel narrowed his eyes on me with a reprimanding tone.

Rohit joined him, "Sash, that's not good on your part. He's been there for you during the club issue, the mid-year appraisal aftermath and every other time..... Didn't you, yourself say that he's not at his desk and his number is unreachable?"

Simbu added the last touch, "You can't take it on him, if he's unaware of your current situation."

I huffed and rolled my eyes, "Yeah, right! In the malware blunder, I'm not wrong but misinterpreting Raghav, I'm wrong!.... You guys are really something..... I get it now, will you'll stop your "Raghav's the best" slogans? It feels like I've been transported to a political gathering, where everyone is praising their party's leader, one after the other."

After sharing a good amount of laughs, we went back to our designated desks. I was feeling thousand times better, that's the effect of good friends. Walking past Raghav's deserted bay, I entered mine. Manoj, my manager rushed over to my desk with creased brows.

"Can we have a quick discussion, Sasha?", he said without wasting any time in pleasant greetings.

"Ye-ss sure", my hesitant reply came.

We walked in to a discussion room and soon after, our porfolio's delivery Manger, Lavanya, barged in too. Both of them together for discussion, rose the suspicions in my mind. Just few moments ago, they were put to rest. Now they were back, jumping up and down like a crazy ping-pong ball in my brain; banging on all it's sidewalls. Taking in a deep breath, I readied myself for their music.

Lavanya broke the silence with her demanding aura. "There's nothing hidden about the agenda of this meeting, so let us divulge the details of the malware detected in your system. Obviously you would have seen the emails generated marking all of us in carbon copy of it.... Please take it as a very serious matter, it has been escalated and gone up to higher levels outside our portfolio too. Not only our delivery head, other protfolio delivery heads and every-one's looking for answers. I know you Sasha, but still it's my duty to tell you -don't hide any facts. It's a stressful situation and even the strongest minds succumb to it. Your answers can help us and the network security team battle this virus that has been detected, to gauge it's destruction..... Please share the details you know of. "

Giving a curt nod in understanding, I narrated the events.

The first question, Lavanya shooted at me,"Did you disclose your official email address in platforms outside the official network, like in your resume or any other website for instance?"

"No. I always give my personal email address only, outside office. Moreover my personal email address has my pet name in contrast to my official one, so even by mistake, there are no chances of it happening", I answered bravely. I wasn't going to cower down to issues I didn't cause. I was a hundred and one percent confident that I didn't invite suspicious mails to my official inbox.

Manoj asked Lavanya, "Has anyone else reported similar mails as Sasha's from same source or having any kind of resemblance or links?", in support of me. Feeling relieved that I had atleast one of their support.

"Not yet. I didn't get such information yet. The network team is looking into it as well as the spam helpdesk. They are doing a global check across all locations, if something has been reported. They need to analyze the scope of destruction, whether it's limited to only our portfolio in our branch location or total portfolio across all locations or only our branch location irrespective of the portfolio. The last one meaning, our entire Coimbatore office has a potential to be prone to destruction". Lavanya's answer made me squirm in my spot. Such a massive affect it could have, was scary.

She continued, "I'm getting so many calls and mails regarding it. I doubt that it could be related to our portfolio or client, as the mail was received in her local mail and not her client mail."

"Yes it came to my local organization mail ID and my remote connection to the client machine was also cut-off, as I was restating my client machine." My disclosure brought waves of relief on both their faces and mine.

Thank God!I hadn't realized this piece of information before. At least there was still some luck shining on my side. If the remote connectivity to my client machine was intact, at the time I had clicked on that malicious link, I was doomed forever. The chances of the malware entering the client machine, would multiplying the issues in hand.

Manoj said, "Good, that's one issue scratched out".

Lavanya phone rang interrupting us, she spoke rapidly into it and turned in on speaker mode. Our branch's head of network security team was at the other side of the line. He wanted to connect with me to touch up on few details, while his team was looking into the issue - scope of destruction, impact of it and restricting the destruction.

He asked the same question as Lavanya and wanted to know how long was the website from the suspicious mail was open on my computer. Some other questions were related to- if any other link in it I had clicked on, any other information I had noticed on the green page. Jotting down my answers, he asked for my phone number incase they require further information. With that, the call came to an end but didn't put a full stop to the chaos situation we were in. It was just the beginning.

We wrapped up our discussion on the note that if any other details pops up in my memory, I should be transparent and keep them in confidence.

After forty five minutes an announcement was being played, across the floor from the speakers on the ceiling. My system was in the network security team's control through remote access, for their inspection. It has turned into their specimen for now. Having nothing else to do, I tuned my ears to the impending announcement. An authoritative voice boomed through the wing.

"Attention! Attention! Attention! Dear colleagues, I request you all to stop whatever important work you are doing and listen up. We have a very important announcement to make."

They gave a small gap before continuing.

"If we have caught your attention, let's continue. This announcement is applicable to each and every employee of the Coimbatore branch and srtict adherence to it is expected. If not stringent actions would be taken against any defaulters.

There has been a very unfortunate event that the organization has come across, threatening the security of our office network. A malicious virus attack has invaded into our network. The concerned department is doing their best to contain it and take necessary actions. Along with that, we require each and everyone's cooperation in fighting against this unforeseen attack."

My breath hitched and heartbeat started to pulsate at a abnormally higher speed. I didn't realize it would lead to such an announcement, meaning it was a dreadful threat.

I need to be calm, relax Sasha, relax.

Starting my breathing exercise, I felt two people stand behind me. Looking over my shoulder I found Rohit and AJ. Rohit squeezed my shoulder slightly to comfort and assuree me that they wouldn't leave me alone.

song:Running out of timeI really thought you were on my side.

We back to listen to the remainder of the announcement.

"To combat this situation and avoid more dire consequences, we are shutting down the Coimbatore branch for 3 days, across all portfolios. It is expected that all employees need to close all their open applications and check if any malware detection or suspicious mails have been received in their respective systems. If found, forward the required details to the spam helpdesk and inform your immediate managers and higher-ups. No employee is susposed to login to their systems in this 3-day shutdown, either from office or from home. No official webmails, apps or anything using your office credentials should be accessed in this time, until further notice. Any official communication will be passed on to your registered mobile numbers via SMS through the admin helpdesk or your managers.

For any concerns or queries related to this, please reach out to your managers. We expect good code of conduct and confidentiality to be maintained related to the virus attack.

Lastly, each employee needs to shutdown their systems and leave the premises by 3pm IST, today.

Thank you all for your time, looking forward for your cooperation."

Resting my elbows on the table, with my head in my hands, I clutched my hair, tugging it in frustration.

Great! What did I do?Full shutdown of an entire branch office, for three days.... All because of me?!

In next five minutes, everyone's phones beeped with a written copy of the announcement. The broadcasted message was replayed through the speakers every fifteen minutes, to ensure everyone was aware of it and served as a hard reminder of my actions. Those who hadn't received the broadcast message were asked to update their phone numbers to their managers. No one was allowed to do any update or anything in their system, apart from closing and scanning through their mails for any suspicious mails.

If the organization had been pushed to take such extreme actions of shutdown, risking 3 day heavy revenue loss across the numerous client accounts the Coimbatore branch was handling; it had to have a severe impact. Revenue loss was a trade-off they had settled for, compared to the security risk and their reputational risk, that was put on stake.

While others rejoiced on the three day off-work leave bestowed on them; some feared their jobs, due to the crippling down of the organization in the face-off with the unidentified virus outbreak. All of this had only one straightforward consequence for me - my termination. Looks like I might have to put my future plans in action, sooner than I had sketched it out for.

Getting kicked out of an organization for breaching security and inviting security threats, would lead to getting blacklisted. Any Indian recruiter wouldn't want to approach or hire a blacklisted profile. For putting myself back in the job market, I needed to change my career path, which I didn't have any alternatives to, at this point of time.

I guess that makes - higher studies at abroad, the only viable option available for me.

That meansGoodbye to this office, Goodbye to India..... and-Goodbye to Raghav??

Where are you, Raghav?

song:Crashing, hit a wallRight now I need a miracleHurry up now, I need a miracle.

22

CHAPTER 22

S asha's POV

song:When the night has comeAnd the land is darkAnd the moon is the only light we'll see.

Speculation about the virus attack, leading to the shutdown of an entire branch, was high among the employees. It obviously wasn't a minuscule issue to shush off. Wagging tongues were murmuring different scenarios around me. Some of the rumors doing the rounds were of the highly feared Ransomware virus. Wherein the hackers, who implanted the virus, would demand huge monetary payment for disabling the virus. They were the creators and destroyers of the virus they had coded. Until they received the payment from the officials, the virus would render the system or network, it had attacked, as unusable and under their hostage.

I knew better than to fall into office gossips but my tensed heart silenced my logical brain. There were chances that the rumors could turn into the truth. In the past few months, some of our counterpart Software companies had reported, of falling prey to the Ransomware. It resulted in increase in the number of anti-virus software providers in the market.

While everybody was busy shutting down their workstations and gathering their things to leave; I sat slumped in my chair, hugging myself. Rubbing my forearms, as a response to the cool air conditioning sting felt due to decrease in the head count at the floor or due to bracing myself for the worst case scenario, was a million dollar question. How just two mouse clicks lead to my downfall, made me realize that it took only a matter of seconds for all my years of hardwork to tumble and fall.

AJ came up to my desk. Seeing my distraught state, he picked me up by my shoulders and walked us to Rohit's. I was in some sort of daze. I felt like a walking zombie in a nightmare, waiting for something to jolt me out of it. Rohit needed some time to wind up, as his system was turning unresponsive with every mouse click.   Engulfed in self-guilt, my conscience pricked me. Due to my oversight error, from the CEO to the employees, from the housekeeping staff to the caterers for the cafeteria; everyone had been affected. All that I could do was pray that it didn't bore a hole in their salaries.

Raghav's POV

Entering our wing, I found it deserted. It didn't look like the usual hustle and bustle of a day in office during the weekday. Instead it replicated the lonely vibes we get when we have to come to office over the weekends for some production release support activities. My teammates hurried back to their desks, while bumping into me from behind. It made me turn right and three floating heads came into my vision. One of them was undoubtedly Sasha's.

Making my way towards Rohit's desk, as I approached closer, I called out to her, "Sasha". She whipped her head sideways and sprung to her feet. Shaking her head, she sprinted and flung onto to me. "Whoa!", escaped my lips as I caught her. I had to take a step back, to form a strong hold due to the force with which she hit me.

   song: No I won't be afraidOh, I won't be afraidJust as long as you stand, stand by me. So darling, darlingStand by me, oh stand by meOh stand, stand by meStand by me.

Sasha clung onto me like I was her life saving vest, she had just found, aiding her from drowning. She wasn't ready to let go anytime soon. Her first PDA from her side, rocket launched me high into the stratosphere. She fit so well into my arms. From the wetness forming at my shoulder and her sudden hug, a clear tell-tale sign, that it wasn't the time for my glory, but to comfort her. Gently storking her back in a comforting gesture similar to that of shushing a baby, I let her hug it out till she felt relieved.

She pulled away from me still caged safely in my arms, I met her wet eyes. "Sshh! Sasha", I spoke softly while letting go of her waist to rub the trails of tears off her cheeks. Caressing her face in my palms, sending her a gaze loaded with care and love, I said. "Hey what happened to my lioness? Where did she go?"Her heavily glistened eyes starred back at me. Tears were threatening to fall at the blink of her eye. Instead a small smile spread across her lips and vanished like a flash of lightening over her gloomy facial canvas.

She held my wrists, removing my palms and moved a step back to distance ourselves, as we were still well within our office premises. She spoke in a dejected tone that pricked my heart. "The virus..... The shutdown..... I think it's because of me." Encouraging her to disclose more, she narrated what she went through in my absence. It made me feel guilty for not being there with her.

I held her hands in mine, rubbing my thumbs across it. "Okay, That's enough", I replied in soothing voice. "You need to wait for their investigation to be over and let them come back to you."

"It's clear as a crystal, Raghav; I'm the root cause of it. They are going to terminate me, all my hard work that would have lead to a promotion, is down the drain. I lost everything in a blink." Sniffing in between her rant, "I'll get blacklisted, no one will select my resume for new opportunities, I will be jobless, penniless... Oh God! I hope they don't penalize me for the damages caused. Do you think they'll fine me?" She squeezed my hand tightly, crushing my bones, questioning me. The wince that reflected from me made her loosen her grasp.

Smiling at her,"First, slow down your galloping thoughts. Like they say — 'Innocent until proven guilty', let's stick to it". I cut her bubbling protests and continued. "If it was black and white, just as you say, don't you think by now the officials would have taken an action against you? They need time to be sure that they aren't making impulsive decisions, so why should we?" I shrugged at her. "Let's go, I need to shutdown my system, then let's have lunch together, separately". I took her hand and made a move to walk but she stood anchored at her position.

"So you aren't leaving me?", her words came from behind me, making me turn and look at her like she had grown two heads.

"What?", I asked in disbelief.

"You know — you mingling with me might tarnish your reputation. I mean..... Being in the same group of an employee who has violated security, can cause you also trouble. Stating I'm bad influence and all". Sasha mumbled away, looking everywhere other than me.

I tugged her hand slightly making her fall a step forward. "The influence you have on me is none of anyone's damn business. They can think whatever hell they want but that's not going to affect me or us."

Her miniature version of my Adam's apple was bobbing as she swallowed, reacting to my intense stare. Happiness flooded my mind internally, as I had rendered my stubborn Sasha— speechless, but masked it well with my stare.

song:Whenever you're in trouble won't you stand by meOh stand by me, oh won't you stand now, standStand by me.

She cleared her throat and said, "You're saying that now, but when things go down south —". She left her words hanging.

Did she actually — actually mean that?She's the only one who could send me to heaven and shoot me down six feet under the ground the next second.

Heaving a long sigh, I shut my eyes to calm my boiling nerves. Opening them, I replied, "Why don't you complete that sentence? I would really like to know the end of it. You see I don't want to make any assumptions".

She stood like a statue, unable to answer my question. Either she didn't want to say it out loud that I would flee leaving her in a knee-deep crisis situation or she didn't want to accept it.

Breaking the lull, "Don't you trust me?", I asked in a mellow tone. "Do you really think that low of me to run away if you fall into trouble? Then what's the point of this?" Gesturing to the space between us. I sobered myself to avoid her stress levels to go any higher up than it already has been. I said, "I will stand by you through thick and thin". I gave her hand a reassuring squeeze and let my words get absorbed into her brain. "Now let's hurry up, I need to shut my system. We need to vacate the premises, these blarring announcements are going to tear my eardrums."

Sasha and me decided to dine in a restaurant instead of the food court in the campus. We placed an order for thai cuisine, our hot favorite white rice with thick white semi gravy loaded wih chicken and veggies. Even after frequenting this place, I couldn't remember the name or how to pronounce it. We usually get confused among the dishes as all look similar but alien to us. I always let Sasha do the honors of placing the order, trusting her she would order it correctly.

We knew exactly at which page and at which corner of the menu booklet it resides. All we had to do is go to the page and point out the name. That's our little secret of figuring out our favorite dish. Once, Sasha tried ordering it verbally, it turned out to be the wrong dish. Thankfully, at that time, we were being served from a familiar waiter and he pointed out that we aren't ordering our usual. Initially I force fed myself to eat her favorite dish but at the end of the meal, it ruled over my taste buds and became my favorite too.

Our dish arrived and was platted by our trusted server. We dug into the not so spicy yet yummy food. While scooping up my morsel of food, I commented.

"Sasha, you have vitamin T deficiency".

"No, I don't", she replied right away."Wait a minute, I don't think there's any vitamin of the type T". She said thoughtfully when her brain recovered from being sidetracked by the delicacy.

"It is there", I replied balantly.

"No it isn't!"

"It is!", I emphasized.

"Nope! It isn't!", she echoed back in the same tone. "Do you want me to look it up?", she challenged with her phone ready to search the internet for it.

Dismissing her hand, "Nah! I know what it stands for."

Sasha raised her eyebrows in question, "Ok, Tell me what is it?"

Turning my body to face her, "Vitamin T stands for Trust and you have inadequate amounts of it."

The reveal of it made Sasha's mouth turn into the shape of an 'O', making her look cute like a baby.

She huffed in regret, "See, it's not about not trusting in you. It's just— I was and still am, paranoid. Yes, there was a flicker of doubt but isn't it acceptable to have it? Considering the situation I was in and that we are still in the process of knowing each other?"

"Hmmm right, I get it. Your apology is accepted". I flashed my toothy grin at her perfect for a toothpaste advertisement.

She arched her eyebrow in response and tried to hide her sly smile in the disguise of chewing her food. "I'm sorry,..... Even if you hadn't hinted for the apology, I was going to say it anyways", she shrugged sending an honest smile in my direction.

"It's fine. I'll feel better if I can get some Vitamin K", I replied conversationally.

"Oh! I didn't know vitamin K is required to boost up one's mood."

"Trust me, it does. To such high levels and doesn't even take long for the result to show."

Sasha had her focus on the plate in front of her while my undue attention was on her.

"Okay, let me think.... I guess carrots have good amounts of Vitamin K.... No that's Vitamin A.... How about fish? I think it should be a vitamin K rich food. Do you want me to order it now?" At last, she looked over at me after the monologue battle she had.

"I know exactly from what I can get it from". A smile grew gradually on my face and I tapped my index finger on my cheek twice. Winking at her playfully, gesturing my vitamin K was a kiss on the cheek.

She shook her head in disbelief, while a light crimson blush spread over her cheeks. "Aren't you so... so..... sooo... Can't even say. I've run out of words to describe you".

"Your thinking power has reduced because of the lack of vitamin K. Here let me give it to you too, so both our levels of vitamin k are fuelled up". Leaning over to claim my reward.

"Oh please! Stop right there mister", she placed her hand on my chest. "Atleast stick to one meaning, if you want to come out convincing. First, it was to improve the happiness quotient and now it is for improving thinking capacity?!" She laughed hard and her eyes glossed up.

This is the kind of water I want to see in her eyes, not the ones earlier. Only happy tears.

I pretend to sulk for a second for being obstructed from leaning further but brighten up a little latter.

"How about vitamin H then? You also like it and have indulged in it happily", I suggested.

Sasha went back to her thinking mode. "I hope this 'vitamin H' is real and not your made up version of it..... I'm now getting confused, don't mess up my head". She hit my forearm playfully.

"It's real. Whether it's made up or not by me, I'm in dire need of it". I kinda pleaded.

"Ya right!", she rolled her eyes getting my underlying hint. "So what does this one mean?"

"Vitamin H is for holding hands". I revealed like an artist pulling down the curtains from his masterpiece.

"Oh! Here I thought it was for a hug", Sasha responded

"Yes, that's also there right!", I scratched my temples. "Let's call it vitamin H+, for the added energy it instills", I concluded winking at her."If it's running on your mind, I don't mind it. I can settle for vitamin H+ for now". I stated and spread out my arms inviting her for a hug. I flapped my fingers signally her to fall into my awaiting arms.

She pushed down my arms, to fall in line with my body. "Didn't I just give you one?", she cocked up her brow. Leaning closer, she whispered, "Overdose of anything, even vitamins, is not good for health, Raghav boy". She pat my cheek playfully in a frequency like the DITs and DAHs of Morse code. Before I could trap her in my armed cage, she ducked and escaped with victorious smile.

Groaning, I warned her, waging my finger playfully. "There's always a next time, Sasha, always!".

She flashed a wide grin and raised her spoon in her defense.

"Really? A fork would have been a better option to scare me off."

We went back to our food after our slight detour.

"So, what's all this about —your cheesy 'vitamins'? Were you a biology student?"

"Yes, I had opted for it. The point is just like how vitamins and minerals are important for our healthy body. These are the essentials required in our relationship if we want it to last, with vitamin T being the most vital one."

Sasha hummed and let out,"Genius!", from her lips. "Nice way to put it, I'm impressed", she added and pat my shoulder.

"Hey, can you repeat that once more?", I requested. "I want to take video and shove it in Vicky's nose that someone called me a 'genius'". My eyes shone on that prospect.

Sasha chuckled and shook her head in amusement. "By the way you can't put the full blame on me, when you were the one having MIA syndrome."

My frown made her elaborate. "MIA means Missing In Action, dumbo. You weren't at your desk, where.were.you?" She questioned with a hard fist punch landing on my forearm, before which I had conveniently beefed up my biceps to lessen the blow.

"Hey! It wasn't my fault that I had a video training with clients at the eleventh floor. If you didn't realize my whole team was missing from the floor. All of us had to attend it, mandatory training". I rolled my eyes at the thought of the training.

Sasha huffed, "Ya right!", her sarcastic reply came. "Client training in our morning hours.... It would be midnight in USA and I highly doubt they would do a night shift just to connect with the offshore team". Pointing towards me, she narrowed her eyed at me. "It's usually the other way around, right? We have client trainings at our midnight hour and their morning time".

I smiled at her adoringly and bent to give quick peck at her forehead. "I get it you missed me a lot, but things happen like this in life. That's life! I'm sorry for not being there but I assure you if it was in my hands I would have left everything to be with you. Also, you know how the eleventh floor video conferencing room is? With all its heavy sound proofing, mobile signals are hard to receive. We didn't even get the broadcasted SMS. Only when we exited the room, cancelling the training mid-way, all our mobiles beeped continuously. "

"Then how did you'll get the information?"

"Vicky usually carries his laptop to such meetings. Selva, our manager pinged him in the official communicator before the announcement boomed from the speakers."

"Oh gosh! Now even our clients know about it", Sasha exclaimed remorsefully and enclosed her face within her palms.

"No, we muted ourselves from the conference before the announcement proceeded. They heard the initial attention and thought a fire alarm was set off". I explained and removed her hands from her face. "Then we excused ourselves stating it was an emergency."

"Hmmmm but still why didn't you'll have live client training in their late night hours?" She questioned, not completely satisfied with the situation.

I chuckled, "Oh my curious lioness", I tapped the bridge of her nose. "They wanted to showcase the new development when our application is down and considering the application downtime is usually in EST night hours, they decided on it". I shrugged.

I was awarded with a weird look. "They could have just manually made the application down in pre-production environment", She suggested.

"Yeah! They tried that too but other upstream and downstream applications were Up and we couldn't ask all of them to be down at the same time. Actually some alternative could have been arranged but we didn't bother. When clients are willing to come online one time in their night hours, why should we object. We escaped from a night shift." Sasha joined in with her giggles.

"Lucky you, but unlucky me!", she scoffed. "Over that you and your dumb cave!"

I smiled to express my thought, "If I had night shift, I wouldn't have been here now, also".

She pursed her lips tightly, "True that!"

I ruffled her bangs fondly, "At the end it all worked out good. Let's hope our lucky streak continues ahead."

"Hope so!", she looked up with optimistic eyes and lifted her hands ti show her crossed fingers.

After our late lunch, we decided to make use of the day off and went to a recreational park to while away the evening. Strolling down the jogging path, hand in hand we enjoyed the breezy air. Admiring the way a group of kids were playing in the park, our conversations weaved around them.

After a while of silence, Sasha spoke. "I was thinking, if I am found guilty, the only option, I have, to revive my shattered career would be to go abroad for higher education."

I nodded my head in understanding but the fear of losing her was building up a storm within me.

"I hope I'm able to get admissions before the term starts. I need to start doing my research on the admission, competitive entrance exams and visa processing". She scoffed, "Who would have thought that I would be pushed into doing this all of a sudden."

I just hummed and nodded my head to her rhetorical statement.

"I hope everything falls in place atleast in my higher education plans", she slummed down onto a bench.

Now it was my turn to cross my fingers behind my back, "Hope so". Internally praying to God to help solve the office issue so that she could retain her job.

We departed after calling off the long day we had. Dropping her off at her home at the stroke of seven, just like how any other official day would end. We grabbed take away dinner parcels to have at our respective homes.

Laying down on my bed, I looked at the clock by my bedside. One day down, two more to go.

Early next morning, I actually visited a temple nearby. Surprising not only Vicky but myself. I performed a small prayer there and made some donations to aged and downtrodden kids available there.

We didn't meet up today as I didn't want to disturb her when she was preparing for her next move. I did check up on her from time-to-time. Around nightfall, my message tone beeped. Picking it up, I saw the message from our office admin helpdesk team. It stated that everyone's expected to report to office the next day and the branch will operate with business as usual.

My first instinct was a Yippee!, then it downed on me, What if Sasha didn't recieve the message?? Before I could dwell on it more, Sasha's incoming voice call came. Sliding my finger to accept the call, I attended it.

"Raghav!", she yelled in excitement, "Did you get the SMS calling all of us back to work? Looks like the issue is solved and the virus has been removed", her happiness bounced was all over the place.

Letting out a relieving sigh, I smiled into the phone wishing it should have been a video call instead.

Thank God she also received it. What if it was a bulk message, in that case all employees would have got it, by default.

"Sasha, did your manager or anyone from network security team contact you or update anything to you?" I asked to get rid of the uncertainty overshadowing us.

"Yup! Manoj called and said that he had something to discuss with me tomorrow. There's nothing to worry about he confirmed."

"That's great to hear!"

"I know right! Finally some ray of sunshine after the past few dark gloomy days.... Ok see you tomorrow at office." We hung up after biding adieu.

The next day at office, an official announcement regarding the recent events was going to held at ten thirty in the morning. Their intention was to put a stop to all gossips as early as possible. All the curious folks flooded the cafeteria, which was the main venue. A webcast of the same would be shared so employees could he part of it from their very desks. Sasha had to attend it and we all tagged along.

The head of the network security team took over the podium, to state the facts. It was revealed that the virus was brought into our network during an external audit. The external auditor while submitting his audit findings report via email, his email's signature was sent as an attachment that had malicious content. The audit firm has been financially penalized heavily and all contracts are cut off. They refrained on disclosing any further details.

He went on to state that no employee played any role in the security breach. This statement declaration eased all our residual suspicions. Suddenly Sasha's name was called out in the microphone, alerting all of us. She turned to look at us with alarm in her eyes. Just when we thought everything was settling down, a new tide was pushed over to us.

The voice from the microphone was heard loud and clear.

"I would like to take this opportunity to highlight a scenario wherein an employee stood with the company's integrity even though they could've backed off. The responsibility and agility shown by the employee is commendable. It also goes without saying a simple action of reporting anything suspicious can safeguard our network from falling prey to any security breaches, be it — malware, phishing, Denial of service or any kind of passive attacks. Each and every attack needs to be reported and not taken lightly.

We as a team need everyone's support in it. Our team can improve our cyber security based on your inputs, so don't ever feel that you are reporting a small issue. Like they say 'a stitch in time saves nine', that's exactly what happened two days earlier when Ms. Sasha Hedge reported a suspicious email. When we all thought we have only one threat at hand, it wasn't the case. Our organization had two cyber attacks on the same day. Thanks to Ms. Sasha Hedge's swift action of forwarding the malicious email to the spam helpdesk, appropriate actions were taken to avoid further attempts. Luckily it was reported early and not many had checked their inbox.

The whole organization is in debt to her and salute her for the brave front she put up when she was under our scanner. "

Another person spoke from an adjacent microphone, "Huge applause to Ms. Sasha Hedge, the entire network security team, spam helpdesk team, leadership team and each and everyone who worked and toiled towards safeguarding our organization from the cyber threats."

Roar of claps echoed in the cafeteria.

Whoever is hearing this via the webcast with headphones, God save them.

Where we thought Sasha would be terminated and here she turned out to be the savior of the day, yet again. Simply we stressed ourselves with our overthinking.

I chuckled reminiscing how she had saved me one morning. It all started from there, leading to a string of events of getting acquainted with the now super star of the organization.

As the applause died, the same executive, continued to speak. "If we haven't fallen prey to such attacks, each and every employee also deserves an applause and pat on their back for being vigilant." This lead to another roar. "With this we come to the end of our announcement, thank you all for your time."

Employees started exiting the cafeteria but the crowd stopped abruptly to some musical beats being played in the speakers. A group of men and women walked over criss cross, before us. At the strikes of three drumstick count ins, they stopped, turned around and took their position. Spotting some familiar faces from the employee dance group, I understood that they had organized a flash mob. It was a really good idea to rejoice and uplift the mood in the office; a warm re-welcome to our office routine.

Spectators started recoding it in their mobile phones, as it was in the reception area and there were no videography constraints in that area. Others clapped along with the music in a rhythm, enjoying it and encouraging the dancer. How they had managed to pull it out off on such a short span of time and execute it with perfection, was beyond my imagination. It looked like they had practiced it for some other occasion but utilized it today.

I turned to search for Sasha and found her thoroughly enjoying the dance performance. Her face lit up in joy, in contrast to her saddened state ever since the cyber attack. Such kind of activities was the need of the hour to release the past day's tensions and who else needed it the most other than Sasha.

I should plan something special for Sasha too.

What should I do?

23

CHAPTER 23

Raghav's POV

song:Caught my heart about one, two timesDon't need to question the reason I'm yours, I'm yoursI'd move the earth or lose a fight just to see you smile'Cause you got no flaws, no flaws.

The official dance group's flash mob turned out to be a good stress buster and Sasha also seemed to have enjoyed it a lot. That sent the wheels in my brain rotating, Why shouldn't I surprise Sasha with one, specially for her?

Make her feel special. Make her feel my love for her. Might be then all the Realtionship based Vitamin deficiency she is having, would vanish.

Giving myself a pat on my back, I set out to put my idea rolling.

All I need now is volunteers..... How about Sasha's hulks and my friends??

After giving it a thought I rejected the idea. Firstly, her hulks wouldn't be able to keep it a secret from her. Secondly, none of us had any dancing bone in our body. I was sure of Vicky and Asim having two left feet, just like me. We were fit only for off-beat dancing. We would all end up making it a disaster or the most, like a gym warm-up routine. It would result in us having second hand embarrassment and nothing else.

No way! It had to be perfect.

I can't approach the same dance group as I wasn't acquainted with them on a one-one basis. The next option was our portfolio's dance group. That would be easier, as I knew most of them and could convince them for it.

Do I need to be part of the flash mob? Of course, you dufus! Are you going to stand in the sidelines and do nothing? Then what difference does the one we just saw and the one you are arranging now?

Sighing, I persuaded myself to actively participate in it and boosted my morale saying it was 'All for Sasha'. Moreover I wouldn't be dancing alone, a bunch of people will surround me and do the same steps. Even if I fumble or mess up with the moves, I could just copy others. I could also request them to keep simpler moves that I would be comfortable in. After all flash mobs were based on simple and easy dance moves, nothing extravagant.

Good! One problem solved.

I got the group together and they were kind enough to help me out. With a promise of a treat, they provided their consent. We met up at the recreation room to chose the songs and the dance routine was being choreographed. They were excited for the non-official flash mob giving them more liberty for their creativity. The plan was to practice after office hours or evening coffee break and execute it in the park adjacent to our block, on a weekend. It would be awkward and unprofessional to have a personalized flash mob during the week in the office premises, with mammoth of prying eyes. I'm not doing it for show.

My dance mates had left, leaving me alone to toil with the steps. I had to learn to sync my moves with the music.

You can do it, Raghav! Practice makes man perfect.

I continued rehearsing on my own when a voice behind me put me to an a abrupt stop.

"What are you doing, Raghav?", Sasha asked from the half-open door. Stepping in inside she sat near the music system and looked at me.

"Hmmm, nothing", I reacted. "Just warming up for my workout". I said and immediately started hopping on the spot and doing chest expansion exercises.

"Why here? Why not in the gym behind?", Sasha pointed her thumb backwards to the next room.

"Uhhh, I—", I was cutoff by a new entrant into the room.

"Hey, relax Raghav, don't overdo it. Don't worry you'll do fine on the flash mob". One of my dance mates returned to grab their flask and towel and departed putting me on the hot spot.

"Do you want to explain something to me over here?", Sasha queried.

I tried to improvise but couldn't. So much for the surprise!

Coming out clean, "We were practising for an upcoming flash mob."

"Wow! That's cool!", Sasha clasped her hands in excitement. "I also want in!"

"What?", my eyes doubled at her.

"Ya, we can do it together. I'm sure they won't mind me joining in. 'The More, the merrier', is usually any flash mob's motto". Sasha shrugged and stood in line with me. "Come on, teach me! Let me catch up with the steps", she urged.

Oh God, how did I land into this situation!

With no other go, I showed her the moves of one song and we danced together. It was good to be with her but it ruined my plan. Later I informed the others to abort our romantic flash mob and remodel it for official purpose. We customized it to exhibit the hype of the upcoming Year End event. After daily practice sessions for three days, we executed it in our floor and had a blast. It might not gone as planned but it did half it's job — making Sasha happy.

It's time for my next plan! This time I'm going to be direct and hit the nail on the head. There's not going to be two ways to it.Simple, sweet and to the point!

After thorough exploration, researching and conducting people's survey for the best celebration cake shops, nearby; I went along with the popular demand. Finalizing on blueberry ganache cake, the glossy blueish-purple ganache covering the top and dripping over the sides, gave it a nice finis. Decoration were kept minimal with elongated triangular chocolate wafers, with zebra criss-crosses on it along with where few fresh medium sized strawberries dipped in chocolate coating, clustered at one end. White butter frosting were piped in the form of roses along the cake's circumference and piped in waves to form the border at the bottom. My personalized touch was the message of the cake.

"Will you be my Girlfriend"

song:I'm not tryna be your part time loverSign me up for that full time, I'm yours, all yours.

On inspection of the delivered cake, it was the perfect image of my instructions to the tee. All I had to do is request one of the stalls in the cafeteria to keep it in the fridge for sometime. Luckily, they agreed and had place for it in the refrigerator.

Wow! This is so easy, heaving a relieved sigh.

The restless me called everyone for an early evening coffee break around four thirty. The gang assembled at a table while I went to get the one kilogram, blueberry cake with my proposal on it. Excitement nervousness and the pounding of my heart increased with every step I took, towards the said table, with the cake parcel in my hands. Others were also clueless of my surprise.

Placing the parcel in front of Sasha, "For you", I smiled at her from across the table.

Sasha's skeptical response came out, "For me?" and she hurriedly went on to open the box carefully. I held my breath for her reaction.

"Oh, Raaaagav! It's lovely", she let out a sigh of longing, admiring the cake.

Giving her time to read through my message in white icing, I stood still. A minute passed, two minutes went by; still nothing. A wave of caution rushed through my blood.

That's it? That was her reaction??

song: So what a man gotta do?What a man gotta do?To be totally locked up by youWhat a man gotta say?What a man gotta pray?To be your last "Goodnight" and your first "Good day".

My puzzled brain had been put to rest with the reveal of the cake out of it's box. Like a jigsaw puzzle solved, the sight in front of me answered my doubts. My proposal was lost into the wade of pool of white icing meshed with the ganache. For the uninformed onlookers it looked like a whirlpool of some abstract art similar to acrylic pour painting at the centre of the cake.

I internally face-palmed. So much for thinking it would be a piece of cakewalk. This is the reason they say don't jinx yourself.

Sasha plucked the chocolate coated strawberry and bit into it; oblivious to the sensual vibes it sent across to me. Smirking at her crunching into the juicy crimson exotic berry, I thrust my hands into my pockets to keep myself in check.

"What's the occasion?", she asked with the half bitten strawberry in her hand.

AJ standing beside her was hastily setting up the knife and plates. "Like it matters! A delicious looking cake is in front of you, waiting to be cut. Can you just do the honors, so that the starving folks at dig into it. Keep your Q&A (Question and Answer) session for later". He pleaded with his mouth watering and thirsty eyes glued onto the cake; while making all of us chuckle.

"Yes, go ahead Sasha. It's —It's for emerging out as the 'Wonder Woman' from the cyber threat", I covered up.

Sasha did the cake cutting, as we cheered for her. She sliced a piece and leant over the table to feed me. AJ sucked his breathe in horror and shifed the cafe. It was on the verge of getting smashed onto Sasha's royal blue with white stripes nylon shirt thrown over a white t-shirt as a shrug. I shook my head in amusement and came forward to take the offered slice of cake. Holding her wrist, I bit into it and fed her back, while tiding the cream smudged off her lower lip.

Then came the blood bath in the form of cream. Everyone battled to get a chance to smear cream onto Sasha's face. I was against wastage of food in such sort of display of affection or fun. Food is food, meant to be devoured not thrown across. Briefly stealing a glance around us, thankful that her hulks didn't go over the top on it and settled for one decent strike on her face; maintaining our decorum at office.

All went back to their plates of cake. I looked over at Sasha's white cream streaked face, like a soldier prepped up with his white camouflage, instead of black. Letting out a short laugh, I handed her a paper napkin to wipe it off. Few minutes ago, I was fussing over a small smudge and now her face was buried in them. The cake was a hit with all, but not for me.

Another flop plan! God! When am I going to taste success?!

I hadn't given up yet. Next few days went by, in thinking for better fool-proof ideas. I pumped myself up, Don't worry, Third time's a charm! One evening was well spent on shopping for the items required to set up my third plan. I glanced at the purchase enclosed inside the shopping bags, This plan better not back-fire. I said to myself and let sleep consume over me.

Arriving early to office to execute the plan, I went over to her desk with the shopping bags. 'Decorate her desk' surprise was full on roll. I placed two boxes of chocolates, neatly gift wrapped, along with a basket of self watered multicolored Gerberas flowers, on either sides of her computer. Purposely I didn't opt for the clichéd roses, as I could literally see Sasha's cringed face. The multicolored flowers were a reflection of how colorful she had turned my life into. Blowing out few white and blue balloons, I stuck them, alternatively on the rim of her wing's panel.

Taking a step back to get a glimpse of my hardwork, a satisfied smile spread across my face. The decorations looked obvious and stuck out from the strict office atmosphere surrounding her cubicle. As soon as one stepped into the wing, their eyes would catch it.

It's ok, no need to feel awkward. Let them think it's some sort of bay decoration activity.

I only hope, Sasha will like it and not go mad at me for pulling such a stunt.

Drumming impatiently over my desk, my eyed fixed at the wing's entrance anxiously waiting for Sasha to arrive. I didn't want to miss any part of her reaction. It was few minutes past ten, in the morning and Sasha walked through the door. With each step, her smile grew, lighting up her face.

That's the reception I wanted for my surprise.

My eyed followed her like a shadow. When she passed my bay, I stood up, and so did my eyebrows.

What the —?

Her cubicle really looked like the epitome for a bay decoration competition. It had shimmering streamers attached from the ceiling to her cubicle, in the form of a pyramid. A beautiful handicraft colorful paper lantern hung at the middle of the pyramid.

I didn't do this?, my eyes squinted at the hanging decorations.

I strode towards her and found her team mates singing birthday songs and wishing her. My head whipped so hard that I would have cracked my neck. The shocks never seem to sieze.

How the hell did I not know her Birthday!?!

I cursed myself mentally. On the other hand, gratefully I had come up with my surprise today, which came handy. Otherwise, I would have looked like a clueless, empty handed idiot. Her teammates also knew her birthday. My decorations blended with theirs, appearing to be like a team effort. I sighed in desperation, things weren't going as planned. I couldn't slump due to my failure, the birthday had to be cherished.

"Happy Birthday Sasha!", I wished her wholeheartedly. "May your following days till forever, be filled with happiness, love, good health and prosperity."

"Thank you Raghav!", she smiled back at me.

Sasha's teammates seemed to have informed her about the gifts I had placed on her desk. She hopped onto her spot on my desk with the chocolate box.

"Thank you so much for these. How did you know it was my birthday today?". She casually asked while popping a chocolate ball into her mouth.

"Just an intuition", I shrugged with small smile.

She wanted to question further but got diverted due to the new flavors that bursted in her mouth.

"These are really yummm. I'm having second thoughts of sharing them with you or anyone". Her honest opinion came out and she clutched the box, safeguarding it from getting snatched away.

Chuckling away, when my head was back to it's position, I said, "It's all yours, enjoy it!"

"Oh trust me I am enjoying it!", she squeaked happily

Me too, my inner voice echoed in my mind, while flashing a hundred watt grin to Sasha.

The note with my confession that I had to slip on to the flower bouquet, was shelved safely inside my trouser's pocket. Ready to be used whenever my next plan of action would roll out. The day flew by with people showering gifts, phone calls, memories with Sasha posted on their social media platforms or as status updates; making the woman ruling my heart be overwhelmed by their love and care.

Let's make the best use of today and end it with a bang!

Chuck the 'surprise' element, our fondness for each other wasn't hidden. It doesn't have to be a surprise to make her feel special.

Holding on to this thought, I invited Sasha to have a cozy dinner with me. I booked a place for a romantic candle lit dinner. We drove into the place and parked the car. The theme based restaurant had a handful of open tree houses, providing the privacy and customizing facility anyone planning for a special evening, could die for. The restaurant beneath the tree houses had decor none lesser in comparison. With open air tables and closed indoor setup options available to choose from.

The maître de ushered us inside and accompanied us to our reserved tree house. The sandy pathway leading to it was bordered with white peebles and diamond shaped solar bricks garden lights on either sides. The illuminated sodium light on the ground and from the lined up twine sphere lanterns overhead alternated with crumpled solar fairy lights trapped inside clear mason jars, depicted a romantic outdoor wedding decor.

I gulped at the sight of it, it's beautiful but was it a little too much for my Tom-Boy Sasha?

Had I known, it would ooze romance and intimacy at every corner of this restaurant, I would have skipped it. I should have known better than to fall for Vicky's suggestion.

The light, from veils of fairy lights in high-low strings, roughly knotted at the edges, was sufficient to aide us in climbing the steps up to the tree house. Inside the tree house was a waiting table and two staff at the corner, where they would assemble our order and one dining table right across it, at the farther end. The breezy air provided the required ventilation. Portable air conditioner with ducts along it's length and bamboo shutters served as substitutes for uncomfortable days.

I could sense the awkwardness of Sasha from beside me. Nearing our table it had two tea candles enclosed within an ornamental Moroccan candle holder. Throwing the light out off it, in symmetrical patterns. At the centre of the table sat a glass dome with a red rose spiraled with sparsely spread out fairy lights, resting on a wooden base. The resemblance to the enchanted red rose from the Beauty and the Beast fairy tale was unbelievable. The tree house was caged with strings of fairy lights scrunched up and lights twinkling from mason jars doubled as lanterns.

Oh God! I wanted to keep it simple and here Sasha would think I went bonkers for putting this together.

"Ma'am", the maître de pulled out a chair for Sasha which seemed to have pulled the two of us from the daze we had fallen into. Sasha smiled and took her seat. While setting the menu card, he said, "The enchanted rose is a souvenir for your stay here, feel free to carry it along when you depart. Feel free to set the music up from your mobiles either from our playlist printed on the last page of the menu or directly from your own device. The music system is wifi operated, the wifi credentials have been sent to the registered number used for the booking. If you have any more specific instructions, let us know. The two stewards at the corner can be asked to exit for complete privacy—"

"No!", I objected within seconds. Calming my voice down, I added, "Thank you. Let them stay".

He smiled back at me, "Hope you enjoy your evening" and left us in each other's company.

The patterns cast on Sasha's face from the candle light made it tough to gauge her expressions.

Breaking the silence engulfing us, 'Ummm, you are awfully quiet ever since we stepped foot in the restaurant. Are you comfortable?"

"Huh! Yes—yes I'm fine. Just caught up in the venue's settings...", Sasha trailed off.

"If you aren't comfortable, we can make a move and go somewhere else", I suggested.

"I didn't mean that".

She's trying to console me when I put her through discomfort.

"I know Sasha". Her silence and stammering made it clear, she felt out of place. I wanted to bang my head to the wall for making her feel like that on her birthday.

"Let's do one thing, we'll order a drink and leave the place. Grab —", I was cut off.

"Why?", Sasha whined making my eyebrows rise. "It's.... This pl ace..... This place is beautiful and out of the world." It took Sasha considerable amount of effort to come to terms with the words splurred out of her mouth. "I haven't been to such a place my entire life..... I know it's polar opposite to my choice or liking but once in awhile it feels good to visit such places". Sending across a genuine smile, she placed her hand over mine and gave it a squeeze. "Thank you so much for bringing me here and making me feel special. It would not have crossed anyone's mind to take out a girl like me to such a fancy place".

Shaking my head in disagreement, for the discrimination Sasha thought she encountered in the eyes of potential suitors. "I beg to differ. The reason why you might not have been brought to such a place has to do with the fact, that the person thought you wouldn't enjoy it. It has nothing to do with you, don't belittle yourself for it."

She scoffed, "Hey it's not like I had a line of suitors for me and nor was I interested in all that".

"Huh?", a spontaneous sound escaped my lips, making her rephrase.

"Nor was I interested in all that, at that time", she emphasized.

"That sounds better", I gave a satisfied nod.

song: You ain't tryna be wasting timeOn stupid people in cheap lines, I'm sure, I'm sureSo I'd give a million dollars just for you to grab me by the collarAnd I'll come build us, build us.

Sasha rolled her eyes and went to add on. "Back to what I was saying.... If it had been anyone else in your shoes, I will bet my money on it; they wouldn't have even thought of bringing me here even if this was their hot favorite."

She was dead serious but all that traveled into my ear and up to my brain cells were, 'If it had been anyone else in your shoes'. After that everything else went blank, pitch black and her voice was muted with only her lips moving. It felt like she was talking into vacuum.

Once her upper and lower lip met each other, I took it as my cue and blurted out. "Why would someone else be in my shoes?", slight undertones of annoyance evident in my voice.

"Oh God, Raghav! That's what you got, from what I said?", she asked hotly.

"Yup! That's of utmost importance right now!", I asserted.

Sasha laughed at my hard expression. "Oh Raghav! You and your pet peeves."

"You haven't answered my question yet?", softening up my tone I asked.

"And what is it?", she tried acting naive.

"Why would you want someone else to be in my shoes?"

"Hmmm it was a generalized observation made for all Tom-Boy's."

"Ok, ok. You are off the hook", I jested. "So you like the place, we can —"

"Raghav, I said it's good to visit it 'once in a while'. Too much of this over-the- top settings will make me puke." She patted my hand before going back to the menu card.

"Puke! Who's going to Puke here? Man! I thought they serve good food here". The familiar male voice bursted the bubble we were in and made us refocus onto the entrance, from where the sound originated.

With that our secluded tree house was infiltrated by four hulks, making their way towards us. I could picture them walking in a slow motion dance walk.

Busted!Just when things were falling in place, these devils had to come to wreck it.

Matching the voice to the face, I deduced it was AJ's remark earlier. Rohit signaled to the stewards for four more chairs, like as if he owned the place. The chairs were brought in no time and our cute candle light dinner table suddenly felt crowded with two of the intruders on each side of us.

Great! They were not passing clouds but were here to stay.

AJ and Rohit were on one side, while Simbu and Daniel on the other, with AJ and Simbu sitting closer to me. I schooled my facial expressions and smiled at them. "Thank you guys for coming", I forced the words out like a dentist plucking out a wisdom tooth.

"Really?", Daniel raised a questioning brow. "And here we thought we came uninvited". He mumbled under his breathe while scanning through the menu. I had caught it but Sasha's preoccupied mind didn't.

I thought Daniel was my supporter?, my suspicions invaded my mind.

Simbu apparently read my thoughts and he whispered, "You got it wrong, none of us are your supporters". After jolting my thoughts with his words, he sat back leaning on the back rest.

AJ winked at me and said, "We know what you've been trying to do. It's not going to be so easy for you to take away our precious Sasha." His tone was soft and hardly above a whisper but had an underlying warning.

Sweeping my eyes across the table, I perceived their actions.

If these three had taken a three sixty degree flip, there were no qualms that Rohit would follow suit. In fact, there were high chances of him being the leader to their pack, in their new found game. I felt like I was on a see-saw, sometimes high up and immediately pulled down my gravitational force.

Superb! Me versus four protective guys, that's the last thing I needed. So much for being happy that she didn't have any over protective brother. Now I had to deal with not one but FOUR.

With no other go we placed our orders and had our so called 'candle light dinner' with Sasha across the table and our four intruders. They played their role to the tee. Anytime I tried making a conversation with Sasha, one of them would butt in. They wouldn't let me even pass a dish to her directly, mid-way someone's hand would take it from me and pass it to her. The R for Romance was changed to R for Ruin, all credits goes to her hulks! Sasha didn't seem to get a whiff of their conspiracy. She thought I had invited them along with her for the dinner —for a candle light dinner! Sasha how could you be so naive??! I let it pass considering it was her birthday and played along their ploy.

At the end of the meal, Sasha excused herself to the ladies room, located in the main indoor hall of the restaurant. Leaving me behind with four muscular men, with a love song playing in the background.

Rohit's confrontation came first."Sorry bro, for giving you a hard time". All I could do react was with a tight smile in his direction. He continued, "But what did you think, we would go easy on you, huh?"

AJ spoke before I opened my mouth. "Not happening, dude. We couldn't just let anyone steal our Sasha away and risk her on getting walked over by a man. We know our breed well and need to protect her."

A sudden thought crossed my mind,Is it due to their meddling ways that Sasha was still single?Not everyone would like to be on the receiving end of heavy scrutiny, with four men go all ape on them.

"Obviously not Rohit! He is the closest to her. He just couldn't let you scoop in and take her away from us", Daniel elaborated.

"I wasn't planning on that", I said honestly. I had come to treat them as my bro's just like Vicky and Asim, before they pulled this stunt.

"To clear the air, we see her as our sister cum friend. Nothing to worry about us including me", Rohit said. He let out a short laugh. "The funny thing is, we go to her for our love advice. I know! What can we do, she's the closest we can ever get to for a lady's insights on things." He shrugged while others hummed in agreement and burst into laughter at their predicament.

She is their love expert but when it comes to her, it's like she is a toddler attending kindergarten for the same subject.

"I came to know that at a later stage. However, I can't deny the fact, that he did give me sleepless nights at the beginning....". Pointing an accusing finger to Rohit. "....With all the 'Sash', 'Rosh', jerseys and the possessiveness and all". I listed out all the times I had been put into a dilemma due to Rohit.

He waved his hand dismissively, "I can't help it, we were in her life before you, so you might have to deal with it. For the record, I was being protective of Sasha like a little sister, whose shoes she filled in for me". He went in to sudden silence like recollecting something in the back of his mind.

Not giving it much a thought, I asked, "Why all this, now?" Gesturing to their agenda of disrupting our dinner date.

"We wanted you to sweat it out a little", AJ chuckled.

"A one-on-one discussion with you to know your intentions for Sasha, was a long pending job", Daniel responded in a serious tone.

"Bro, this is no way a one-on-one discussion", I stated, encircling my hand in the air over the table.

"You obviously know what he is implying". Simbu said in a no nonsense tone, making me look at him in a different light.

Huh?! The usually tight lipped guy seemed to be in a different mood all together. Like they say beware of the silent killers.

I gulped down water from my tumbler and said, "Ok, hit me up with all your questions. I didn't realize I was under your surveillance, nor did I expect such an interrogation. Nevertheless I'm ready, so shoot, whatever you need to ask". Folding my hands, I reclined on my chair exuding confidence. I wasn't going to whimper in front of them. Even if confronted with hundred replicas of them, I could stand my ground, as I didn't have any wrong intentions for Sasha.

They seemed impressed. Yay! Raghav score 1, Hulks score 0. I maintained a mental scorecard and updated it after each shot fired.

Sasha's entry put an abrupt end to the interrogation which was almost as it's closure. My eyes moved between her walking figure and her Hulks. She was all rough and tough at the exterior but had an untainted fragile heart. That's when it downed on me that these guys saw her as one among themselves but protected her with all their heart. They say Blood is thicker than water but their friendship ran way deeper.

How many people had been put under their vigilance?

The count didn't bother me. One thing was sure, I would be their last specimen.

I was here to stay!

Walking towards the steward's waiting table to pay the bill, a photograph hung on the hall of fame board caught my eye. It was of Vicky with his arm secured tightly around a pretty lady's waist, pulling her into his side. They were a picture perfect happy couple. The lady had a bunch of red roses in her hand.

"Vicky?!", I blurted out, it caught the attention of steward who was busy formulating the bill.

"You know him?", the steward asked.

"Yes! What's his photo doing here? Who's that girl with him?"

"That's really nice, then you must be a friend of Vicky.... They were our first customers to inaugurate this tree house concept in this restaurant. In fact, the enchanted red rose at the table is inspired by the golden couple, as we used to call them. He made it at this very place to gift his girlfriend".

Wow! This was news to me. Vicky, his girlfriend, the romantic side of him.

"They were our frequent visitors and due to them we gained popularity. Needless to say, his enchanted rose gift became an instant hit with our customers. The bottom of the wooden panel has his name as the proprietor. We sometimes customize them to engrave our customer's names, if requested".

While I was starring shell shocked at the framed photograph, the steward rambled on.

Might be this would shed some light on Vicky's love life, that he had successfully kept under wraps from me.

"You know where they are? They haven't visited us in years. They are ok, right? We just assumed they relocated or went abroad."

"Vicky is fine, he's the one who suggested this place to me."

"That's really humble of him. We are providing you ten percent discount on the bill, as you are Vicky's friend", the steward stated with a smile. "A more generous discount would be applicable if Vicky Sir would have been here. Try to bring him here, our eyes and this place is missing our golden couple. If they re-visit, tell them, their bill is on the house."

I blinked at him in astonishment. The way he spoke of the couple in question, it seemed they embodied the Romeo-Juliet kind of love. The steward had no idea that their most loved couple also faced the tragic end of Romeo and Juliet. I put on a small smile and thanked him for the discount.

Pulling out my card, Rohit stopped me. "We will pay for us, you can pay for Sasha and yourself". My protests died down my throat with his stance. He really could be intimidating.

Sasha picked up her enhanted rose gift and held it hugging to herself. She looked happy and relaxed. Her smile was all that I had aimed for, the remaining half of my plans to woo her —my proposal, could be done in due course of time.

After all a man had to take some time off to sharpen his skills after four failures in a row.

My plans turned out to be just like an half boiled egg. I would strive to perfect them.

song:So what a man gotta do?What a man gotta do?To be totally locked up by youWhat a man gotta do?What a man gotta prove?To be totally locked up by you.

24

CHAPTER 24

Raghav's POV

song: Take my hand, take a breathPull me close and take one stepKeep your eyes locked on mineAnd let the music be your guide.

The entire office was in festival mode and the week long year end celebrations were in full swing. Multiple events taking place at the same time in different venues of the office. The two blocks that were occupied by our company in this huge IT campus had a cheerful cloud on it. Other company's employees looked at the grand entrances of our blocks with envy. Obviously when their companies had such functions, it would be our turns to burn in jealousy. Like a baton passed around the companies, they made sure their annual events didn't clash with others, due to the space constraints of the shared campus.

Green and blue balloons tangled together to form arches, welcomed us at the entrance. The reception area was also adorned with balloon decorations and glittering cutouts of i-Fest 2019 stuck on the wall. Major events were listed on roll up banner displays, stationed at prominent places for awareness.

Vicky came up to Asim's desk and turned towards me. "Let's participate in some event, it'll be fun. I heard today's the last day for the registration of treasure hunt and prelims will start after lunch. Shall we send our nominations for it?" He placed his hand in Asim's shoulder to catch his attention too.

"Hmmmmm. These events only freshers and juniors participate. We will look odd, let them enjoy. This is the only time they can. Later when they become seniors like us drowned with work, they won't get a chance". I replied back looking at my desktop, busy typing away an email.

"Oh come on man, don't make us sound like oldies. We still have young blood. So what if we are seniors, there are no restrictions on who can participate. It's for all employees, even if the CEO wants he can!" Vicky fought back.

"Why do you even want to participate now, all of a sudden?", Asim questioned him, titling his head to look up to him.

"It's been years since we all are together during the annual fest. Don't know when we will get this opportunity later. Don't be a spoil sport now! Come on you lazy asses." Vicky grumbled.

"Ok ok fine. I'm in", I surrendered.

"We need five people in a team as per the rules", Asim stated with his hands folded.

"That's not going to be a problem", Vicky dismissed him with his hand. "We can loop in Bala and -".

Asim cut him off, "Each team needs to have a girl in it to qualify". Vicky's eye gleamed with mischief and I knew what it indicated. Before Vicky could open his mouth, Asim beat him to it. "And no Sasha can't be the girl".

"Why?", came my instant objection.

Asim turned to me with an amused look. "It's because she's already participating in it with her gang. You didn't know?"

"Daniel and Simbu too? They are from different portfolios so how can they be part of the same team? Isn't it a competion between portfolios and at the end the one with most points lifts the championship trophy?" I questioned.

"The competition is still there but they have modified the rules. For off-stage events employees from different portfolios can participate together as a team to foster employee bondings. This has always been the case, didn't you know that, Raghav?" Asim creased out my doubts.

"Ya, I didn't know, never gave those rules a second look" I shrugged and said in a wooden tone.

"So what, Chitra can join us. I'll ask Bala and Chitra, you go ahead and send the nominations". Vicky said to Asim while fishing out his phone to make the calls.

He gave the green signal to Asim, in the form of a thumbs up, after ending the second call. Asim clicked on the send button of the ready-to-go drafted mail. Our nominations were sent in the nick of time before closure of registrations for it. The organizers of the treasure hunt event sent out a reminder to all participating teams. In which, it stated that, the link to questionaire for the prelims will be sent out at 3:30 pm IST on the dot and responses recieved by 4 o'clock will only be eligible.

As soon as the 'Race against time' quiz link made it's entry to our mailboxes, we all swarmed onto Asim's desk to solve it. The first eight teams with highest correct responses would make it through to win a spot for the actual event. The results were announced after an hour and luckily our team and Sasha's team made it through. The qualified teams and their participants were listed on in the announcement mail. Seeing Sasha's hulk's names, a fire ignited within me.

See you there, hulks! This time the battleground is fair and square. Last time I was caught off guard, now let's see who wins.

I had to avenge them for the debacle they brought on my romantic candle light dinner with Sasha. The event would be kicked off at ten in the morning, the following day and the teams were asked to assemble at the designated starting point of the treasure hunt - the reception.

Gearing up for the treasure hunt to start, we were chatting away and sizing up our competitors. Sasha walked up to me and pat my shoulder from behind me. She pulled me slightly to the corner and asked in a hushed tone.

"Is there something between Vicky and Chitra?", nudging her head towards them.

Briefly glancing at Vicky and Chitra having a private conversation, I looked back at Sasha. "No, that was just to trick us. To satisfy the rules of minimum one girl per team, Vicky called her."

Sasha nodded her hand and was interrupted by her message tone. While she was looking into it, my eyes averted back to Vicky and Chitra. They seemed to have entered into a heated argument with Chitra leaving his side in fumes.

Could it be?

I opened my phone and went to the photo I had successfully snucked to click at the restaurant.

The girl in the photo isn't Chitra. Who was she?

Sasha's words dragged me out of my sneaky detective thoughts. "You know, you guys are going to lose, right!" She stated in confidence as she tipped on her black cap secured on her head. "We are the reigning champions. Last year we had a jolt and ended up as runners up. After that setback, we are fully charged up to take back our crown and we will are going to fight tooth and nail for it".

I chuckled to say, "It's just a game, Sasha".

"Yes, but don't think I'll go soft on you. This is competition and it means war", she stated with her chin up.

Letting out another short laugh, I accepted the challenge. "Ok, bring it on! May the best man -uh best team, win".

"We will see". On that note we shook hands and went back to join our respective teams.

Vicky narrowed his eyes on me, "Put your head in the game. You are the weak link of this team".

Feeling insulted I spat out, "And, how is that?"

"Obviously, with your 'Ms. Sneakers' and her magical effect on you", he shrugged and pushed his hands into his pockets.

I snorted and rolled my eyes.

"Huh! What was I telling? .... Yeah, if I see you pull our team down and we lose, I won't let you in the house". He warned me with an intense stare, his competitive streak mode was switched on.

"Hey, that's my home if you are forgetting". I stood up to him closer and jabbed my chest, stifling my laugh.

"Whatever! Make sure we win", he left after a brisk thud on my back.

The organizers asked one representative from each team to walk up to collect the first clue of the treasure hunt, without opening it. Once they fell in place with their teams, with the blow of the whistle, all opened the chit to read the starting clue.

"#1 ~ It all started over here"

The buzzing murmurs started erupting in the reception area as everyone started guessing the location of the next clue.

The main gate of the whole IT Campus, the reception area we were in, training rooms, the auditorium that doubled as an induction room on employees day of joining; were some of the options we thought of. Hunters from other teams had already started making a move. Some searched the reception area, while we stood in a circle like a rugby team crowding up to strategize.

Chitra complained, "Hurry up guys! Look at the other teams, they have already started searching. I didn't accept to join a loosing team". She ended with a groan, folding her arms.

Vicky rolled his eyes, "Oh God! Who did I choose for my team!" and grunted.

"Ya right! You are the one to be blamed. You have a good track record of making all the wrong decisions". She bickered back, making me wonder if this was an extension of their earlier argument.

"Guys! GUYS! Chill, let's focus on the game, alright". I tried playing the water to cease the fire catching up.

"Yes, Raghav's right", Asim agreed. Turning to Chitra he said, "Chitra, like they say - slow and steady wins the race. And who else will know better than Raghav, the brand ambassador of it". His short laugh gained momentum as others joined him. I shot a lazer gaze at him, for his explicit reference to my love story, which everyone seemed to have picked up so quickly.

While the four of us were busy coming up with rebuts like we are at a face off competition, where the person with the witty remarks or one liners would win; Bala was trying to solve the clue. The snap from his fingers, made all of us shift our eyes to him.

He said barely above a whisper, motioning us to cuddle up more, to avoid getting eavesdroped. "I found it, it's the training room at our mother campus..... In the beginning while announcing the rules they said the clues could be anywhere in this whole IT campus, not limited to only our two blocks but also remaining ten blocks. They also said it could be at our next door parent company's campus. "

Asim added,"Yeah it could be potential location as all new employees have to first report at our parent company's campus on the date of joining for a tour of it."

"Right! Let's make a move. But we need to be sneaking about it so other teams who haven't solved it yet don't follow our trail", Vicky said.

"To save time we can go in our two wheelers, I have mine. Anyone wants to hop in with me?", Chitra suggested and sent an open invitation.

If something was brewing between Vicky and her, he would have grabbed the opportunity. Instead he backed down and doubled with Bala on the latter's bike, while Asim and me decided to jog up and try to potray we were going towards the main entrance in search of the second clue. For any team to collect the next clue all the hunters of that team had to be physically present at the spot.

Vicky called us up stating to make a faster move as our guess was right and he could see three employees wearing our IT company's yellow ID card tags hung aroynd their necks, in contrast to the blue ones of our mother company.

Entering into the familiar ground, a wave of nostalgia hit me, reminiscing my initial three months of stringent training period we had undergone here. For us it seemed to be nothing less than a military training. We had to report at sharp eight thrity in the morning and leave the campus at eight in the evening. The extra long tweleve working hours were steneous but on the same hand most enjoyable phase of our professional life. It was an amalgamation of our college days and new office life routine. We didn't actually work due tweleve hours but had to clock it daily.

Four years back, all freshers training took place at the block designated for the Software division in the parent company's campus. The parent company had ventured out into a number of different businesses, each having a building designated to it. With the fast growth of the IT sector, a single block had fallen short to meet its employees needs; leading up to shifting the whole IT sector to the next door IT campus. My freshers batch was the last one to have spent their training days in this lovely campus.

We sped up and reached the main training room of our olden days, the volunteers congratulated us for being the first team to have made it to them. They handed a yellow token named clue to us. Bala examined it, rotating the coin sized token. "What's this? Where's the second clue?"

"It's a token to the second clue. All clues outside our IT campus will be obtained from the reception area - the starting point of the hunt", the male volunteer replied.

"Great!", Chitra scoffed, "They are making us run around... . Thankfully I have my bike".

"That's what a treasure hunt is all about, running around", Vicky shot her a look. Making peace between them we retraced our steps all the way back to our block. Midway we found Sasha and her hulks making their way to the mother campus.

I chuckled and smirked at them, looks like they had now only cracked the clue.

Panting towards the reception we showed our yellow token and in exchange we obtained the second clue.

"#2 ~ We plant the seed and it grows"

Vicky said "Now this has to be this block's training room, it can't be the same mother campus one's. The other block over here doesn't have a training room".

Asim said, "It could also be the library as there are many techinal and management related books there apart from newspapers, magazines and few novels".

"Vicky's sounds good to me. That's where we are trained in different skills by experts and we incorporate those skills in our professional day-to-day". I elaborated the meaning.

"Ok Asim you goto the library, we will go to the training rooms. Whoever finds the clue call the others".

Swiftly Chitra made a group in the text messaging mobile application with the five of us in it. "Or give a text message or call to this group". She beamed while waving her phone showing the group chat with her single 'Hi' on it.

"Great, let's move", Vicky smiled at her.

We rushed up the staircase instead of wasting time for the elevator, as the training rooms resided in the first floor. Stumbling into the four rooms, we found the clue stuck on edge of the white board. This time they made each volunteer to sit in all the rooms, confusing us, but still we found it.

Vicky picked the sticky note and read it.

"Elimination Round; State the 5 principles of our company to the volunteer to collect the third clue"

Running up to the volunteer, we ticked off three correct principles and contemplated the remaining two. Shooting out all varuous kinds of words that could suit, the volunteer was smiling at us at our failed attempts. The volunteer was so close to disqualifying us for the number of attempts and told that next attempt would our be our last one. Vicky and Chitra were going to oppose it but were cut-off with another team's entry. Asim took out his mobile and on net surfing landed up in our company's website. Reading through our company's mission statement, we whispered the other two principles into the volunteers ears and obtained our third clue.

"#3 ~ The Pride of the company"

The five of us waded towards the elevator section away from the other sniffing hunters, to brainstorm on the third clue.

"Employees are the pride", Bala quipped to which Chitra rebuked. "As if! Come out of your dream world", she scoffed. "I think it's the board room on the eleventh floor. If any clients or delegates come, they have all the meetings over there and that floor has posh, sleek interiors compared to the other floors".

"It could be it", I said after a thought. Asim and Bala went to pressed all the call buttons of the six elevators.

We waited for anyone of them to open up at our floor. Being still in the lead and climbing up stairs of ten floors didn't seem to be a wise decision. As soon as, one of the elevator's dinged, it seemed to have light up an idea in Vicky's brain. I made a move to enter it but was caught from behind by him.

Vicky let out two words that seemed to change our direction and we sprinted downstairs without any qualms. "The museum!"

While climbing onto the bikes, Chitra said, "Be thankful to me. You got the hint because of my guess".

Vicky laughed, "You are right, Chitra. I stole it from your guess. Happy now, let's be go".

Asim and me spotted one of our friends in the two wheelers open parking lot adjacent to our building and borrowed his for the time being. Another round of a two-way jog to the main campus would be tiring and drain out all our energy. The museum built in the mother campus was a must spot in the campus tour for new employees, clients, delegates and any important occasion. It exhibited our companies heritage and important events and objects developed or manufactured by any of it's related businesses. All the prestigious awards won in the business world were also put up there. No doubt it was the pride of the company.

The volunteer checked our previous clue papers before handing over the note to us, to check if we didn't skip any round.

"Elimination Round; Name the first and last three CEOs of the company"

Bala groaned, "Uff! Another elimination round!"

The volunteer replied, "Yes we have only four chits here", lifting them up.

Asim stated the current and previous CEO, now we needed answers to the first and third last CEO. Just then the team we met at the training room bursted in, with Sasha's team closely behind them. Seeing our competitors had caught up with us, sent Bala and Vicky frantically dialing up people. Asim searched for clues in the hall of fame list of prominent leaders, while Chitra and myself searched the net for answers.

Bala and Vicky had stepped out as to avoid letting out hints to others. Bala called a known personal from the finance department as whatever finance related transactions were done had to be signed and sealed by the then CEO. Making them to be highly aware of the CEO names as it was related to their daily office work. While

Vicky called up someone from HR department as they would be the next best shot to remember the CEO names.

Our team struggled to obtain the answers whereas Sasha's team bet us to it with Rohit's contacts and Sasha's manager, Manoj providing them with the answers. She playfully waved at me with her fingers moving rapidly. After her few failed winking attempts, she gave up and exited the museum. With their exit, marked the entry of two more teams, now the competition was neck-to-neck. Four teams were present at the museum but only the first three to give the right answers would proceed to the next round. From the leading position we had dropped down the chart and were on the verge of getting eliminated due to two CEO names.

On succeeding in getting the right answers, we exited the campus as the third team to make it through. Collecting the fourth clue from the reception, back in our block, we set our minds racing immediately.

"#4 ~ All work and no play makes Jack a dull boy"

Our gang no longer held the leading position and with other teams catching up, we had to buckle up to stay in the running. Recreation room, gym, cafeteria, sports court and the park where the options we had thought of. We spilt up into three with Chitra and Asim to inspect the indoor options, while I checked out the park. Bala and Vicky sprinted towards the sportd court, two blocks apart, as they were fast runners and in case we found the next clue they could make it back at a faster pace. Our strategy boomeranged on us, with the sports court turning out to be the right choice.

Vicky's group call stated that they found the clue but as the five of us weren't at the spot, the clue wasn't handed to them.

I spoke back in the phone, "No worries bro, we are all making our way to it". I turned around and jogged backwards for a few steps to check if other teams were behind us. The route was clear and I continued, "One good news, the park is the destination for the next clue. I found the volunteers but when they checked the number of clues they rejected me, stating there's wasn't the right stop for me."

"Great bro! Hurry up now Sasha's team is also here, they are waiting for Daniel to join", Vicky replied.

"Shit! Daniel made it too. Come soon guys!", Bala exclaimed and they cut the call.

We reached the spot with us catching our breath while Vicky read out the elimination clause.

"Elimination Round;Sing the official anthem"

Great!Our official anthem was always the butt for our jokes. Whenever it was played, we had made fun of its lyrics but never had actually memorized it.

All of us searched the net and found it. Vicky jogged up to one of the volunteers and showed the lyrics while Rohit started reading out the lyrics to the other volunteer. The volunteers didn't give in until all the five hunters of the team sang it out. Only two teams had reached it, and it being the only answer we sung it out aloud to one of the three volunteers. Sasha's team beat us here too they finished the last verse a minute before us. Getting the next clue before us, but we still had the upper hand, due to me, we knew the next destination.

"#5 ~ Latest addition to us"

I could hear their options while trying to figure out the right one. The new cafeteria and gym at the other block, the new stall at the cafeteria at our block were some of their choices.

Food is all they could think of, I laughed internally.

We waited for them to leave the court in the pretense that we were thinking of the options of the next destination. They made their move to the left of the court, stating that till now not one clue was in the other block and hence it had higher chances. While we turned to the right towards our block, behind which was the new park - the correct destination.

Sasha turned back and saw us walking and high fiving each other. Picking up the wind she halted her friends and it downed on them the correct location. They ran towards us and in no time were in line with us. Finding them next to us, both the teams started off an unofficial 200 meters running race. Sasha ran next to me and gave me a tough competition. She glanced sideways at me and smiled, battling her eyelashes rapidly.

"That's so not you, Sasha! You can't charm me into losing ". I remarked at her attempts.

"Oh Really? There's a saying- don't enrage a charging bull", she cocked her eyebrows in surprise with a mischievous smile playing on her lips.

I chuckled with my head bobbing backwards, "How are you going to butt me, you don't have any horns?" I stated the obvious while running with Sasha.

She let out a laugh, "Not everything should be taken literally, my dear Raghav!". She extended her hand out to fondly play with the hair on my crown. Making me lower my speed, taking it to her advantage she picked up speed and turned around to a halt. Her next actions caught me by surprise, and made me stumble and fall backwards onto my back. She had locked her eyes with mine and kissed her palms and blew a kiss in the air in my direction.

S-S-Sasha blew a kiss to me??!! My inner voice stammered not able to agree to what my eyes had witnessed. It sure was a shocking experience, anyone would fall by it's impact.

She clasped her hands in joy and winked at me before speeding off.

Not only she blew a kiss but she gave me wink after all the failed attempts.She sure is learning the art of tease fast.

All your effect, Raghav!, my mind voice echoed.

song: It's like catching lightning,The chances of findingSomeone like youIt's one in a million, the chances of feeling.

Her hulks had already had a head start and by now would have reached the point and she would join them in no time. Whereas, I was laying on the ground with Asim and Chitra helping me up. While dusting off my clothes Vicky's call came and he glowered, "Where are you?".

Sprinting up with my slightly limping leg, we joined Vicky and Bala, to collect our next clue. I turned to Sasha and she mimicked the shrugging emoji present in our smartphones, with her palms open in the air. The glint in her eyes and stature implied on the lines of, 'All's fair in love and war'. I just nodded to her with a smile. I couldn't be mad at her, she was making me taste my cup of Tea. To top it, I had earned a flying kiss, what could have been the downside to it.

Luckily Sasha's team seemed to have misplaced one of their clues. By the time they found it, our team of five also had landed up right in time, making up for the lag. Both the teams were handed over the chits at the same time.

"Elimination Round; Write a letter to your manager asking for leave, top two hilarious letters make it to the finale"

The third team also had succeeded to get to the park. All the three teams hurdled up and wretched their brains for hilarious ideas. I swept my glance over the other two teams and landed on to an animated Sasha. I didn't get a chance to observe her today with all the running around for the treaasure hunt.

Her black cap had cast a shadow over her eyes and covered her pixie hair. Her trademark red lipstick, adoring her lips, hadn't smudged after a day of running under the hot sun and sweat. The outfit projected the preparations she had done to beat the heat. Her cap, her breezing oversized white cotton shirt with thin red stripes, upto her mid thigh, doubling as a short top along with limestone grey cotton straight pants. Upon studying her, the desire to take her out took over me.

Voila! Got the perfect idea!

"Here give me the pen", I grabbed the sheet and pen from Vicky who was skeptical. "Trust me, I got it!".

I started writing the leave application letter.

"Respected Sir,

Sub: Leave Application

Sir, as you know I have been working so hard lately and would like to take a day off to re-energize myself. On my return, I will be able to take up more work with the extra energy pumped in me. Also, I want to put my love life back on track. Considering tomorrow, you will be having back-to-back meetings, I can take your daughter out for a date without any tension of getting caught.

Looking at it as a win-win situation for my professional and personal life along with your's, requesting you to kindly grant me one day off work, tomorrow.

Yours sincerely, To-be-son-in-law."

Vicky looked at me like a proud father and slammed my back with appreciation. We were the first team to hand over the letter with Sasha's just behind us. The volunteers read my letter and let out a short laugh.

Vicky jumped on the opportunity, "See you smiled and he laughed, it means we passed the round". He kinda urged them to pass on the final clue to us. After securing it, I turned to look at the surprise Sasha's eyes. Brushing past her and our shoulders grazing each other, I dipped my head to whisper into her ears.

"Rabbits may hop, fox may be sly but at the end it's the honest tortoise that always wins the race". I turned her cap around backwards and tapped it. "Be ready for the date", winking at her, I jogged to catch up with my troupe.

"#6 ~ I'm odd, I'm even and many use me. I know only three colors"

The finale clue, true to it's requirement was the most bizarre and difficult clue. Walking out of the park we started rummaging through our brain for picking up on any hint. We went up to the point of thinking the '#6' also played a part of the clue. We sat down on the risen pavement and drank some water, knowing that it would take long time to crack this puzzle. With no leads, we thought of things, places that could have odd and even numbers. The apparent choices upfront were - lift, floors, parking lot.

How are we going to search all the floors! That's hell of a work.

Sasha and her hulks walked past us and were busy in their discussion world, implying that they made it to the finals. It had now boiled down to both our gangs and the one who cracks this first would be the winner.

This is exactly what I wanted.The finish line is not too far away.

After searching non-stop for thirty minutes, at the elevators in both the blocks and sixth floor of both buildings, Asim gave a group call. "Guys, It's the sixth floor of the parking lot, come soon. I can see the volunteers but I haven't found the treasure neither has the other team."

Spending close to an hour looking around the sixth floor of the parking lot but still no success, the organizers felt sorry for us and themselves. They decided to give us a hint, to bring the event to it's closure.

"We knew the last one will be hard to crack, but never thought it'll be so hard", the volunteer said. "The team whose all participants are here amd have all clues will get a hint".

Both the teams had one missing person, all rushed to call them asking them to report to this spot immediately. The missing hunters joined us together, thus giving no team an added advantage.

"The treasure is present only within these four pillars and a stop-watch of thirty minutes will be ticked off. You need to find it within the time limit or else no winners will be declared. Points to the respective profolios scoreboard will be added as per the runners up position". Some nodded, others groaned first before agreeing.

"Your time starts now!", one of the organizer announced making us fan out in all directions within the said boxed area.

The bounded area between the four pillars had many cars and two wheelers. We seived through the ones that had odd and even numbers on their license plates but still not fruitful.

The last ten minutes countdown started, half of our teams flocked around the organizers asking for more hints. The others gave up and rested on some cars for support.

Rohit all of a sudden forcefully opened the driver's door of the same car I had rested on. I glanced at him weirdly, this guy is breaking into someone's car just to get a seat to sit!?

Refocusing my eyes back to Sasha to continue our eye flirting, making her squirm. No doubt it was my all time favorite pass time activity.

Rohit emerged out of the car yelling, with a box held in the air, "Found it!".

My head whipped to his side and my eyes popped out of their sockets. He found the treasure in the eleventh hour and the time-keeper announced "Time's up", just a second later.

Whilst Sasha and the hulks were rejoicing over the win, Vicky glared at me as both Rohit and me were near the car. Even after Rohit opened it, I hadn't picked up. It was a close win, only if I hadn't diverted my attention we could have been the team yelling in joy. I raised my hands in surrender with an apologetic expression to Vicky.

I went up to Sasha when her lane was clear and congratulated her. "Hmmm so where are you taking me for our date?", I casually asked.

"What date?", she asked. For a person who just won a treasure hunt event solving clues, she stood there in front of me with a clueless look.

"The one I mentioned in my leave letter", I replied with a smug look. "My leave's approved, so we can go", I stated.

"Uh? If you had applied for leave and asked me out for a date in the letter, May I know why I'm supposed to be taking you out, instead?" She reasoned out with her hands on her hips.

"That's because we lost, and I'm sad", pretending to sulk, I gloom-ly said with sagged shoulders. "Don't you want to cheer me up with a date?", I asked her with hopefully eyes while pulling a sad, long face.

Sasha raised her brow, "Shameless!", she bursted out in laughter. "Ok ok, my dear petty Raghav boy, will think about it".

"Wow!", my face lit up, "I'm looking forward to it", I said as we departed.

The next two days had the gaming event, adzap, prelims of adapt tune and light music competitions. Just one day before the Grand event, the fashion show was scheduled for which Sasha had asked me to her partner in. The rehearsal for the choreography of it took place in the gym, in allocated slots to the various teams. Looking at our mirror images walking down, hands looped in with each other, was delightful. In a closed room, to strut and pause to give away model postures, didn't feel like a hard task but I dreaded the final event on the stage.

The fashion show would be followed by a mini DJ night. The DJ night, final rounds of adapt tune and light music along with the group dance would be held on the D-day interrupted by the awards ceremony. The dinner buffet of the main event was also the highlight. None of that mattered to me. Today, the day of the fashion show was my D-day.

Standing dressed in my uncomfortable costume in the green room, I tried peeping through to catch a glimpse of the crowd. The roar of applause and the cheers already gave me hint of the extent of audience present. Sasha placed a comforting hand on my shoulder. "Relax Raghav, all you have to do is stick to what we rehearsed. I'll be there by your side. You just have to walk and pause, it's not hard", she said in a soothing tone.

song: Take my hand, I'll take the leadAnd every turn will be safe with meDon't be afraid, afraid to fallYou know I'll catch you through it all.

Coming into my vision's scope, she stood in matching costumes. The theme of the fashion show was Love. While other teams were going to depict love in all kinds of relationship to get a wide range of costumes to pull off, we stuck to the 'romantic love'. Dressed in attire of different eras and Red being the central color of each ensemble. Depicting that love is the feeling that is passed on from generations after generations. Sasha and me had landed up with the olden era of warriors.

I scoffed, I didn't know calling her Wonder woman the other day would end us being dressed like them. She seemed pleased to have been thrust with the warrior look.

She wore thick engraved bronzed clutches like bracelets on her hands and dark brown lined with golden border, three layered elvish pauldron as a shoulder armour. They were crossed strapped to her body from leftover pieces of brown belts. A thick royal maroon velvet shawl with golden twirl designs was clutched to her neck and hung behind like a cape.

A large circular shaped bronze shield with spider web design in sparkling red made for her top over a glittering skin hugging t-shirt. The centre of the web had large pentagon shaped artificial ruby stuck on it. She teamed it with deep red tight leather pants. A mix of golden and bronze linked chains hung in loops around her waist with a fantasy golden handle dagger sneaking out of it. Golden with bronze self designed boots rode upto her calves. One layer of the shoulder armour made up as her knee armour. Her look completed with a thick golden chain with a circlar sun shaped pendant as her head gear.

She looked every bit of a deadly warrior princess ready to kick some ass.

While she adored her look, also getting her hands dirty in designing and making her costume; I was far from being comfortable. The elvish pauldron, bronze hand braces and thick golden curtain with red creepers look alike pattern as my cape, were the similarities with her outfit. The reference for mine was from the movie Gladiator.

Wearing knee high Roman multiple strapped brown sandals with golden studs on it. Dark brown shorts just above the knee, hidden under heavy pleated gladiator leather kilt of same colour, lined with golden buds, giving it a more prominent look. With a large sword tucked into the waist band, protruding outside upto my calf along with a shield on one hand, comprised my armour. The long curved rectangular scutum red shield with golden wings drawn over it, made me feel a little better as I could hide my hideous costume with it. I opted for a simple golden Caeser leafed circlet as my headgear but Sasha disagreed with it. She went all out and rented a golden Roman soldier helmet minus the jaw and cheekbone protectors, so that my face was visible. A long trail of red features, fanned out on top of my crown. She didn't leave me a chance to hide my face.

The only part of my face that was hidden by the helmet was my sideburns, like it did any good!

I was under the impression they would apply bronzer on my chest and make me go on stage half-naked and shirtless. Thankfully they felt pity on me and gave a steel upper body armour with a sun engraved on it with wavy rays coming out of it. An enlarged version of Sasha's pendant, with a shiny red stone in the middle, giving me Iron man feels.

Our team was second last in order to go on stage. A last minute change in our execution was done, on analyzing other team's outfits. We would depict the era's in descending order now, which made Sasha and me the showstopper of our team. Like every coin has two sides to it, this spur of the moment change also did.

Being the showstopper, would put me directly in the spotlight and right in the middle of the stage, but for a shorter duration. All my hopes of garnering minimim attention standing in one corner of the stage but for a longer duration, went down the hill.

Our team's turn came and it was time to face the music for me. Our teammates had already walked down and stood at their designated spots in a semi-circle, leaving the centre spot vacant for us. On our entry beat, Sasha entered the stage from the left and me from the right. Meeting at the middle, we paused to look into each other's and turned on our heels to face the crowd. I gulped and my heart beat faster than the upbeat music. Sasha slid her hand into my outstretched arm and settled it in nook of my inner elbow, clutching it tightly to comfort me.

Strutting down the stage, as practised, Sasha swayed her cape to emanate a strong persona. Filling the vacant spot and with the spotlight on us, Sasha turned towards me. We gave an instense glare to the audience, with a light thud of my shield on the stage, to make an impact. She removed the dagger and grazed it seductively along by jaw, while capturing my undue attention and an arm secured around her waist possessively.

Uff! The stage was getting hot. It was like we were announcing ourselves as a couple to the entire office. Better watch out, don't mess with us.

If only my proposal to her was done before this, it would have been great and more meaningful.

The hoots and whistles heard from every corner proved that our team's performance was enjoyed by many. We seemed to have enacted the deadly warrior couple and pulled it off quite well. With the music drowning, others slowly synchronously exited the stage from the either side of us and retraced our steps and forked back to our entry points.

The last team made their performance and we watched them from the sidelines. Sasha came to green room and was standing next to me intently watching the fashion show. Till the results were released, we were asked to stay in out outfits. The last minute change in our choreography was the strike of gold we hit. Overall we stood second, sharing the spot we another team but Sasha and me won the Showstopper couple award plus the best ensemble award. She leaped in joy into my arms and we hugged it out briefly, before making our second appearance on the stage to recieve the award.

With that, the stage and ground was open for the DJ night. Blarring music blasted with everyone joining in it, despite being in their fashion show outfits. Sasha's and mine were the only uncomfortable costumes and needed to be changed. The green room was empty with only the two of us. Sasha turned to go back to her green room for a quick change, but I caught by her elbow.

"What is it Raghav?", turning in her heels she asked.

My eyed averted to the single fresh long stemmed red rose reciding in cup of water, hidden from the naked eye. I gestured her to wait while I grabbed the rose and held it at my back.

Standing toe-to-toe her, I heaved lightly before starting.

"I've been thinking alot lately, about us. I think we have spent enough time in getting to know each other in the past few months. After our small confession, we embarked a new journey together and it has been blissful ever since. No matter how much we fought or had misunderstandings, at the end we were back together in our happy place. And I think that's what really matters....."

song: Let it rain, let it pour, what we have is worth fighting forYou know I believe that we were meant to be! Oh!

Taking a short break, I continued.

"With you by my side, I am a happy person.... You are my happy place and I want me to be yours too."

song:The way we doAnd with every step togetherWe just keep on getting betterSo can I have this dance?

I got down on knee and extended the rose towards her.

"So, Sasha, I have one question for you.....

Can I have this dance, with you as my girlfriend?"

25

CHAPTER 25

Sasha's POV

song:I gotta say what's on my mindSomething about us doesn't seem right these daysLife keeps getting in the wayWhenever we try somehow the planIs always rearranged.

We looked into each other's eyes, like the world had been put to a stand still. The earsplitting music radiating from outside, seemed to be the only proof, to defy it. I whipped my head to glance around to check if a potrait of us was being snapped.

I was really tired after all the fashion show related prep; ensuring everything was in place. Some issues related to our costumes had sprouted out in the eleventh hour, sending me into a frenzy. After calming my hysterical self, I was able to come up with a backup plan and it fit well. Following that, was the nervousness to pull off our role of a warrior couple and making sure Raghav didn't get cold feet. I didn't want him to regret doing it for me.

The whole day felt like climbing up a ladder slowly, one step at a time, tackling one issue at a time. With our successful exit from the stage, my mind jumped to do a happy dance. The euphoric mood had soon converted to intense suspense till the results were declared. To top it all, how could I forget the bomb dropped on me by my manager, in the morning.

Now, when I thought my over worked brain could get some moments of relaxation and tranquility, here Raghav was on his knee with a rose in his hand.

What else could it be?

I constricted the sudden dialation of pupils to reach it's maximum capacity and subdued myself instantly. I took a deep breath and tried to see the scenario with a calm mind. Within seconds my mind was blown off with reality hitting me.

Nooooo! It can't be.

But looks like it is Sasha, why else will he be on his knee and try rewinding his words, he spelled it out to you.

Not now!

A train of thoughts were battling it out against each other in my mind but oblivious to Raghav. I came up with the idea of sidelining it as a prank or a gig. Covering my mouth, I burst out laughing.

Facing Raghav again, I hiccupped in giggles, to ask. "Is this an extension of our act on stage?", circling his posture. "Are you by any chance, videographing all of this for some skit or role play event?? If you had done this back on the stage, it would have been a sure shot win for us".

Raghav frowned and then raised his brow in response.

Looks like he didn't buy it.

Raghav shook his head in disagreement and pointed his eyes to the rose in his hand. Getting tired of waiting for my response, he pulled back his outstretched hand and rested it on his knee. An awkward silence filled between us.

You can't keep him hanging like that forever, Sasha. He's waiting and he has the right to know it.

I picked him by his shoulders and could sense his body stiffening up. It was time to come out in the clear, taking his hands in mine, "Ra-ghav, you know I like you too, but —"

song:It's so hard to sayBut I gotta do what's best for meYou'll be okay.

The sudden change in Raghav's expression faltered me for a moment but with determination I proceeded.

"But, what?", Raghav's voice had an edge to it.

"Listen, I have just been offered an onsite opportunity. Manoj called me in, this morning, to inform that all the visa processing is set. Date is set and everything is finalized. Only thing that's pending is the date of travel to arrive and for me to on-board the flight". I swallowed the lump in my throat. "Which means.... Everything is falling in place for my dream of an onsite opportunity..... Everything is perfect". I lifted and shook his hands in desperation, "But..... Only the timing isn't correct.... I'm sorry, but I have to leave...to follow my dreams... I hope you understand".

song:I've got to move on and be who I amI just don't belong here, I hope you understandWe might find our place in this world somedayBut atleast for now, I gotta go my own way.

I sprinted out of the door, unable to bear the distraught look on Raghav's face as he slumped down on the bench.

Raghav's POV

I sat down with Sasha's words replaying in repeat mode in my mind, when Vicky entered.

"Hey man! Here you are and we've been searching for you, all over. You haven't changed out of your outfit yet?", He asked.

"Raghav, Raghav". He snapped his fingers in front of me and released me from my momentarily hypnotic state.

"Uh-Huh!", I replied in confusion.

Vicky took a seat beside me and asked, "What happened bro? What's this rose?—" He took a moment, to put two and two together and figured it out. "D-did, did you pr-propose to Sasha?... And she said no?" He also sounded astonished at the unlikely outcome.

Asim too had joined us and stood in front of me. I just nodded in slow motion. They gave me time to open up and after silencing the voices in my head, I spoke up.

"For past few days I was checking out ideas to cheer her up, off the cyber threat stress...That's when I came to know that though Actions speak louder than words, woman want both actions and words. So I decided to propose officially?" I said with a dejected tone.

"Did she tell any reason for turning you down?", Asim cautiously asked.

"Ya! Her damn onsite role came in the way", my bubbling anger seeped out.

"Onsite!", Vicky exclaimed with a hitch. I thought he would continue but he had only blurted that word and fell silent.

Asim let out a long sigh before speaking, "So what have you guys decided?"

"What's there to decide, when the entire universe is only conspiring to separate us!". I spat out in frustration and brushed my hand over my hair till it reached my nape. "She said sorry, she needs to take up the offer. Hell! No one would close the door to the golden opportunity."

They let me vent out my feelings while being there beside me as my support system.

"Do you wanna know, what else sucks?!! It sucks to be a failure in both my professional and personal life." Halting after each sentence tumbling out of my mouth. I turned right and jolted Vicky's forearm to meet his face. "Sasha is approximately one year junior to me experience-wise, if we neglect the months. Still she's able to secure an onsite job but not me!" I yelled, all my insecurities were coming out.

Vicky squeezed my shoulder to calm me and said, "Relax bro".

All of my myriad emotions were getting the worse out of me. "No man!", I pushed his hand off me. "You are a witness of how much effort I'm putting in to get an onsite role, with all the automations and work I have done.... But where, where is the output?? Zero, Nil, nothing! It's not done Vicky, it's not done... Life is outright unfair!!"

"What am I doing wrong to deserve this, tell me guys?". Swapping my focus between Asim and Vicky, with angry questioning eyes. The anger wasn't directed to them but reflected the rage I was feeling at this moment.

Leaning on the table behind him, Asim spoke, "Do you really want to go down that road now? Don't you think you are getting sidetracked?"

"It's all interconnected, Bhai", like a deflated balloon, I slumped more into my seat. My voice too trailed down in defeat. "Whichever door I see open, before I can enter it, it slams on my face. Onsite I didn't get, that's ok; but the same thing is happening with Sasha and me. I feel like I'm going to be thrown out and shut out of her life."

song:Don't wanna leave it all behindBut I get my hopes up, and I watch them fall everytimeI know the color turns to grayAnd it's just so hard to watch it allSlowly fade away.

"You are overthinking it. Did Sasha really say anything on those lines?", Asim questioned with folded arms.

I shook my head, "If she goes abroad, it's like a dead end for us. I can't tell her not to go, that's wrong in so many ways...... Why do girls have to compromise always?? Had it been me, there would have never been such expectations.... I agree, I am jealous, after all I'm also a human being not a saint! That doesn't mean I will ask her to step back from her achievements. She's studied and worked hard for years for it, and deserves every bit of the fruits for her efforts. It's just, this stupid onsite had to butt in, at the wrong time and play with my life!" I scoffed in irritation.

song:What about us?What about everything we've been through?What about trust?You know I never wanted to hurt youAnd what about me?What am I supposed to do?

Vicky stood up and went towards the window at his side. Clutching the grill on the window, looking out of it, he said. "That's what it does, creates havoc in one's self. Onsite is overrated, all glittery-glamorous initially but empty lonely life later". Heaving a deep sigh and spinning on his heels, he turned towards me. "But everyone doesn't have the same fate, Raghav. Take it as a God's sign and try to find a loophole in it."

"Ya right!", I replied sarcastically, with my head down, looking at the floor.

"Vicky's right", Sasha's voice came from the doorstep, grabbing all of our attention instantly.

What's she doing here.... after thirty minutes of running away from me?

She walked in, "Can I talk to you alone, Raghav?". Without waiting for my response, Vicky and Asim made their way out. She replaced Asim's spot and took a step closer to stand in front of me.

"What are you doing here? I thought you ran away from me, even before boarding your flight". An undertone of accusation laced my tone. "Sasha — the Runaway Tom-Boy", gesturing an imaginary pluck card with the label I gave her, on it.

"More like, the Run-way Tom-Boy". Her emphasis on the word with her pupils rolling towards the stage side, implied the catwalk we did earlier.

"It's not the time to crack jokes, Sasha", I reprimanded her, shaking my head in oscillation.

"Oh come on, Raghav. Take a chill-pill, Lighten up a bit."

"Don't push the wrong buttons. I'm not in the mood now, Sasha", I gloomly replied.

"Look at me, you'll feel better!", she chirped with insistence and wore a wide grin.

"You have all the rights to be cheerful.... Your dreams are all coming true", I stated in a wooded voice.

Her eyes dreamily sparkled, "Ya right! My dreams are certainly coming true. In fact! I'm getting more than I bargained for."

I wore a tight smile. "Don't get me wrong Sasha, I am truly happy for you and wish you success and happiness from the bottom of my heart.....But, you don't know what I'm going through, so please don't rub it in my face".

Saying that I got up and took a step, only to be abruptly stopped by Sasha's side-stepping me.

"I can understand but Raghav, hear me out. I came to talk to you and I'm not leaving without a discussion".

Letting out a deep breath, I concided. "Ok, go ahead. What did you want to talk about?"

She cast her mesmerizing smile that tugged my heartstrings.

Oh! I'm going to miss it so much.

"The thing is, I've had alot going on with me today. First the fashion show preps and all, then the sudden confirmation of my onsite and everything. I needed some time off to think it through and I just did it".

I kept nodding my head and she took a break from delivering her speech.

"Did what?", I asked.

"Found it!", she exclaimed like it was obvious.

"Found what?", a deep valley formed at the middle of my forehead conjoinimg my eyebrows.

"The loophole, silly!", her fingers pushed my forehead back.

Seeing no change in my deadpan expression, she continued.

"Will we be able to pull off a long distance relationship?!?"

26

CHAPTER 26

Raghav's POV

song:There goes my heart beating'Cause you are the reasonI'm losing my sleepPlease come back now. And there goes my mind racingAnd you are the reasonThat I'm still breathingI'm hopeless now.

Sasha stood in front of me with her question hanging in the air. It took me by surprise. In less than an hour, I've been hit by so many shockwaves, it was unbelievable. I wasn't in an ambulance or hospital getting treated, then why did I have to undergo the shocks!? I pushed that thought aside as I had a more important issue at hand.

Did she really suggest for a long distance relationship?!

"Hell ya!", I dammed in determination. "Sasha does that mean a 'yes' to my proposal?", I enquired.

Just the thought that she hadn't outright dismissed me due to her onsite situation, inflated my chest with pride and hopes. Her suggestion hinted of an indirect yes but my ears and brain were hungry for her words to get registered inside me. I needed words and only words to hurl out the negative voice booming within me. They had to be thrown out of the same window, through which they made their way in poisoning my mind.

"Yes, dumbo!" She rolled her eyes as if she couldn't believe I was dim-witted, to not have understood it.

"Yay!", I exclaimed in ecstasy and picked her up to twirl her. My happiness knew no bounds. A squeal of surprise escaped her mouth, "Whoaaa!", followed by her continuous giggles. Her laced fingers rested on my nape for support, when she was up in the air. I couldn't stop myself from twirling, even with our uncomfortable warrior get-up.

song:There goes my hand shakingAnd you are the reasonMy heart keeps bleedingI need you now.

In between her laughs she half-protested, "Ok Raghav, enough now. Put me down! My head is spinning and your's too".

"Girl! Let me bask in my glory for sometime", I shook my head.

She huffed and let out a short laugh, "Put me down, Raghav!". She slammed her palm on my chest to hit me playfully.

"Are you scared that I'll drop you?" I cocked my brow up and stopped the blissful twirls, but didn't let her down.

She scoffed, "Firstly, I weigh like a feather and if you drop me, it just shows your strength. Secondly, if you drop me, you are going to get it nicely from me, after the fall. So, let me down this moment!". She tried to pull up a stern face while demanding, but failed miserably.

I chuckled and shook my head in disagreement. Instead of letting her down, I tossed her higher up and secured her tightly.

"I'm not a baby you know!", she retorted.

"Oh! I'm not so sure about that though", I replied with a thoughtful expression.

Again a playful slap flung onto my chest, making me chuckle.

"Don't worry Sasha, no one's seeing. All are busy dancing away". I whispered in her ears, as I slowly let her down.

She throw a reprimanding glare from the rim of her spectacles. I hugged her tightly but metal clinking against each other was heard.

Stupid body armours! I can't even feel her against me and enjoy our hug.

Nevertheless, I didn't break the hug. It felt like the medicine for my wounded heart. Her cuddly hug provided all the solace I needed right now. Of course, Sasha had a string of patience related to touchy emotional feels. Once that thread broke, she brought some space between us. My hands slid to her waist and encircled her to hold her within an arm's distance.

She smiled and ruffled my front hair playfully. "Feeling better?"

I nodded my head happily and returned her smile. Leaning forward I placed a kiss on her cheeks and let my lips linger on her skin. A slight blushing smile grew on her face, making me return back to catch a proper holistic front view of it.

She grabbed my forearms trying to free herself. "Ok, let's go change and join others for the DJ night outside."

"Uh-huh!", I disagreed. "Your not leaving my embrace so soon, Sasha. My wounds haven't healed yet. Just stay here like this for some more time, please.... It feels like I've just been resurrected.... When are you going to stop giving me such heartattacks?!"

song:If I could turn back the clockI'd make sure the light defeated the darkI'd spend every hour of every dayKeeping you safe.

"Never!", she stuck her tongue out and made a funny face. "You signed up for it. Actually, you came up with the proposed document!" She taunted and raised her eyebrow in amusement. "Are you having second thoughts already, mister?"

"Excuse me there were no clause in my proposal that states you have a license to give me a heartattack?", I chided.

Patting my biceps, "Poor boy, didn't know what he signed up for". After her giggles ended, she said, "Didn't anyone tell you not to sign anything without prior knowledge on it?" She shrugged mischievously, "It's ok, you can still annul it, if you want?"

"Never!", I protested with a stern stare.

"Good. Then learn the nuisances of it, Raghav boy. I and only I have the rights to make your heart beat faster or cause glitches in it". Sasha leaned forward to state it with her penetrating stare. Resting back, she placed her hand on my shoulders and beamed. "Don't worry they'll all be happy shocks from here after. You won't die of it, I assure you".

"Whoa! You really are a surprise package". She left me impressed and half-shell-shocked with her words. She just claimed me, my heart and soul, marking her territory. "Where did you hide this side of yours? Are you sure you are my romantic deficient, Sasha?" I asked and moved my head around in search of her in jest.

She blew on her maroon streaked bangs adoring a cute irritated look. "Do you want to do this now!". She grabbed my lower jaw and maneuvered it to bring it in her line of sight. "I'm the same bold, fiesty Sasha, if you have forgotten. I'm brushing up my skills that you said, I lacked in. I'm just a fast learner Raghav". She shrugged her shoulders casually and lifted her chin up in pride.

It was a very tempting offer, her action closed the distance between our lips.

"Good to know! Shall we put your skills to test then?" A devilish smirk played on my lips. I pretended to pout and get ready for another kiss but it landed on her own palm blocking my entire face.

"Oh God, Raghav! You just need a key to wind up. Calm your horses down, ok!" She whipped her head around to look for onlookers and there, within seconds Sasha's bold demeanor shifted gears to her shy side.

I let out a loud laugh, "Welcome back!". I greeted her with a wide grin and raised eyebrows.

She huffed and scoffed, mumbling something under her breath. Cuteness overloaded!!

The half-open greenroom door banged shut and we averted our eyes to it. Sasha's pupils grew on size thinking of a sneaking intruder but it was just the wind's doing. She blew a relieved sigh and we turned our focus back to each other.

"Do you really have no problems with a long distance relationship?", she asked with slight hesitance.

"Long distance, short distance, no distance; nothing makes a difference to me, as long as we have a 'relationship', Sasha". I replied earnestly.

"Do you think we can manage it? You know it'll be tough—"

I placed peck on her other cheek to stop her. "Nothing's easy in life, Sasha. It's all about survival of the fittest".

"But still. We won't get to see each other".

"Technology has grown, dear. What's video calls for then? We just need a strong internet connectivity and unlimited pack". I answered her with a peck, back on her left cheek.

"Ok! The time difference! It's going to be huge. When it's day there, it'll be night over here. Basically when you'll be awake, I'll be snoring away in deep sleep".

I jerked my head back, "Do you snore?"

She rolled her eyes, "You know what I meant, Raghav!"

I smiled at her irriated tone. "When will voice messages come in handy?! We can still hear each other's voice. Might be record and keep it, so whenever we feel lonely or other person is not available, we can get some sort of comfort". I suggested in a soothing voice, before pecking her right cheek.

I was so enjoying our conversation. She was immersed in her queries and I was getting surplus of Vitamin K.

She let out a deep breath, "Hmmmm, It's going to be a tough battle ahead for us, but I think we can fight it".

"There you go! That's my Sasha! Ready for any challenge". I pepped her up and placed a peck at the centre of her forehead. Lowering my mouth to her ears I whispered. "I'm available for you 24/7, just bear with my sleepy voice at odd hours. I'm sure you're half-sleepy voice is going to be really seductive, waiting to hear it."

Instantly she pushed me back slightly and narrowed her eyes on me. "I'm going to put up a time table chart for you, for our voice or video calls. Anything aside from those time-slots, unless it's really urgent and important, you better not call. And I mean really urgent, do or die situation, literally, not for your flirty antics. Got it!" She stated hotly, pointing her index finger at it.

I couldn't help myself from laughing and said. "You know me very well. I'm impressed." I tried placing a kiss on the finger pointed at me but her reflexes were fast enough to dodge it. She placed her hands on her hips with a ready-to-fight stance within my caged arms. "Cool! Cool! I agree with all your terms and conditions", I beamed and continued my kissing strikes, pecking her both her cheeks.

"You better abide by the rules", she stated.

"There's going to be a rule book?", I questioned on surprise.

She shrugged, "May be, may not be. It all depends on your behavior". She ended with stern glare at me, like I'm going to get scared of it. Her doubts again rose back to the surface, "Are you okay with it? Do you need time to think about it?"

Sliding my hands from her spine to either sides of her waist, I gave her a slight jerk. "Sasha look at me.... We will be fine as long as we are honest with each other. Till this arrangement doesn't get suffocating, we will push through it. But if you ever feel that it's not working out, it's putting a toll on you or anything, just voice it out to me. You are the one, going to leave all your family, friends and go to an unknown land, to be among unknown people. It's going to have a heavy toll on you more than me. So promise me if you can't take it, you'll let me know. Same way, if I'm not able to handle the hurdles, we will talk it out. I don't want us to drag it, if we are not happy and I will stand by my word to end it with dignity for our betterment."

song:(I don't wanna fight no more)(I don't wanna hurt no more)(I don't wanna cry no more)(Come back, I need you to hold me closer now)You are the reason, oh(Just a little closer now)(Come a little closer now)(I need you to hold me tonight).

Sasha nodded and said, "I promise. Lot's of adjustments are required".

"True that! I'll make adjustments from my side, you make from your side and we will meet midway. Efforts are required from both sides to make it through. Just like how two people come forward and meet in the middle while smooching".

"Oh God, Raghav! Can you ever be serious?"

"Excuse me! I was serious. It just took a turn, it's not my fault, its all your doing."

"Ya right!", she scoffed. "Why do I have a feeling you just overtook my loophole idea and selling it to me like a cunning salesperson?"

"I'm not claiming any ownership on it. The long distance relationship idea has your intellectual propriety stamp. I'm only providing support to it. I just needed a spark of hope and your idea did that. Then there was no turning back for the spark to grow in size into a full blown out flame". I said in my defense. Switching to a gentler tone, "I'm so happy you came up with it and rescued our ship. I can't thank you enough for it."

She sent a warm understanding smile, "I know you were under alot of stress and it resulted in playing haywire with your emotions."

"You saw all of that?", I spat out im bewilderment.

"Not all of it, but the last leg of it".

"Oh God! I'm sorry you had to see my meltdown. On the other hand, it's good you saw it. In spite of it, we are still standing locked up in each other's arms. Bearing testimony, that we can survive through tough waters. You've seen me in my worst but that didn't deter you from coming forward to put forth your idea, that says it all..... Sasha, we have faced many testing times and flew out in flying colors. This is going to be one of the most difficult test to our bond, without trying it we won't know if it'll make us or break us."

"Absolutely! I agree with you on everything, except one."

"What's that?"

"It's not sorry but it's 'Happy Pongal'", Sasha's lips gradually curled up along with her words to make a perfect smile.

"Happy Pongal to you too, Sasha", I mirrored her smiling face.

"I shouldn't have run away just like that earlier and pushed you into the dark phase".

"Nah! It's all good. It's better to vent out your emotions rather than pile it up. I unloaded and emptied my heart before you came back with your idea. You needed time to sneak something out of our situation and you did it. Proud of you! Your were willing to walk the path with me, instead of taking the easy way out by declining as soon as trouble knocks our door, that shows how much you value and cherish our bond. You really made me a happier man today. Not everyone will have that guts." I pecked her all over her face—forehead, temples, cheeks and tip of her nose to show my gratitude and love for her.

"Ok, ok now relax", saying that she nudged her head towards my arms and glanced at me. Implying to release her from my embrace, I pretended to misread her eyes.

"Raghav, I think you have been revived back to your normal self with all your cheesy vitamin K's and H's and what not. It's time to unplug the ventilator, as it's job is done here." She said with finality.

It was my turn to scoff and I pried my hands off her slowly. Just then my phone's ringtone was heard. I fished it out to see it was Asim's call. I held Sasha's hand with my other hand and spoke into the phone.

"Are you fine?", Asim asked over the phone.

"Yes, more than fine". I stated, sliding my eyes to glance at Sasha at my side, I continued speaking on the phone. "We are official now! Let Vicky know too". My eyes were trained on Sasha while continuing the conversation with Asim.

"Congrats man! Happy for Sasha and you. So you guys decided the long distance way?", he asked casually.

"Yup! How did you know?", I quipped.

"It's obvious and the only way out. Are you guys even planning to come out of that room?.... You know you are still in the office, just reminding you guys". Asim warned mischievously with underlying puns. In the background I could hear a song from the hindi movie Bobby, being played on Asim's side. Proving that Vicky was around and had received the breaking news.

song: Bahar se koi andar na aa sake (No one from outside can come inside) Andar se koi bahar na ja sake(No one from inside can go outside) Socho kabhi aisa ho toh kya ho(Imagine what would happen in such a situation) Socho kabhi aisa ho toh kya ho(Imagine what would happen in such a situation) Hum tum ek kamre mein band ho (If you and I were locked in a room) Aur chaabi kho jaaye(And the keys are lost) Hum tum ek kamre mein band ho(If you and I were locked in a room) Aur chaabi kho jaaye(And the keys are lost).

I rolled my eyes, "Yes, we will join you in five, just need a change of clothes and you'll find us at the ground."

"Ok, come soon. Everyone's waiting for you guys. Bye". Asim ended the quick call.

Pecking Sasha's hands, I let her leave to change. Picking her up from her green room, we made our way to the ground, hand in hand. Guiding our way through the dancing crowd, we reached the spot our gang was dancing at. Daniel and Simbu, the only two true blue Coimbatorites of our gang, were busy doing some wacky moves to the beats of Tamil songs — 'Daddy Mommy' and 'Why this Kolaveri di'. As the music of the latter started, I glanced sideways at Sasha for the situation song, of how she put me in distress. She innocently shrugged and let go off my hands. Walking to her hulks, she informed them about our official status and they all congratulated us with hugs and handshakes.

Rohit hugged me and before breaking it off, he yelled into my ears due to the loud music. "Take good care of Sasha, bro, if you want your bones to be intact." Parting away he flashed a smile at me, making me gulp. His hard slams on my back earlier felt like congratulatory pats but now came out as warning threats. I received similar warnings from the other three but mellowed down versions.

Rohit's aura was similar to that of a street fighter— you mess with her, you'll be the one gasping for life.

I have heard some rumors of his fights. Also witnessed his rage in the Manoj-Sasha misunderstanding and now this. He does have a deadly streak to his side.

I better watch out!

With his aura, he's going to scare everyone. How's he even going to find his partner then?

Shrugging it off, I swept my gaze around to watch all employees having fun and dancing away. Sasha came up to me and stood beside me. I bent down and whisper-yelled in her ears, "How do you want to celebrate our officiating?"

A frown grew in her face, "Haven't you had enough?", she asked in disbelief.

"Uh?"

"This is the celebrations", with her open palm she gestured the DJ night. "The whole office is dancing and celebrating, what more do you want?!"

I chuckled into her ears sending waves of vibrations ringing in her ear and entire bloodstream. "Ya right, how much more bolder and grandeur could it have been. We declared ourselves as a couple on the ramp walk and you, also gave out a warning to the onlookers as you claimed me, in front of everyone. Now, see everyone's part of the after party of our announcement. Just perfect! " I said coolly and stood back in my position stifling my laugh, watching Sasha's expressions change like an on-off switch.

"I didn't do anything of that sort", she hissed sidewards.

"Sasha, I didn't take you for someone with a short term memory loss. Let me walk you through it, you don't remember the dagger act you pulled off on the stage?!" I innocently put forth the reminder.

Her eyes doubled in astonishment and hissed. "It didn't mean that! I was playing my part in the role play, that's it."

"Okay, what ever makes you sleep at night, Hun." I chirped avoiding Sasha's glare for not agreeing with her.

Making a childish face at me, she took a step sideways, away from me, to show her displeasure. I followed her footsteps and closed the distance she put. She took one step right, then I took another step right. This went on for few steps till she didn't have space to move without colliding into her neighbor.

The group next to her were dancing with full energy and kept moving. This made her distance from them and step closer to me with the back of our hands and shoulders grazing each other. My fingers were twitching to pull her against me, flesh to flesh, bone to bone and enjoy the musical night under the stars. Replicating the couple pose we depicted at the fashion show but more intimately.

However, I kept myself in check. Constantly reminding myself that this wasn't a club or concert we had gone to attend but we were at office among our colleagues and higher officials. Even if I did something of that sort, there were no qualms that Sasha would get into her earlier warrior princess character and pull out all her

Kungfu Panda moves on me, then and there. Leaving no mercy on me, for pulling out such a stunt in front of numerous eyes.

I didn't mind dying in her arms but not dying from her hands.

I would do anything to keep her happy. Like they say —Happy girlfriend, Happy life.

Whoa! That sounds great!

Sasha, my one and only official girlfriend!

song:I'd climb every mountainAnd swim every oceanJust to be with youAnd fix what I've broken'Cause I need you to seeThat you are the reason.

27

CHAPTER 27

R aghav's POV

song:Oh, her eyes, her eyesMake the stars look like they're not shinin'Her hair, her hairFalls perfectly without her tryingShe's so beautiful and I tell her everyday.

The Monday, following the annual fest; the entire office looked like it had been engulfed in sorrow. Devoid of the fun and frolic mood, that loomed over it for the past week. The company conveniently held the event on a Friday to ensure the employees recovered over the weekend from its aftermath and reported back to work promptly. Keeping a healthy attendance, resulting in zero revenue leakage from the clients.

I had picked Sasha up, at her paying guest accommodation for breakfast and we rode together to office. We decided to utilize the three month period in our kitty, before her onsite deputation, to it's maximum extent. Squeezing out, whatever time we could offer each other to spend in each one's company. As a result of it, daily breakfast, to and fro office rides were our couple's package with additional few dinners thrown occasionally, as a cashback reward. Just like any cashback reward, sometimes it worked, sometimes it didn't. We didn't stress on it too much as we needed to have our personal space too.

Inside the office premises we maintained a healthy distance as before, donning the role of dignified professionals. Still, I didn't want any unwanted attention or fingers pointing towards us. With one high priority agenda on my mind, I entered our floor.

Checked my inbox for any new tasks thrown in my way and my calendar for today's meeting. Figuring out two suitable time slots for my main agenda, I swapped the control from the remotely connected client machine back to my local machine. I shot a ping to the human resource executive handling our client account. Once the greetings were exchanged, I conveyed that I needed her time to discuss an important topic. Luckily, our availability matched and I went ahead to schedule the meeting.

Grabbing my employee ID card, I wore the tag around my neck and left for the said meeting venue.

"Hi Sneha, Raghav here", extending my hand for a handshake, I greeted. "Thank you for taking out your time in such a short duration".

Smiling away, she gestured me to take a seat across the table, in the closed discussion room. "It's part of my job, not a problem. So what's the important thing you wanted to discuss about, Raghav?"

I nervously cleared my throat, how much ever focused I was to get this done, it took some time for me to voice it out. "I am not sure if there is a process in place for this.... I would like to know if apart from married relationship, are other relationships with co-workers can be updated with the organization?"

Sneha smiled back, "As far as I know only married, ex-employees information are to be declared".

Rubbing my nape nervously, I asked, "For Girlfriend and Boyfrie nd?... Ummm few organizations ask employees to declare them to avoid.... You know... Any sticky issues."

"That's a good thought Raghav. To be transparent, you want to share your professional and personal equations with your co-workers and keep the officials posted". After giving it a thought she said, "Hmm I think there is a provision for it but its in the initial stages of enforcement. Here, this is the option you need to find in your personal details in your company profile. You can update in the remarks section the name of the co-worker and your relationship, until the new option is enabled for all employees."

"Sure, will do that. Anything else that I need to take care of?"

"Try to ask the related co-worker to update in their profile too. Upon updation, it'll go to your manager and senior manager for acknowledgment. If the related co-worker doesn't update from their side within 25 days, there will be a round of discussions with both of you to check if everyone's on the same page and the stated relationship is consented or a false information. Please keep that in mind. Also, request you to undergo the 'Code of Conduct' training. I'm sure it won't be needed, seeing that you have come forth with the declaration. Nevertheless, it would benefit you'll and it's recommended to complete it."

On agreeing to it, we parted ways with a relieved me, going back to my desk. Sasha too agreed on declaring our relationship in the required portal. My fingers were trembling while entering the details. It felt surreal along with the splash of reality hitting me, that we were taking the next step in our relationship. Professionally we had finished announcing it, but when was it going to happen on the personal front— to our families; still had a big question mark.

I had a very busy day due to my relationship status change task, and wasn't able to spend time with my friends. When all the hoopla around it died, it was time for a late evening break. Sasha's hulks along with Vicky and Asim were crowded over a table in our break-out zone, when both of us walked in together. Pulling out the chair for Sasha as a gentleman, raised eyebrows from my troupe and her too.

Clapping my hands on my thigs, as we settled in, Vicky took it as his cue to start his business.

Vicky opened his mouth and directed his words towards me. "Just because you have a new confirmed friend, you'll neglect us, is it?" His brows bounced high and low.

Returning a puzzled look, I asked, "Which friend?"

"Sasha", he nudged his chin in her direction and continued, "your girl friend".

Scoffing, I answered with a deadpan expression, "She's not my friend now. She's my Girlfriend."

"You just said she's not your friend and later stated that she is your girl friend. Gosh! Raghav, get your relationship tag straightened out", Vicky ridiculed.

AJ joined in, to support his new partner in crime. "Yes Raghav, a friend is a friend. Like how I'm your friend, so I'm your boy friend. Similarly, Sasha being a girl, is your girl friend". He reasoned out like a four year old kid. A round of stifled and muffled laughs were heard from our table when he proclaimed to my boy friend.

Oh God! Wasn't Vicky enough to poke fun at me?Did he really need a co-conspirator to find thousand and one ways to pull my leg? If you had to send supporters to Earth, couldn't you have sent some to be on my side?I looked heavenwards while letting out my frustration.

I sent a speed text message to Sasha.

Help me pls! ~R

Why, can't handle your friend? ~S

Sasha! Vicky alone would have been a task. But now AJ has joined him like aBuy 1, Get 1 free offer.

ROFL Can't keep mylaugh in check

Meanie!! What happened to 'I'm your man and only I can claim me'??? Here, your dear friend is staking claims on me ashis boy friend & you are lips are zipped....

Oh! Please I didn'tsay anything like that

Ya right! Liar cock!

So childish!

My time will also come. You just wait and watch

I'm waiting

Her last message made me look at her in surprise.

Winkie wink and allWah! The prim and proper,Tom-Boy is opening upher can of emotions. You're challengeing me! Ok, Game on!!

Looking forward to it

Sasha, don't ask for things which you may not be able to handle. For now let me handlethis Vicky-AJ duo

Sasha shrugged and a private smile playing on her lips.

Letting out a grunt, I turned to Aj, "I'm not your boy friend, I'm just your friend."

"Ah! You had the time to come to Earth? So where did your spaceship take the two of you this time? Saturn? Mars or Lovey-Dovey planet?", Vicky teased.

"Asim, tell your friend there, to shut up". I stated in a stern no nonsense tone.

"Oh! I'm not your friend, now? Looks like what people say is true. The entry of one person in someone's life, marks the exit of some other person. I didn't know I would be the one to be shown the doors!" Vicky pulled out an over-dramatic act from some godforsaken movie.

I understood my best bet for it to die down soon was to be ignorant. I continued sipping through the hot beverage in my hand.

All of a sudden, AJ morphed into an innocent toddler shooting questions to his teacher, Vicky. "Sir-Sir!", he mimicked a toddler, "Where is the Lovey-Dovey planet? Is it next to our planet Earth?"

Vicky patted his back, "Yes, my child it seems near but yet very far at the same time. Some people visit it too often and they lose contact with the people on the earth."

Sasha dipped her head at the indirect insuniation. I could see her cheeks were flaming up in shyness.

Enacting a jumping toddler, AJ continued his play, "Can we also go there?"

"Oh! No, no, child. It's only reserved for the people who discovered it. That's Raghav and Sasha. The access for entry into their own planet, is restricted to them only."

These two are not putting a full-stop to it! I groaned out aloud.

The Girlfriend banter was much better than this.

I was having second thoughts to interrupt their impromptu skit. Just then AJ turned and pointed at Sasha and me.

"Hmmm, so these two friends have their own planet?", AJ questioned.

"For the love of God!" I raised my hands in air and shook them in agitation.

Falling back to square one, Vicky folded his arms. "What did he say wrong, Raghav boy? You only said Sasha is your girl 'friend'". He air quoted and emphasized on the word —friend.

"She's not my 'girl' 'friend' but 'girlfriend'. Please note the space between the two words, that makes the difference. Sasha is my 'GIRLFRIEND'! No space between girl and friend".

I heaved a long sigh, Hope our discussion above it was a closed chapter now, after the umpteenth time.

By now the whole breakout area felt like a cave echoing the words Girlfriend and a headache was creeping into me.

With a evil smirk, AJ teased, "Just like there's no space with the two of you, right now."

Immediately Sasha shifted her chair slightly away from me. Earning a round of chuckles from the boys, while rewarding me with a stern sideways glare.

"Ok-ok. Now that you have had a good amount of entertainment at our expense, let's cut it out now." I suggested.

We made smalltalk on the news making headlines in the city, grabbing everyone's eyeballs. One female employee brushed past our table and did a double take. She came back and stood beside me and said. "You guys were fantastic in the fashion show. From your outfit to your expression, everything was perfect."

I leaned a little towards Sasha and away from our newly encountered fan. "Thank you!", Sasha and me, replied in sync.

Our fan, smiled at us and before retreating, she said. "I didn't know you guys were together in real. You'll made a really good couple on the stage. Wish you the best for the future!"

A combined gratitude from us resulted in the girl's remark, "What a wavelength, you guys share!" With that, she left our table.

Her sweet words of appreciation and wishes made me feel lucky abd elated. Vicky fished out a small circular box from his pockets. While opening it's lid, he off-handedly spoke. "You guys are attracting too much attention now itself."

"What do you mean?", I quipped.

"Means at the start of your relationship". Asim replied while Vicky was struggling to open the box, no larger than that of a coin's size, in his hand.

"True! True", Daniel and Rohit agreed.

"Being newbies in the land of the love, I suggest you to dial it down in front of jealous eyes". Vicky stated, his eyes and hands trained on breaking open the lid.

"Don't jinx us guys and don't scare us", Sasha stated casually.

Whereas I objected to the new tag given to us, "We are not newbies!"

Vicky scoffed, "Ya right. You are still like newborn babies who need to learn their way around the romance world. But you don't have to worry about anything, like always I have a fix! Ta-da!" He exclaimed when he succeeded in his task with the circular box.

Rubbing his ring finger in circular motion inside the box, he leant over the table to reach me. Within a fraction of a second, his finger made a hard press on my cheek and then he settled down in his seat. As a reflex, I touched the point of contact and saw black color on my fingers. With the help of the front camera in my phone, I saw a jet black dot marking my cheek.

"What's this?", I questioned.

"That's Kaala Teeka to wade off evil eyes, in other words nazar. Your grandparents would've done that to you went you were babies. I'm not your grandfather but I think it was my duty to safeguard you. You can thank me later."

Vicky had a proud smile smeared on his face. It became difficult to decipher if it was just another trick or a genuine act. However, his words and expression emoted sincerity. He moved on to Sasha, who jerked her head back.

"I'm out of here. You guys don't have any work to do, is it?", she exclaimed.

"Sash, it's nearly the end of the day, what work do you have now?", Rohit asked.

She scrunched her nose, "Hmm, I'm going to pack up then". She stood up and made a move but I held her forearm.

'What?', her eyes screamed at me.

'It's just a dot, let him do it', my eyes replied back.

She blew out a deep breath and gave in. Sasha put her hand forward instructing Vicky to put it at the back of her hand. I didn't know Vicky was superstitious but if had gone all the way to buy a kajal box and had a sincere concern, I couldn't deny him. Knowing very well it had roots to his own love life. When we all dispersed, leaving Sasha and me alone in my car, I pecked her cheek as token of thanks. She looked down at her kaala teeka and smiled.

Days flew by, turning into weeks; and they were nothing but blissful times. Sasha and me gelled like anything and our love journey was smooth as butter. We stole our precious private moments and got to know each other more. We became the IT couple in our IT office, what an irony. Obviously, our friends left no chance to find moments to tease us. Without doubt, AJ and Vicky were the ones milking away all the chances. They would put up an act and imitate us as a couple. It felt like immediately our office cafeteria was revamped into a live theatre stage.

One day, Sasha and me were having our private time at the secluded semi-cicular bench behind our block. It was an area hidden by trees on either two sides and our building behind us, with no such great view, just a plain parapet wall. She asked something out of the blue, that shifted my attention from my phone to her.

"How and why did you fall for me?"

Sasha's question came out as meare whisper, while she was rotating a white plumeria flower with a yellow tinge at it's centre. The ornamental plants surrounding us had white flowers with both yellow and pink centered flowers. The one that fell on me, I handed it to Sasha.

"What do you mean why and how? Love doesn't have reasons nor logic, it just happens." I shrugged.

"It does have. Everything in this world runs on logic."

"Not everything but most of the things", I retorted.

"Let's not deviate from the topic. I asked how did you fall for a Tom-Boy?"

"The heart knows what it wants". I smiled at her to ease her nerves.

She scoffed, "Ya right! Stop talking around the bush. You could have got any girl, why me?"

"You could have got any other guy, but why me?" I threw her words back to her.

"You see, there was an invisible line of long queue of guys trailing behind me, right!".

I narrowed my eyes on her, "Are you implying that you settled with me since I was the only option?"

"Don't point the gun at me, first answer my question". She insisted like a stubborn kid.

"You aren't denying it, so what should I take from it?" I replied back exasperatedly.

"First come, first served. So it's your turn to answer, first. Aren't you a software engineer, don't you know about FIFO (First-In First-Out) queue?"

"For your kind information, there's also something called LIFO (Last-in Last-out) queue".

She groaned, "Raghav, we can do this all day long. Can you please just come back to the point?" Her dejected tone in her plea made be resign.

song:Yeah, I know, I knowWhen I compliment her she won't be-lieve meAnd it's so, it's soSad to think that she don't see what I seeBut every time she asks me, "Do I look okay?"I say.

"Ok relax! To tell the truth, I, myself don't know when and how our friendship blossomed into fondness to eventually culminate to our current status. I can't pin-point a single occasion to say that this was the defying moment. Everything as such fell in place, like it had been God's plan from the word go. About your other question why you and not any other girl, others didn't leave an impact on me I guess" I shrugged nonchalantly. "Sometimes being different makes you stand out and catch attention."

"In my case, it was the other way around. I always stood out from the crowd but was sidelined due to the choices I took. Being a plain boring Tom-Boy, doesn't catch attention to spark something, but only to be ridiculed or picked at. At the most, left out alone as an outcast. "

I placed my hand over hers, that was resting on the bench. "I can understand that, after all I was single too, all these years. No one took interest in a shy guy —"

She raised her brow in question, "You and Shy Guy, please tell that to someone else. You are anything but that."

"Trust me I was the shy, quiet boy, more like a geek, always in my own world. As I grew up, my only aim was to succeed in my studies and have a good career. Neither did I pay attention to girls nor did they too. It was mutual repulsion, I guess. I didn't think about it much because I thought no one would have been interested in me, anyways. So I can understand what you are trying to say. You don't need tons of people gushing over you, one person is more than enough."

She stole a glance at me and sent a tantalizing smile, "True that".

"You are like the shining pearl inside an oyster. The oyster shell being not pleasing to the eye, people abandon it. Not realizing that the true beauty is hidden enclosed in it. Your shell helped me in a way though. If someone else had been attracted to it, I would have lost my chance right". I winked at her.

song:When I see your faceThere's not a thing that I would change'Cause you're amazingJust the way you areAnd when you smileThe whole world stops and stares for a while'Cause girl you're amazingJust the way you areYeah.

"You are such an opportunist. Always on the lookout for a chance".

"Hundred percent true in your case, I'm certainly not going to deny it", I stated proudly. "Now your turn. What did you see in me, to accept my proposal?" I fluffed my hair and tugged my collar; dusted my shirt to show off my style.

She laughed at my antics. "You were the first guy to see me as a potential love interest. From the beginning you came off as a genuine, easy-going, decent guy. I guess our frequent chats and mutual interest in each other played some role. And yes, you are a lovable guy, so who wouldn't fall for you. You made a person allergic to romance, sprout such feelings within them, kudos to you! The most important fact, you accepted me for the way I am."

I leaned in closer to peck her forehead. With my hand snaked to the back of her head, to form a firm hold; the lip to forehead contact lingered for a couple of seconds. I could sense her insecurities and felt her self-esteem drop low in this topic. I didn't like seeing her in self-doubt.

"You are Sasha, the best version of yourself". I said when we separated.

She hunmed and nodded in agreement. "So, you too were a closed bud all these years? I knew it takes time for a flower to open up and blossom but this long?"

"It was waiting for the right kind of sunshine to be cast upon it. And you walked in". Winking and smirking at her, I replied.

Her fisted hand landed on my biceps, playfully, "Raghav you should be called as the Winking pro."

"Oh! I'm a pro at many things, Hun". I suggested mischievously, loving the endearment I use for her.

She rolled her eyes and huffed, "You and your Hun!"

"Yes, what should me and my Hun, do?"

"Nothing!", she snorted.

"Why, when we can do so many things?" I continued baiting her and thoroughly enjoying her cute, innocent expressions.

She wore a sweet, saccharine dripping smile with an equally laced tone. "You like your vitamins alot right, you want some?"

I rapidly nodded my head in eagerness, without any hesitancy.

She laughed her heart out and exclaimed, "Such an excited puppy dog". Leaning in forward she rested her palm along the left side of my face and moved to kiss on my right cheek.

My excitement was bubbling like boiling water.

She stopped mid-way and her eyes roamed all over my face, as if memorizing each contour of it. I turned to face her to see a teasing smirk growing on hers. With the help of her free hand, she blew a air kiss in my direction.

"There you go! Your dose of vitamin K". Stating that, she slid her hand down my cheek upto my chin and nudged it playfully.

I have been played! All the living cells in my body screamed.

Casting her a disapproving gaze, "I don't like it when you're such a tease". I huffed in protest and folded my arms.

Sasha giggled, "Look who's talking, the master of tease. By the way, I'm learning from my teacher and he seems to be pretty good at it". She jabbed softly at the center of my chest. She cocked her brow in question, "Are you worried that the student is catching up with the teacher and you'll be dethroned?"

I looked down at her finger resting on me. Moving back to meet her black orbs, I advised grumblingly. "Learn other things too, Sasha."

After a moment of stillness, we burst out laughing. I thought I was getting my first real kiss from her but on introspection, I knew it will take some more time for her to come out of her cocoon. For now,

I was happy that she was comfortable with me and I could see her progress.

In a jiff, two months flew by, marking the countdown of thirty days for Sasha's departure to onsite. Luckily, our first Valentine's Day together, could be celebrated before she left. Needless to say, I wanted ot to be super special. Here we go again in preparations for my Valentine's day proposal. It was cheesy and cliché but we didn't have time on our hand. I didn't want to spare any moment, that had the potential to make our bond more stronger and memorable, to pass by unnoticed.

Considering the not-so fantastic outcome of my previous ideas, I was skeptical. Wih renowed zeal and confidence I said to myself.

They have to be executed once again, failure is only the stepping stone to success.I can now learn from the previous mistakes and mend them to fit perfectly now.

If I search for new ideas, they may face the same fate as the earlier ones.

Going against the famous proverb — Don't put all balls in the same basket, I decided on a proposal marathon. Showering her with all the failed ideas one after the one, a day before Valentine's. This time God's angels were looking down on me and guarding. Valentine's fell on a Monday, so I had full Sunday without any office disturbance to carry out the plan.

Kicking off with a Sunday brunch, I let us have the required extra hours of sleep to keep us energized throughout the busy day. After our south Indian brunch with the pomegranate juice, that became her go-to drink now, we started the marathon proposal. I knew she was full till the brim of her food pipe. Of course, devouring a cone shaped ghee masala roast with a plate of poori-aloo and topping it with basundi, anyone would be in a state of daze.

Turning the car towards our office, made her frown a little. I covered it up by telling I had left something at my desk, that I needed to pick it up before we goto our next date destination. Little did she know that office was the real destination. Taking advantage of deserted office on a Sunday, I lead her to the park beside our block. We sat on a bench and suddenly music started picking up a notch.

"What's this?" She questioned, whipping her head left and right, trying to narrow down the source and it's location.

While she was busy in her quest, I sprung to my feet and stood in front of her. Tapping her shoulder to catch her attention, I said, "This is for you, my Sasha". With a snap of my fingers, my dancing troupe emerged from their hideouts and making my moves I joined them.

The flash mob we had practiced last time was executed perfectly. She stood up and swayed with the music. Towards the end of it, I moved towards her and went down on my knees with my gift hidden away from her sight. Her hands flew to her mouth in surprise and squealed. Revealing the gift — a beautifully blown Glass Rose and asked, "Will you be my Valentine, Sasha?"

She took it from my head and exclaimed, "Obviously! Who else will it be..... Thank you and it is a yes!"

Hooting and applause was heard behind me from my dancemates on her acceptance. I stood up and pressed my lips on forehead.

"This rose symbolizes our relationship — everlasting and fragile. Care needs to be taken to cherish it, just like our love. It can break if cracks develop, but if handled with care, it'll be forever and not wither away."

She smiled and nodded in agreement, I think I just stunned her. Placing another peck on her forehead, I motioned my troupe to join in our celebrations. They brought the cake we had ordered with the same words piped on it when I was down on my knees. This time I had ordered for a simpler version — Plum cake with thick chocolate sauce piping, leaving very little room for a melting disaster. Moreover it represented us and our likes more than anything.

After cutting the cake and devouring it, I turned to Sasha.

"Do you know why I chose a plum cake?"

She shrugged and bit into it, "Because it's one of our favorites".

I shook my head. "That too, but mainly because it resembles us. We, are all about substance and little show. Similarly, plum cakes have all the flavors imbibed inside them and don't need additional decorations or frosting to make it delicious or appetizing."

Her eyebrows shooted up and an impressed look over her face. "You really a something, Raghav! With your positive attitude and way with words". She took my hand and sandwiched it between her palms. "Thank you for making me feel so good about myself. I don't know what good deeds did I do in my past life, to have been rewarded with you". Her eyes turned glossy as she was getting emotional and overwhelmed with joy at the same time.

song:Oh, you know, you knowYou know I'd never ask you to changeIf perfect's what you're searching for then just stay the same-So don't even bother asking if you look okayYou know I'll say.

I swept her bangs to the side, away from her eyes and rested my free palm on her cheek. Caressing it in gentle stokes with my thumb. Acknowledging it, she leaned into my palm, titling her head. "Me too, Sasha. Can't thank God enough for sending you down as my angel on Earth". She cringed at my words and we shared another round of laughter.

The message tone of my phone interrupted us, my smile grew wider when I saw what it was. Making her sit beside me, I shared her the video clip I had made with the help of our friends. It started with a musical slideshow of our photos together, with our marathon photo sneakily taken by Asim and Vicky, as the first.

The photos faded and short video messages from our friends about us reeled out. Vicky, Asim, Daniel, Simbu, Ruhi, Chitra had some nice cute messages for us. Wishing us years of togetherness and reminiscing their favorite moments of Sasha and me. Rohit also had some good stuff to say but as usual he didn't end his message without a subdued warning to me. AJ was full on in fun mode and continued his pulling our legs in it too.

The surprise package was an audio clip of Mrs Hedge, Sasha's mom, giving us blessings. On which Sasha rolled her eyes, "I can't believe you got her also to agree for the video? Are you talking with my mom behind my back? Don't steal my mother, Raghav, she is my mom!" She threw a hard stare at me. I responded with a small smile and shrugged innocently.

"No one's trying to steal your mom, Hun." I tried pacifying her and outright disregarded her other question. With the attempt to bring back the conversation on track, I said. "I'll mail the video clip to you and when you are in doubt about our relationship, please view it. It might change you mind if we are going through a rough patch".

"Oh! So this is supposed to be reminder for me?"

"Take it however you want but don't forget your mom's blessings for us and her consent". I said proudly.

She knitted her eyebrows together, "You are so chaloo, you think you can sway my mind using my nother as your trump card? "

At that thought, I chuckled, "Hello! She's your mother, she'll take your side obviously".

"Ya right!", she remarked sarcastically. Sasha knew I had a good bond with her mother but how much ever strong it was, it wasn't deeper than the mother - daughter bond.

"Relax Sasha! I'm just saying before we think of taking any drastic step, we can watch this video. It may or may not sway our mind. No doubt your mom will agree to whatever you decide, same with me". Glancing at my wristwatch, "Okay, it's time for our next destination, let's go". I stood up and extended my hand towards her.

She slammed her's into mine in tiredness and whined. "Isn't it over yet, how many more destinations have you planned for one day?"

"Hmmm, I think two more".

We rode to the next stop, an old age home. Sasha liked volunteering work, I had seen her enthusiasm for it in office. As her days in Coimbatore were limited, I thought of planning the things she likes to do. Moreover, she was going to embark a new journey professionally and would require all the blessings she could gather. That made me transform my previous ruined romantic candle light dinner into a luncheon and game time at the old age home.

I had extended the invite to our friends too, who happily joined us. We spent our afternoon with the senior citizens, some played carrom, cards, chess and other indoor board games. Some read stories to the cute grannies over there. I sang few songs on my guitar as a closing note to them. We left he place with a promise of returning soon, with ot without Sadha, alone with photographs of the memories we shared.

The rosy sky signalled the early evening tea-time, the perfect time for our entry to our next station. When we remembered our elders, how could we forget the cute little beings on the opposite side of the same spectrum. Orphanage was our next stop. Our visit, started off with skits, from us and the children, who displayed their talents. Dividing amongst ourselves, some of us played cricket with the children and others played indoor games with those who weren't fit enough for cricket. Another cake cutting ceremony along with chocolates and new clothes distribution took place. The only mistake we did was, we took selfies at the end. Wide smiles over sweating faces were snapped as result of it.

The day ended with both of us reclining in our respective car seats of my car in front of a societal park near her accommodation.

"Thank you, for planning this day for me, it really felt special. I didn't take you for person who would celebrate Valentine's day to such an extent". Sasha was the one to break the comfortable silence.

"Hmmm, even I didn't know", I blew out a short laugh.

"So you are Romantic Raghav then?", she jested while turning to face me.

"Yes for you. You made me become one. The romance quotient grew on me like wildfire, just like you". I playfully nudged her straight nose.

She tried her best to throw a reprimanding glare but failed miser-ably. "Since we celebrated Valentine's day a day in prior, tomorrow will be back to normal routine?!" She let out a long sigh.

"Looks like my lioness hasn't had enough of her surprises!" I said playfully. "Dil maange more, is it?", I asked in surprise.

"Hmmm, nothing of that sorts.... We had our day but tomorrow everyone will have there's and rub it in my face".

Grinning in bewilderment, "You want to indulge in some PDA, oh my God, am I hearing things now?"

"Don't make fun of me, Raghav", she scolded me with a punch me. Anicipating her move, I quickly beefed-up my biceps to lesser the blow.

"I'm not, it took me by surprise, Sasha", I replied honestly with a undertone of amusement.

Our gaze met a couple seated cozily at a corner of the park and they were smooching. It was a heavy duty make-out session. Luckily it was slightly dark and no onlookers except us. We immediately averted our eyes and peeked a glance at each other. Our eyes spoke volumes and conveyed the unsaid words — 'No to PDA, that's not us.'

Seeing her dull face over the end to the V-Day celebrations, I revealed. "Don't worry, you still have two more surprises", raising my fingers to show the number.

"Wow! Where's it?". She immediately jumped in joy and scanned through my car in search of it. She turned to look behind at the back seat. Unable to locate anything special around, she repeated her question, "I can't see it, where did you hide it, Raghav?"

"Hun, relax!" Her creased lines straightened out a little. She was warming up to my endearment for her, implying it to be a sign of improvement. "They are lined up for tomorrow, you'll get your gifts then."

She snorted, ready to put a tantrum if required. "Then why did you tell me today!", she crossed her arms annoyedly.

"You were looking sad and dull, so I wanted to cheer up".

"Give me the gift now", she held her open palm in my direction. "I'll cheer up instantly."

Casting a smile, I replied. "Nope! It doesn't work like that, they are scheduled for tomorrow. Besides I don't have them with me now. Didn't the day full of surprises, fill your stomach?"

"It did!" She said with dejected tone and her hand fell back on her lap. "But you, you had to open your damn mouth and ruin it. Now, you don't want to disclose it fully. Urgh!! Raghav! You know very well that I don't like having only half-eaten information. Either spill the beans fully or don't spill anything. How difficult is that! Why don't you ever do that. Now my mind is going to start it's over analysis to churn out thousand and one possibilities. For sure, they won't even be a mile close to what you are actually going to do."

"Chill Hun! The wait time is only a day, actually only a night. Tomorrow you'll know what's the special Valentine's Gift."

"You are so mean!", she announced with piercing eyes.

I chuckled at her adorable behavior, "Have patience, baby. Anyways, few moments ago you were sad you won't get pampered tomorrow. Sasha, I think you have split personality, or at least, bipolar."

She raised her eyes in challenge and it returned to it's usual place, when I raised my hands in surrender. "If you had already decided to give the gifts tomorrow, then why did you plan the day-long date today?"

"I wanted to spend a together outside the office walls. Keeping in mind your thirty day ticking countdown also has started, you will get busy with packing and other stuff. Making today the ideal choice for it." I said and pecked her cheeks.

Firing up the engine, I made way to her paying guest accommodation, as her deadline for entry into the said premises was closing.

I'm also eagerly waiting for tomorrow, to give her the special Valentine's Gift.

28

CHAPTER 28

Raghav's POV

song: Heart beats fastColors and promisesHow to be brave-How can I love when I'm afraid to fallBut watching you stand aloneAll of my doubt, suddenly goes away somehow.

The most anticipated day had arrived, it was 14th February! Sasha had bombarded me with text messages over the night to give her hints, to guess what the remaining surprise gifts were. Her impatience was one thing and mine was to see my Reaction Queen's expression when her special gift was uncovered.

Seated in my car, parked a little away from her gate, my eyes followed her every move as she walked towards the car. Her burgandy bangs flopped up and down with each step she took. Her trademark black winged eyes were shielded by her spectacles. Clutching her sling bag, thrown over her left shoulder, she hopped down the steps at her gate. Pushing back the centre of her sliding eyewear, to make it rest properly at the nose juncture. The metallic edge of the frame caught a ray of light and sparkled, giving her a touch of a dazzling shining star.

Dressed in plain white shirt teamed with olive green cargo pants. A loose fit, long sleeved, mid thigh long, open grey cardigan was thrown over it, to keep her warm. Though the winter season had conveyed it's goodbye to the city, the chill February winds still lingered around.

I opened the door from inside for her, stretching over the passenger seat. As she took her place and was fastening her seatbeat midway, I spoke.

"I thought you'll come dressed in pink, today".

"Why?", she asked and looked up from her task to meet my eyes.

"I heard wearing pink on V-Day denotes that a person is in a committed relationship". I stated matter-of-factly.

She huffed and sat back after securing her safety belt. Turning sideways carefully in her seat to face me, she narrowed her eyes. "I don't see any shades of pink on you!" Her gaze did a quick once-over of my ensemble, proving her accusation.

"But, I'm a —". I held my tongue in check when she bouched up her sleeves and folded her arms. The perfect arc of her brows made me accept defeat and let it pass.

"Good!", she lauded me and bent over to my side. Pulling the keys out, drowned the roar of the car engine to a complete stop.

"First things first, where's the gift? Cut the suspense now", she demanded.

I paused for few minutes and said coolly, "It's not a gift-gift."

A suspicious shadow overtook her face along with a deep frown. "If you are thinking of anything stupid, like PDA or something on those lines, you can forget it."

Her look of a stern no-nonsense teacher made me chuckle. "Sasha, now you are putting ideas in my head".

"Oops!", she retreated from her conjecture. "Ok, then what is it?", she asked softly.

I inhaled and exhaled a deep breathe and built up the atmosphere. It was huge. I didn't time to organize my words before they escaped my mouth and messed it up.

"Lately, I've been burning the candles at both ends to impress the clients and worked few late hours from home. Providing overlap of my working hours with theirs. Everything paid off, in acquiring my reward for my sweat and blood. Each task that earned praises, found it's entry into a piggybank account of mine and when it was full, my prize was ready to be claimed". I beamed with happiness as I spoke.

"What's the reward?", Sasha quipped.

"Patience hun, let me finish". She nodded and gestured to carry on.

"You remember the Navratri client visit?" I asked her.

Rolling her eyes, "Obviously".

"When I thought only my work as in the dollar save automation collaboration with Vicky, other individual automations, taking up extra work and then that damn task which I had wrongly estimated; did all the talking, looks like I sidelined the client visit. Do you remember how many clients came over during the floor visit, that time?"

"Cathy, Dave, Ethan and Lisa, if I'm not wrong?" She ticked them off on her fingers.

"Your missing one person, just like I did. It was Cathy and her team of four. The fourth person was Michael, he was a silent spectator but turned out to be the most important one. His observant eyes, liked the Navratri based bay decoration and how I had conceptualized it, mixing fun and work. The parallels we drew with the festival and work, were etched in his memory. When it drilled down to my competitor and me, for the prized spot; he was the decision maker.

He selected me, stating that we needed young blood like me who knew how to do a job well and have an out-of-box thinking. If we train ourselves in that lane, we can come up with many more dollar save projects and automation ideas. Adding to it, for the client organization to put up tough competition and earn laurels in the business world, automation was the need of the hour."

"Congratulations Raghav! I'm so proud of you". She gave me an enthusiastic short hug, before resting back in her seat. "Are you getting a promotion for it?"

"Huh-uh!", I shook my head in disagreement. With an ear-to-ear smile, "Even better than that.... I.... secured an onsite assignment!" I announced in excitement whilst playing drumrolls on the steering wheel for additional effect.

Her eyes doubled, tripled in size. Clearly unable to believe it, she blurted out, "What!... Wow!"

"Luckily, two weeks back they confirmed my deputation. You won't believe, both of us have been assigned to the same office, same city; to top it all, on the very same day". My voice notched up an octane as the reveal of my reward progressed. I continued to say, "They sped up the process and formalities, to send all the employees going on onsite deputation, together in one-shot. My visa is short term for now, due to insufficient time. After landing over there, they'll extend it to one year, same as yours. How lucky are we!?" I exclaimed with my happiness to the peak.

She was overwhelmed and squealed in joy. "This is the best Valentine's Gift ever, Raghav! It's just perfect."

I teased her a bit, "What did you think, I will let you spill away from my hands, just like that, without a fight? Now, you can't escape me". I ended in laughter. "I tried my level best to secure the onsite role and thanks to all my stars for shining on me, cumulatively. I did this for us! Everyone was scaring me about long distance relationship and how it's tough. When couples who have been together for ages couldn't withstand the pressure of it, we being at our initial stages, made me uneasy. I hope you liked the surprise?"

If I thought my happiness knew no bounds, her's was thousand folds of mine. She jumped in her seat and leapt on to me for another round of Vitamin H+. It seriously was excessive showering of H+. She would retreat and before reclining back, she would come forward for another cuddling hug. Felt like she was reciprocating all my gifts with interest. While breaking one hug, she slowly left my arms and stole a peep of my face, before doing what left me spell bound.

My cute, innocent, Tom-Boy Girlfriend — Sasha; gifted me with a quick peck on my lips!!! Instantly she fell back into the passenger seat, feeling shy and flustered to the core.

On my lips! On my lips! Sasha just kisssd me on my lips! My heart and mind were dancing around it.

I had been waiting for her first kiss from her side, since forever, if I'm exaggerating. Never in my wildest dreams would I have ever imagined, that it would land on my lips in the first try! She hit the bull's eye like in a game of archery.

song:One step closer. I have died everyday, waiting for youDarling, don't be afraid, I have loved you for a thousand yearsI'll love you for a thousand more.

"Now this is what you call a perfect Valentines Day and the best gift ever!"

I scremed out it euphoria, unable to contain it within me. Her face resembled a red tomato, due to her growing blush. Before

Sasha could fall back to her romance deficient nutshell, I sent her an apologetic smile for my over enthusiasm. She responded back with an understanding smile and a nod.

"So, now the thirty day countdown is applicable for you too?" She broke the ice burg creeping up between us, after her surprising kiss.

"Ummm, yes. So many things to do. It's going to be tightly packed days ahead. I still can't believe it's happening so fast, it's like living a dream".

"It's all your hard work and your never say die attitude that made it happen, for you and for us. Like they say — every cloud has it's silver lining!, I'm witnessing one right now."

I nodded in agreement, "You're right! Sometimes when a shadow of darkness hovers over us, we think it's 'The End for us'. Actually, it's just that our seeds of success are being planted under the shadow. I remember learning in my childhood that during the initial stages, all seeds need some shadow, a little bit of sunshine and occasional watering. Only then, do they shoot up to grow into a tree."

She broke into a wide proud grin, "And you did just that! Worked in silence and let the success make all the noise! I can't be more proud of you. Oh my Gosh! I don't know why my vision is getting blurry".

I had roared up the engine and maneuvered the car towards the office, to have our breakfast at the office cafeteria.

"Here, take this tissue. Don't cry, I'm not that bad of a company. That you need to shed tears thinking that you couldn't get rid of me in Coimbatore to enjoy your freedom, abroad". I pulled her leg, stealing a glance at her before training them on the road.

Anticipating a punch from her on my biceps, as usual, instead, I earned a soft peck on my left cheek. I couldn't help but sneak a peek at her and raised my brow in surprise. She conveniently averted her eyes and focused them out of her window. Kinda turning her back to me, to sneak away from responding.

"Today's really my lucky day, I guess", I casually commented. "Now I'm realizing the truth behind the proverb — Uparwala jab bhi deta hai, chapar phaad ke deta hai! (When the Lord gives, His bounty is limitless)". Smirking playfully, I stated looking straight through the windshield, at the road ahead.

"Oh! Just shut up and drive, Raghav!". She shushed me and there her dismissive slap met my biceps, as expected earlier.

My last surprise for her was waiting at her office desk. I converted the decorations and chocolates from the previous failed proposal into meaningful gifts. A stressbuster smiley ball and a coffee mug with our photo on it, welcomed her at her desk.

While she was scrutinizing it, I demanded. "You better be using the coffee mug in your new office. Your new colleagues should get the message loud and clear that you're in a relationship and are off-limits." I damned with no ounce of faltering. Adjusting it's position on the desk, I said, "Keep in mind that it needs to be faced this way, to show our photo".

Her train of giggles didn't seem to find a stopping point. "Is it really necessary? Anyways, you are going to be like a satellite, revolving around me, all the time!" She shrugged, unashamed to call the truth out.

I snorted, "I wish I could that! By the way, why is everyone suddenly talking about planets and solar system lately, are you'll brushing up your astronomy skills?

My reply seemed to irk her, "Why are you insecure? You are coming along too, right?"

"Yeah, I'm coming with you to onsite, but can't trust this management. Remember, they canceled Chitra's onsite deputation in the last moment, stating that the clients were not on the same terms on the choice of employee selection. Just few hours before she had to leave for the airport, they conveyed it to her, it was devastating! I have my full trust on the clients but its wavery when it comes to our management...... Besides, whether I'm there or not, this better be with you all the time, got it?!"

"Okay, Mr. Possessive freak", she saluted me, obeying my instructions.

song:Time stands stillBeauty in all she isI will be braveI will not let anything,take awayWhat's standing in front of me.

At the end of the long day, Sasha was waiting for me to wrap up my work. It had unceremoniously dragged on till eight thirty in the night, due to a client meeting. I had insisted on her leaving without me and taking a ride home with one of her hulks. She refused outright and said she didn't mind waiting for me. She would stay inside the floor within my vision and if she got bored, would do her next day's work prior, to make room for some leisure time tomorrow.

My call ended atlast and I went to the men's room to relieve myself and freshen up. We decided on having a cup of piping hot coffee before we make a headstart for home, to energize ourselves after the long day. Sasha head to the breakout area, as we parted ways to join back afterwards, for the coffee.

Hot chocolate aroma, right from a bakery, hit my nostrils; when I entered the coffee area. As I took few steps into the room, my eyes shone in surprise and wandered around to meet Sasha's. She had set up a long overdue date for us at office, at our floor in the breakout area, at a table next to the entrance door.

She motioned me to sit at the said table were two cups of coffee with hot steam emerging out of it, was visible. She stood near the microwave oven and when the timer set off, she opened it. In her gloved hands, she held two mugs of make-on-the-go chocolate lava cake. As she came near to the table and arranged them on it, she depicted a domesticated version of my Sasha. She even wore an apron for heating the cake in the microwave oven.

So adorably cute!

Clearly it was an alien field of work, which she hadn't ventured out in, yet.

Taking her seat, she removed the apron and said. "After the maggi noodles disaster, I thought this would be a safer option. This cake required only pre-heating the mixture before serving. Seeing how much efforts you took to organize things for me, I thought this was the closest I could get for a successful homemade cooked dish. Hope it works fine for you, instead of ordering from the restaurant!"

"This is picture perfect, Sasha! With no one around, a simple and cozy date, at the very place where it all started from". I nudged towards the swipe machine at the floor's entrance where our magical first meet took place.

song: Every breath, every hour has come to thisOne step closer.

She played an instrumental melody from her phone, as a soft background music. We had a good relaxing time, unwinding the day's toil with the right combination of coffee and chocolate lava cake and subtle music. Her simple carefree effort outdid mine. I would anytime choose this moment over any other date. At that note, I realized the latent truth that hit me like a lightening strike.

I found my love and tranquility... And-and, I think I'm ready to take it to the next step....

song:And all along I believed,I would find youTime has brought your heart to me, I have loved you for a thousand yearsI'll love you for a thousand more. One step closerOne step closer.

29

CHAPTER 29

Raghav's POV

song:Don't have to leave this townto see the world'Cause it's something that I gotta doI don't wanna look back in thirty yearsAnd wonder who you're married toWanna say it now, wanna make it clearFor only you and God to hear.

Two days later I confronted Sasha with the new brain wave that hit me. No, I didn't do another round of proposal, it would be taxing for me and rub Sasha on the wrong side. Too many proposals in such short span of time. Also, it required a man-to-man discussion, before plunging into it. Her consent was essential. Just because I had comprehended, it didn't mean the same brain wave would have hit her yet. During our lone time, before calling it a night, we spent some extra moments in the seclusion of my car outside her accommodation.

Placing her right hand in between my palms, I rested our sandwiched hands on her lap. Looking down at it and fondly caressing to fuel up the courage I required for the upcoming discussion. It was time for the crawling caterpillars in my mind to transform into butterfly and fly off my mouth. My words would need to withstand strong opposition initially. Similar to the initial struggle of the flapping wings until they found the hang of flying. I knew a smooth gliding journey was awaiting, once we emerged victorious of the first phase.

Drawing in a deep breathe, prying my eyes off our hands, I looked up. On straightening, I found her vision too was stuck at our hands.

"Sasha, I want to talk to you about something. It's huge. Please think it through, before you give me your final decision on it. Take how much ever time you want. The only thing I can hope is, that you should be completely honest with me". Squeezing her hands to provide solace, to which one of us, could be debatable.

"Raghav, you know, you are creeping me out, right?", she jerked her head back.

Sending her a reassuring smile, "Nothing's creepy, just need your point of view on something."

"Then, dive into it. Why are you running around the bushes for?" She insisted.

"You know we only have twenty-eight days over here, before we touch down on foreign land.... I—I was wondering if you would be fine, if I introduced you officially to my family...on the lines of taking the next step in our relationship".

song:When you love someone, they say you set 'em freeBut that ain't gonna work for me.

Instantly her pupils dialated till there was no room for further expansion. "What?! Raghav have you gone nuts?! It's too soon to be thinking about such stuff". She panicked, as anticipated.

"Stuff?", I spat out in surprise, "It's our life, our future I'm talking about. Tell me something, marriage has never crossed your mind? Or did you not forsee, going through it with me?" By now, our respective hands were to ourselves with the topple of our shaky foundation.

"Raghav!", she groaned, "Obviously the first option. Do you see me as the kind of girl who's going to be dreaming and planning out a wedding?"

"Not immediately but eventually, yes!" Folding my arms in affirmatiom, I damned.

"Really?" Her arched eyebrows rose in challenge.

"I mean, not a dreamy extravagant wedding. I thought somewhere in the back of your mind, you would have thought that marriage is on the cards for us." I could feel my confidence levels drop down.

Sasha took my hand in hers and entangled her fingers, filling the gaps between mine. Looking straight into my eyes, she said. "It is! I feel we need to slow down a bit. We are taking, way too many steps, too fast. Don't you think so?" Her soft voice tried pushing some reasons through my thick skull.

"Glad to hear that", I heaved a sigh of relief. "You should have said it clearly at the beginning. Your reaction scared the living daylights off me". I scoffed like a child and fidgetted with my legs, trying to find leg space.

"Like Asim said stop being a Kang-ga-roo". Thankfully, her tease cut the tension in the air, with both of us, breaking into smiles.

Rolling my eyes, I brought back our discussion on tracks. "This great idea didn't just dawn on me, this instant. I slept over it for two days, before coming to you. You should also give it a thought. I know it's early for us but do you think we have time on our hands, especially with our onsite assignment?"

She thought for, what could be ten seconds, before giving her opinion. "Have you ever heard of 'metamorphosim' or 'evolution'?

Everything requires time for it to evolve and speeding up the process, isn't going to result in a good way."

"Are we going to be answering each other with questions?" When she wore a deadpan expression, I continued. "Let's come out of the 'theorical' world to a practical world".

"My answers were aligned with both", she debated with a stern glare.

"Chill Sasha! Let's suppose, we don't disclose it to our families and leave for abroad. In the span of one year, away from here, are you telling me that there aren't going to be marriage alliance discussions at our homes?"

"No one's going to force us into marriage. We'll have a say in it too". She lifted her nose, making her point.

"Yes, true that! I don't want to wait till the last moment, with prospective 'suitors' banging at your doorstep. I don't like the possibility of it hanging around in our absence. In that case, if now it's too early, then it may be too late, then and that unsettles me". Just think about the probability of it happening, sent the pit of my stomach churning. The thought needed to pass away, this very moment, before bile could come out of my mouth.

song:I don't wanna live without youI don't wanna even breatheI don't wanna dream about youWanna wake up with you next to me.

I could see her mind was battling on it. "Okay! I agree with you, but still feel you are hopping on a bullet train, when we need to take things slow. I'm a goods carrier train, it's difficult for me to keep up with you". She gestured to herself.

I smirked, "You—you are calling me a bullet train? I'm sure Vicky and Asim would beg to differ on it. I'm the slowest of the lot, did you forget I'm the renowned tortoise?" Pulling my collar in pride to emphasize it.

She rolled her eyes, "You are not, at this point!"

Turning back to her, I said mustering up all my convincing skills. "I'm not suggesting to get married right now. We can just make our sides of the families be aware of our relationship status and our future intentions. Marriage can happen on a much later stage."

"It could backfire too!"

"How's that?"

"What if they don't agree to our selection of partners?"

"See now you are following! We have a limited time frame over here. We'll just drop the idea on them and scurry off to America. Then, we will have one year to convince them and potray that we are an ideal match. In the meanwhile, we will also be closer and figure out whether what we started will meet it's desirable destiny."

Her eyes squinted at me and her hard glare was kind of scary under the dim light of the overhead interior light, which was switched on throughout our discussion. "So you still have doubts?"

I pursed my lips to disguise my smile. "Never say never, right? More over, it's for you— your benefit of doubt."

She snorted, "Ya right!" and crossed her arms, annoyed with my reply.

"Sasha! Hun!" I leaned over slightly and shook her upper arm as she was purposely avoiding my eye contact. Rubbing her arm to ease her irritated look, I said. "I'm just sticking to my words I said when we spoke about our long distance relationship."

"Which one?", she immediately responded.

"That if you think I am or our relationship is over-bearing, we will call it quits". Gently and slowly I stated as not to aggravate more than she already was.

"You don't seem to have trust. Mr. Raghav Srivatsav, it's you who has Vitamin T deficiency, not me". A forceful jab stabbed at centre of ny chest. Now her blazing gaze found the perfect line of sight with me. "If you want to have an escape route out of us, then why involve our families and burden them? Let's figure it out ourselves and then when you have hundred percent surety, then we can bother our parents with it".

"You do have a valid point, but you are getting me wrong. I said it's for Your benefit of doubt. If I wasn't sure or had commitment issues, why would I have come up with the suggestion of meeting our families. There's no one in the world with whom I would want to take this step. I already have your mother's vote of confidence on my side, I want that to be extended to the whole family."

song:I don't wanna go down any other road nowI don't wanna lovenobody but you.

She huffed, "Such a greedy man, you are. Can't you be happy with what you have now?"

"Nope!", I grinned at her. "Moreover, my family is unaware about us. It'll give them an opportunity to see us in a different light."

"Whose fault is that?", she snorted.

"If they come to know that there's something more than friend-ship, they will surely pester me in bringing you home to meet them. Do you want the scrutiny to happen at my home or in your safe haven? I'm suggesting all this for your comfort. When I know that an official introduction is inevitable, why not have both the parties at the same time? This way we all can be on the same page. If you want to meet my family separately, it's fine by me". I shrugged as I concluded.

"I'm not! What will I tell my parents? Without their knowledge I'm not taking such a huge step and getting acquainted with your family on a personal basis. I could speak to them on phone."

"Just as I thought. That's the reason I didn't want to put you on the spot. Speaking on the phone is different and meeting face to face is entirely different."

When silence took over, I added. "Sasha, I don't want to force you into anything, nor will I ever do. What came to my mind and what I thought would do us good, I said. If you feel uncomfortable and feel it's too early getting are parents involved in our equation, it's fine. I wanted to convey my point of view and wanted to hear yours. So relax, nothing you agree or disagree to, is going to change the dynamics between us". I hugged her and placed a long kiss on her forehead and temples, to ease the tension I gave her.

She mumbled under me, "Why do we keep inviting trouble? Can't we just go and enjoy onsite together and push these things for a later stage?"

I held her shoulders and kept her in an arm's distance. "I didn't know my Ms. Sneakers was looking forward for us to enjoy together in abroad? What did you exactly have in mind by 'enjoy'?" With my recent favorite teasing expression, I smirked at her.

"Raghav!", she reprimanded me for my pun.

"We haven't set foot on foreign soil, but looks like their winds are already having an effect on you, now itself". My smirk grew into an enormous grin with a sparkle of mischievous glint in my eyes. Rubbing my palms together, I said, "I can't wait to see what happens when we land there".

Her infamous, predictable punch flew onto my biceps, this time it didn't stop with one but a train of them. Chuckling away, I pulled her closee for my much need Vitamin H+.

"Stop baiting me always, Raghav!", she mumbled into my chest softly.

I kissed her hair on top of her hand, "Sorry Hun!" Another kiss landed on her crown and I said. "Sorry, but I can't help it!" I shrugged and she playful pat on my chest before pulling me closer to her. Her hands traced my body and rested on my back, as she snuggled into the hug.

"This is heaven", I let out in a soft breath. "Wish we could stay forever like this Sasha, but the security gates will close in another ten minutes or so."

I felt her ball up her fist and hit my back. "Why do you open your mouth to ruin the moment, Raghav?" With that she parted away.

I knew both of us wanted to be in the moment and never leave each other's arms. We were getting carried away, but now wasn't the moment to lose track of time.

"We will have all the time in the world to recreate such moments, but I want to be on my best behavior until we are packed off to America."

She narrowed her eyes at me, "Don't read too much into this ok. Don't fog your head with anything." She replied sternly.

Rolling my eyes, I replied. "My eyes and mind aren't clouded with anything, they are clear as crystal. Ok, before you leave, can you tell me why you don't want to make an official announcement at our homes? You didn't mind it when we declared it at office." I voiced out the question that lingered in my mind and which would surely result in a sleepless night, if I didn't ask her now.

She groaned,"Your questions never die, is it?"

"That's the last one, I swear. We don't have much time, only seven more minutes till the gates are closed". Looking into my wristwatch, I hurried her to get her reply.

Her shoulders slummed down and she said. "I'm not the ideal girl for marriage, everyone knows that. You wear a different color of glasses and saw me as someone special. But, I can't expect the same out of your family. I'm scared, no worried. What if they reject me? Everything will be ruined. It'll spoil our mood and going to my dream job with a sore mindset, isn't something to look forward to."

I pecked her forehead "Sometimes I really want to open your brain and see what's in it, that gives you such ideas." She responded with an emotionalless expression. "Sasha, they are my family, they'll want to see me happy. When they see my happiness is with you, even if they have any reservations, they'll accept you wholeheartedly. If they don't, why am I there for? I'll convince them. Don't forget I was born in that family, so if I have such viewpoints, they did play some role in it. They might have similar views too, so I don't see any issues in it. Leave that to me, don't stress on it. Did you ever think, objection could come from your end too? "

"You have already charmed my mother, what more do you want. What is there unlikable about you?"

I beamed with pride, "Hundred percent correct!"

She shook her head in amusement and smiled. Collecting her things and stuffing it into her backpack, she opened her door to leave. I took her hand and pecked the back of her palm. "Stress isn't a good colour on you, leave it to me. Sleep tight. Good night, Sweet dreams Hun".

I could see her visibly relax more and she convey her good night, before rushing to get past the gates. Once she passed the said territory, breathlessly she waved towards me as I backed up the car to leave.

song: Looking in your eyes now, if I had to die nowI don't wanna love nobody but you (you)I don't wanna lovenobody but you (you).

Sasha took three days time to agree with my decision to make our parents aware of our love. She said, "Let's inform them, it's upto them if they want to have a formal meet or not." That sounded good to my ears and I nodded in agreement. Now we had twenty-five days to decide on how and when to disclose it. The office had granted us a week's leave for spending time with our families before leaving for our new assignment, as one year would be a long duration away from our loved ones. Luckily me, I would be taking one of my loved ones with me.

We decided to avail out time off on our second last week of stay in India. If any official work or transfer of tasks or KT (knowledge transfer) sessions were pending, we could attend to it on the last week and depart from Coimbatore.

Bangalore, being our hometowns, on an early friday evening we started off on our long drive together. A mini road trip together to our hometown was kicked off.

After leaving behind the traffic of the main city, Sasha turned on the radio. She had packed some wraps for our journey. I had cooked the chicken for the filling, while she heated the ready-made tortillas and diced some vegetables to add to the filling, along with mustard, honey-chili sauce and mayonnaise. We had made a few extras and has a pre-snack before we left. Shared a few with our friends due to their ogling eyes while we were packing the wraps.

This felt so right, in so many ways. I could picture us picnicking like this on weekends at our new home— abroad, far away from home.

song:All the wasted days, all the wasted nightsI'll blame it all on being youngGot no regrets 'cause it got me hereBut I don't wanna waste another one.

Just then a question crossed my mind. "Why did you settle for an IT job in Coimbatore, when Bangalore is the IT hub?" I asked her casually.

"I got the call letter from this company first and considering that I had spent my entire life in Bangalore, I wanted to explore other places. Try to be independent and all. It's not too far too just 6-7hrs journey on road and in case of emergencies a forty-five minute flight. My dad was fine with it, after he selected my place of start. What about you?"

I hummed in acknowledgment. "Same with me too, also the climate is good compared to the other cities. Didn't you think of asking for relocation after spending three years here?"

"Relocate for what? All of my friends are here, without them office would be boring and dull. I didn't have a solid reason for relocation, but if they weren't going to give me promotion or onsite, I would have pressurized them to grant it within two months. All this hardwork and no reward, at the expense of staying away from family for so many years, wasn't worth it. "

I nodded in agreement. "In onsite too, your hulks wouldn't be there", I pointed out.

"You'll be there right", came her swift reply.

I whipped my head sideways and smiled at her before focusing back on the road. She didn't realize her one line reply, meant the world to me. I took her hand and placed it on the gear. Resting my palm over hers, I intertwined our fingers and clamped on the gear. Shifting the gears of the car, hand-in-hand, along with hers; I could only wish we did the same while shifting the gears of our life in synchrony.

song:I've been thinking about what I want in my lifeIt begins and ends the sameIf I had to choose what I couldn't loseThere'd only be one thing.

We disclosed our relationship status to our respective families on the third day of our arrival. Sasha's family had already got the hint thanks to Mrs. Hedge. What stunned me was that my parents too had whiff of it. Like they say you can't hide anything from your parents, they know each and every expression of ours. After all they saw us growing up in front of their eyes. I couldn't read them like an open book, like they did, though. They had a very neutral response, nothing over the top. None of our families spoke about it for next two days. If I thought they weren't giving it any attention, I was proven wrong.

By the third last day of our stay in Bangalore, we had completed most of our shopping and packing. Suddenly while having lunch, my Dadi (paternal grandmother) said, "Call the girl's family and tell them we will visit them at five in the evening."

Her announcement stunned not only me but my parents too. "So soon, Dadi? We should have informed them in prior." I replied hesitantly.

"Yes we are giving them three hours prior notice, what more do they want? It's not like we are asking them to prepare a wedding lunch that they need more time". She responded back arrogantly.

That's her nature but I think it was too fast, I mean such short notice, what will the Hedge's think. Oh Godness! The first impression was going to get ruined. I started getting nervous. I knew no one would go against her words, being the oldest member of the family. Somewhere amidst this, I tried convincing myself that we didn't have time and procrastinating it wasn't going to be of any help. I swallowed my food quickly and excused myself, to inform Sasha with the latest developments.

"What?!? Three hours?", she screamed into the phone. Involuntarily making me move away from the phone and return once she had calmed down.

I cut her off before she could ramble on. "Hun, relax! We have only three hours, let's make the most of it. There's no use of worrying about it, sooner or later it was going to happen. Be happy this way we have only three hours of worry now. If it had been a planned meet, the number of hours would have added to it."

She let out a sigh and we spoke a few words before conveying, Best of Luck to each other. Our 'Meet the family' exam was due in less than three hours. The preparation time was less and we didn't know how long would the real test last for.

Hope we don't flunk at it. I prayed as I looked heavenwards.

We arrived at Sasha's residence sharp on the dot, as my Dadi and father regarded punctuality very high. To my relief, the Hedge's were ready and well prepared. The welcome, initial greetings and discussion about family background went smooth.

So far so good.

Just then my Dadi turned towards me asked. "Where is the girl, tell them to bring her out? Her brother is also here."

My eyes doubled and I wore an embarrassed expression as I swept my eyes across the room. Mr. Hedge looked pissed but held his tongue in check due to his wife's calming hand on his knee. While she wore a tight smile, my gaze moved on to Sasha. She wore a worried look and I could see hurt cloaking her pupils. I gulped my saliva and shook my head to let her know she didn't need to feel sad.

The only person who could save us from this, was me. I turned to my Dadi and took out her spectacles from her eyes. Cleaning it with my handkerchief, I placed it back slowly on her nose.

She smiled at me and pat my lap, "Thank you".

"Dadi, Sasha is here. The one sitting in the navy blue kurtha and stripped red and white dupatta". I pointed to Sasha sitting in front of me. At the mention of the dupatta, Sasha immediately pulled it back up on her shoulder. It had slid down behind her due to the blowing air from the fan. She had secured the dupatta on one side of her shoulder at the back but didn't secure it in front.

Obviously she wasn't used to handling dupatta's on a daily basis, so it didn't hit her mind to catch it from being blown away. Over that, her navy blue kurtha resembled a punjabi men's kurtha with wooded buttons at the centre and sleeves till her elbows having a loop. She had teamed with similar stripped leggings kind of clothing.

"Oh! Ok ok!", Dadi replied as she pushed her spectacles up her nose. She gave Sasha a look over that was way too obvious, making Sasha squirm under her scrutinizing eyes. I squeezed my grandmother's hand a couple of times but her gaze didn't falter or soften up. I looked over her bent head to my mother and sent her a signal of alarm.

My mom caught it and quickly handled the situation. "She is short sighted and far sighted, with old age, vision gets distorted. I guess the spectacles weren't cleaned properly before we came here. Sorry about her words, she's always blunt, don't mind her."

Mrs. Hedge picked up the conversation before anyone else could. Smiling away she said, "Yes, we can understand. Everyone goes through it, old age happens. Even when my spectacles are hanging on my neck, I search for it for half a day". She let out a forced laugh, which my mom joined in too. They were trying to break the thick tension looming around, like two friends working together on a mission.

Atleast two people were getting along, I smiled at them, swapping my gaze between them.

A roar of laughter erupted from my grandmother beside me and all eyes turned towards her.

Now what's this? What's the next bomb she's going to drop? Please let me be something nice.

Once her laughter died, she said, "Now I know, what's the problem." My breath hitched with each word that was being expelled out of her mouth. What she did next stunned everyone. She winked at Sasha and said, "Her hair is the problem."

Oh God! Have mercy.

"Now all problems are solved!" Announcing that, she turned towards me and beamed, as wide as she could, showing off her dentures.

"Huh?", I reacted out loud in confusion.

"Raghav, shabaash (congrats)! You did a better job than your father over here". She stole a dig at my mother and father. She turned to view the puzzled expression, mirroring on the Hedge's and continued to elaborate. "Raghav's grandfather had always one problem at home, my long hair. It used to lay around everywhere

—living room, bedroom, bathroom; how much ever I tried these untamed hair strands didn't stay in one place, neither on my head nor in my home. He had an obsession with cleanliness and majority of our arguments were due to my hair floating around everywhere."

Everyone's expression dialed down to a relaxed one and I heaved a sigh of relief.

She looked into my eyes and clutched my chin fondly. "My grandson made the perfect choice, now no problems due to hair will be there. Your choice surely would have been approved by your late grandfather. You made his soul rest in peace. I'm so proud of you!" She kissed me on my forehead. Returning back to the others, she happily stated, "Approved from my side!"

Uff! One down, three more to go.

My mother got up and put a teeka on Sasha and me. When she went back to her seat, she said. "Wherever my son's happiness lays, my happiness is there too. Sasha, the name is itself unique, no wonder my son's heart is wrapped around you. If you have impressed his Dadi in your first meet, that's just the icing on the cake." My Dadi scoffed on that note and lowering her voice my mother said. "You better be on my side okay and help me earn some brownie points from, you know whom".

Everyone let out a short laugh.

"My dear daughter-in-law, I might be hard of hearing but I heard that. Don't spoil the new daughter-in-law of the house. Sasha Magu, don't get swayed by her sweet talks. She promised me the same with my mother-in-law, but zero outcome." She gestured with a thumbs down and shook her head in dejection. "Raghav's wife will obviously be on my side, because Raghav loves me the most, right Raghav Magu?"

Out of nowhere I got dragged into their battle. Just a second ago I was happy and thrilled that both the ladies of my home were accepting the union of Sasha and me, with open arms. Now I had three pairs of eyes trained at me with hope in them. I hurriedly took the glass of water in front of me.

How does one escape from such a situation? Who could choose, who do you love the most— Dadi, mom or Sasha?

My dad, who was seated between his mother and wife, chuckled. "Poor boy, don't put him on the spot in front of his futures in-laws. It feels like Déjà vu. Mr. Hedge you also might have undergone similar situation, right?"

He smiled and nodded in response.

"Uff! Thank God now I'll be spared. Raghav, take your baton". My dad passed on to me an imaginary baton. "Now they'll fight over you, instead of me. I pity you, I had only two competitors but you have three". He burst out laughing again.

I rolled my eyes, he sure is enjoying it way too much. My mother pat his knee softly to make him control his laugh. She turned to-wards the Hedge's and said. "To wrap it up, it's a yes from our side." Dad's faint laugh still did the background score for my mother's words. "Let us know if you need time to think and feel free to ask any questions, if you have any?"

Mrs. Hedge's chirpy voice came first. "I liked Raghav from the start. He's perfect for my Sasha. With his entry in her life, I was able to breathe comfortably. I didn't think this day would ever come. Thank you so much Raghav and thank you so much all of you for accepting Sasha. Tomorrow I will donate double at the temple. The Almighty's blessings have brought us together in this joyous occasion."

Sasha and me heaved a relaxed sigh and blinked at each other in understanding. We exhanged smiles through our glasses of water.

Mr. Hedge's turn to speak came. "There's no doubt your son here is a good man. I have heard way too many stories and praises from my wife here. She has a tendency to get carried away in emotions, obviously that's how I secured her hand in marriage.....but not me."

I didn't know theirs was a love marriage too. I had started to ponder on their story, when Mr. Hedge's ending words echoed in my eyes.

What! Don't tell me he has an objection?!?

I briefly glanced at Sasha, who was sitting beside her dad. She emoted the same question as me.

"Your family seems nice and witnessing your love and whole hearted welcome of my daughter, I'm overwhelmed." His words made me refocus my vision on him. "Raghav, son, Sasha has been brought up to be an independent woman. She might not allows agree to you, due to her strong willed mind but she sure won't disrespect you or your family. You already know she's different from other girls but still were headstrong and persuasive on going forward, it's commendable. It reflects your true character that you value inner beauty than exterior, kudos to you. I can't believe my daughter had grown so big and time has come to send her off to her new home". His eyes started to water and voice was getting wobbly. He pecked her forehead and looked straight into my eyes, "Take good care of her, she's as innocent as she was at the time I taught her how to ride her bicycle. It's a yes from us too."

"Kya bhai saheb, you are getting emotional now itself? Bidaai ke time par kya hoga?", my dad consoled Mr. Hedge. ("What's this repected brother, you are getting emotional now itself? What will happen during the bridal farewell then?")

My mother joined in too. "We don't have a daughter, but still can understand your sentiments. Don't worry, she'll be like a daughter in our home."

Sasha handed a tissue and a glass of water to her father and she was sipping through hers too.

"Trust me, she'll be valued at our home, I'm not just saying for namesake. We don't disrespect God's footsteps. Sasha's truly our Lakshmi, as soon as she entered Raghav's life, everything good started happened in his life." My mother added stated with pride and honesty.

Sasha choked and spit out the water, at the same time. I knew exactly what made her respond in that way. I rolled my eyes and face-palmed internally.

Way to ruin a moment, Sasha!

Once everyone was satisfied that Sasha was fine, we resumed eating our samosas and snacks. Others were gibber-gabbering away, while my fingers started getting fidgety. It seemed to be the winding up of the evening and I hadn't spent a minute alone with Sasha. We had to celebrate our moment of victory, it couldn't wait.

I cleared my throat and caught everyone's attention. Mrs. Hedge enquired if I needed water or juice, to which I shook my head. My Dadi replied back, "Arrey! We forgot one important part of the discussion". She clapped her hands in sudden realization.

Now, what is it?

"Which part?", Mr. Hedge asked cautiously.

"The bride and the groom didn't get a chance to talk alone, separately. I know they know each other from before, in fact on their insistence only we have all gathererd here. But customs are customs, we shouldn't leave it like that." My Dadi explained. I wanted to leap and hug her in joy but controlled my actions.

"Yes, they deserve this much. Let them spend some alone time. I'm sure they are getting bored among us, adults". My father also sided with his mother.

Mr. Hedge sighed and said, "Okay! Keep in mind, no hanky-panky business at my home..... Or in onsite, got it?"

I nodded my head, "Yes, sir. I assure you, our relation will be pure and respectful."

We excused ourselves and made way to the front porch. It was hidden from their vision and had a bench attached to the wall and a bamboo cane curved swing hanging from the ceiling. Sasha took her place on the swing, she looked happy and relaxed.

"Our line is clear now", I flashed her a wide grin.

"Uh- what?"

"For marriage!", I replied in an obvious tone.

Her smile grew wider, "Hmmm yes. I didn't imagine it to be so easy."

"Me too. I guess they were all waiting for us to get married".

She giggled, "True that! I'm sure my mother is waiting for her grandchildren."

I raised my brow and smirked, "Then what are we waiting for? We should all obey our parents, Hun".

She threw me a deadly glare. "Need I remind you what my dad said earlier — no hanky-panky business."

"Oh my God Sasha! You are so naughty, I didn't say we need to grant your mother's wish, this instant. Wait let me tell your dad, who is the one eager to go agains his orders". I pretended to move towards the front door and Sasha jumped out off swing to catch me. I chuckled at her shock and hugged her sideways.

"Oh my dear Sasha! What am I going to do with you?!" I placed a peck on her cheek, which sent her hurriedly two meters away from me.

"Behave!" She scowled cutely, trying to overlook over my shoulder for any of our family members.

I stole another peck on the cheek that would have felt lonely, without my lips gracing it. She responded with her hands on hips and a stern glare.

"Relax, my quota of Vitamin K has been fulfilled", I raised my hands is surrender. "If yours is not, feel free to claim it". I tapped my cheeks and brought it front of her.

She pushed me slightly, "Raghav, please!"

"Okay fine", I shoved my hands into my pockets and felt my smartphone.

Taking it out, I took a snap of her in her attire.

"What was that for?", she questioned.

"I'm not sure when I'll be able to see you again in Indian wear. So this is for memory." She snorted in response.

"Hun, will you please model for me? Only one photo, the earlier one isn't clear."

She agreed and posed silently with a smile. I took a head-to-toe photograph. After taking a couple of snaps in burst mode, I stood beside her with my arm secured around her shoulder. "This is for our memory, our first official 'meet the parents' photograph. Say cheese!"

song:I don't wanna lovenobody but you (you)I wanna say it now, wanna make it clearFor only you and God to hear.

30

EPILOGUE

Raghav's POV

song:What would I do without your smart mouth?Drawing me in, and you kicking me outYou've got my head spinning,no kidding,I can't pin you downWhat's going on in that beautiful mind?I'm on your magical mystery rideAnd I'm so dizzy,don't know what hit me, but I'll be alright.

We had a tearful farewell while bidding goodbye to our family and friends at the airport. After entering into our economy class cabin, I heaved a long sigh, it was going to be a long journey. Securing our hand luggage in the overhead compartment I raised my brow at Sasha, she had occupied my favorite window seat. The departure was scheduled in the night and the prospect of sparkling lights image dancing in the dark, enticed me, into gaining back my window seat.

Sasha turned towards me, patting the seat next to her, she smiled. "Come and fasten your seat belt, it'll soon be the time to take off." Her smiling invitation tugged my heartstings.

I cannot believe, so soon, we were having our first couple air travel. Every day, something or the other is a 'first' for us. So many journeys are yet to be traversed and I just couldn't wait to unravel them all.

The flight took off smoothly, Sasha was enjoying her dazzling lights view; while I enjoyed mine.

"You know that's my favorite seat, the window side?". I stated and she hummed in response still engrossed by the view from her oval window.

I continued, "I never offer my window seat to anyone, even during family travel with toddlers around. "

"That's so mean, Raghav! You are really a baby, sometimes". Sasha whipped her head towards me and frowned. Resting her palm on my upper arms, she said, "Thanks for making the exception for me." My eyes were still trained at her palm slowly caressing my biceps.

I raised my brow in question. "What are you upto? Are you bribing me, indirectly?!"

"Huh?", she looked confused.

I nudged towards her hand with my eyes. "Oh God! Raghav you have such a one track mind!". She slapped my arm playing, before removing her hand.

Wiggling my eyebrows in pure mischief, "How else should I perceive it?"

"Nowadays anything I do or say, you somehow try to find a double meaning to it". She huffed, "I was trying to pacify you, considering you lost your favorite spot to me. Just like how you try to console a kid, when he doesn't get his chocolate. It was a plain straight act of empathy. Sometimes, Raghav boy, take things at face value."

I rested by back on my armrest and faced her. "I don't mind losing to you."

She scoffed, "Okay, whatever makes you happy, Raghav boy."

"On the contrary, though, I have a better view angle than yours". I said confidently.

"Really?" Sasha fell into my words and tried jerking back parallel to my line of vision, to check the angle.

A smile grew on my face watching her experiment the various angles. Patting her shoulder, "Hun, you won't find the right angle."

"Why?" She questioned while sweeping her focus back to me.

"You won't be able to find the same view as mine because mine is an interpolation of two of my favorite scenes — you and the sparkling night view from the sky". I tried my level best to maintain a straight look while saying it. The deflation of Sasha's sincere interested look, for some knowledge flash, to an utter disappointment, was worth my efforts. She rolled her eyes and moved back to her window, downright ignoring me.

song:My head's under waterBut I'm breathing fineYou're crazy andI'm out of my mind.

"Sasha!" "Hun!" "Sorry!" "Happy Pongal!"

I kept calling her out and placed my hands on her elbow, which she successfully shrugged off, off her.

"Hun, I swear I won't tease you or say anything cheesy. Come on, let's not ruin our first couple trip to abroad."

"Couple?" She turned left and looked at me. "We aren't going on a honeymoon or anything, we are going on an official business travel. To work in America and not for vacationing over there." She reminded me like a strict officer.

Honeymoon! My eye lit up but I held my tongue, to avoid making the situation worsen than it had already been. "I know", I said in a deflated tone with my shoulders sagging an inch.

Just then an air-hostess came by our seats and asked politely. "Sir, Ma'am, what would like to have as your drink? We have some healthy fresh fruit juices, tomato juice and some alcoholic beverages to choose from."

"Healthy!", Sasha scoffed. "All does this man knows is his Vitamin K, Vitamin H and Vitamin H+, and that's not even vaguely related to anything healthy."

"Eh? Pardon me? Vitamin what, Ma'am?". The confused air-hostess asked, while I wore a baffled look.

Gosh! Sasha!She's going to spill all our code words.

Once the words she had let out spontaneously got registered in her head, she sent an embarrassed smile in our direction. "Fresh orange juice for me, please." Giving her a curt nod, the air-hostess, started serving her glass. "I meant orange juice is healthy and has lots of Vitamin C. It'll keep me healthy and combat my on-sight of flu". Sasha rambled on, trying to cover up her slip of the tongue, disastrously. She even faked a couple of coughs to prove she is catching the flu. "Hope the weather at our final destination doesn't aggravate it. Do you have any idea of our destination's prevailing weather conditions. Is it warm or cold?". She asked the dutiful air-hostess, who was pre-occupied in filling our glasses.

"It's warm over there. You'll be fine Ma'am. Here you go, your healthy glass of orange juice." With a smile she handed over it to Sasha. I sheepishly smiled and gestured the same for me.

Once the cabin crew along with their trolley of beverages were out of sight and hearing range, Sasha punched my arm and threw an accusation on me.

"Urgh! It was so embarrassing. All because of you ", she scowled emphasizing the last line.

"What did I do?" I shrugged innocently. "I didn't ask you to divulge our code words or ask you to put on an act of falling sick. Want my suggestion, you need more training for your acting skills". I flashed a smirk, before taking a gulp of her Vitamin C loaded juice.

When she was about to turn around again and dial into her do not disturb mode, I grabbed her elbow to turn her back. I lifted my hands and clutched my earlobes to mouth — 'Happy Pongal'. I knew she wouldn't be able resist my innocent chocolate boy charm.

"Hopeless! Change your name to 'Hopeless Raghav Srivatsav'."

With that I knew I had won over her and broken her 'no talking' stance.

After all, you can't stay mad at a person, who makes you laugh.

song:'Cause all of meLoves all of youLove your curves and all your edgesAll your perfect imperfections.

Pulling her sideways, into my embrace, I placed a kiss on her temple before hugging her. Taking her free hand into mine, I said. "I like all our bittersweet moments too. Don't make fun of me, if you find it funny." Like an opening and closing vote of thanks quote, I pecked her temple again. I pat my back internally thinking of my accomplishment.

All three Vitamins in one go. What a masterstroke!

song:Give your all to meI'll give my all to youYou're my end and my beginningEven when I lose I'm winning'Cause I give you all of meAnd you give me all of you, oh-oh.

Sasha stayed comfortable in my embrace and didn't make a move to break it. In fact, she snuggled into it even more. While sipping into her juice and faintly admitted. "Me too." To which I looked down at her cuddled figure resting on my chest and raised an eyebrow. She smiled at me and started to come out of my embrace. "We need such moments to act as a nazar tod (break evil eye) for us."

My already arched eyebrow, shot up an inch higher up. "You believe in such stuff?"

"Not exactly, but better safe than never. I'm not telling to be blindly superstitious. Why don't you just take it as like this — always having lovey-dovey moments will become boring. We need fights to spice it up."

"Huh??", my eyes nearly popped out of their sockets. "Spice it up, I see", I repeated her words in a completely different playful tone. Humming in agreement, "I heard kiss and makeup after fights, increases the intensity of love." She shook her head in amusement.

"Vicky's going to be so proud of you..... For taking his suggestions, one step higher."

The dinner trolley rolled up to our aisle and we started our meal alongside the homemade sides packed by Sasha's mother. It was going to be nearly a day's long journey in the plane, with a switchover at Dubai. Considering it, our mother's had turned masterchefs and packaging experts. Their packages contained few special delicacies for our flight journey and not to forget the nearly double digit number of tins with unperishable edibles part of our cargo luggage.

After an enjoyable meal, I bent over Sasha's seat and viewed the twinkling lights in awe together, chatting away about their sources. My arms like a boundary wall surrounded Sasha on either sides. Her back rested on my chest and my chin on her left shoulder. Our cute back hug image reflected on the window panel. 'Click!', my phone sound emerged while capturing our ghost image overlaying over the sparkling sodium lights on a black canvas. We turned to inspect the snap and it was just Picture perfect!

The lights had dimmed, signaling the quiet hours and too fell in slumber. She rested her head on her headrest. My fingers twitched to remove the armrest barrier between us to cuddle together for the whole night. It took every ounce of my self-control to avoid doing so.

I woke up before Sasha at the announcement of nearing our stopover destination and were expected to land in another forty-five minutes. Cracking my sore neck muscles, my eyes found my Ms. Sneakers, who had sneaked her hands around my arms with her head on my shoulder. She seemed to be sleeping peacefully. Looking over her head, the sight of dawn with fluffy clouds spread over the sky like separated cotton balls, was a sight to behold.

I'm literally in air with my loved one in my arms, it couldn't have been any better. How I wish the moment would seize. Even better, I wish I could wake up to this sight, everyday.

That day isn't far away.

A wide grin beamed on my face at that thought. Sasha's eyes started fluttering to open and the first thing she saw was ME! Her cute smile changed to shock at our position, making her straighten up in her seat faster than usual. The remaining journey glided away in watching movies or napping.

The first week on American soil was hectic in settling down at office and our thirty day accommodation provided by the company. We declared our relationship at the client office too. They had strict rules on workplaces romance and the officials had authority to take stringent action against us if found guilty of breaking them. Also, non-disclosure of workplace relationships, of any kind, could be subjected to the law. We were mature adult and as it is, we weren't the ones who indulge in public display of affection. Neither did we nuture our relationship to garner any kind of professional gains. We were good as long as we didn't do anything to sabotage each other's work and kept our professional and personal lives separate. Nor were we the kind of couple who would not see eye to eye in office and not meet for coffee breaks or lunch, just to be extra cautious. We so needed the break time to spend in each other's company.

We spent our weekdays slogging at office while our weekends for discovering nearby places and sight-seeing. Sasha loved being adventurous, going on hikes, camping and there were so many places to visit, to quench her thirst. I was a mediocre person in terms of venturing out, but I didn't mind as long as I had Sasha's company and we were safe.

The time had come to shift out to a more permanent place of stay. The lookout for it had started almost since we landed, actually even before. While in Coimbatore, we got in touch with family, friends, friends of friends and the list goes on, to gather information of the suburbs and cost of living. After working hours we used to squeeze in sometime for site visits, in order to keep our weekends free of such important but boring tasks.

"Sasha, I think I like this place. The locality is also good and centralized, surrounded with supermarkets. There's a metro station in walkable distance and it's only a fifteen minutes ride in the metro to our office. What do you think?"

"Hmmm, yes. It looks good and ticks off majority of the checklist items. I like that it has a balcony too."

"Attached to your room or common area?", I asked.

"Common area. But it's wide and it'll do."

I nodded. As we stepped out of the inspected flat, making our way to the elevator, I said. "It's a three bedroom apartment with two bedrooms ready to occupy."

"Hmmm", she hummed in response while putting her phone back in her backpack.

"Both are available at the same time."

"Yes, Raghav."

"So-so —", I trailed off.

"So what?", she questioned.

"How do feel, meeting your new roommate?" Casting a gentle smile, I enquiried.

"Who? Where?" She whipped her head all around in search of the person.

I tapped her shoulder and when her attention was on me, I jerked both my thumbs and announced. "Me!"

She let out a train of speedbreaker giggles. "You? You got to be kidding me?"

"Why? How do you like the idea of a live-in relationship, of course in separate rooms. After all, I'm also a decent, traditional guy too." I hurried up the explanation part of it.

She puffed out a blow of air and replied sarcastically. "Yes-yes, there is no doubt that you a good traditional guy. We can stay in separate rooms..... in separate apartments too."

"But—".

"Raghav, do you really want to have this conversation now? You know my dad warned you that sometimes I might not agree with you and you need to accept it." She said in a flat tone. I knew it was a ridiculous hasty idea for us.

The day to move in to our new respective rooms came. We had unloaded our luggage from the cab and shifting it to her flat. Once her boxes had been placed inside her room. I bid goodbye to her at her doorstep.

Catching the doorframe on either sides and leaning in towards her, I said. "Before I start unpacking, just wanted to re-check if your thoughts have changed about my live-in offer?" Shooting my gaze to the vacant room opposite hers. "Wiggling my eyebrows," Your one yes and one phone call away to the landlords, is the only thing stopping me from unloading my luggage in that room."

She let out a chuckle, "You never give up is it?"

"My never say die attitude, lead me to my onsite assignment. I'm hoping it works in my personal life too", I smirked.

She placed both her palms on my flexed muscles and took a step forward. I briefly glanced at her hand when she squeezed them and met her eyes again. "My dear Raghav boy, you are so correct. It worked for your career and it will, definitely, work in your personal life too." By now her palms had traced a long path on my upper body. They had roamed up to my shoulders, glided along the shoulder bone towards my neck and slid down sensually to my chest.

Alarm started ringing within me with each movement of her hand trail. My breath hitched and I swallowed hard. Now her palms seemed to have stationed on my chest. She took a tiny step forward, making me take an equal amount of step back.

"Sasha!", I called out but in no vain.

She progressed to take another step forward. I whipped my head both sides, to check for any audience in the corridor.

"Sa-asha....", her name came out breathlessly. "I don't think it's the right time or place for —".

She didn't seem to pay any heed to my shaky warning. All she did was close the distance between us and I kept adding the distance. This lead to me standing on her doormat, entirely outside her flat.

Out of nowhere, she pushed me away with slight force, making me loose the grip on the doorframe and stumble backwards. A puzzled expression crept gradually over my face.

"Like I said, your 'never say die' attitude will work for your personal life too but—but not in this case, sweetheart!". She dust-clapped her hands in victory and folded her hands to lean on one side of the door frame.

I huffed and straightened my shirt to stand upright. "Did you have to push me, to convey your point?!"

She closed her eyes for a second and bobbed her head in acceptance. "Yes!" Drawing an incomprehensible figure in the air with her fingers, she asked. "What were you telling earlier? You don't think it's the right time and place for— for what Raghav?!?" She tightly pursed her lips to stifle her forth coming laugh.

I scrunched my face in slight humiliation and grumbled. "Nothing Sasha!" Unable to withstand my second hand embarrassment, I averted my attention by focusing on rolling down my folded sleeves.

"Ah! Let me guess!", Sasha suggested with her finger on her cheek. Tapping her cheek, she tried to showcase that she was searching for the answers. "You are always right, Raghav", she stated, in over-excitement.

Now what is she upto?! My eyeballs jolted up to steal a peek at her.

She continued, with laughter in her eyes, when our gaze met. "This isn't the right place or time, for —". She gave a dramatic pause, before completing her sentence. "For unpacking your things! As you need to do it over there". She bent her head forward to look at her right and jerked her thumb in the same direction. "I think it'll take approximately five more minutes for you to start, too." She stole a glance at her wristwatch and exclaimed. Looking back at my face she said, "That's why I'm going to call you from here on, Mr. Right Raghav!" She announced happily, flashing all her teeth in full contentment with her leg pulling stunt.

Once again I scoffed in annoyance, which I felt I had done an umpteen number of times within the span of ten minutes. I took a deep breath.

"It's ok Hun, I prefer being called Sweetheart, as earlier". I winked at her and her surprised expression vouched for the correct intepretion of my tongue-in-cheek reference.

Taking advantage of her stunned stance, I stole a peck on the cheek; she had patted awhile ago, in pretense of coming up with her witty reply. It did the needful to break her frozen state.

"That, was for your earlier invitation". With a mischievous smile, I tapped her nose adoringly and stepped back to make way towards my room in the next-door flat.

She called out, "When did I do such a thing."

Taking small strides backwards, I repeated her actions to answer her question. "When you did this!", I tapped my cheek. "I thought you were asking me for a kiss on your cheek. Sorry Sasha, sometimes I'm a late bloomer, I understood it a little late. Hope you don't mind, a five minutes delayed kiss?!?" I shrugged innocently. I had to stop, to laugh my heart out when she scoffed and mumbled something under her breath.

"You can't beat your teacher, in a subject he has mastered, my dear Sasha."

Before she could reply anything else in her defense, I said. "One more thing hun, I'm not just 'Mr. Right Raghav' but I'm 'YOUR Mr. Right Raghav'. She stood tongue-tied and settled with shaking her head repeatedly in amusement. "Bye, Hun! Meet you for dinner later. Take rest till then". I sent a curt salute in her direction and entered my flat.

song:How many times do I have to tell you?Even when you're crying, you're beautiful tooThe world is beating you down, I'm around through every moodYou're my downfall, you're my museMy worst distraction, my rhythm and bluesI can't stop singing, it's ringing, in my head for you.

One year later

How fast one year glided away, I couldn't believe. It felt like only yesterday Sasha and me were at the baggage carousel, waiting for our luggage to appear on the rotating conveyor belt. It was a year well spent at onsite — roaming around, clicking photographs everywhere we went, checking out new places to eat along with new cuisines. All-in-all, it was a splendid experience. I couldn't have wished for a better dating period.

Our respective mother's were the ones that faced the brunt of our enjoyment. Sasha's mother spent the days in worry, that we might break up and kept insisting for an engagement or a formal betrothal ceremony. On the other hand, my mother lived in fear of our safety, when we shared our camping and hiking experiences and photographs. Her point of view was that we were taking life for granted and chilling out like the world was going to end. Her take was, if we got engaged, only then we would behave responsibly and cut down on our adventurous trips. Little did she know we didn't require that step to keep our camping trips in check. I, being a slight scaredy cat, played the role of the anchor; whenever Sasha's want for thrilling experiences went over-board.

On successful stalling of the engagement for a year, our families had had enough of it. They scheduled a group video call on one fine Sunday morning, eastern standard time. Sasha and me joined through the same laptop and sat side-by-side in her flat's living room. The Hedge family and mine were in full attendance, even though it late in the night for them. My Dadi too was an attendee, indicating it was a very important video call.

My mom played the role of addressing the elephant in the room. "Sasha - Raghav, now it's been one year since we agreed to your excuses for the engagement. Now I have put my foot down and unanimously, vote for it to happen soon."

"Ma, we also want it happen soon. It's just that our definition of soon isn't matching with all of yours." I said politely, well aware of the fact that my would-be in-laws are part of the call too. The fact was both Sasha and me wanted to enjoy the 'Boyfriend-Girlfriend' Tag to the fullest.

"I don't know which dictionary are you referring to for your definition of 'soon'. Soon in no language and in no dictionary means one year Raghav!"

Sensing my mother's impatience, I had to do something before it converting into anger. Trying to think of something to up with, before I'm scolded like a small kid in front of the Hedge family, but in vain.

"Aunty, for the engagement to take place we need to come to Bangalore, but we are still stuck, here." Sasha voiced out an appropriate concern and emoted it perfectly well with a sincere disappointed emotions. It felt like she really wanted it to happen but couldn't help it, but I knew it was otherwise.

That's my girl! I leapt in joy internally.

My mother wasn't having it, this time, she came well prepared. Flashing a smile, she responded back, "I knew both of you would say this but I have a solution for it too."

"We are going to have an online engagement ceremony!" Both the mothers announced in unison, happily.

Sasha and me snapped our heads at each other and immediately dialed into our eye conversation.

'Oh God! We are trapped this time', her eyes emoted.

'Relax Sasha, I'm there!', my eyes responded back.

'Think something soon'

'Will do, don't panic', my eyes conveyed to her.

song:Cards on the table, we're both showing heartsRisking it all, though it's hard.

We could hear all sorts of background noises from clearing of throats, awkward coughs to kisses blown in the air.

My dad's voice boomed, "Raghav continue your romance after the call. Concentrate over here now. Err-uh! Need I remind you that your in-laws are also watching". Dad did a commendable job in bringing us back to earth from our parallel universe.

Great! Busted!

The kissing sounds were still being heard, I let my eyes roam across the laptop screen to find the culprit. It was none other than my Dadi, it shocked me to the core.

"Oh! Sshh!", my Dadi outrightly shushed her son. "He's not like you, he is my grandson. Danke ki chot pe, seena thok ke; pyaar karega bhi, pyaar jatayega bhi. (With all the hype and hoopla and fanfare, proudly he will show as well as declare, his love)".

Oh Gosh! Dadi please control! How much more second hand embarrassment I need to face.

She was rooting and hooting for us, the only thing left was whistling. If she knew how to whistle, that wouldn't have stopped her too. Smiling awkwardly, I shrugged in humiliation looking at the Hedge family's video slot. Whether they understood it was directed to them or not, I wasn't sure.

Mrs Hedge giggled and said, "See this is the only option available for you'll. Everyone here has agreed to it. Just decided the date and let us know. If that also you want us to do, we will happily do it."

"But —but, online? Won't it be weird?", Sasha questioned.

"Sasha Magu (child), what's weird in it? Be modern like me! The 21st century cool, Dadi. Why do you want to follow some boring age old format, leave that behind. Try something new and exciting. Don't you want me to witness something special, that I can brag about, to my friends when I meet them in afterlife? I don't know how much more time I have left on Earth." Dadi explained, more like emotionally blackmailed by pulling out her age card, smoothly.

Dadi was turning out to be extra ultra-modern for our liking.

Sasha innocently asked her father, "Dad do you also agree with it?"

"Great! We all told, is that not enough? Ok hear it from the horse's mouth", Mrs. Hedge replied, slightly irritated. She turned to her husband, "You itself tell else your daughter, she won't believe, after all Father's daughter she is! I didn't do anything at all, right!" She grumbled, scarcasm dripping from her tongue.

Sasha rolled her eyes as she knew this was the usual reaction from her mother, when she feels neglected in her daughter's eyes. "Ma! I didn't mean it, in that sense. He's been awfully quiet the whole time so wanted to check with him."

Mrs. Hedge dramatically put her hand on her heart and sucked her breath. "Oh God! Now you are telling I'm not letting him speak". She nudged her husband, "Say something soon before she accuses me of putting words in your mouth too."

Now it was Sasha's turn for experiencing the embarrassment in front of her in-laws.

"MA!", Sasha gasped. Her gaze kept sweeping to my family's video box, to gauge their reactions.

"It's ok Sasha, it's ok Mr. and Mrs. Hedge. It's Har Ghar ki kahani (the story of everyone's home). Same situation here also, Mr. Hedge, don't worry." My dad jerked his head sideways towards my mother and winked to the screen, directing it to Sasha's father. His not-so wise declaration, resulted in earning him a jab from my mother, in return. Setting off a laughter riot.

Looks like today everyone's on a roll!

Mr. Hedge spoke, "Yes Sasha, we are all happy with the decision. On contrary, we are more than happy for this arrangement. It bears less expenses and reduces unnecessary extra pompousness, people attach to such affairs. Right Mr. Srivatsav?"

My father damned, "Cent percent right!". They even hi-fied over the internet.

Both the families are putting a united front against us. There's no turning back now! How come they are all agreeing to each other, usually in such marriage talks, disagreements were inevitable.

These people are all so W-E-I-RD! Did they practice or do a rehearsal of some sorts this meeting?

"Okay!", Sasha's bummed reply came. She seemed to have accepted defeat and our fate.

I too was falling prey to their well executed plan. A moment before I was also about to convey my consent, the bulb in my brain lit. That's the perfect escape, my inner voice validated my brilliant get-us-off-the-hook idea.

"I'm also fine, but Ma, only one issue is there. You are aware that we can schedule a vacation back to India once every year, with a one-way flight trip sponsored by the company, right?" When my mother nodded and urged me to go on, I glanced at my in-laws. "However due to some high priority project, we had to postpone our vacation a little. I was going to use 'our engagement' as an excuse to get our vacation plans approved. As they seem to be always coming up with some sort lame excuses in making us postpone or discouraging us from availing our vacation. If we have an online engagement, our vacation plans may be stalled further. Will you be fine, not able to meet us in person for another few months or maybe another year, based on responses we got earlier at office?!?"

"What! Another year!", my mother shrieked.

"They can't do that, that's so unprofessional!", Mrs. Hedge said in accusatory tone.

"No, nothing is unprofessional. The vacation leaves will be carry forwarded and be available to avail in the future. This is business peak time, so lots of new mini projects are coming back-to-back. If you put ourselves in their shoes, they have a valid reason." I reasoned out.

"Also, there's a rule if an employee hasn't availed his or her vacation in eighteen months, in his first onsite visit, the company will bare the two-way ticket expenses. This is applicable only for the first trip." Sasha added to my point.

"Just don't inform them you are engaged", Mrs. Hedge suggested matter-of-factly.

"Aunty, I don't think so that's a good idea. In States, at least in our client organization, they take relationships between employees very seriously. It may result in termination and immediate extradition. Worse case scenario, we can even end up behind the bars. I've earned shocking goosebump-ridden stories of the number of years it sometimes takes to come out of the jail, while trying to prove not-guilty. That's not a situation we want to invite, right Aunty?"

I wasn't even fully sure upto what extent the information, I had shared was true or not. I didn't give it a damn even if it was zero per-cent, the truth. Right now my mission — 'Sabotage the engagement', was in full motion. The gasps let out by my mother and others, punctuating each information I had revealed, indicated that I had hit the rod when it was hot.

While everyone busied themselves in talking and thinking a way out of the pickle I had put them in, Sasha and me shared private smiles. Admits their murmurs in Kanada, I fist-bumped Sasha, be-hind our backs, hidden from the camera lens. On a concluding note, we decided that we would wait for another six months time, then we would be flying down to India for our engagement.

Six months later

On our engagement day, a small to medium sized banquet hall was booked and decorated. It was only for close-knit family mem-bers and friends. Our gang had ordered a choco-scotch crunchy cake, which had butterscotch crunches plastered around its circumference and on the top. Miniature dome shaped chips, made up of white and normal chocolate, along with the butterscotch crunches decorated the top. The message that adorned the cake was -

"To-Be Mr. & Mrs. Sneakers "

This is surely Vicky's doing, especially the pair of sneakers.

It was made of fondant icing protruding out in three dimensions, below the written message. The colors were the same as that of the sneakers Sasha wore when I met her. It was the first part of her that came into my vision, and since then there was no turning back.

On the muhuruth (auspicious time), we slipped our engagement rings on each other's fingers. Thankfully everyone had crowded on the stage to congratulate each other and conveniently moved a few meters away from us. Milking the opportunity, I stole a kiss on Sasha's cheek and whispered into her ears.

"Congratulations to-be wifey!"

She clutched my self-desigbed neru jacket and pulled me slightly down. Tip-toeing to bridge the gap between us, she pecked my cheek in return in lightening speed. Mirroring my actions she whispered into my ear.

"Congratulations to you too, to-be hubby."

If I thought her quick peck was the evening's surprising and bold move from her side, the word 'Hubby' escaping out from lips stunned me. Her next set of words left me spellbound. Looking right into my eyes with her hands gently resting on my upper arm, she said. "I love you, Raghav!"

Even in my dazzled state of mind, my lips moved rapidly to reply back. "I love you too, Sasha!"

It then struck me, that this was very first time we had confessed our feelings to each other with the four letter L-word. This time around our confession had a different word, thought it started with 'L' and ended with 'E', similar to the earlier one. The centre two letters were swapped and which made all the difference. Sasha, being the first to confess, between the two of us, blew my mind away.

In the span of nearly two years of companionship, it never crossed our minds that we hadn't said 'I love you' to each other. I guess we can blame it on our naïveté. Our bond wasn't dependent on such words but on the love we had in our hearts for the other. Nevertheless, stating it out aloud, gave a sense of trademark certified stamp on it.

Her surprises for the joyous evening, didn't seem to cease. The exchange of kisses and love declaration happened right in the middle of the stage among guests on-stage as well as off-stage.

Where did my innocent, people - cautious Sasha go?

The second the thought crossed my mind, it seems to have telepathically sent to Sasha. She tugged on the dangling sides of her dupatta, falling on either sides of her face and whipped her head to catch any onlookers red-handed. I was about to inform her that it was of no use, surely our display of affection wouldn't have gone unnoticed, atleast not by the photographer. Out of fear of ruining this moment, I let it pass. Luckily her dupatta securely pinned to her hair on the crown of her head, set the dupatta cascading on either sides of her face, providing the discretion for our sneaky kisses.

After the exchange of the rings and rituals, I picked up my guitar and dedicated a song to Sasha, my fiancé. Half seated on a circular rotatable chair, with only lower back support, that was specifically brought to the stage, I held Sasha's gaze. She was seated at the center of the stage in our love seat. I sang, 'All of Me' by John Legend.

song:Cause all of meLoves all of youLove your curves and all your edgesAll your perfect imperfectionsGive your all to meI'll give my all to youYou're my end and my beginningEven when I lose I'm winning'Cause I give you all of meAnd you give me all of you.

When the music and applause died down, my Dadi started to complain. "Raghav you changed a lot. I didn't know when we sent you off to America, you'll return back as a foreigner! The song was nice but sing something desi too."